the street
lawyer

John Grisham is the bestselling author of twenty-two novels, one work of non-fiction, a collection of short stories, and a novel for young readers. He lives in Virginia and Mississippi.

john grisham

the street lawyer

arrow books

Reissued in the United Kingdom by Arrow Books in 2010

9 10

Copyright © John Grisham 1998

John Grisham has asserted his right under the Copyright, Designs and
Patents Act, 1988 to be identified as the author of this work

First published in the United Kingdom in 1998 by Century
First published in paperback in 1999 by Arrow books

Arrow Books
The Random House Group Limited
20 Vauxhall Bridge Road, London, SW1V 2SA

www.rbooks.co.uk

Addresses for companies within The Random House Group Limited can
be found at: www.randomhouse.co.uk/offices.htm

The Random House Group Limited Reg. No. 954009

A CIP catalogue record for this book
is available from the British Library

ISBN 9780099537199

Penguin Random House is committed to a sustainable future for
our business, our readers and our planet. This book is made from
Forest Stewardship Council® certified paper.

Printed and bound in Great Britain by Clays Ltd, Elcograf S.p.A.

ONE

The man with the rubber boots stepped into the elevator behind me, but I didn't see him at first. I smelled him though – the pungent odor of smoke and cheap wine and life on the street without soap. We were alone as we moved upward, and when I finally glanced over I saw the boots, black and dirty and much too large. A frayed and tattered trench coat fell to his knees. Under it, layers of foul clothing bunched around his midsection, so that he appeared stocky, almost fat. But it wasn't from being well fed; in the wintertime in D.C., the street people wear everything they own, or so it seems.

He was black and aging – his beard and hair were half-gray and hadn't been washed or cut in years. He looked straight ahead through thick sunglasses, thoroughly ignoring me, and making me wonder for a second why, exactly, I was inspecting him.

He didn't belong. It was not his building, not his elevator, not a place he could afford. The lawyers on all eight floors worked for my firm at hourly rates that still seemed obscene to me, even after seven years.

Just another street bum in from the cold. Happened all the time in downtown Washington. But we had security guards to deal with the riffraff.

We stopped at six, and I noticed for the first time that he had not pushed a button, had not selected a floor. He was following me. I made a quick exit, and as I stepped into the splendid marble foyer of Drake & Sweeney I glanced over my shoulder just long enough to see him standing in the elevator, looking at nothing, still ignoring me.

Madam Devier, one of our very resilient receptionists, greeted me with her typical look of disdain. 'Watch the elevator,' I said.

'Why?'

'Street bum. You may want to call security.'

'Those people,' she said in her affected French accent.

'Get some disinfectant too.'

I walked away, wrestling my overcoat off my shoulders, forgetting the man with the rubber boots. I had nonstop meetings throughout the afternoon, important conferences with important people. I turned the corner and was about to say something to Polly, my secretary, when I heard the first shot.

Madam Devier was standing behind her desk, petrified, staring into the barrel of an awfully long handgun held by our pal the street bum. Since I was the first one to come to her aid, he politely aimed it at me, and I too became rigid.

'Don't shoot,' I said, hands in the air. I'd seen enough movies to know precisely what to do.

'Shut up,' he mumbled, with a great deal of composure.

There were voices in the hallway behind me. Someone yelled, 'He's got a gun!' And then the voices disappeared into the background, growing fainter and fainter as my colleagues hit the back door. I could almost see them jumping out the windows.

To my immediate left was a heavy wooden door that led to a large conference room, which at that moment happened to be filled with eight lawyers from our

2

litigation section. Eight hard-nosed and fearless litigators who spent their hours chewing up people. The toughest was a scrappy little torpedo named Rafter, and as he yanked open the door saying 'What the hell?' the barrel swung from me to him, and the man with the rubber boots had exactly what he wanted.

'Put that gun down,' Rafter ordered from the doorway, and a split second later another shot rang through the reception area, a shot that went into the ceiling somewhere well above Rafter's head and reduced him to a mere mortal. Turning the gun back to me, he nodded, and I complied, entering the conference room behind Rafter. The last thing I saw on the outside was Madam Devier shaking at her desk, terror-stricken, headset around her neck, high heels parked neatly next to her wastebasket.

The man with the rubber boots slammed the door behind me, and slowly waved the gun through the air so that all eight litigators could admire it. It seemed to be working fine; the smell of its discharge was more noticeable than the odor of its owner.

The room was dominated by a long table, covered with documents and papers that only seconds ago seemed terribly important. A row of windows overlooked a parking lot. Two doors led to the hallway.

'Up against the wall,' he said, using the gun as a very effective prop. Then he placed it very near my head, and said, 'Lock the doors.'

Which I did.

Not a word from the eight litigators as they scrambled backward. Not a word from me as I quickly locked the doors, then looked at him for approval.

For some reason, I kept thinking of the post office and all those horrible shootings – a disgruntled employee returns after lunch with an arsenal and wipes out fifteen of his co-workers. I thought of the playground massacres – and the slaughters at fast-food restaurants.

And those victims were innocent children and otherwise decent citizens. We were a bunch of lawyers!

Using a series of grunts and gun thrusts, he lined the eight litigators up against the wall, and when their positions suited him he turned his attention to me. What did he want? Could he ask questions? If so, he could get anything he damned well pleased. I couldn't see his eyes because of the sunglasses, but he could see mine. The gun was pointed at them.

He removed his filthy trench coat, folded it as if it were new, and placed it in the center of the table. The smell that had bothered me in the elevator was back, but not important now. He stood at the end of the table and slowly removed the next layer – a bulky gray cardigan.

Bulky for a reason. Under it, strapped to his waist, was a row of red sticks, which appeared to my untrained eye to be dynamite. Wires ran like colored spaghetti from the tops and bottoms of the sticks, and silver duct tape kept things attached.

My first instinct was to bolt, to lunge with arms and legs flapping and flailing for the door, and hope for luck, hope for a bad shot as I scrambled for the lock, then another bad shot as I fell through the doorway into the hallway. But my knees shook and my blood ran cold. There were gasps and slight moans from the eight against the wall, and this perturbed our captor. 'Please be quiet,' he said in the tone of a patient professor. His calmness unnerved me. He adjusted some of the spaghetti around his waist, then from a pocket in his large trousers produced a neat bundle of yellow nylon rope and a switchblade.

For good measure, he waved the gun at the horrified faces in front of him, and said, 'I don't want to hurt anybody.'

That was nice to hear but hard to take seriously. I counted twelve red sticks – enough, I was certain, to make it instantaneous and painless.

Then the gun was back on me. 'You,' he said, 'tie them up.'

Rafter had had enough. He took one very small step forward and said, 'Look, pal, just exactly what do you want?'

The third shot sailed over his head into the ceiling, where it lodged harmlessly. It sounded like a cannon, and Madam Devier or some female shrieked in the foyer. Rafter ducked, and as he attempted to stand upright the beefy elbow of Umstead caught him squarely in the chest and returned him to his position against the wall.

'Shut up,' Umstead said with clenched jaws.

'Do not call me Pal,' the man said, and Pal was instantly discarded as a reference.

'What would you like us to call you?' I asked, sensing that I was about to become the leader of the hostages. I said this very delicately, with great deference, and he appreciated my respect.

'Mister,' he said. Mister was perfectly fine with everyone in the room.

The phone rang, and I thought for a split second he was going to shoot it. Instead he waved it over, and I placed it squarely before him on the table. He lifted the receiver with his left hand; his right still held the gun, and the gun was still pointed at Rafter.

If the nine of us had a vote, Rafter would be the first sacrificial lamb. Eight to one.

'Hello,' Mister said. He listened briefly, then hung up. He carefully backed himself into the seat at the end of the table and sat down.

'Take the rope,' he said to me.

He wanted all eight of them attached at the wrists. I cut rope and tied knots and tried my best not to look

5

at the faces of my colleagues as I hastened their deaths. I could feel the gun at my back. He wanted them bound tightly, and I made a show of practically drawing blood while leaving as much slack as possible.

Rafter mumbled something under his breath and I wanted to slap him. Umstead was able to flex his wrists so that the ropes almost fell loose when I finished with him. Malamud was sweating and breathing rapidly. He was the oldest, the only partner, and two years past his first heart attack.

I couldn't help but look at Barry Nuzzo, my one friend in the bunch. We were the same age, thirty-two, and had joined the firm the same year. He went to Princeton, I went to Yale. Both of our wives were from Providence. His marriage was working – three kids in four years. Mine was in the final stage of a long deterioration.

Our eyes met and we both were thinking about his kids. I felt lucky to be childless.

The first of many sirens came into range, and Mister instructed me to close the blinds over the five large windows. I went about this methodically, scanning the parking lot below as if being seen might somehow save me. A lone police car sat empty with its lights on; the cops were already in the building.

And there we were, nine white boys and Mister.

At last count, Drake & Sweeney had eight hundred lawyers in offices around the world. Half of them were in D.C., in the building Mister was terrorizing. He instructed me to call 'the boss' and inform him that he was armed and wired with twelve sticks of dynamite. I called Rudolph, managing partner of my division, antitrust, and relayed the message.

'You okay, Mike?' he asked me. We were on Mister's new speakerphone, at full volume.

'Wonderful,' I said. 'Please do whatever he wants.'

6

'What does he want?'

'I don't know yet.'

Mister waved the gun and the conversation was over.

Taking my cue from the pistol, I assumed a standing position next to the conference table, a few feet from Mister, who had developed the irritating habit of playing absent-mindedly with the wires coiled against his chest.

He glanced down and gave a slight tug at a red wire. 'This red one here, I give it a yank and it's all over.' The sunglasses were looking at me when he finished this little warning. I felt compelled to say something.

'Why would you do that?' I asked, desperate to open a dialogue.

'I don't want to, but why not?'

I was struck by his diction – a slow, methodical rhythm with no hurry and each syllable getting equal treatment. He was a street bum at the moment, but there had been better days.

'Why would you want to kill us?' I asked.

'I'm not going to argue with you,' he announced. No further questions, Your Honor.

Because I'm a lawyer and live by the clock, I checked my watch so that whatever happened could be duly recorded, if we somehow managed to survive. It was one-twenty. Mister wanted things quiet, and so we endured a nerve-racking period of silence that lasted fourteen minutes.

I could not believe that we were going to die. There appeared to be no motive, no reason to kill us. I was certain that none of us had ever met him before. I remembered the ride on the elevator, and the fact that he seemed to have no particular destination. He was just a nut in search of hostages, which unfortunately would have made the killings seem almost normal by today's standards.

7

It was precisely the kind of senseless slaughter that would grab the headlines for twenty-four hours and make people shake their heads. Then the dead lawyer jokes would start.

I could see the headlines and hear the reporters, but I refused to believe it would happen.

I heard voices in the foyer, sirens outside; a police radio squawked somewhere down the hallway.

'What did you eat for lunch?' Mister asked me, his voice breaking the silence. Too surprised to consider lying, I hesitated for a second, then said, 'A grilled chicken Caesar.'

'Alone?'

'No, I met a friend.' He was a law school buddy from Philly.

'How much did it cost, for both of you?'

'Thirty bucks.'

He didn't like this. 'Thirty bucks,' he repeated. 'For two people.' He shook his head, then looked at the eight litigators. If he polled them, I hoped they planned to lie. There were some serious stomachs among the group, and thirty bucks wouldn't cover their appetizers.

'You know what I had?' he asked me.

'No.'

'I had soup. Soup and crackers at a shelter. Free soup, and I was glad to get it. You could feed a hundred of my friends for thirty bucks, you know that?'

I nodded gravely, as if I suddenly realized the weight of my sin.

'Collect all the wallets, money, watches, jewelry,' he said, waving the gun again.

'May I ask why?' I asked.

'No.'

I placed my wallet, watch, and cash on the table,

and began rummaging through the pockets of my fellow hostages.

'It's for the next of kin,' Mister said, and we all exhaled.

He instructed me to place the loot in a briefcase, lock it, and call 'the boss' again. Rudolph answered on the first ring. I could envision the SWAT leader camped in his office.

'Rudolph, it's me, Mike, again. I'm on the speaker-phone.'

'Yes, Mike. Are you okay?'

'Just fine. Look, this gentleman wants me to open the door nearest the reception area and place a black briefcase in the hallway. I will then close the door and lock it. Understand?'

'Yes.'

With the gun touching the back of my head, I slowly cracked the door and tossed the briefcase into the hallway. I did not see a person anywhere.

Few things can keep a big-firm lawyer from the joys of hourly billing. Sleep is one, though most of us slept little. Eating actually encouraged billing, especially lunch when the client was picking up the check. As the minutes dragged on, I caught myself wondering how in the world the other four hundred lawyers in the building would manage to bill while waiting for the hostage crisis to end. I could just see them out there in the parking lot, most of them sitting in their cars to keep warm, chatting away on cell phones, billing somebody. The firm, I decided, wouldn't miss a beat.

Some of the cutthroats down there didn't care *how* it ended. Just hurry up and get it over with.

Mister seemed to doze for a second. His chin dipped, and his breathing was heavier. Rafter grunted to get my attention, then jerked his head to one side as if to suggest I make a move. Problem was, Mister held the gun with his right hand, and if he was indeed napping, then he was doing so with the dreaded red wire held firmly in his left hand.

And Rafter wanted me to be the hero. Though Rafter was the meanest and most effective litigator in the firm, he was not yet a partner. He was not in my division, and we weren't in the Army. I didn't take orders.

'How much money did you make last year?' Mister, very much awake, asked me, his voice clear.

Again, I was startled. 'I, uh, gosh, let me see –'

'Don't lie.'

'A hundred and twenty thousand.'

He didn't like this either. 'How much did you give away?'

'Give away?'

'Yes. To charities.'

'Oh. Well, I really don't remember. My wife takes care of the bills and things like that.'

All eight litigators seemed to shift at once.

Mister didn't like my answer, and he was not about to be denied. 'Who, like, fills in your tax forms?'

'You mean for the IRS?'

'Yeah, that's it.'

'It's handled by our tax division, down on the second floor.'

'Here in this building?'

'Yes.'

'Then get it for me. Get me the tax records for everybody here.'

I looked at their faces, and a couple wanted to say, 'Just go ahead and shoot me.' I must've hesitated too long, because Mister shouted, 'Do it now!' And he used the gun when he shouted.

I called Rudolph, who also hesitated, and so I shouted at him. 'Just fax them in here,' I demanded. 'Last year's only.'

10

We stared at the fax machine in the corner for fifteen minutes, afraid Mister might start executing us if our 1040's didn't hurry along.

TWO

Freshly anointed as scribe for the group, I sat where Mister pointed with the gun and clutched the faxes. My buddies had been standing for almost two hours, backs to the wall, still joined together, barely able to move, and they were beginning to slouch and slump and look miserable.

But their level of discomfort was about to rise significantly.

'You first,' he said to me. 'What's your name?'

'Michael Brock,' I answered politely. Nice to meet you.

'How much money did you make last year?'

'I've already told you. A hundred and twenty thousand. Before taxes.'

'How much did you give away?'

I was certain I could lie. I was not a tax lawyer, but I was confident I could dance around his questions. I found my 1040 and took my time flipping through the pages. Claire had earned thirty-one thousand dollars as a second-year surgical resident, so our gross income looked quite handsome. But we paid fifty-three thousand in taxes – federal income and an amazing variety of others – and after repayment of student loans, Claire's educational expenses, twenty-four hundred a month for a very nice apartment in Georgetown, two late-model cars with the obligatory mortgages, and a host of other costs naturally related to a comfortable lifestyle, we had invested only twenty-two thousand in mutual funds.

Mister was waiting patiently. In fact, his patience was beginning to unnerve me. I assumed that the SWAT boys were crawling in the air vents, climbing nearby trees, scampering across the roofs of buildings next door, looking at blueprints of our offices, doing all the things you see on TV with the goal of somehow placing a bullet through his skull, and he seemed oblivious to it. He had accepted his fate and was ready to die. Not true for the rest of us.

He continually toyed with the red wire, and that kept my heart rate over a hundred.

'I gave a thousand dollars to Yale,' I said. 'And two thousand to the local United Way.'

'How much did you give to poor people?'

I doubted if the Yale money went to feed needy students. 'Well, the United Way spreads the money around the city, and I'm sure some of it went to help the poor.'

'How much did you give to the hungry?'

'I paid fifty-three thousand dollars in taxes, and a nice chunk of it went for welfare, Medicaid, aid to dependent children, stuff like that.'

'And you did this voluntarily, with a giving spirit?'

'I didn't complain,' I said, lying like most of my countrymen.

'Have you ever been hungry?'

He liked simple answers, and my wit and sarcasm would not be productive. 'No,' I said. 'I have not.'

'Have you ever slept in the snow?'

'No.'

'You make a lot of money, yet you're too greedy to hand me some change on the sidewalk.' He waved the gun at the rest of them. 'All of you. You walk right by me as I sit and beg. You spend more on fancy coffee

13

than I do on meals. Why can't you help the poor, the sick, the homeless? You have so much.'

I caught myself looking at those greedy bastards along with Mister, and it was not a pretty sight. Most were staring at their feet. Only Rafter glared down the table, thinking the thoughts all of us had when we stepped over the Misters of D.C.: If I give you some change you'll (1) run to the liquor store, (2) only beg more, (3) never leave the sidewalk.

Silence again. A helicopter hovered nearby, and I could only imagine what they were planning in the parking lot. Pursuant to Mister's instructions, the phone lines were on hold, so there was no communication. He had no desire to talk to or negotiate with anyone. He had his audience in the conference room.

'Which of these guys makes the most money?' he asked me.

Malamud was the only partner, and I shuffled the papers until I found his.

'That would be me,' Malamud offered.

'What is your name?'

'Nate Malamud.'

I flipped through Nate's return. It was a rare moment to see the intimate details of a partner's success, but I got no pleasure from it.

'How much?' Mister asked me.

Oh, the joys of the IRS code. What would you like, sir? Gross? Adjusted gross? Net? Taxable? Income from salaries and wages? Or income from business and investments?

Malamud's salary from the firm was fifty thousand dollars a month, and his annual bonus, the one we all dreamed about, was five hundred and ten thousand. It had been a very good year, and we all knew it. He was one of many partners who had earned over a million dollars.

I decided to play it safe. There was lots of other

income tucked away near the back of the return – rental properties, dividends, a small business – but I guessed that if Mister somehow grabbed the return he would struggle with the numbers.

'One point one million,' I said, leaving another two hundred thousand on the table.

He contemplated this for a moment. 'You made a million dollars,' he said to Malamud, who wasn't the least bit ashamed of it.

'Yes, I did.'

'How much did you give to the hungry, and the homeless?'

I was already scouring his itemized deductions for the truth.

'I don't recall exactly. My wife and I give to a lot of charities. I know there was a donation, I think for five thousand, to the Greater D.C. Fund, which, as I'm sure you know, distributes money to the needy. We give a lot. And we're happy to do it.'

'I'm sure you're very happy,' Mister replied, with the first hint of sarcasm.

He wasn't about to allow us to explain how generous we *really* were. He simply wanted the hard facts. He instructed me to list all nine names, and beside each write last year's income, then last year's gifts to charities.

It took some time, and I didn't know whether to hurry or be deliberate. Would he slaughter us if he didn't like the math? Perhaps I shouldn't hurry. It was immediately obvious that we rich folks had made lots of money while handing over precious little of it. At the same time, I knew the longer the situation dragged on, the crazier the rescue scenarios would become.

He hadn't mentioned executing a hostage every hour. He didn't want his buddies freed from jail. He didn't seem to want anything, really.

I took my time. Malamud set the pace. The rear was

brought up by Colburn, a third-year associate who grossed a mere eighty-six thousand. I was dismayed to learn my pal Barry Nuzzo earned eleven thousand more than I did. We would discuss it later.

'If you round it off, it comes to three million dollars,' I reported to Mister, who appeared to be napping again, with his fingers still on the red wire.

He slowly shook his head. 'And how much for the poor people?'

'Total contributions of one hundred eighty thousand.'

'I don't want total contributions. Don't put me and my people in the same class with the symphony and the synagogue, and all your pretty white folks clubs where you auction wine and autographs and give a few bucks to the Boy Scouts. I'm talking about food. Food for hungry people who live here in the same city you live in. Food for little babies. Right here. Right in this city, with all you people making millions, we got little babies starving at night, crying 'cause they're hungry. How much for food?'

He was looking at me. I was looking at the papers in front of me. I couldn't lie.

He continued. 'We got soup kitchens all over town, places where the poor and homeless can get something to eat. How much money did you folks give to the soup kitchens? Any?'

'Not directly,' I said. 'But some of these charities –'

'Shut up!'

He waved the damned gun again.

'How about homeless shelters? Places we sleep when it's ten degrees outside. How many shelters are listed there in those papers?'

Invention failed me. 'None,' I said softly.

He jumped to his feet, startling us, the red sticks fully visible under the silver duct tape. He kicked his chair back. 'How 'bout clinics? We got these little

16

clinics where doctors – good decent people who used to make lots of money – come and donate their time to help the sick. They don't charge nothing. Government used to help pay the rent, help buy the medicine and supplies. Now the government's run by Newt and all the money's gone. How much do you give to the clinics?'

Rafter looked at me as if I should do something, perhaps suddenly see something in the papers and say, 'Damn! Look here! We gave half a million bucks to the clinics and soup kitchens.'

That's exactly what Rafter would do. But not me. I didn't want to get shot. Mister was a lot smarter than he looked.

I flipped through the papers as Mister walked to the windows and peeked around the mini-blinds. 'Cops everywhere,' he said, just loud enough for us to hear. 'And lots of ambulances.'

He then forgot about the scene below and shuffled along the edge of the table until he stopped near his hostages. They watched every move, with particular attention paid to the explosives. He slowly raised the gun, and aimed it directly at Colburn's nose, less than three feet away.

'How much did you give to the clinics?'

'None,' Colburn said, closing his eyes tightly, ready to cry. My heart froze and I held my breath.

'How much to the soup kitchens?'

'None.'

'How much to the homeless shelters?'

'None.'

Instead of shooting Colburn, he aimed at Nuzzo and repeated the three questions. Nuzzo had identical responses, and Mister moved down the line, pointing, asking the same questions, getting the same answers. He didn't shoot Rafter, much to our dismay.

'Three million dollars,' he said in disgust, 'and not a

dime for the sick and hungry. You are miserable people.'

We felt miserable. And I realized he was not going to kill us.

How could an average street bum acquire dynamite? And who would teach him how to wire it?

At dusk he said he was hungry, and he told me to call the boss and order soup from the Methodist Mission at L Street and Seventeenth, Northwest. They put more vegetables in the broth, Mister said. And the bread was not as stale as in most kitchens.

'The soup kitchen does carryout?' Rudolph asked, his voice incredulous. It echoed around the room from the speakerphone.

'Just do it, Rudolph!' I barked back at him. 'And get enough for ten people.' Mister told me to hang up, and again put the lines on hold.

I could see our friends and a squadron of cops flying across the city, through rush-hour traffic, and descending upon the quiet little mission where the ragged street people hunched over their bowls of broth and wondered what the hell was going on. Ten orders to go, extra bread.

Mister made another trip to the window when we heard the helicopter again. He peeked out, stepped back, tugged at his beard, and pondered the situation. What type of invasion could they possibly be planning that would involve a helicopter? Maybe it was to evacuate the wounded.

Umstead had been fidgeting for an hour, much to the dismay of Rafter and Malamud, who were joined to him at the wrists. He finally couldn't stand it any longer.

'Uh, sir, excuse me, but I really have to, uh, go to the boys' room.'

Mister kept tugging. 'Boys' room. What's a boys' room?'

'I need to pee, sir,' Umstead said, very much like a third-grader. 'I can't hold it any longer.'

Mister looked around the room, and noticed a porcelain vase sitting innocently on a coffee table. With another wave of the gun, he ordered me to untie Umstead.

'The boys' room is over there,' Mister said.

Umstead removed the fresh flowers from the vase, and with his back to us urinated for a long time while we studied the floor. When he finally finished, Mister told us to move the conference table next to the windows. It was twenty feet long, solid walnut like most of the furniture at Drake & Sweeney, and with me on one end and Umstead grunting on the other, we managed to inch it over about six feet until Mister said stop. He made me latch Malamud and Rafter together, leaving Umstead a free man. I would never understand why he did this.

Next, he forced the remaining seven bound hostages to sit on the table with their backs to the wall. No one dared ask why, but I figured he wanted a shield from sharpshooters. I later learned that the police had snipers perched on a building next door. Perhaps Mister had seen them.

After standing for five hours, Rafter and company were relieved to be off their feet. Umstead and I were told to sit in chairs, and Mister took a seat at the end of the table. We waited.

Life in the streets must teach one patience. He seemed content to sit in silence for long periods of time, his eyes hiding behind the glasses, his head perfectly still.

'Who are the evictors?' he mumbled, to no one in particular, and he waited a couple of minutes before saying it again.

19

We looked at each other, confused, with no clue what he was talking about. He appeared to be staring at a spot on the table, not far from Colburn's right foot.

'Not only do you ignore the homeless, you help put them in the streets.'

We, of course, nodded along, all singing from the same sheet. If he wanted to heap verbal abuse on us, we were perfectly willing to accept it.

Our carryout arrived at a few minutes before seven. There was a sharp knock on the door. Mister told me to place a call and warn the police that he would kill one of us if he saw or heard anyone outside. I explained this carefully to Rudolph, and I stressed that no rescue should be attempted. We were negotiating.

Rudolph said he understood.

Umstead walked to the door, unlocked it, and looked at Mister for instructions. Mister was behind him, with the gun less than a foot from Umstead's head.

'Open the door very slowly,' Mister said.

I was standing a few feet behind Mister when the door opened. The food was on a small cart, one of our paralegals used to haul around the enormous amounts of paper we generated. I could see four large plastic containers of soup, and a brown paper bag filled with bread. I don't know if there was anything to drink. We never found out.

Umstead took one step into the hallway, grabbed the cart, and was about to pull it back into the conference room when the shot cracked through the air. A lone police sniper was hiding behind a credenza next to Madam Devier's desk, forty feet away, and he got the clear look he needed. When Umstead bent over to grab the cart, Mister's head was exposed for a split second, and the sniper blew it off.

Mister lurched backward without uttering a sound,

and my face was instantly covered with blood and fluids. I thought I'd been hit too, and I remember screaming in pain. Umstead was yelling somewhere in the hall. The other seven scrambled off the table like scalded dogs, all yelling and digging toward the door, half of them dragging the other half. I was on my knees, clutching my eyes, waiting for the dynamite to explode, then I bolted for the other door, away from the mayhem. I unlocked it, yanked it open, and the last time I saw Mister he was twitching on one of our expensive Oriental rugs. His hands were loose at his sides, nowhere near the red wire.

The hallway was suddenly filled with SWAT guys, all clad in fierce-looking helmets and thick vests, dozens of them crouching and reaching. They were a blur. They grabbed us and carried us through the reception area to the elevators.

'Are you hurt?' they asked me.

I didn't know. There was blood on my face and shirt, and a sticky liquid that a doctor later described as cerebrospinal fluid.

THREE

On the first floor, as far away from Mister as they could get, the families and friends were waiting. Dozens of our associates and colleagues were packed in the offices and hallways, waiting for our rescue. A loud cheer went up when they saw us.

Because I was covered with blood, they took me to a small gym in the basement. It was owned by our firm and virtually ignored by the lawyers. We were too busy to exercise, and anyone caught working out would almost certainly be assigned more work.

I was instantly surrounded by doctors, none of whom happened to be my wife. Once I convinced them the blood was not mine, they relaxed and conducted a routine exam. Blood pressure was up, pulse was crazy. They gave me a pill.

What I really wanted was a shower. They made me lie on a table for ten minutes while they watched my blood pressure. 'Am I in shock?' I asked.

'Probably not.'

I certainly felt like it. Where was Claire? For six hours I was held at gunpoint, life hanging by a thread, and she couldn't be bothered to come wait with the rest of the families.

The shower was long and hot. I washed my hair three times with heavy shampoo, then I stood and dripped for an eternity. Time was frozen. Nothing mattered. I was alive, breathing and steaming.

I changed into someone else's clean gym clothes, which were much too big, and went back to the table for another check of my blood pressure. My secretary, Polly, came in and gave me a long hug. I needed it desperately. She had tears in her eyes.

'Where's Claire?' I asked her.

'On call. I've tried calling the hospital.'

Polly knew there wasn't much left of the marriage.

'Are you okay?' she asked.

'I think so.'

I thanked the doctors and left the gym. Rudolph met me in the hall and gave me a clumsy embrace. He used the word 'congratulations,' as if I had accomplished something.

'No one expects you to work tomorrow,' he said. Did he think a day off would cure all my problems?

'I haven't thought about tomorrow,' I said.

'You need some rest,' he added, as if the doctors hadn't thought of this.

I wanted to speak to Barry Nuzzo, but my fellow hostages had already left. No one was injured, just a few rope burns on the wrists.

With the carnage held to a minimum, and the good guys up and smiling, the excitement at Drake & Sweeney waned quickly. Most of the lawyers and staff had waited nervously on the first floor, far away from Mister and his explosives. Polly had my overcoat, and I put it on over the large sweat suit. My tasseled loafers looked odd, but I didn't care.

'There are some reporters outside,' Polly said.

Ah, yes, the media. What a story! Not just your garden-variety on-the-job shooting, but a bunch of lawyers held hostage by a street crazy.

But they didn't get their story, did they? The lawyers escaped, the bad guy took a bullet, the

23

explosives fizzled when their owner hit the floor. Oh, what could've been! A shot, then a bomb, a flash of white light as the windows shattered, arms and legs landing in the street, all duly recorded live by Channel Nine for the evening's lead story.

'I'll drive you home,' Polly said. 'Follow me.' I was very thankful someone was telling me what to do. My thoughts were slow and cumbersome, one still-frame after another, with no concept of plot or setting.

We left the ground floor through a service door. The night air was sharp and cold, and I breathed its sweetness until my lungs ached. As Polly ran to get her car, I hid at the corner of the building and watched the circus out front. There were police cars, ambulances, television vans, even a fire truck. They were packing and leaving. One of the ambulances was parked with its rear to the building, no doubt waiting to carry Mister to the morgue.

I'm alive! I am alive! I said this over and over, smiling for the first time. I'm alive!

I closed my eyes tightly and offered a short but sincere prayer of thanks.

The sounds began coming back. As we sat in silence, Polly behind the wheel, driving slowly and waiting for me to say something, I heard the piercing clap of the sniper's rifle. Then the thud as it found its mark, and the stampede as the other hostages scrambled off the table and through the door.

What had I seen? I had glanced at the table where the seven were staring intently at the door, then back to Mister as he raised the gun and pointed it at Umstead's head. I was directly behind him when he was hit. What stopped the bullet from leaving him and getting me? Bullets go through walls and doors and people.

'He was not going to kill us,' I said, barely loud enough to be heard.

Polly was relieved to hear my voice. 'What was he doing then?'

'I don't know.'

'What did he want?'

'He never said. It's amazing how little was actually said. We sat for hours just looking at each other.'

'Why wouldn't he talk to the police?'

'Who knows? That was his biggest mistake. If he'd kept the phones open, I could've convinced the cops that he was not going to kill us.'

'You don't blame the cops, do you?'

'No. Remind me to write them letters.'

'Are you working tomorrow?'

'What else would I do tomorrow?'

'Just thought you might need a day off.'

'I need a year off. One day won't help.'

Our apartment was the third floor of a rowhouse on P Street in Georgetown. Polly stopped at the curb. I thanked her and got out, and I could tell from the dark windows that Claire was not home.

I met Claire the week after I moved to D.C. I was just out of Yale with a great job in a rich firm, a brilliant future like the other fifty rookies in my class. She was finishing her degree in political science at American University. Her grandfather was once the governor of Rhode Island, and her family has been well connected for centuries.

Drake & Sweeney, like most large firms, treats the first year as a boot camp. I worked fifteen hours a day, six days a week, and on Sundays Claire and I would have our weekly date. Sunday nights I was in the office. We thought that if we got married, we would have more time together. At least we could share a bed, but sleep was about all we did.

25

The wedding was large, the honeymoon brief, and when the luster wore off I was back at the office ninety hours a week. During the third month of our union, we actually went eighteen days without sex. She counted.

She was a sport for the first few months, but she grew weary of being neglected. I did not blame her, but young associates don't complain in the hallowed offices of Drake & Sweeney. Less than ten percent of each class will make partner, so the competition is ruthless. The rewards are great, at least a million bucks a year. Billing lots of hours is more important than a happy wife. Divorce is common. I didn't dream of asking Rudolph to lighten my load.

By the end of our first year together, Claire was very unhappy and we had started to quarrel.

She decided to go to med school. Tired of sitting at home watching TV, she figured she could become as self-absorbed as I was. I thought it was a wonderful idea. It took away most of my guilt.

After four years with the firm, they started dropping hints about our chances of making partner. The hints were collected and compared among many of the associates. It was generally felt that I was on the fast track to a partnership. But I had to work even harder.

Claire became determined to spend more time away from the apartment than I did, and so both of us slid into the silliness of extreme workaholism. We stopped fighting and simply drifted apart. She had her friends and interests, I had mine. Fortunately, we did not make the mistake of reproducing.

I wish I had done things differently. We were in love once, and we let it get away.

As I entered the dark apartment, I needed Claire for the first time in years. You come face to face with death and you need to talk about it. You need to be needed, to be stroked, to be told that someone cares.

I fixed a vodka with ice and sat on the sofa in the den. I fumed and pouted because I was alone, then my thoughts switched to the six hours I'd spent with Mister.

Two vodkas later, I heard her at the door. She unlocked it, and called, 'Michael.'

I didn't say a word because I was still pouting and fuming. She walked into the den, and stopped when she saw me. 'Are you all right?' she asked with genuine concern.

'I'm fine,' I said softly.

She dropped her bag and overcoat, and walked to the sofa, where she hovered over me.

'Where have you been?' I asked.

'At the hospital.'

'Of course.' I took a long drink. 'Look, I've had a bad day.'

'I know all about it, Michael.'

'You do?'

'Of course I do.'

'Then where the hell were you?'

'At the hospital.'

'Nine of us held hostage for six hours by a crazy man. Eight families show up because they're somewhat concerned. We get lucky and escape, and I have to catch a ride home with my secretary.'

'I couldn't be there.'

'Of course you couldn't. How thoughtless of me.'

She sat down in a chair next to the sofa. We glared at each other. 'They made us stay at the hospital,' she began, very icy. 'We knew about the hostage situation, and there was a chance there could've been casualties. It's standard procedure in that situation – they notify the hospitals, and everyone is placed on standby.'

Another long drink as I tried to think of something sharp to say.

'I couldn't help you at your office,' she continued. 'I was waiting at the hospital.'

'Did you call?'

'I tried. The phone lines were jammed. I finally got a cop, and he hung up on me.'

'It was over two hours ago. Where have you been?'

'In OR. We lost a little boy in surgery; he was hit by a car.'

'I'm sorry,' I said. I could never comprehend how doctors faced so much death and pain. Mister was only the second corpse I had ever laid eyes on.

'I'm sorry too,' she said, and with that she went to the kitchen and returned with a glass of wine. We sat in the semi-darkness for a while. Because we did not practice communication, it did not come easy.

'Do you want to talk about it?' she asked.

'No. Not now.' And I really didn't. The alcohol mixed with the pills, and my breathing became heavy. I thought of Mister, how calm and peaceful he was, even though he waved a gun and had dynamite strapped to his stomach. He was thoroughly unmoved by long stretches of silence.

Silence was what I wanted. Tomorrow I would talk.

FOUR

The chemicals worked until four the next morning, when I awoke to the harsh smell of Mister's sticky brain fluid weaving through my nostrils. I was frantic for a moment in the darkness. I rubbed my nose and eyes, and thrashed around the sofa until I heard someone move. Claire was sleeping in a chair next to me.

'It's okay,' she said softly, touching my shoulder. 'Just a bad dream.'

'Would you get me some water?' I said, and she went to the kitchen.

We talked for an hour. I told her everything I could remember about the event. She sat close to me, rubbing my knee, holding the glass of water, listening carefully. We had talked so little in the past few years.

She had to make her rounds at seven, so we cooked breakfast together, waffles and bacon. We ate at the kitchen counter with a small television in front of us. The six o'clock news began with the hostage drama. There were shots of the building during the crisis, the mob outside, some of my fellow captives hurriedly leaving when it was over. At least one of the helicopters we had heard belonged to the news station, and its camera had zoomed down for a tight shot of the window. Through it, Mister could be seen for a few seconds as he peeked out.

His name was DeVon Hardy, age forty-five, a Vietnam vet with a short criminal record. A mug shot from an arrest for burglary was put on the screen behind the early morning newsperson. It looked nothing like Mister – no beard, no glasses, much younger. He was described as homeless with a history of drug use. No motive was known. No family had come forward.

There were No comments from our side, and the story fizzled.

The weather was next. Heavy snow was expected to hit by late afternoon. It was the twelfth day of February, and already a record had been set for snowfall.

Claire drove me to the office, where at six-forty I was not surprised to see my Lexus parked among several other imports. The lot was never empty. We had people who slept at the office.

I promised to call her later in the morning, and we would try to have lunch at the hospital. She wanted me to take it easy, at least for a day or two.

What was I supposed to do? Lie on the sofa and take pills? The consensus seemed to be that I needed a day off, after which I guessed I would be expected to return to my duties at full throttle.

I said good morning to the two very alert security guards in the lobby. Three of the four elevators were open, waiting, and I had a choice. I stepped onto the one Mister and I had taken, and things slowed to a crawl.

A hundred questions at once: Why had he picked our building? Our firm? Where had he been in the moments before he entered the lobby? Where were the security guards who usually loitered near the front? Why me? Hundreds of lawyers came and went all day long. Why the sixth floor?

And what was he after? I did not believe DeVon

Hardy went to the trouble of wrapping himself with explosives and risking his life, humble as it was, to chastise a bunch of wealthy lawyers over their lack of generosity. He could've found richer people. And perhaps greedier ones.

His question, 'Who are the evictors?,' was never answered. But it wouldn't take long.

The elevator stopped, and I stepped off, this time without anyone behind me. Madam Devier was still asleep at that hour, somewhere, and the sixth floor was quiet. In front of her desk I paused and stared at the two doors to the conference room. I slowly opened the nearest one, the one where Umstead stood when the bullet shot over his head and into Mister's. I took a long breath and flipped a light switch.

Nothing had happened. The conference table and chairs were in perfect order. The Oriental rug upon which Mister died had been replaced with an even prettier one. A fresh coat of paint covered the walls. Even the bullet hole in the ceiling above Rafter's spot was gone.

The powers that be at Drake & Sweeney had spent some dough the previous night to make sure the incident never occurred. The room might attract a few of the curious throughout the day, and there certainly could be nothing to gawk at. It might make folks neglect their work for a minute or two. There simply couldn't be any trace of street trash in our pristine offices.

It was a cold-blooded cover-up, and, sadly, I understood the rationale behind it. I was one of the rich white guys. What did I expect, a memorial? A pile of flowers brought in by Mister's fellow street people?

I didn't know what I expected. But the smell of fresh paint made me nauseous.

On my desk every morning, in precisely the same spot, were *The Wall Street Journal* and *The Washington*

Post. I used to know the name of the person who put them there, but it was long forgotten. On the front page of the *Post*'s Metro section, below the fold, was the same mug shot of DeVon Hardy, and a large story about yesterday's little crisis.

I read it quickly because I figured I knew more details than any reporter. But I learned a few things. The red sticks were not dynamite. Mister had taken a couple of broom handles, sawed them into little pieces, wrapped the ominous silver tape around them, and scared the living hell out of us. The gun was a .44 automatic, stolen.

Because it was the *Post*, the story dealt more with DeVon Hardy than with his victims, though, in all fairness, and much to my satisfaction, not a single word had been uttered by anyone at Drake & Sweeney.

According to one Mordecai Green, Director of the 14th Street Legal Clinic, DeVon Hardy had worked for many years as a janitor at the National Arboretum. He'd lost his job as a result of budget cutting. He had served a few months in jail for burglary, then landed in the streets. He'd struggled with alcohol and drugs, and was routinely picked up for shoplifting. Green's clinic had represented him several times. If there was family, his lawyer knew nothing about it.

As to motive, Green had little to offer. He did say that DeVon Hardy had been evicted recently from an old warehouse in which he had been squatting.

An eviction is a legal procedure, carried out by lawyers. I had a pretty good idea which one of the thousands of D.C. firms had tossed Mister into the streets.

The 14th Street Legal Clinic was funded by a charity and worked only with the homeless, according to Green. 'Back when we got federal money, we had seven lawyers. Now we're down to two,' he said.

Not surprisingly, the *Journal* didn't mention the story. Had any of the nine corporate lawyers in the nation's fifth-largest silk-stocking firm been killed or even slightly wounded, it would've been on the front page.

Thank God it wasn't a bigger story. I was at my desk, reading my papers, in one piece with lots of work to do. I could've been at the morgue alongside Mister.

Polly arrived a few minutes before eight with a big smile and a plate of homemade cookies. She was not surprised to see me at work.

In fact, all nine of the hostages punched in, most ahead of schedule. It would've been a glaring sign of weakness to stay home with the wife and get pampered.

'Arthur's on the phone,' Polly announced. Our firm had at least ten Arthurs, but only one prowled the halls without the need of a last name. Arthur Jacobs was the senior partner, the CEO, the driving force, a man we admired and respected greatly. If the firm had a heart and soul, it was Arthur. In seven years, I had spoken to him three times.

I told him I was fine. He complimented me on my courage and grace under pressure, and I almost felt like a hero. I wondered how he knew. He had probably talked to Malamud first, and was working his way down the ladder. So the stories would begin, then the jokes. Umstead and his porcelain vase would no doubt cause much hilarity.

Arthur wanted to meet with the ex-hostages at ten, in the conference room, to record our statements on video.

'Why?' I asked.

'The boys in litigation think it's a good idea,' he said, his voice razor-sharp in spite of his eighty years. 'His family will probably sue the cops.'

33

'Of course,' I said.

'And they'll probably name us as defendants. People will sue for anything, you know.'

Thank goodness, I almost said. Where would we be without lawsuits?

I thanked him for his concern, and he was gone, off to call the next hostage.

The parade started before nine, a steady stream of well-wishers and gossipers lingering by my office, deeply concerned about me but also desperate for the details. I had a pile of work to do, but I couldn't get to it. In the quiet moments between guests, I sat and stared at the row of files awaiting my attention, and I was numb. My hands wouldn't reach.

It was not the same. The work was not important. My desk was not life and death. I had seen death, almost felt it, and I was naive to think I could simply shrug it off and bounce back as if nothing had happened.

I thought about DeVon Hardy and his red sticks with the multicolored wires running in all directions. He'd spent hours building his toys and planning his assault. He'd stolen a gun, found our firm, made a crucial mistake that cost him his life, and no one, not one single person I worked with, gave a damn about him.

I finally left. The traffic was getting worse, and I was getting chatted up by people I couldn't stand. Two reporters called. I told Polly I had some errands to run, and she reminded me of the meeting with Arthur. I went to my car, started it and turned on the heater, and sat for a long time debating whether to participate in the reenactment. If I missed it, Arthur would be upset. No one misses a meeting with Arthur.

I drove away. It was a rare opportunity to do something stupid. I'd been traumatized. I had to leave.

34

Arthur and the rest of the firm would just have to give me a break.

I drove in the general direction of Georgetown, but to no place in particular. The clouds were dark; people scurried along the sidewalks; snow crews were getting ready. I passed a beggar on M Street, and wondered if he knew DeVon Hardy. Where do the street people go in a snowstorm?

I called the hospital and was informed that my wife would be in emergency surgery for several hours. So much for our romantic lunch in the hospital cafeteria.

I turned and went northeast, past Logan Circle, into the rougher sections of the city until I found the 14th Street Legal Clinic. Fourteenth at Q, NW. I parked at the curb, certain I would never again see my Lexus.

The clinic occupied half of a three-story red-brick Victorian mansion that had seen better days. The windows on the top floor were boarded with aging plywood. Next door was a grungy Laundromat. The crack houses couldn't be far away.

The entrance was covered by a bright yellow canopy, and I didn't know whether to knock or to just barge in. The door wasn't locked, and I slowly turned the knob and stepped into another world.

It was a law office of sorts, but a very different one from the marble and mahogany of Drake & Sweeney. In the large room before me there were four metal desks, each covered with a suffocating collection of files stacked a foot high. More files were placed haphazardly on the worn carpet around the desks. The wastebaskets were filled, and wadded sheets of legal paper had rolled off and onto the floor. One wall was covered with file cabinets in a variety of colors. The word processors and phones were ten years old. The wooden bookshelves were sagging. A large fading photograph of Martin Luther King hung crookedly on

35

the back wall. Several smaller offices branched off the front room.

It was busy and dusty and I was fascinated with the place.

A fierce Hispanic woman stopped typing after watching me for a moment. 'You looking for somebody?' she asked. It was more of a challenge than a request. A receptionist at Drake & Sweeney would be fired on the spot for such a greeting.

She was Sofia Mendoza, according to a nameplate tacked to the side of her desk, and I would soon learn that she was more than a receptionist. A loud roar came from one of the side rooms, and startled me without fazing Sofia.

'I'm looking for Mordecai Green,' I said politely, and at that moment he followed his roar and stomped out of his side office and into the main room. The floor shook with each step. He was yelling across the room for someone named Abraham.

Sofia nodded at him, then dismissed me and returned to her typing. Green was a huge black man, at least six five with a wide frame that carried a lot of weight. He was in his early fifties, with a gray beard and round eyeglasses that were framed in red. He took a look at me, said nothing, yelled again for Abraham while sauntering across the creaking floor. He disappeared into an office, then emerged seconds later without Abraham.

Another look at me, then, 'Can I help you?'

I walked forward and introduced myself.

'Nice to meet you,' he said, but only because he had to. 'What's on your mind?'

'DeVon Hardy,' I said.

He looked at me for a few seconds, then glanced at Sofia, who was lost in her work. He nodded toward his office, and I followed him into a twelve-by-twelve room with no windows and every square inch of

36

available floor space covered with manila files and battered law books.

I handed him my gold-embossed Drake & Sweeney card, which he studied with a deep frown. Then he gave it back to me, and said, 'Slumming, aren't you?'

'No,' I said, taking the card.

'What do you want?'

'I come in peace. Mr. Hardy's bullet almost got me.'

'You were in the room with him?'

'Yep.'

He took a deep breath and lost the frown. He pointed to the only chair on my side. 'Have a seat. But you might get dirty.'

We both sat, my knees touching his desk, my hands thrust deep into the pockets of my overcoat. A radiator rattled behind him. We looked at each other, then looked away. It was my visit, I had to say something. But he spoke first.

'Guess you had a bad day, huh?' he said, his raspy voice lower and almost compassionate.

'Not as bad as Hardy's. I saw your name in the paper, that's why I came.'

'I'm not sure what I'm supposed to do.'

'Do you think the family will sue? If so, then maybe I should leave.'

'There's no family, not much of a lawsuit. I could make some noise with it. I figure the cop who shot him is white, so I could squeeze a few bucks out of the city, probably get a nuisance settlement. But that's not my idea of fun.' He waved his hand over the desk. 'God knows I got enough to do.'

'I never saw the cop,' I said, realizing it for the first time.

'Forget about a lawsuit. Is that why you're here?'

'I don't know why I'm here. I went back to my desk this morning like nothing happened, but I couldn't think straight. I took a drive. Here I am.'

He shook his head slowly, as if he was trying to understand this. 'You want some coffee?'

'No thanks. You knew Mr. Hardy pretty well.'

'Yeah, DeVon was a regular.'

'Where is he now?'

'Probably in the city morgue at D.C. General.'

'If there's no family, what happens to him?'

'The city buries the unclaimed. On the books it's called a pauper's funeral. There's a cemetery near RFK Stadium where they pack 'em in. You'd be amazed at the number of people who die unclaimed.'

'I'm sure I would.'

'In fact, you'd be amazed at every aspect of homeless life.'

It was a soft jab, and I was not in the mood to spar. 'Do you know if he had AIDS?'

He cocked his head back, looked at the ceiling, and rattled that around for a few seconds. 'Why?'

'I was standing behind him. The back of his head was blown off. I got a face full of blood. That's all.'

With that, I crossed the line from a bad guy to just an average white guy.

'I don't think he had AIDS.'

'Do they check them when they die?'

'The homeless?'

'Yes.'

'Most of the time, yes. DeVon, though, died by other means.'

'Can you find out?'

He shrugged and thawed some more. 'Sure,' he said reluctantly, and took his pen from his pocket. 'Is that why you're here? Worried about AIDS?'

'I guess it's one reason. Wouldn't you be?'

'Sure.'

Abraham stepped in, a small hyper man of about forty who had public interest lawyer stamped all over him. Jewish, dark beard, horn-rimmed glasses, rumpled blazer, wrinkled khakis, dirty sneakers, and the weighty aura of one trying to save the world.

He did not acknowledge me, and Green was not one for social graces. 'They're predicting a ton of snow,' Green said to him. 'We need to make sure every possible shelter is open.'

'I'm working on it,' Abraham snapped, then abruptly left.

'I know you're busy,' I said.

'Is that all you wanted? A blood check.'

'Yeah, I guess. Any idea why he did it?'

He removed his red glasses, wiped them with a tissue, then rubbed his eyes. 'He was mentally ill, like a lot of these people. You spend years on the streets, soaked with booze, stoned on crack, sleeping in the cold, getting kicked around by cops and punks, it makes you crazy. Plus, he had a bone to pick.'

'The eviction.'

'Yep. A few months ago, he moved into an abandoned warehouse at the corner of New York and Florida. Somebody threw up some plywood, chopped up the place, and made little apartments. Wasn't a bad place as far as homeless folk go – a roof, some toilets, water. A hundred bucks a month, payable to an ex-pimp who fixed it up and claimed he owned it.'

'Did he?'

'I think so.' He pulled a thin file from one of the stacks on his desk, and, miraculously, it happened to be the one he wanted. He studied its contents for a moment. 'This is where it gets complicated. The property was purchased last month by a company called RiverOaks, some big real estate outfit.'

'And RiverOaks evicted everyone?'

'Yep.'

'Odds are, then, that RiverOaks would be represented by my firm.'

'Good odds, yes.'

39

'Why is it complicated?'

'I've heard it secondhand that they got no notice before the eviction. The people claim they were paying rent to the pimp, and if so, then they were more than squatters. They were tenants, thus entitled to due process.'

'Squatters get no notice?'

'None. And it happens all the time. Street folk will move into an abandoned building, and most of the time nothing happens. So they think they own it. The owner, if he's inclined to show up, can toss 'em without notice. They have no rights at all.'

'How did DeVon Hardy track down our firm?'

'Who knows? He wasn't stupid, though. Crazy, but not stupid.'

'Do you know the pimp?'

'Yeah. Completely unreliable.'

'Where did you say the warehouse was?'

'It's gone now. They leveled it last week.'

I had taken enough of his time. He glanced at his watch, I glanced at mine. We swapped phone numbers and promised to keep in touch.

Mordecai Green was a warm, caring man who labored on the streets protecting hordes of nameless clients. His view of the law required more soul than I could ever muster.

On my way out, I ignored Sofia because she certainly ignored me. My Lexus was still parked at the curb, already covered with an inch of snow.

FIVE

I drifted through the city as the snow fell. I couldn't recall the last time I had driven the streets of D.C. without being late for a meeting. I was warm and dry in my heavy luxury car, and I simply moved with the traffic. There was no place to go.

The office would be off-limits for a while, what with Arthur mad at me; and I'd have to suffer through a hundred random drop-ins, all of which would start with the phony 'How you doin'?'

My car phone rang. It was Polly, panicky. 'Where are you?' she asked.

'Who wants to know?'

'A lot of people. Arthur for one. Rudolph. Another reporter called. There are some clients in need of advice. And Claire called from the hospital.'

'What does she want?'

'She's worried, like everybody else.'

'I'm fine, Polly. Tell everybody I'm at the doctor's office.'

'Are you?'

'No, but I could be. What did Arthur say?'

'He didn't call. Rudolph did. They were waiting for you.'

'Let 'em wait.'

A pause, then a very slow 'Okay. When might you be dropping by?'

'Don't know. I guess whenever the doctor releases me. Why don't you go home; we're in the middle of a storm. I'll call you tomorrow.' I hung up on her.

The apartment was a place I had rarely seen in the light of day, and I couldn't stand the thought of sitting by the fire and watching it snow. If I went to a bar, I'd probably never leave.

So I drove. I flowed with the traffic as the commuters began a hasty retreat into the Maryland and Virginia suburbs, and I breezed along near-empty streets coming back into the city. I found the cemetery near RFK where they buried the unclaimed, and I passed the Methodist Mission on Seventeenth where last night's uneaten dinner originated. I drove through sections of the city I had never been near and probably would never see again.

By four, the city was empty. The skies were darkening, the snow was quite heavy. Several inches already covered the ground, and they were predicting a lot more.

Of course, not even a snowstorm could shut down Drake & Sweeney. I knew lawyers there who loved midnights and Sundays because the phones didn't ring. A heavy snow was a delightful respite from the grueling drudgery of nonstop meetings and conference calls.

I was informed by a security guard in the lobby that the secretaries and most of the staff had been sent home at three. I took Mister's elevator again.

In a neat row in the center of my desk were a dozen pink phone messages, none of which interested me. I went to my computer and began searching our client index.

RiverOaks was a Delaware corporation, organized in 1977, headquartered in Hagerstown, Maryland. It was privately held, thus little financial information was available. The attorney was N. Braden Chance, a name unknown to me.

I looked him up in our vast database. Chance was a partner in our real estate division, somewhere down on the fourth floor. Age forty-four, married, law school at Duke, undergrad at Gettysburg, an impressive but thoroughly predictable résumé.

With eight hundred lawyers threatening and suing daily, our firm had over thirty-six thousand active files. To make sure our office in New York didn't sue one of our clients in Chicago, each new file was entered immediately into our data system. Every lawyer, secretary, and paralegal at Drake & Sweeney had a PC, and thus instant access to general information about all files. If one of our probate attorneys in Palm Beach handled the estate of a rich client, I could, if I were so inclined, punch a few keys and learn the basics of our representation.

There were forty-two files for RiverOaks, almost all of them real estate transactions in which the company had purchased property. Chance was the attorney of record on every file. Four were eviction actions, three of which took place last year. The first phase of the search was easy.

On January 31, RiverOaks purchased property on Florida Avenue. The seller was TAG, Inc. On February 4, our client evicted a number of squatters from an abandoned warehouse on the property – one of whom, I now knew, was Mister DeVon Hardy, who took the eviction personally and somehow tracked down the lawyers.

I copied the file name and number, and strolled to the fourth floor.

No one joined a large firm with the goal of becoming a real estate lawyer. There were far more glamorous arenas in which to establish reputations. Litigation was the all-time favorite, and the litigators

43

were still the most revered of all God's lawyers, at least within the firm. A few of the corporate fields attracted top talent – mergers and acquisitions was still hot, securities was an old favorite. My field, antitrust, was highly regarded. Tax law was horribly complex, but its practitioners were greatly admired. Governmental relations (lobbying) was repulsive but paid so well that every D.C. firm had entire wings of lawyers greasing the skids.

But no one set out to be a real estate lawyer. I didn't know how it happened. They kept to themselves, no doubt reading fine print in mortgage documents, and were treated as slightly inferior lawyers by the rest of the firm.

At Drake & Sweeney, each lawyer kept his current files in his office, often under lock and key. Only the retired files were accessible by the rest of the firm. No lawyer could be compelled to show a file to another lawyer, unless requested by a senior partner or a member of the firm's executive committee.

The eviction file I wanted was still listed as current, and after the Mister episode I was certain it was well protected.

I saw a paralegal scanning blueprints at a desk next to a secretarial pool, and I asked him where I might find the office of Braden Chance. He nodded to an open door across the hall.

To my surprise, Chance was at his desk, projecting the appearance of a very busy lawyer. He was perturbed by my intrusion, and rightfully so. Proper protocol would have been for me to call ahead and set up a meeting. I wasn't worried about protocol.

He didn't ask me to sit. I did so anyway, and that didn't help his mood.

'You were one of the hostages,' he said irritably when he made the connection.

'Yes, I was.'

'Must've been awful.'

'It's over. The guy with the gun, the late Mr. Hardy, was evicted from a warehouse on February 4. Was it one of our evictions?'

'It was,' he snapped. Because of his defensiveness, I guessed the file had been picked through during the day. He'd probably reviewed it thoroughly with Arthur and the brass. 'What about it?'

'Was he a squatter?'

'Damned sure was. They're all squatters. Our client is trying to clean up some of that mess.'

'Are you sure he was a squatter?'

His chin dropped and his eyes turned red. Then he took a breath. 'What are you after?'

'Could I see the file?'

'No. It's none of your business.'

'Maybe it is.'

'Who is your supervising partner?' He yanked out his pen as if to take down the name of the person who would reprimand me.

'Rudolph Mayes.'

He wrote in large strokes. 'I'm very busy,' he said. 'Would you please leave?'

'Why can't I see the file?'

'Because it's mine, and I said no. How's that?'

'Maybe that's not good enough.'

'It's good enough for you. Why don't you leave?' He stood, his hand shaking as he pointed to the door. I smiled at him and left.

The paralegal heard everything, and we exchanged puzzled looks as I passed his desk. 'What an ass,' he said very quietly, almost mouthing the words.

I smiled again and nodded my agreement. An ass and a fool. If Chance had been pleasant and explained that Arthur or some other honcho from above had ordered the file sealed, then I wouldn't have been as

45

suspicious. But it was obvious there was something in the file.

Getting it would be the challenge.

With all the cell phones Claire and I owned – pocket, purse, and car, not to mention a couple of pagers – communication should've been a simple matter. But nothing was simple with our marriage. We hooked up around nine. She was exhausted from another one of her days, which were inevitably more fatiguing than anything I could possibly have done. It was a game we shamelessly played – my job is more important because I'm a doctor/lawyer.

I was tiring of the games. I could tell she was pleased that my brush with death had produced aftershocks, that I'd left the office to wander the streets. No doubt her day had been far more productive than mine.

Her goal was to become the greatest female neurosurgeon in the country, a brain surgeon even males would turn to when all hope was lost. She was a brilliant student, fiercely determined, blessed with enormous stamina. She would bury the men, just as she was slowly burying me, a well-seasoned marathon man from the halls of Drake & Sweeney. The race was getting old.

She drove a Miata sports car, no four-wheel drive, and I was worried about her in the bad weather. She would be through in an hour, and it would take that long for me to drive to Georgetown Hospital. I would pick her up there, and we would try to find a restaurant. If not, it would be Chinese carryout, our standard fare.

I began arranging papers and objects on my desk, careful to ignore the neat row of my ten most current files. I kept only ten on my desk, a method I'd learned from Rudolph, and I spent time with each file every day. Billing was a factor. My top ten invariably included the wealthiest clients, regardless of how pressing their legal problems. Another trick from Rudolph.

I was expected to bill twenty-five hundred hours a year. That's fifty hours a week, fifty weeks a year. My average billing rate was three hundred dollars an hour, so I would gross for my beloved firm a total of seven hundred and fifty thousand dollars. They paid me a hundred and twenty thousand of this, plus another thirty for benefits, and assigned two hundred thousand to overhead. The partners kept the rest, divided annually by some horrendously complex formula that usually caused fistfights.

It was rare for one of our partners to earn less than a million a year, and some earned over two. And once I became a partner, I would be a partner for life. So if I made it when I was thirty-five, which happened to be the fast track I was on, then I could expect thirty years of glorious earnings and immense wealth.

That was the dream that kept us at our desks at all hours of the day and night.

I was scribbling these numbers, something I did all the time and something I suspect every lawyer in our firm did, when the phone rang. It was Mordecai Green.

'Mr. Brock,' he said politely, his voice clearly audible but competing with a din in the background.

'Yes. Please call me Michael.'

'Very well. Look, I made some calls, and you have nothing to worry about. The blood test was negative.'

'Thank you.'

'Don't mention it.'

'Just thought you'd want to know as soon as possible.'

'Thanks,' I said again, as the racket rose behind him. 'Where are you?'

'At a homeless shelter. A big snow brings 'em in faster than we can feed them, so it takes all of us to keep up. Gotta run.'

The desk was old mahogany, the rug was Persian, the chairs were a rich crimson leather, the technology was state-of-the-art, and as I studied my finely appointed office, I wondered, for the first time in many years there, how much all of it cost. Weren't we just chasing money? Why did we work so hard; to buy a richer rug, an older desk?

There in the warmth and coziness of my beautiful room, I thought of Mordecai Green, who at that moment was volunteering his time in a busy shelter, serving food to the cold and hungry, no doubt with a warm smile and a pleasant word.

Both of us had law degrees, both of us had passed the same bar exam, both of us were fluent in the tongue of legalese. We were kindred to some degree. I helped my clients swallow up competitors so they could add more zeros to the bottom line, and for this I would become rich. He helped his clients eat and find a warm bed.

I looked at the scratchings on my legal pad – the earnings and the years and the path to wealth – and I was saddened by them. Such blatant and unashamed greed.

The phone startled me.

'Why are you at the office?' Claire asked, each word spoken slowly because each word was covered with ice.

I looked in disbelief at my watch. 'I, uh, well, a client called from the West Coast. It's not snowing out there.'

I think it was a lie I'd used before. It didn't matter.

'I am waiting, Michael. Should I walk?'

'No. I'll be there as fast as I can.'

48

I'd kept her waiting before. It was part of the game –
we were much too busy to be prompt.

I ran from the building, into the storm, not really
too concerned that another night had been ruined.

SIX

The snow had finally stopped. Claire and I sipped our coffee by the kitchen window. I was reading the paper by the light of a brilliant morning sun. They had managed to keep National Airport open.

'Let's go to Florida,' I said. 'Now.'

She gave me a withering look. 'Florida?'

'Okay, the Bahamas. We can be there by early afternoon.'

'There's no way.'

'Sure there is. I'm not going to work for a few days, and –'

'Why not?'

'Because I'm cracking up, and around the firm if you crack up, then you get a few days off.'

'You are cracking up.'

'I know. It's kinda fun, really. People give you space, treat you with velvet gloves, kiss your ass. Might as well make the most of it.'

The tight face returned, and she said, 'I can't.'

And that was the end of that. It was a whim, and I knew she had too many obligations. It was a cruel thing to do, I decided as I returned to the paper, but I didn't feel bad about it. She wouldn't have gone with me under any circumstances.

She was suddenly in a hurry – appointments, classes, rounds, the life of an ambitious young surgical resident. She showered and changed and was ready to go. I drove her to the hospital.

We didn't talk as we inched through the snow-filled streets.

'I'm going to Memphis for a couple of days,' I said matter-of-factly when we arrived at the hospital entrance on Reservoir Street.

'Oh really,' she said, with no discernible reaction.

'I need to see my parents. It's been almost a year. I figure this is a good time. I don't do well in snow, and I'm not in the mood for work. Cracking up, you know.'

'Well, call me,' she said, opening her door. Then she shut it – no kiss, no good-bye, no concern. I watched her hurry down the sidewalk and disappear into the building.

It was over. And I hated to tell my mother.

My parents were in their early sixties, both healthy and trying gamely to enjoy forced retirement. Dad was an airline pilot for thirty years. Mom had been a bank manager. They worked hard, saved well, and provided a comfortable upper-middle-class home for us. My two brothers and I had the best private schools we could get into.

They were solid people, conservative, patriotic, free of bad habits, fiercely devoted to each other. They went to church on Sundays, the parade on July the Fourth, Rotary Club once a week, and they traveled whenever they wanted.

They were still grieving over my brother Warner's divorce three years earlier. He was an attorney in Atlanta who married his college sweetheart, a Memphis girl from a family we knew. After two kids, the marriage went south. His wife got custody and moved to Portland. My parents got to see the grandkids once a year, if all went well. It was a subject I never brought up.

I rented a car at the Memphis airport and drove east into the sprawling suburbs where the white people lived. The blacks had the city; the whites, the suburbs. Sometimes the blacks would move into a subdivision, and the whites would move to another one, farther away. Memphis crept eastward, the races running from each other.

My parents lived on a golf course, in a new glass house designed so that every window overlooked a fairway. I hated the house because the fairway was always busy. I didn't express my opinions, though.

I had called from the airport, so Mother was waiting with great anticipation when I arrived. Dad was on the back nine somewhere.

'You look tired,' she said after the hug and kiss. It was her standard greeting.

'Thanks, Mom. You look great.' And she did. Slender and bronze from her daily tennis and tanning regimen at the country club.

She fixed iced tea and we drank it on the patio, where we watched other retirees fly down the fairway in their golf carts.

'What's wrong?' she said before a minute passed, before I took the first sip.

'Nothing. I'm fine.'

'Where's Claire? You guys never call us, you know. I haven't heard her voice in two months.'

'Claire's fine, Mom. We're both alive and healthy and working very hard.'

'Are you spending enough time together?'

'No.'

'Are you spending any time together?'

'Not much.'

She frowned and rolled her eyes with motherly

concern. 'Are you having trouble?' she asked, on the attack.

'Yes.'

'I knew it. I knew it. I could tell by your voice on the phone that something was wrong. Surely you're not headed for a divorce too. Have you tried counseling?'

'No. Slow down.'

'Then why not? She's a wonderful person, Michael. Give the marriage everything you have.'

'We're trying, Mother. But it's difficult.'

'Affairs? Drugs? Alcohol? Gambling? Any of the bad things?'

'No. Just two people going their separate ways. I work eighty hours a week. She works the other eighty.'

'Then slow down. Money isn't everything.' Her voice broke just a little, and I saw wetness in her eyes.

'I'm sorry, Mom. At least we don't have kids.'

She bit her lip and tried to be strong, but she was dying inside. And I knew exactly what she was thinking: two down, one to go. She would take my divorce as a personal failure, the same way she broke down with my brother's. She would find some way to blame herself.

I didn't want the pity. To move things along to more interesting matters, I told her the story of Mister, and, for her benefit, downplayed the danger I'd been in. If the story made the Memphis paper, my parents had missed it.

'Are you all right?' she asked, horrified.

'Of course. The bullet missed me. I'm here.'

'Oh, thank God. I mean, well, emotionally are you all right?'

'Yes, Mother, I'm all together. No broken pieces. The firm wanted me to take a couple of days off, so I came home.'

'You poor thing. Claire, and now this.'

'I'm fine. We had a lot of snow last night, and it was a good time to leave.'

'Is Claire safe?'

'As safe as anybody in Washington. She lives at the hospital, probably the smartest place to be in that city.'

'I worry about you so much. I see the crime statistics, you know. It's a very dangerous city.'

'Almost as dangerous as Memphis.'

We watched a ball land near the patio, and waited for its owner to appear. A stout lady rolled out of a golf cart, hovered over the ball for a second, then shanked it badly.

Mother left to get more tea, and to wipe her eyes.

I don't know which of my parents got the worst end of my visit. My mother wanted strong families with lots of grandchildren. My father wanted his boys to move quickly up the ladder and enjoy the rewards of our hard-earned success.

Late that afternoon my dad and I did nine holes. He played; I drank beer and drove the cart. Golf had yet to work its magic on me. Two cold ones and I was ready to talk. I had repeated the Mister tale over lunch, so he figured I was just loafing for a couple of days, collecting myself before I roared back into the arena.

'I'm getting kind of sick of the big firm, Dad,' I said as we sat by the third tee, waiting for the foursome ahead to clear. I was nervous, and my nervousness irritated me greatly. It was my life, not his.

'What's that supposed to mean?'

'Means I'm tired of what I'm doing.'

'Welcome to the real world. You think the guy working a drill press in a factory doesn't get tired of what he's doing? At least you're getting rich.'

So he took round one, almost by a knockout. Two

holes later, as we stomped through the rough looking for his ball, he said, 'Are you changing jobs?'

'Thinking about it.'

'Where are you going?'

'I don't know. It's too early. I haven't been looking for another position.'

'Then how do you know the grass is greener if you haven't been looking?' He picked up his ball and walked off.

I drove alone on the narrow paved trail while he stalked down the fairway chasing his shot, and I wondered why that gray-haired man out there scared me so much. He had pushed all of his sons to set goals, work hard, strive to be Big Men, with everything aimed at making lots of money and living the American dream. He had certainly paid for anything we needed.

Like my brothers, I was not born with a social conscience. We gave offerings to the church because the Bible strongly suggests it. We paid taxes to the government because the law requires it. Surely, somewhere in the midst of all this giving some good would be done, and we had a hand in it. Politics belonged to those willing to play that game, and besides, there was no money to be made by honest people. We were taught to be productive, and the more success we attained, the more society would benefit, in some way. Set goals, work hard, play fair, achieve prosperity.

He double-bogeyed the fifth hole, and was blaming it on his putter when he climbed into the cart.

'Maybe I'm not looking for greener pastures,' I said.

'Why don't you just go ahead and say what you're trying to say?' he said. As usual, I felt weak for not facing the issue boldly.

'I'm thinking about public interest law.'

'What the hell is that?'

'It's when you work for the good of society without making a lot of money.'

'What are you, a Democrat now? You've been in Washington too long.'

'There are lots of Republicans in Washington. In fact, they've taken over.'

We rode to the next tee in silence. He was a good golfer, but his shots were getting worse. I'd broken his concentration.

Stomping through the rough again, he said, 'So some wino gets his head blown off and you gotta change society. Is that it?'

'He wasn't a wino. He fought in Vietnam.'

Dad flew B-52's in the early years of Vietnam, and this stopped him cold. But only for a second. He wasn't about to yield an inch. 'One of those, huh?'

I didn't respond. The ball was hopelessly lost, and he wasn't really looking. He flipped another onto the fairway, hooked it badly, and away we went.

'I hate to see you blow a good career, son,' he said. 'You've worked too hard. You'll be a partner in a few years.'

'Maybe.'

'You need some time off, that's all.'

That seemed to be everybody's remedy.

I took them to dinner at a nice restaurant. We worked hard to avoid the topics of Claire, my career, and the grandkids they seldom saw. We talked about old friends and old neighborhoods. I caught up on the gossip, none of which interested me in the least.

I left them at noon on Friday, four hours before my flight, and I headed back to my muddled life in D.C.

SEVEN

Of course, the apartment was empty when I returned
Friday night, but with a new twist. There was a note
on the kitchen counter. Following my cue, Claire had
gone home to Providence for a couple of days. No
reason was given. She asked me to phone when I got
home.

I called her parents' and interrupted dinner. We
labored through a five-minute chat in which it was
determined that both of us were indeed fine, Memphis
was fine and so was Providence, the families were fine,
and she would return sometime Sunday afternoon.

I hung up, fixed coffee, and drank a cup staring out
the bedroom window, watching the traffic crawl along
P Street, still covered with snow. If any of the snow
had melted, it wasn't obvious.

I suspected Claire was telling her parents the same
dismal story I had burdened mine with. It was sad and
odd and yet somehow not surprising that we were
being honest with our families before we faced the
truth ourselves. I was tired of it and determined that
one day very soon, perhaps as early as Sunday, we
would sit somewhere, probably at the kitchen table,
and confront reality. We would lay bare our feelings
and fears and, I was quite sure, start planning our
separate futures. I knew she wanted out, I just didn't
know how badly.

I practiced the words I would say to her out loud until they sounded convincing, then I went for a long walk. It was ten degrees with a sharp wind, and the chill cut through my trench coat. I passed the handsome homes and cozy rowhouses, where I saw real families eating and laughing and enjoying the warmth, and moved onto M Street, where throngs of those suffering from cabin fever filled the sidewalks. Even a freezing Friday night on M was never dull; the bars were packed, the restaurants had waiting lines, the coffee shops were filled.

I stood at the window of a music club, listening to the blues with snow packed around my ankles, watching the young couples drink and dance. For the first time in my life, I felt like something other than a young person. I was thirty-two, but in the last seven years I had worked more than most people do in twenty. I was tired, not old but bearing down hard on middle age, and I admitted that I was no longer fresh from college. Those pretty girls in there would never look twice at me now.

I was frozen, and it was snowing again. I bought a sandwich, stuffed it into a pocket, and slogged my way back to the apartment. I fixed a strong drink, and a small fire, and I ate in the semi-darkness, very much alone.

In the old days, Claire's absence for the weekend would have given me guilt-free grounds to live at the office. Sitting by the fire, I was repulsed by that thought. Drake & Sweeney would be standing proudly long after I was gone, and the clients and their problems, which had seemed so crucial, would be tended to by other squads of young lawyers. My departure would be a slight bump in the road for the firm, scarcely noticeable. My office would be taken minutes after I walked out.

At some time after nine, the phone rang, jolting me

from a long, somber daydream. It was Mordecai Green, speaking loudly into a cell phone. 'Are you busy?' he asked.

'Uh, not exactly. What's going on?'

'It's cold as hell, snowing again, and we're short on manpower Do you have a few hours to spare?'

'To do what?'

'To work. We really need able bodies down here. The shelters and soup kitchens are packed, and we don't have enough volunteers.'

'I'm not sure I'm qualified.'

'Can you spread peanut butter on bread?'

'I think so.'

'Then you're qualified.'

'Okay, where do I go?'

'We're ten blocks or so from the office. At the intersection of Thirteenth and Euclid, you'll see a yellow church on your right. Ebenezer Christian Fellowship. We're in the basement.'

I scribbled this down, each word getting shakier because Mordecai was calling me into a combat zone. I wanted to ask if I should pack a gun. I wondered if he carried one. But he was black, and I wasn't. What about my car, my prized Lexus?

'Got that?' he growled after a pause.

'Yeah. Be there in twenty minutes,' I said bravely, my heart already pounding.

I changed into jeans, a sweatshirt, and designer hiking boots. I took the credit cards and most of the cash out of my wallet. In the top of a closet, I found an old wool-lined denim jacket, stained with coffee and paint, a relic from law school, and as I modeled it in the mirror I hoped it made me look non-affluent. It did not. If a young actor wore it on the cover of *Vanity Fair*, a trend would start immediately.

I desperately wanted a bulletproof vest. I was

59

scared, but as I locked the door and stepped into the snow, I was also strangely excited.

The drive-by shootings and gang attacks I had expected did not materialize. The weather kept the streets empty and safe, for the moment. I found the church and parked in a lot across the street. It looked like a small cathedral, at least a hundred years old and no doubt abandoned by its original congregation.

Around a corner I saw some men huddled together, waiting by a door. I brushed past them as if I knew exactly where I was going, and I entered the world of the homeless.

As badly as I wanted to barge ahead, to pretend I had seen this before and had work to do, I couldn't move. I gawked in amazement at the sheer number of poor people stuffed into the basement. Some were lying on the floor, trying to sleep. Some were sitting in groups, talking in low tones. Some were eating at long tables and others in their folding chairs. Every square inch along the walls was covered with people sitting with their backs to the cinder blocks. Small children cried and played as their mothers tried to keep them close. Winos lay rigid, snoring through it all. Volunteers passed out blankets and walked among the throng, handing out apples.

The kitchen was at one end, bustling with action as food was prepared and served. I could see Mordecai in the background, pouring fruit juice into paper cups, talking incessantly. A line waited patiently at the serving tables.

The room was warm, and the odors and aromas and the gas heat mixed to create a thick smell that was not unpleasant. A homeless man, bundled up much like Mister, bumped into me and it was time to move.

I went straight to Mordecai, who was delighted to see me. We shook hands like old friends, and he introduced me to two volunteers whose names I never heard.

'It's crazy,' he said. 'A big snow, a cold snap, and we work all night. Grab that bread over there.' He pointed to a tray of sliced white bread. I took it and followed him to a table.

'It's real complicated. You got bologna here, mustard and mayo there. Half the sandwiches get mustard, half get mayo, one slice of bologna, two slices of bread. Do a dozen with peanut butter every now and then. Got it?'

'Yeah.'

'You catch on quick.' He slapped me on the shoulder and disappeared.

I hurriedly made ten sandwiches, and declared myself to be proficient. Then I slowed, and began to watch the people as they waited in line, their eyes downcast but always glancing at the food ahead. They were handed a paper plate, a plastic bowl and spoon, and a napkin. As they shuffled along, the bowl was filled with soup, half a sandwich was placed on the plate, then an apple and a small cookie were added. A cup of apple juice was waiting at the end.

Most of them said a quiet 'Thanks' to the volunteer handing out the juice, then they moved away, gingerly holding the plate and bowl. Even the children were still and careful with their food.

Most seemed to eat slowly, savoring the warmth and feel of food in their mouths, the aroma in their faces. Others ate as fast as possible.

Next to me was a gas stove with four burners, each with a large pot of soup cooking away. On the other side of it, a table was covered with celery, carrots, onions, tomatoes, and whole chickens. A volunteer with a large knife was chopping and dicing with a vengeance. Two more volunteers manned the stove.

61

Several hauled the food to the serving tables. For the moment, I was the only sandwich man.

'We need more peanut butter sandwiches,' Mordecai announced as he returned to the kitchen. He reached under the table and grabbed a two-gallon jug of generic peanut butter. 'Can you handle it?'

'I'm an expert,' I said.

He watched me work. The line was momentarily short; he wanted to talk.

'I thought you were a lawyer,' I said, spreading peanut butter.

'I'm a human first, then a lawyer. It's possible to be both – not quite so much on the spread there. We have to be efficient.'

'Where does the food come from?'

'Food bank. It's all donated. Tonight we're lucky because we have chicken. That's a delicacy. Usually it's just vegetables.'

'This bread is not too fresh.'

'Yes, but it's free. Comes from a large bakery, their day-old stuff. You can have a sandwich if you like.'

'Thanks. I just had one. Do you eat here?'

'Rarely.' From the looks of his girth, Mordecai had not maintained a diet of vegetable soup and apples. He sat on the edge of the table and studied the crowd. 'Is this your first trip to a shelter?'

'Yep.'

'What's the first word that comes to mind?'

'Hopeless.'

'That's predictable. But you'll get over it.'

'How many people live here?'

'None. This is just an emergency shelter. The kitchen is open every day for lunch and dinner, but it's not technically a shelter. The church is kind enough to open its doors when the weather is bad.'

I tried to understand this. 'Then where do these people live?'

62

'Some are squatters. They live in abandoned build-ings, and they're the lucky ones. Some live on the streets; some in parks; some in bus stations; some under bridges. They can survive there as long as the weather is tolerable. Tonight they would freeze.'

'Then where are the shelters?'

'Scattered about. There are about twenty – half privately funded, the other half run by the city, which, thanks to the new budget, will soon close two of them.'

'How many beds?'

'Five thousand, give or take.'

'How many homeless?'

'That's always a good question because they're not the easiest group to count. Ten thousand is a good guess.'

'Ten thousand?'

'Yep, and that's just the people on the street. There are probably another twenty thousand living with families and friends, a month or two away from homelessness.'

'So there are at least five thousand people on the streets?' I said, my disbelief obvious.

'At least.'

A volunteer asked for sandwiches. Mordecai helped me, and we made another dozen. Then we stopped and watched the crowd again. The door opened, and a young mother entered slowly, holding a baby and followed by three small children, one of whom wore a pair of shorts and mismatched socks, no shoes. A towel was draped over its shoulders. The other two at least had shoes, but little clothing. The baby appeared to be asleep.

The mother seemed dazed, and once inside the basement was uncertain where to go next. There was not a spot at a table. She led her family toward the food, and two smiling volunteers stepped forward to

63

help. One parked them in a corner near the kitchen and began serving them food, while the other covered them with blankets.

Mordecai and I watched the scene develop. I tried not to stare, but who cared?

'What happens to her when the storm is over?' I asked.

'Who knows? Why don't you ask her?'

That put me on the spot. I was not ready to get my hands dirty.

'Are you active in the D.C. bar association?' he asked.

'Somewhat. Why?'

'Just curious. The bar does a lot of pro bono work with the homeless.'

He was fishing, and I wasn't about to get caught. 'I work on death penalty cases,' I said proudly, and somewhat truthfully. Four years earlier, I had helped one of our partners write a brief for an inmate in Texas. My firm preached pro bono to all its associates, but the free work had damned well better not interfere with the billings.

We kept watching the mother and her four children. The two toddlers ate their cookies first while the soup was cooling. The mother was either stoned or in shock.

'Is there a place she can go to right now and live?' I asked.

'Probably not,' Mordecai answered nonchalantly, his large feet swinging from the edge of the table. 'As of yesterday, the waiting list for emergency shelter had five hundred names on it.'

'For emergency shelter?'

'Yep. There's one hypothermia shelter the city graciously opens when the temperature drops below freezing. That might be her only chance, but I'm sure it's packed tonight. The city is then kind enough to close the shelter when things thaw.'

The sous-chef had to leave, and since I was the nearest volunteer who wasn't busy at the moment, I was pressed into duty. While Mordecai made sandwiches, I chopped celery, carrots, and onions for an hour, all under the careful eye of Miss Dolly, one of the founding members of the church, who'd been in charge of feeding the homeless for eleven years now. It was her kitchen. I was honored to be in it, and I was told at one point that my chunks of celery were too large. They quickly became smaller. Her apron was white and spotless, and she took enormous pride in her work.

'Do you ever get used to seeing these people?' I asked her at one point. We were standing in front of the stove, distracted by an argument in the back somewhere. Mordecai and the minister intervened and peace prevailed.

'Never, honey,' she said, wiping her hands on a towel. 'It still breaks my heart. But in Proverbs it says, "Happy is the man who feeds the poor." That keeps me going.'

She turned and gently stirred the soup. 'Chicken's ready,' she said in my direction.

'What does that mean?'

'Means you take the chicken off the stove, pour the broth into that pot, let the chicken cool, then bone it.'

There was an art to boning, especially using Miss Dolly's method. My fingers were hot and practically blistered when I finished.

EIGHT

Mordecai led me up a dark stairway to the foyer. 'Watch your step,' he said, almost in a whisper, as we pushed through a set of swinging doors into the sanctuary. It was dim, because people were trying to sleep everywhere. They were sprawled on the pews, snoring. They were squirming under the pews, mothers trying to make children be still. They were huddled in the aisles, leaving a narrow path for us as we worked our way toward the pulpit. The choir loft was filled with them too.

'Not many churches will do this,' he whispered as we stood near the altar table and surveyed the rows of pews.

I could understand their reluctance. 'What happens Sunday?' I whispered back.

'Depends on the weather. The Reverend is one of us. He has, on occasion, canceled worship instead of running them out.'

I was not sure what 'one of us' meant, but I didn't feel like a member of the club. I heard the ceiling creak, and realized that there was a U-shaped balcony above us. I squinted and slowly focused on another mass of humanity layered in the rows of seats up there. Mordecai was looking too.

'How many people . . .' I mumbled, unable to finish the thought.

'We don't count. We just feed and shelter.'

A gust of wind hit the side of the building and rattled the windows. It was considerably colder in the sanctuary than in the basement. We tiptoed over bodies and left through a door by the organ.

It was almost eleven. The basement was still crowded, but the soup line was gone. 'Follow me,' Mordecai said.

He took a plastic bowl and held it forth for a volunteer to fill. 'Let's see how well you cook,' he said with a smile.

We sat in the middle of the pack, at a folding table with street people at our elbows. He was able to eat and chat as if everything was fine; I wasn't. I played with my soup, which, thanks to Miss Dolly, was really quite good, but I couldn't get beyond the fact that I, Michael Brock, an affluent white boy from Memphis and Yale and Drake & Sweeney, was sitting among the homeless in the basement of a church in the middle of Northwest D.C. I had seen one other white face, that of a middle-aged wino who had eaten and disappeared.

I was sure my Lexus was gone, certain I could not survive five minutes outside the building. I vowed to stick to Mordecai, whenever and however he decided to leave.

'This is good soup,' he pronounced. 'It varies,' he explained. 'Depends on what's available. And the recipe is different from place to place.'

'I got noodles the other day at Martha's Table,' said the man sitting to my right, a man whose elbow was closer to my bowl than my own.

'Noodles?' Mordecai asked, in mock disbelief. 'In your soup?'

'Yep. 'Bout once a month you get noodles. Course everybody knows it now, so it's hard to get a table.'

I couldn't tell if he was joking or not, but there was a

67

twinkle in his eye. The idea of a homeless man lamenting the lack of tables in his favorite soup kitchen struck me as humorous. Hard to get a table; how many times had I heard that from friends in Georgetown?

Mordecai smiled. 'What's your name?' he asked the man. I would learn that Mordecai always wanted a name to go with a face. The homeless he loved were more than victims; they were his people.

It was a natural curiosity for me too. I wanted to know how the homeless became homeless. What broke in our vast system of public assistance to allow Americans to become so poor they lived under bridges?

'Drano,' he said, chomping on one of my larger celery chunks.

'Drano?' Mordecai said.

'Drano,' the man repeated.

'What's your last name?'

'Don't have one. Too poor.'

'Who gave you the name Drano?'

'My momma.'

'How old were you when she gave you the name Drano?'

''Bout five.'

'Why Drano?'

'She had this baby who wouldn't shut up, cried all the time, nobody could sleep. I fed it some Drano.' He told the story while stirring his soup. It was well rehearsed, well delivered, and I didn't believe a word of it. But others were listening, and Drano was enjoying himself.

'What happened to the baby?' Mordecai asked, playing the straight guy.

'Died.'

'That would be your brother,' Mordecai said.

'Nope. Sister.'

'I see. So you killed your sister.'

'Yeah, but we got plenty of sleep after that.'

Mordecai winked at me, as if he'd heard similar tales.

'Where do you live, Drano?' I asked.

'Here, in D.C.'

'Where do you stay?' Mordecai asked, correcting my vernacular.

'Stay here and there. I got a lot of rich women who pay me to keep them company.'

Two men on the other side of Drano found this amusing. One snickered, the other laughed.

'Where do you get your mail?' Mordecai asked.

'Post office,' he replied. Drano would have a quick answer for every question, so we left him alone.

Miss Dolly made coffee for the volunteers after she had turned off her stove. The homeless were bedding down for the night.

Mordecai and I sat on the edge of a table in the darkened kitchen, sipping coffee and looking through the large serving window at the huddled masses. 'How late will you stay?' I asked.

He shrugged. 'Depends. You get a coupla hundred people like this in one room, something usually happens. The Reverend would feel better if I stay.'

'All night?'

'I've done it many times.'

I hadn't planned on sleeping with these people. Nor had I planned on leaving the building without Morde-cai to guard me.

'Feel free to leave whenever you want,' he said. Leaving was the worst of my limited options. Midnight, Friday night, on the streets of D.C. White boy, beautiful car. Snow or not, I didn't like my odds out there.

'You have a family?' I asked.

'Yes. My wife is a secretary in the Department of

Labor. Three sons. One's in college, one's in the Army.' His voice trailed away before he got to son number three. I wasn't about to ask.

'And one we lost on the streets ten years ago. Gangs.'

'I'm sorry.'

'What about you?'

'Married, no kids.'

I thought about Claire for the first time in several hours. How would she react if she knew where I was? Neither of us had found time for anything remotely related to charity work.

She would mumble to herself, 'He's really cracking up,' or something to that effect.

I didn't care.

'What does your wife do?' he asked, making light conversation.

'She's a surgical resident at Georgetown.'

'You guys'll have it made, won't you? You'll be a partner in a big firm, she'll be a surgeon. Another American dream.'

'I guess.'

The Reverend appeared from nowhere and pulled Mordecai deep into the kitchen for a hushed conversation. I took four cookies from a bowl and walked to the corner where the young mother sat sleeping with her head propped on a pillow and the baby tucked under her arm. The toddlers were motionless under the blankets. But the oldest child was awake.

I squatted close to him, and held out a cookie. His eyes glowed and he grabbed it. I watched him eat every bite, then he wanted another. He was small and bony, no more than four years old.

The mother's head fell forward, jolting her. She looked at me with sad, tired eyes, then realized I was playing cookie man. She offered a faint smile, then rearranged the pillow.

'What's your name?' I whispered to the little boy. After two cookies, he was my friend for life.

'Ontario,' he said, slowly and plainly.

'How old are you?'

He held up four fingers, then folded one down, then raised it again.

'Four?' I asked.

He nodded, and extended his hand for another cookie, which I gladly gave him. I would have given him anything.

'Where do you stay?' I whispered.

'In a car,' he whispered back.

It took a second for this to sink in. I wasn't sure what to ask next. He was too busy eating to worry about conversation. I had asked three questions; he'd given three honest answers. They lived in a car.

I wanted to run and ask Mordecai what you do when you find people who live in a car, but I kept smiling at Ontario. He smiled back. He finally said, 'You got more apple juice?'

'Sure,' I said, and walked to the kitchen, where I filled two cups.

He gulped one down, and I handed him the second cup.

'Say thanks,' I said.

'Thanks,' he said, and stuck out his hand for another cookie.

I found a folding chair and took a position next to Ontario, with my back to the wall. The basement was quiet at times, but never still. Those who live without beds do not sleep calmly. Occasionally, Mordecai would pick his way around the bodies to settle some flare-up. He was so large and intimidating that no one dared challenge his authority.

With his stomach filled again, Ontario dozed off, his little head resting on his mother's feet. I slipped into the kitchen, poured another cup of coffee, and went back to my chair in the corner.

Then the baby erupted. Its pitiful voice wailed forth with amazing volume, and the entire room seemed to ripple with the noise. The mother was dazed, tired, frustrated at having been aroused from sleep. She told it to shut up, then placed it on her shoulder, and rocked back and forth. It cried louder, and there were rumblings from the other campers.

With a complete lack of sense or thought, I reached over and took the child, smiling at the mother as I did so in an attempt to win her confidence. She didn't care. She was relieved to get rid of it.

The child weighed nothing, and the damned thing was soaking wet. I realized this as I gently placed its head on my shoulder and began patting its rear. I moved to the kitchen, desperately searching for Mordecai or another volunteer to rescue me. Miss Dolly had left an hour earlier.

To my relief and surprise, the child grew quiet as I walked around the stove, patting and cooing and looking for a towel or something. My hand was soaked.

Where was I? What the hell was I doing? What would my friends think if they could see me in the dark kitchen, humming to a little street baby, praying that the diaper was only wet?

I didn't smell anything foul, though I was certain I could feel lice jumping from its head to mine. My best friend Mordecai appeared and turned on a switch. 'How cute,' he said.

'Do we have any diapers?' I hissed at him.

'Big job or little job?' he asked happily, walking toward the cabinets.

'I don't know. Just hurry.'

He pulled out a pack of Pampers, and I thrust the child at him. My denim jacket had a large wet spot on the left shoulder. With incredible deftness he placed the baby on the cutting board, removed the wet diaper, revealing a baby girl, cleaned her with a wipe of some sort, rediapered her with a fresh Pamper, then thrust her back at me. 'There she is,' he said proudly. 'Good as new.'

'The things they don't teach you in law school,' I said, taking the child.

I paced the floor with her for an hour, until she fell asleep. I wrapped her in my jacket, and gently placed her between her mother and Ontario.

It was almost 3 A.M., Saturday, and I had to go. My freshly pricked conscience could take only so much in one day. Mordecai walked me to the street, thanked me for coming, and sent me away coatless into the night. My car was sitting where I left it, covered with new snow.

He was standing in front of the church, watching me as I drove away.

NINE

Since my run-in with Mister on Tuesday, I had not billed a single hour for dear old Drake & Sweeney. I'd been averaging two hundred a month for five years, which meant eight per day for six days, with a couple left over. No day could be wasted and precious few hours left unaccounted for. When I fell behind, which rarely happened, I would work twelve hours on a Saturday and perhaps do the same on a Sunday. And if I wasn't behind, I would do only seven or eight hours on Saturday and maybe a few on Sunday. No wonder Claire went to med school.

As I stared at the bedroom ceiling late Saturday morning, I was almost paralyzed with inaction. I did not want to go to the office. I hated the thought. I dreaded the neat little rows of pink phone messages Polly had on my desk, the memos from higher-ups arranging meetings to inquire about my well-being, the nosy chitchat from the gossipers, and the inevitable 'How you doin'?' from friends and those genuinely concerned and those who couldn't care less. What I dreaded most, though, was the work. Antitrust cases are long and arduous, with files so thick they require boxes, and what was the point anyway? One billion-dollar corporation fighting another. A hundred lawyers involved, all cranking out paper.

I admitted to myself that I'd never loved the work. It

was a means to an end. If I practiced it with a fury, became a whiz and perfected a specialty, then one day soon I would be in demand. It could've been tax or labor or litigation. Who could love antitrust law?

By sheer will, I forced myself out of bed and into the shower.

Breakfast was a croissant from a bakery on M, with strong coffee, all taken with one hand on the wheel. I wondered what Ontario was having for breakfast, then told myself to stop the torture. I had the right to eat without feeling guilty, but food was losing its importance for me.

The radio said the day's high would be twenty degrees, the low near zero, with no more snow for a week.

I made it as far as the building's lobby before being accosted by one of my brethren. Bruce somebody from communications stepped onto the elevator when I did, and said gravely, 'How you doin', pal?'

'Fine. You?' I shot back.

'Okay. Look, we're pulling for you, you know. Hang in there.'

I nodded as if his support was crucial. Mercifully, he left on the second floor, but not before favoring me with a locker-room pat on the shoulder. Give 'em hell, Bruce.

I was damaged goods. My steps were slower as I passed Madam Devier's desk and the conference room. I went down the marble hallway until I found my office and slumped into the leather swivel, exhausted.

Polly had several ways of leaving behind the phone litter. If I had been diligent in returning calls, and if she happened to be pleased with my efforts, she would leave one or two message slips near my phone. If, however, I had not, and if this happened to displease her, then she liked nothing better than to line them up in the center of my desk, a sea of pink, all perfectly arranged in chronological order.

I counted thirty-nine messages, several urgent, several from the brass. Rudolph especially seemed to be irritated, judging by Polly's trail. I read them slowly as I collected them, then set them aside. I was determined to finish my coffee, in peace and without pressure, and so I was sitting at my desk, holding the cup with both hands, staring into the unknown, looking very much like someone teetering on the edge of a cliff, when Rudolph walked in.

The spies must have called him; a paralegal on the lookout, or maybe Bruce from the elevator. Perhaps the entire firm was on alert. No. They were too busy.

'Hello, Mike,' he said crisply, taking a seat, crossing his legs, settling in for serious business.

'Hi, Rudy,' I said. I had never called him Rudy to his face. It was always Rudolph. His current wife and the partners called him Rudy, but no one else.

'Where have you been?' he asked, without the slightest hint of compassion.

'Memphis.'

'Memphis?'

'Yeah, I needed to see my parents. Plus the family shrink is there.'

'A shrink?'

'Yes, he observed me for a couple of days.'

'Observed you?'

'Yeah, in one of those swanky little units with Persian rugs and salmon for dinner. A thousand bucks a day.'

'For two days? You were in for two days?'

'Yeah.' The lying didn't bother me, nor did I feel bad because the lying didn't bother me. The firm can be harsh, even ruthless, when it decides to be, and I was in no mood for an ass-chewing from Rudolph. He had marching orders from the executive committee, and he would make a report minutes after leaving my office. If I could thaw him, the report would go soft, the brass would relax. Life would be easier, for the short term.

'You should've called somebody,' he said, still hard, but the crack was coming.

'Come on, Rudolph. I was locked down. No phones.' There was just enough agony in my voice to soften him.

After a long pause, he said, 'Are you okay?'

'I'm fine.'

'You're fine?'

'The shrink said I'm fine.'

'One hundred percent?'

'A hundred and ten. No problems, Rudolph. I needed a little break, that's all. I'm fine. Back at full throttle.'

That was all Rudolph wanted. He smiled and relaxed and said, 'We have lots of work to do.'

'I know. I can't wait.'

He practically ran from my office. He would go straight to the phone and report that one of the firm's many producers was back in the saddle.

I locked the door and turned off the lights, then spent a painful hour covering my desk with papers and scribblings. Nothing was accomplished, but at least I was on the clock.

When I couldn't stand it any longer, I stuffed the phone messages in my pocket and walked out. I escaped without getting caught.

I stopped at a large discount pharmacy on Massachusetts, and had a delightful shopping spree. Candy and small toys for the kids, soap and toiletries for them all, socks and sweatpants in a variety of children's sizes. A large carton of Pampers. I had never had so much fun spending two hundred dollars.

And I would spend whatever was necessary to get them into a warm place. If it was a motel for a month, no problem. They would soon become my clients, and I would threaten and litigate with a vengeance until they had adequate housing. I couldn't wait to sue somebody.

I parked across from the church, much less afraid than I had been the night before, but still sufficiently scared. Wisely, I left the care packages in the car. If I walked in like Santa Claus it would start a riot. My intentions were to leave there with the family, take them to a motel, check them in, make sure they were bathed and cleaned and disinfected, then feed them until they were stuffed, see if they needed medical attention, maybe take them to get shoes and warm clothes, then feed them again. I didn't care what it would cost or how long it might take.

Nor did I care if people thought I was just another rich white guy working off a little guilt.

Miss Dolly was pleased to see me. She said hello and pointed to a pile of vegetables with skins in need of removal. First, though, I checked on Ontario and family, and couldn't find them. They were not in their spot, so I roamed through the basement, stepping over and around dozens of street people. They were not in the sanctuary, nor in the balcony.

I chatted with Miss Dolly as I peeled potatoes. She remembered the family from last night, but they had already left when she arrived around nine.

'Where would they go?' I wondered.

'Honey, these people move. They go from kitchen to kitchen, shelter to shelter. Maybe she heard they're giving out cheese over in Brightwood, or blankets somewhere. She might even have a job at McDonald's and she leaves the kids with her sister. You never know. But they don't stay in one place.'

I seriously doubted if Ontario's mother had a job,

but I wasn't about to debate this with Miss Dolly in her kitchen.

Mordecai arrived as the line was forming for lunch. I saw him before he saw me, and when our eyes made contact his entire face smiled.

A new volunteer had sandwich duty; Mordecai and I worked the serving tables, dipping ladles into the pots and pouring the soup into the plastic bowls. There was an art to it. Too much broth and the recipient might glare at you. Too many vegetables and there would be nothing left but broth. Mordecai had perfected his technique years ago; I suffered a number of glaring looks before I caught on. Mordecai had a pleasant word for everyone we served – hello, good morning, how are you, nice to see you again. Some of them smiled back, others never looked up.

As noon approached, the doors grew busier and the lines longer. More volunteers appeared from nowhere, and the kitchen hummed with the pleasant clutter and bang of happy people busy with their work. I kept looking for Ontario. Santa Claus was waiting, and the little fella didn't have a clue.

We waited until the lines were gone, then filled a bowl each. The tables were packed, so we ate in the kitchen, leaning against the sink.

'You remember that diaper you changed last night?' I asked between bites.

'As if I could forget.'

'I haven't seen them today.'

He chewed and thought about it for a second. 'They were here when I left this morning.'

'What time was that?'

'Six. They were in the corner over there, sound asleep.'

'Where would they go?'

'You never know.'

'The little boy told me they stayed in a car.'
'You talked to him?'
'Yeah.'
'And now you want to find him, don't you?'
'Yeah.'
'Don't count on it.'

After lunch, the sun popped through and the movement began. One by one they walked by the serving table, took an apple or an orange, and left the basement.

'The homeless are also restless,' Mordecai explained as we watched. 'They like to roam around. They have rituals and routines, favorite places, friends on the streets, things to do. They'll go back to their parks and alleys and dig out from the snow.'

'It's twenty degrees outside. Near zero tonight,' I said.

'They'll be back. Wait till dark, and this place will be hopping again. Let's take a ride.'

We checked in with Miss Dolly, who excused us for a while. Mordecai's well-used Ford Taurus was parked next to my Lexus. 'That won't last long around here,' he said, pointing at my car. 'If you plan to spend time in this part of town, I'd suggest you trade down.'

I hadn't dreamed of parting with my fabulous car. I was almost offended.

We got into his Taurus and slid out of the parking lot. Within seconds I realized Mordecai Green was a horrible driver, and I attempted to fasten my seat belt. It was broken. He seemed not to notice.

We drove the well-plowed streets of Northwest Washington, blocks and sections of boarded-up rowhouses, past projects so tough ambulance drivers refused to enter, past schools with razor wire glistening on top of the chain link, into neighborhoods permanently scarred by riots. He was an amazing tour guide.

Every inch was his turf, every corner had a story, every street had a history. We passed other shelters and kitchens. He knew the cooks and the Reverends. Churches were good or bad, with no blurring of the lines. They either opened their doors to the homeless or kept them locked. He pointed out the law school at Howard, a place of immense pride for him. His legal education had taken five years, at night, while he worked a full-time job and a part-time one. He showed me a burned-out rowhouse where crack dealers once operated. His third son, Cassius, had died on the sidewalk in front of it.

When we were near his office, he asked if it would be all right to stop in for a minute. He wanted to check his mail. I certainly didn't mind. I was just along for the ride.

It was dim, cold, and empty. He flipped on light switches and began talking. 'There are three of us. Me, Sofia Mendoza, and Abraham Lebow. Sofia's a social worker, but she knows more street law than me and Abraham combined.' I followed him around the cluttered desks. 'Used to have seven lawyers crammed in here, can you believe it? That was when we got federal money for legal services. Now we don't get a dime, thanks to the Republicans. There are three offices over there, three here on my side.' He was pointing in all directions. 'Lots of empty space.'

Maybe empty from a lack of personnel, but it was hard to walk without tripping over a basket of old files or a stack of dusty law books.

'Who owns the building?' I asked.

'The Cohen Trust. Leonard Cohen was the founder of a big New York law firm. He died in eighty-six; must've been a hundred years old. He made a ton of money, and late in life he decided he didn't want to die with any of it. So he spread it around, and one of his many creations was a trust to help poverty lawyers assist the homeless. That's how this place came to be. The trust operates three clinics – here, New York, and Newark. I was hired in eighty-three, became the director in eighty-four.'

'All your funding comes from one source?'

'Practically all. Last year the trust gave us a hundred and ten thousand dollars. Year before, it was a hundred fifty, so we lost a lawyer. It gets smaller every year. The trust has not been well managed, and it's now eating the principal. I doubt if we'll be here in five years. Maybe three.'

'Can't you raise money?'

'Oh, sure. Last year we raised nine thousand bucks. But it takes time. We can practice law, or we can raise funds. Sofia is not good with people. Abraham is an abrasive ass from New York. That leaves just me and my magnetic personality.'

'What's the overhead?' I asked, prying but not too worried. Almost every nonprofit group published an annual report with all the figures.

'Two thousand a month. After expenses and a small reserve, the three of us split eighty-nine thousand dollars. Equally. Sofia considers herself a full partner. Frankly, we're afraid to argue with her. I took home almost thirty, which, from what I hear, is about average for a poverty lawyer. Welcome to the street.'

We finally made it to his office, and I sat across from him.

'Did you forget to pay your heating bill?' I asked, almost shivering.

'Probably. We don't work much on weekends. Saves money. This place is impossible to heat or cool.'

That thought had never occurred to anyone at Drake & Sweeney. Close on weekends, save money. And marriages.

'And if we keep it too comfortable, our clients won't

leave. So it's cold in the winter, hot in the summer, cuts down on the street traffic. You want coffee?'

'No thanks.'

'I'm joking, you know. We wouldn't do anything to discourage the homeless from being here. The climate doesn't bother us. We figure our clients are cold and hungry, so why should we worry about those matters. Did you feel guilty when you ate breakfast this morning?'

'Yes.'

He gave me the smile of a wise old man who'd seen it all. 'That's very common. We used to work with a lot of young lawyers from the big firms, pro bono rookies I call them, and they would tell me all the time that they lost interest in food at first.' He patted his ample midsection. 'But you'll get over it.'

'What did the pro bono rookies do?' I asked. I knew I was moving toward the bait, and Mordecai knew I knew.

'We sent them into the shelters. They met the clients, and we supervised the cases for them. Most of the work is easy, it just takes a lawyer on the phone barking at some bureaucrat who won't move. Food stamps, veterans' pensions, housing subsidies, Medicaid, aid to children – about twenty-five percent of our work deals with benefits.'

I listened intently, and he could read my mind. Mordecai began to reel me in.

'You see, Michael, the homeless have no voice. No one listens, no one cares, and they expect no one to help them. So when they try to use the phone to get benefits due them, they get nowhere. They are put on hold, permanently. Their calls are never returned. They have no addresses. The bureaucrats don't care, and so they screw the very people they're supposed to help. A seasoned social worker can at least get the bureaucrats to listen, and maybe look at the file and maybe return a phone call. But you get a lawyer on the phone, barking and raising hell, and things happen. Bureaucrats get motivated. Papers get processed. No address? No problem. Send the check to me, I'll get it to the client.'

His voice was rising, both hands waving through the air. On top of everything else, Mordecai was the consummate storyteller. I suspected he was very effective in front of a jury.

'A funny story,' he said. 'About a month ago, one of my clients went down to the Social Security office to pick up an application for benefits, should've been a routine matter. He's sixty years old and in constant pain from a crooked back. Sleep on rocks and park benches for ten years, you got back problems. He waited in line outside the office for two hours, finally got in the door, waited another hour, made it up to the first desk, tried to explain what he wanted, and proceeded to get a tongue lashing from a hard-ass secretary who was having a bad day. She even commented on his odor. He was humiliated, of course, and left without his paperwork. He called me. I made my calls, and last Wednesday we had a little ceremony down at the Social Security office. I was there, along with my client. The secretary was there too, along with her supervisor, her supervisor's supervisor, the D.C. office director, and a Big Man from the Social Security Administration. The secretary stood in front of my client, and read a one-page apology. It was real nice, touching. She then handed me his application for benefits, and I got assurances from everybody present that it would receive immediate attention. That's justice, Michael, that's what street law is all about. Dignity.'

The stories rolled on, one after the other, all ending with the street lawyers as the good guys, the homeless as the victors. I knew he had tucked away in his repertoire just as many heartbreaking tales, probably more, but he was laying the groundwork.

I lost track of time. He never mentioned his mail. We finally left and drove back to the shelter.

It was an hour before dark, a good time, I thought, to get tucked away in the cozy little basement, before the hoodlums began roaming the streets. I caught myself walking slowly and confidently when Mordecai was at my side. Otherwise, I would've been slashing through the snow, bent at the waist, my nervous feet barely touching the ground.

Miss Dolly had somehow procured a pile of whole chickens, and she was laying for me. She boiled the birds; I picked their steaming flesh.

Mordecai's wife, JoAnne, joined us for the rush hour. She was as pleasant as her husband, and almost as tall. Both sons were six six. Cassius had been six nine, a heavily recruited basketball star when he was shot at the age of seventeen.

I left at midnight. No sign of Ontario and his family.

TEN

Sunday began with a late morning call from Claire, another stilted chat she initiated only to tell me what time she would be home. I suggested we have dinner at our favorite restaurant, but she was not in the mood. I didn't ask her if anything was wrong. We were beyond that.

Since our apartment was on the third floor, I had been unable to make satisfactory arrangements to have the Sunday *Post* home-delivered. We had tried various methods, but I never found the paper half the time.

I showered and dressed in layers. The weatherman predicted a high of twenty-five, and as I was getting ready to leave the apartment the newsperson rattled off the morning's top story. It stopped me cold; I heard the words, but they didn't register immediately. I walked closer to the TV on the kitchen counter, my feet heavy, my heart frozen, my mouth open in shock and disbelief.

Sometime around 11 P.M., D.C. police found a small car near Fort Totten Park, in Northeast, in a war zone. It was parked on the street, its bald tires stuck in the frozen slush. Inside were a young mother and her four children, all dead from asphyxiation. The police suspected the family lived in the car, and was trying to stay warm. The automobile's tailpipe was buried in a pile of snow plowed from the street. A few details, but no names.

I raced to the sidewalk, sliding in the snow but staying on my feet, then down P Street to Wisconsin, over to Thirty-fourth to a news-stand. Out of breath and horrified, I grabbed a paper. On the bottom corner of the front page was the story, obviously thrown in at the last minute. No names.

I yanked open Section A, dropping the rest of the paper onto the wet sidewalk. The story continued on page fourteen with a few standard comments from the police and the predictable warnings about the dangers of clogged tailpipes. Then the heartbreaking details: The mother was twenty-two. Her name was Lontae Burton. The baby was Temeko. The toddlers, Alonzo and Dante, were twins, age two. The big brother was Ontario, age four.

I must have made a strange sound, because a jogger gave me an odd look, as if I might be dangerous. I began walking away, holding the paper open, stepping on the other twenty sections.

'Excuse me!' a nasty voice called from behind. 'Would you like to pay for that?' I kept walking.

He approached from the rear and yelled, 'Hey, pal!' I stopped long enough to pull a five-dollar bill from my pocket and throw it at his feet, hardly looking at him.

On P, near the apartment, I leaned on a brick retaining wall in front of someone's splendid rowhouse. The sidewalk had been meticulously shoveled. I read the story again, slowly, hoping that somehow the ending would be different. Thoughts and questions came in torrents, and I couldn't keep up with them. But two repeated themselves: Why didn't they return to the shelter? And, did the baby die wrapped in my denim jacket?

Thinking was burden enough. Walking was almost impossible. After the shock, the guilt hit hard. Why

87

didn't I do something Friday night when I first saw them? I could have taken them to a warm motel and fed them.

The phone was ringing when I entered my apartment. It was Mordecai. He asked if I'd seen the story. I asked if he remembered the wet diaper. Same family, I said. He'd never heard their names. I told him more about my encounter with Ontario.

'I'm very sorry, Michael,' he said, much sadder now.

'So am I.'

I couldn't say much, the words wouldn't form, so we agreed to meet later. I went to the sofa, where I remained for an hour without moving.

Then I went to my car and removed the bags of food and toys and clothing I'd bought for them.

Only because he was curious, Mordecai came to my office at noon. He'd been in plenty of big firms in his time, but he wanted to see the spot where Mister fell. I gave him a brief tour with a quick narration of the hostage affair.

We left in his car. I was thankful for the light Sunday traffic because Mordecai had no interest in what the other cars were doing.

'Lontae Burton's mother is thirty-eight years old, serving a ten-year sentence for selling crack,' he informed me. He'd been on the phone. 'Two brothers, both in jail. Lontae had a history of prostitution and drugs. No idea of who the father, or fathers, might be.'

'Who's your source?'

'I found her grandmother in a housing project. The last time she saw Lontae she had only three kids, and she was selling drugs with her mother. According to the grandmother, she cut her ties with her daughter and granddaughter because of the drug business.'

'Who buries them?'

'Same people who buried DeVon Hardy.'

'How much would a decent funeral cost?'

'It's negotiable. Are you interested?'

'I'd like to see them taken care of.'

We were on Pennsylvania Avenue, moving past the mammoth office buildings of Congress, the Capitol in the background, and I couldn't help but offer a silent curse or two at the fools who wasted billions each month while people were homeless. How could four innocent children die in the streets, practically in the shadow of the Capitol, because they had no place to live?

They shouldn't have been born, some people from my side of town would say.

The bodies had been taken to the Office of the Chief Medical Examiner, which also housed the morgue. It was a two-story brown aggregate building at D.C. General Hospital. They would be held there until claimed. If no one came forward within forty-eight hours, they would receive a mandatory embalming, be placed in wooden caskets, and quickly buried in the cemetery near RFK.

Mordecai parked in a handicapped space, paused for a second, and said, 'Are you sure you want to go in?'

'I think so.'

He'd been there before, and he had called ahead. A security guard in an ill-fitting uniform dared to stop us, and Mordecai snapped so loud it scared me. My stomach was in knots anyway.

The guard retreated, happy to get away from us. A set of plate-glass doors had the word MORGUE painted in black. Mordecai entered as if he owned the place.

'I'm Mordecai Green, attorney for the Burton family,' he growled at the young man behind the desk. It was more of a challenge than an announcement.

The young man checked a clipboard, then fumbled with some more papers.

'What the hell are you doing?' Mordecai snapped again.

The young man looked up with an attitude, and then realized how large his adversary really was. 'Just a minute,' he said, and went to his computer.

Mordecai turned to me and said loudly, 'You'd think they have a thousand dead bodies in there.'

I realized that he had no patience whatsoever with bureaucrats and government workers, and I remembered his story about the apology from the Social Security secretary. For Mordecai, half of the practice of law was bullying and barking.

A pale gentleman with badly dyed black hair and a clammy handshake appeared and introduced himself as Bill. He wore a blue lab jacket and shoes with thick rubber soles. Where do they find people to work in a morgue?

We followed him through a door, down a sterile hallway where the temperature began dropping, and, finally, to the main holding room.

'How many you got today?' Mordecai asked, as if he stopped by all the time to count bodies.

Bill turned the doorknob and said, 'Twelve.'

'You okay?' Mordecai asked me.

'I don't know.'

Bill pushed the metal door, and we stepped in. The air was frigid, the smell antiseptic. The floor was white tile, the lighting blue fluorescent. I followed Mordecai, my head down, trying not to look around, but it was impossible. The bodies were covered from head to ankle with white sheets, just like you see on television. We passed a set of white feet, a tag around a toe. Then some brown ones.

We turned and stopped in a corner, a gurney to the left, a table to the right.

Bill said, 'Lontae Burton,' and dramatically pulled the sheet down to her waist. It was Ontario's mother all right, in a plain white gown. Death had left no marks on her face. She could've been sleeping. I couldn't stop staring at her.

'That's her,' Mordecai said, as if he'd known her for years. He looked at me for verification, and I managed a nod. Bill wheeled around, and I held my breath. Only one sheet covered the children.

They were lying in a perfect row, tucked closely together, hands folded over their matching gowns, cherubs sleeping, little street soldiers finally at peace.

I wanted to touch Ontario, to pat him on the arm and tell him I was sorry. I wanted to wake him up, take him home, feed him, and give him everything he could ever want.

I took a step forward for a closer look. 'Don't touch,' Bill said.

When I nodded, Mordecai said, 'That's them.'

As Bill covered them, I closed my eyes and said a short prayer, one of mercy and forgiveness. Don't let it happen again, the Lord said to me.

In a room down the hall, Bill pulled out two large wire baskets containing the personal effects of the family. He dumped them on a table, and we helped him inventory the contents. The clothing they wore was dirty and threadbare. My denim jacket was the nicest item they owned. There were three blankets, a purse, some cheap toys, baby formula, a towel, more dirty clothes, a box of vanilla wafers, an unopened can of beer, some cigarettes, two condoms, and about twenty dollars in bills and change.

'The car is at the city lot,' Bill said. 'They say it's full of junk.'

'We'll take care of it,' Mordecai said.

We signed the inventory sheets, and left with the

personal assets of the Lontae Burton family. 'What do we do with this stuff?' I asked.

'Take it to the grandmother. Do you want your coat back?'

'No.'

The funeral parlor was owned by a minister Mordecai knew. He didn't like him because the Reverend's church was not friendly enough to the homeless, but he could deal with him.

We parked in front of the church, on Georgia Avenue near Howard University, a cleaner part of town without as many boards over windows.

'It's best if you stay here,' he said. 'I can talk to him a lot plainer if we're alone.'

I didn't want to sit in the car by myself, but by then I trusted him with my life anyway. 'Sure,' I said, sinking a few inches and glancing around.

'You'll be all right.'

He left, and I locked the doors. After a few minutes, I relaxed, and began to think. Mordecai wanted to be alone with the minister for business reasons. My presence would've complicated matters. Who was I and what was my interest in the family? The price would rise immediately.

The sidewalk was busy. I watched the people scurry by, the wind cutting them sharply. A mother with two children passed me, bundled in nice clothing, all holding hands. Where were they last night when Ontario and family were huddled in the frigid car, breathing the odorless carbon monoxide until they floated away? Where were the rest of us?

The world was shutting down. Nothing made sense. In less than a week, I had seen six dead street people, and I was ill-equipped to handle the shock. I was an educated white lawyer, well fed and affluent, on the fast track to serious wealth and all the wonderful things it would buy. Sure the marriage was over, but I would bounce back. There were plenty of fine women out there. I had no serious worries.

I cursed Mister for derailing my life. I cursed Mordecai for making me feel guilty. And Ontario for breaking my heart.

A knock on the window jolted me. My nerves were shot to hell anyway. It was Mordecai, standing in the snow next to the curb. I cracked the window.

'He says he'll do it for two thousand bucks, all five.'

'Whatever,' I said, and he disappeared.

Moments later he was back, behind the wheel and speeding away. 'The funeral will be Tuesday, here at the church. Wooden caskets, but nice ones. He'll get some flowers, you know, make it look nice. He wanted three thousand, but I convinced him that there would be some press, so he might get himself on television. He liked that. Two thousand isn't bad.'

'Thanks, Mordecai.'

'Are you okay?'

'No.'

We said little as we drove back to my office.

Claire's younger brother James had been diagnosed with Hodgkin's disease – thus the family summit in Providence. It had nothing to do with me. I listened to her talk about the weekend, the shock of the news, the tears and prayers as they leaned on each other and comforted James and his wife. Hers is a family of huggers and criers, and I was thrilled she had not called me to come up. The treatment would start immediately; the prognosis was good.

She was happy to be home, and relieved to have someone to unload on. We sipped wine in the den, by the fire, a quilt over our feet. It was almost romantic, though I was too scarred to even think of being sentimental. I made a valiant effort at hearing her words, grieving appropriately for poor James, interjecting fitting little phrases.

This was not what I had expected, and I wasn't sure if it was what I wanted. I thought we might shadow-box, perhaps even skirmish. Soon it had to get ugly, then hopefully turn civil as we handled our separation like real adults. But after Ontario, I was not prepared to deal with any issue involving emotion. I was drained. She kept telling me how tired I looked. I almost thanked her.

I listened hard until she finished, then the conversation slowly drifted to me and my weekend. I told her everything – my new life as a volunteer in the shelters, then Ontario and his family. I showed her the story in the paper.

She was genuinely moved, but also puzzled. I was not the same person I'd been a week earlier, and she was not sure she liked the latest version any better than the old. I was not sure either.

ELEVEN

As young workaholics, Claire and I did not need alarm clocks, especially for Monday mornings, when we faced an entire week of challenges. We were up at five, eating cereal at five-thirty, then off in separate directions, practically racing to see who could leave first.

Because of the wine, I had managed to sleep without being haunted by the nightmare of the weekend. And as I drove to the office, I was determined to place some distance between myself and the street people. I would endure the funeral. I would somehow find the time to do pro bono work for the homeless. I would pursue my friendship with Mordecai, probably even become a regular in his office. I would drop in occasionally on Miss Dolly and help her feed the hungry. I would give money and help raise more of it for the poor. Certainly I could be more valuable as a source of funds than as another poverty lawyer.

Driving in the dark to the office, I decided that I needed a string of eighteen-hour days to readjust my priorities. My career had suffered a minor derailment; an orgy of work would straighten things out. Only a fool would jump away from the gravy train I was riding.

I chose a different elevator from Mister's. He was history; I shut him out of my mind. I did not look at the conference room where he died. I threw my briefcase and coat on a chair in my office and went for coffee. Bouncing down the hallway before six in the morning, speaking to a colleague here, a clerk there, removing my jacket, rolling up my sleeves – it was great to be back.

I scanned *The Wall Street Journal* first, partly because I knew it would have nothing to do with dying street people in D.C. Then, the *Post*. On the front page of the Metro section, there was a small story about Lontae Burton's family, with a photo of her grandmother weeping outside an apartment building. I read it, then put it aside. I knew more than the reporter, and I was determined not to be distracted.

Under the *Post* was a plain manila legal-sized file, the kind our firm used by the millions. It was unmarked, and that made it suspicious. It was just lying there, exposed, on the center of my desk, placed there by some anonymous person. I opened it slowly.

There were only two sheets of paper inside. The first was a copy of yesterday's story in the *Post*, the same one I'd read ten times and shown to Claire last night. Under it was a copy of something lifted from an official Drake & Sweeney file. The heading read: EVICTEES – RIVEROAKS/TAG, INC.

The left-hand column contained the numbers one through seventeen. Number four was DeVon Hardy. Number fifteen read: Lontae Burton, and three or four children.

I slowly laid the file on the desk, stood and walked to the door, locked it, then leaned on it. The first couple of minutes passed in absolute silence. I stared at the file in the center of the desk. I had to assume it was true and accurate. Why would anyone fabricate such a thing? Then I picked it up again, carefully. Under the second sheet of paper, on the inside of the file itself, my anonymous informant had scribbled with a pencil: The eviction was legally and ethically wrong.

It was printed in block letters, in an effort to avoid detection should I have it analyzed. The markings were faint, the lead hardly touching the file.

I kept the door locked for an hour, during which time I took turns standing at the window watching the sunrise and sitting at my desk staring at the file. The traffic increased in the hallway, and then I heard Polly's voice. I unlocked the door, greeted her as if everything was swell, and proceeded to go through the motions.

The morning was packed with meetings and conferences, two of them with Rudolph and clients. I performed adequately, though I couldn't remember anything we said or did. Rudolph was so proud to have his star back at full throttle.

I was almost rude to those who wanted to chat about the hostage crisis and its aftershocks. I appeared to be the same, and I was my usual hard-charging self, so the concerns about my stability vanished. Late in the morning, my father called. I could not remember the last time he'd called me at the office. He said it was raining in Memphis; he was sitting around the house, bored, and, well, he and my mother were worried about me. Claire was fine, I explained; then to find safe ground, I told him about her brother James, a person he had met once, at the wedding. I sounded properly concerned about Claire's family, and that pleased him.

Dad was just happy to reach me at the office. I was still there, making the big money, going after more. He asked me to keep in touch.

Half an hour later, my brother Warner called from his office, high above downtown Atlanta. He was six years older, a partner in another megafirm, a no-holds-barred litigator. Because of the age difference, Warner and I had never been close as kids, but we enjoyed each other's company. During his divorce three years earlier, he had confided in me weekly.

He was on the clock, same as I, so I knew the conversation would be brief. 'Talked to Dad,' he said. 'He told me everything.'

'I'm sure he did.'

'I understand how you feel. We all go through it. You work hard, make the big money, never stop to help the little people. Then something happens, and you think back to law school, back to the first year, when we were full of ideals and wanted to use our law degrees to save humanity. Remember that?'

'Yes. A long time ago.'

'Right. During my first year of law school, they took a survey. Over half my class wanted to do public interest law. When we graduated three years later, everybody went for the money. I don't know what happened.'

'Law school makes you greedy.'

'I suppose. Our firm has a program where you can take a year off, sort of a sabbatical, and do public interest law. After twelve months, you return as if you never left. You guys do anything like that?'

Vintage Warner. I had a problem, he already had the solution. Nice and neat. Twelve months, I'm a new man. A quick detour, but my future is secure.

'Not for associates,' I said. 'I've heard of a partner or two leaving to work for this administration or that one, then returning after a couple of years. But never an associate.'

'But your circumstances are different. You've been traumatized, damned near killed simply because you were a member of the firm. I'd throw my weight around some, tell 'em you need time off. Take a year, then get your ass back to the office.'

98

'It might work,' I said, trying to placate him. He was a type A personality, pushy as hell, always one word away from an argument, especially with the family. 'I gotta run,' I said. So did he. We promised to talk more later.

Lunch was with Rudolph and a client at a splendid restaurant. It was called a working lunch, which meant we abstained from alcohol, which also meant we would bill the client for the time. Rudolph went for four hundred an hour, me for three hundred. We worked and ate for two hours, so the lunch cost the client fourteen hundred dollars. Our firm had an account with the restaurant, so it would be billed to Drake & Sweeney, and somewhere along the way our bean counters in the basement would find a way to bill the client for the cost of the food as well.

The afternoon was nonstop calls and conferences. Through sheer willpower, I kept my game face and got through it, billing heavily as I went. Antitrust law had never seemed so hopelessly dense and boring.

It was almost five before I found a few minutes alone. I said good-bye to Polly, and locked the door again. I opened the mysterious file and began making random notes on a legal pad, scribblings and flow-charts with arrows striking RiverOaks and Drake & Sweeney from all directions. Braden Chance, the real estate partner I'd confronted about the file, took most of the shots for the firm.

My principal suspect was his paralegal, the young man who had heard our sharp words, and who, seconds later, had referred to Chance as an 'ass' when I was leaving their suite. He would know the details of the eviction, and he would have access to the file.

With a pocket phone to avoid any D&S records, I called a paralegal in antitrust. His office was around the corner from mine. He referred me to another, and with little effort I learned that the guy I wanted was

Hector Palma. He'd been with the firm about three years, all in real estate. I planned to track him down, but outside the office.

Mordecai called. He inquired about my dinner plans for the evening. 'I'll treat,' he said.

'Soup?'

He laughed. 'Of course not. I know an excellent place.'

We agreed to meet at seven. Claire was back in her surgeon's mode, oblivious to time, meals, or husband. She had checked in mid-afternoon, just a quick word on the run. Had no idea when she might be home, but very late. For dinner, every man for himself. I didn't hold it against her. She had learned the fast-track lifestyle from me.

We met at a restaurant near Dupont Circle. The bar at the front was packed with well-paid government types having a drink before fleeing the city. We had a drink in the back, in a tight booth.

'The Burton story is big and getting bigger,' he said, sipping a draft beer.

'I'm sorry, I've been in a cave for the past twelve hours. What's happened?'

'Lots of press. Four dead kids and their momma, living in a car. They find them a mile from Capitol Hill, where they're in the process of reforming welfare to send more mothers into the streets. It's beautiful.'

'So the funeral should be quite a show.'

'No doubt. I've talked to a dozen homeless activists today. They'll be there, and they're planning to bring their people with them. The place will be packed with street people. Again, lots of press. Four little coffins next to their mother's, cameras catching it all for the six o'clock news. We're having a rally before and a march afterward.'

100

'Maybe something good will come from their deaths.'

'Maybe.'

As a seasoned big-city lawyer, I knew there was a purpose behind every lunch and dinner invitation. Mordecai had something on his mind. I could tell by the way his eyes followed mine.

'Any idea why they were homeless?' I asked, fishing.

'No. Probably the usual. I haven't had time to ask questions.'

Driving over, I had decided that I could not tell him about the mysterious file and its contents. It was confidential, known to me only because of my position at Drake & Sweeney. To reveal what I had learned about the activities of a client would be an egregious breach of professional responsibility. The thought of divulging it scared me. Plus, I had not verified anything.

The waiter brought salads, and we began eating. 'We had a firm meeting this afternoon,' Mordecai said between bites. 'Me, Abraham, Sofia. We need some help.'

I was not surprised to hear that. 'What kind of help?'

'Another lawyer.'

'I thought you were broke.'

'We keep a little reserve. And we've adopted a new marketing strategy.'

The idea of the 14th Street Legal Clinic worried about a marketing strategy was humorous, and that was what he intended. We both smiled.

'If we could get the new lawyer to spend ten hours a week raising money, then he could afford himself.'

Another series of smiles.

He continued. 'As much as we hate to admit it, our survival will depend on our ability to raise money. The

101

Cohen Trust is declining. We've had the luxury of not begging, but now it's gotta change.'

'What's the rest of the job?'

'Street law. You've had a good dose of it. You've seen our place. It's a dump. Sofia's a shrew. Abraham's an ass. The clients smell bad, and the money is a joke.'

'How much money?'

'We can offer you thirty thousand a year, but we can only promise you half of it for the first six months.'

'Why?'

'The trust closes its books June thirtieth, at which time they'll tell us how much we get for the next fiscal year, beginning July first. We have enough in reserve to pay you for the next six months. After that, the four of us will split what's left after expenses.'

'Abraham and Sofia agreed to this?'

'Yep, after a little speech by me. We figure you have good contacts within the established bar, and since you're well educated, nice-looking, bright, and all that crap, you should be a natural at raising money.'

'What if I don't want to raise money?'

'Then the four of us could lower our salaries even more, perhaps go to twenty thousand a year. Then to fifteen. And when the trust dries up, we could hit the streets, just like our clients. Homeless lawyers.'

'So I'm the future of the 14th Street Legal Clinic?'

'That's what we decided. We'll take you in as a full partner. Let's see Drake & Sweeney top that.'

'I'm touched,' I said. I was also a bit frightened. The job offer was not unexpected, but its arrival opened a door I was hesitant to walk through.

Black bean soup arrived, and we ordered more beer.

'What's Abraham's story?' I asked.

'Jewish kid from Brooklyn. Came to Washington to work on Senator Moynihan's staff. Spent a few years on the Hill, landed on the street. Extremely bright. He

spends most of his time coordinating litigation with
pro bono lawyers from big firms. Right now he's suing
the Census Bureau to be certain the homeless get
counted. And he's suing the D.C. school system to
make sure homeless kids get an education. His people
skills leave a lot to be desired, but he's great in the
back room plotting litigation.'

'And Sofia?'

'A career social worker who's been taking night
classes in law school for eleven years. She acts and
thinks like a lawyer, especially when she's abusing
government workers. You'll hear her say, "This is
Sofia Mendoza, Attorney-at-Law," ten times a day.'

'She's also the secretary?'

'Nope. We don't have secretaries. You do your own
typing, filing, coffee making.' He leaned forward a few
inches, and lowered his voice. 'The three of us have
been together for a long time, Michael, and we've
carved out little niches. To be honest, we need a fresh
face with some new ideas.'

'The money is certainly appealing,' I said, a weak
effort at humor.

He grinned anyway. 'You don't do it for the money.
You do it for your soul.'

My soul kept me awake most of the night. Did I have
the guts to walk away? Was I seriously considering
taking a job which paid so little? I was literally saying
good-bye to millions.

The things and possessions I longed for would
become fading memories.

The timing wasn't bad. With the marriage over, it
somehow seemed fitting that I make drastic changes
on all fronts.

TWELVE

I called in sick Tuesday. 'Probably the flu,' I told
Polly, who, as she was trained to do, wanted specifics.
Fever, sore throat, headaches? All of the above. Any
and all, I didn't care. One had better be completely
sick to miss work at the firm. She would do a form and
send it to Rudolph. Anticipating his call, I left the
apartment and wandered around Georgetown during
the early morning. The snow was melting fast; the
high would be in the fifties. I killed an hour loitering
along Washington Harbor, sampling cappuccino from
a number of vendors, watching the rowers freeze on
the Potomac.

At ten, I left for the funeral.

The sidewalk in front of the church was barricaded.
Cops were standing around, their motorcycles parked
on the street. Farther down were the television vans.

A large crowd was listening to a speaker yell into a
microphone as I drove by. There were a few hastily
painted placards held above heads, for the benefit of
the cameras. I parked on a side street three blocks
away, and hurried toward the church. I avoided the
front by heading for a side door, which was being
guarded by an elderly usher. I asked if there was a
balcony. He asked if I was a reporter.

He took me inside, and pointed to a door. I thanked

104

him and went through it, then up a flight of shaky stairs until I emerged on the balcony overlooking a beautiful sanctuary below. The carpet was burgundy, the pews dark wood, the windows stained and clean. It was a very handsome church, and for a second I could understand why the Reverend was reluctant to open it to the homeless.

I was alone, with my choice of seating. I walked quietly to a spot above the rear door, with a direct view down the center aisle to the pulpit. A choir began singing outside on the front steps, and I sat in the tranquillity of the empty church, the music drifting in. The music stopped, the doors opened, the stampede began. The balcony floor shook as the mourners poured into the sanctuary. The choir took its place behind the pulpit. The Reverend directed traffic – the TV crews in one corner, the small family in the front pew, the activists and their homeless down the center section. Mordecai ambled in with two people I didn't know. A door to one side opened, and the prisoners marched out – Lontae's mother and two brothers, clad in blue prison garb, cuffed at the wrists and ankles, chained together and escorted by four armed guards. They were placed in the second pew, center aisle, behind the grandmother and some other relatives.

When things were still, the organ began, low and sad. There was a racket under me, and all heads turned around. The Reverend assumed the pulpit and instructed us to stand.

Ushers with white gloves rolled the wooden coffins down the aisle, and lined them end to end across the front of the church with Lontae's in the center. The baby's was tiny, less than three feet long. Ontario's, Alonzo's, and Dante's were midsized. It was an appalling sight, and the wailing began. The choir started to hum and sway.

The ushers arranged flowers around the caskets,

and I thought for one horrifying second they were going to open them. I had never been to a black funeral before. I had no idea what to expect, but I had seen news clips from other funerals in which the casket was sometimes opened, the family kissing the corpse. The vultures with the cameras were ever ready.

But the caskets remained closed, and so the world didn't learn what I knew – that Ontario and family looked very much at peace.

We sat down, and the Reverend served up a lengthy prayer. Then a solo from sister somebody, then moments of silence. The Reverend read Scripture, and preached for a bit. He was followed by a homeless activist who delivered a scathing attack on a society and its leaders who allowed such a thing to happen. She blamed Congress, especially the Republicans, and she blamed the city for its lack of leadership, and the courts, and the bureaucracy. But she saved her harshest diatribe for the upper classes, those with money and power who didn't care for the poor and the sick. She was articulate and angry, very effective, I thought, but not exactly at home at a funeral.

They clapped for her when she finished. The Reverend then spent a very long time blasting everyone who wasn't of color and had money.

A solo, some more Scripture, then the choir launched into a soulful hymn that made me want to cry. A procession formed to lay hands upon the dead, but it quickly broke down as the mourners began wailing and rubbing the caskets. 'Open them up,' someone screamed, but the Reverend shook his head no. They bunched toward the pulpit, crowding around the caskets, yelling and sobbing as the choir cranked it up several notches. The grandmother was the loudest, and she was stroked and soothed by the others.

I couldn't believe it. Where were these people during the last months of Lontae's life? Those little bodies lying up there in boxes had never known so much love.

The cameras inched closer as more and more mourners broke down. It was more of a show than anything else.

The Reverend finally stepped in and restored order. He prayed again with organ music in the background. When he finished, a long dismissal began as the people paraded by the caskets one last time.

The service lasted an hour and a half. For two thousand bucks, it wasn't a bad production. I was proud of it.

They rallied again outside, and began a march in the general direction of Capitol Hill. Mordecai was in the middle of it, and as they disappeared around a corner, I wondered how many marches and demonstrations he had been in. Not enough, he would probably answer.

Rudolph Mayes had become a partner at Drake & Sweeney at the age of thirty, still a record. And if life continued as he planned, he would one day be the oldest working partner. The law was his life, as his three former wives could attest. Everything else he touched was disastrous, but Rudolph was the consummate big-firm team player.

He was waiting for me at 6 P.M. in his office behind a pile of work. Polly and the secretaries were gone, as were most of the paralegals and clerks. The hall traffic slowed considerably after five-thirty.

I closed the door, sat down. 'Thought you were sick,' he said.

'I'm leaving, Rudolph,' I said as boldly as I could, but my stomach was in knots.

He shoved books out of the way, and put the cap on his expensive pen. 'I'm listening.'

107

'I'm leaving the firm. I have an offer to work for a public interest firm.'

'Don't be stupid, Michael.'

'I'm not being stupid. I've made up my mind. And I want out of here with as little trouble as possible.'

'You'll be a partner in three years.'

'I've found a better deal than that.'

He couldn't think of a response, so he rolled his eyes in frustration. 'Come on, Mike. You can't crack up over one incident.'

'I'm not cracking up, Rudolph. I'm simply moving into another field.'

'None of the other eight hostages are doing this.'

'Good for them. If they're happy, then I'm happy for them. Besides, they're in litigation, a strange breed.'

'Where are you going?'

'A legal clinic near Logan Circle. It specializes in homeless law.'

'Homeless law?'

'Yep.'

'How much are they paying you?'

'A bloody fortune. Wanna make a donation to the clinic?'

'You're losing your mind.'

'Just a little crisis, Rudolph. I'm only thirty-two, too young for the midlife crazies. I figure I'll get mine over with early.'

'Take a month off. Go work with the homeless, get it out of your system, then come back. This is a terrible time to leave, Mike. You know how far behind we are.'

'Won't work, Rudolph. It's no fun if there's a safety net.'

'Fun? You're doing this for fun?'

'Absolutely. Think how much fun it would be to work without looking at a time clock.'

'What about Claire?' he asked, revealing the depths of his desperation. He hardly knew her, and he was the least qualified person in the firm to dispense marital advice.

'She's okay,' I said. 'I'd like to leave Friday.'

He grunted in defeat. He closed his eyes, slowly shook his head. 'I don't believe this.'

'I'm sorry, Rudolph.'

We shook hands and promised to meet for an early breakfast to discuss my unfinished work.

I didn't want Polly to hear it secondhand, so I went to my office and called her. She was at home in Arlington, cooking dinner. It ruined her week.

I picked up Thai food and took it home. I chilled some wine, fixed the table, and began rehearsing my lines.

If Claire suspected an ambush, it wasn't evident. Over the years we had developed the habit of simply ignoring each other, as opposed to fighting. Therefore, our tactics were unrefined.

But I liked the idea of a blindside, of being thoroughly prepared with the shock, then ready with the quips. I thought it would be nice and unfair, completely acceptable within the confines of a crumbling marriage.

It was almost ten; she had eaten on the run hours earlier, so we went straight to the den with glasses of wine. I stoked the fire and we settled into our favorite chairs. After a few minutes I said, 'We need to talk.'

'What is it?' she asked, completely unworried.

'I'm thinking of leaving Drake & Sweeney.'

'Oh really.' She took a drink. I admired her coolness. She either expected this or wanted to seem unconcerned.

'Yes. I can't go back there.'

'Why not?'

'I'm ready for a change. The corporate work is suddenly boring and unimportant, and I want to do something to help people.'

'That's nice.' She was already thinking about the money, and I was anxious to see how long it would take to get around to it. 'In fact, that's very admirable, Michael.'

'I told you about Mordecai Green. His clinic has offered me a job. I'm starting Monday.'

'Monday?'

'Yes.'

'So you've made your decision already.'

'Yes.'

'Without any discussion with me. I have no say in the matter, is that right?'

'I can't go back to the firm, Claire. I told Rudolph today.'

Another sip, a slight grinding of the teeth, a flash of anger but she let it pass. Her self-control was amazing.

We watched the fire, hypnotized by the orange flames. She spoke next. 'Can I ask what this does for us financially?'

'It changes things.'

'How much is the new salary?'

'Thirty thousand a year.'

'Thirty thousand a year,' she repeated. Then she said it again, somehow making it sound even lower. 'That's less than what I make.'

Her salary was thirty-one thousand, a figure that would increase dramatically in the years to come – serious money was not far away. For purposes of the discussion, I planned to have no sympathy for any whining about money.

'You don't do public interest law for the money,' I said, trying not to sound pious. 'As I recall, you didn't go to med school for the money.'

Like every med student in the country, she had

110

begun her studies vowing that money was not the attraction. She wanted to help humanity. Same for law students. We all lied.

She watched the fire and did the math. I guessed she was probably thinking about the rent. It was a very nice apartment; at twenty-four hundred a month it should've been even nicer. The furnishings were adequate. We were proud of where we lived – right address, beautiful rowhouse, swanky neighborhood – but we spent so little time there. And we seldom entertained. Moving would be an adjustment, but we could endure it.

We had always been open about our finances; nothing was hidden. She knew we had around fifty-one thousand dollars in mutual funds, and twelve thousand in the checking account. I was amazed at how little we'd saved in six years of marriage. When you're on the fast track at a big firm, the money seems endless.

'I guess we'll have to make adjustments, won't we?' she said, staring coldly at me. The word 'adjustments' was dripping with connotations.

'I suppose so.'

'I'm tired,' she said. She drained her glass, and went to the bedroom.

How pathetic, I thought. We couldn't even muster enough rancor to have a decent fight.

Of course, I fully realized my new status in life. I was a wonderful story – ambitious young lawyer transformed into an advocate for the poor; turns back on blue-chip firm to work for nothing. Even though she thought I was losing my mind, Claire had found it hard to criticize a saint.

I put a log on the fire, fixed another drink, and slept on the sofa.

THIRTEEN

The partners had a private dining room on the eighth floor, and it was supposed to be an honor for an associate to eat there. Rudolph was the sort of klutz who would think that a bowl of Irish oatmeal at 7 A.M. in their special room would help return me to my senses. How could I turn my back on a future filled with power breakfasts?

He had exciting news. He'd spoken with Arthur late the night before and there was in the works a proposal to grant me a twelve-month sabbatical. The firm would supplement whatever salary the clinic paid. It was a worthy cause, they should do more to protect the rights of the poor. I would be treated as the firm's designated pro bono boy for an entire year, and they could all feel good about themselves. I would return with my batteries recharged, my other interests quelled, my talents once again directed to the glory of Drake & Sweeney.

I was impressed and touched by the idea, and I could not simply dismiss it. I promised him I would think about it, and quickly. He cautioned that it would have to be approved by the executive committee since I was not a partner. The firm had never considered such a leave for an associate.

Rudolph was desperate for me to stay, and it had little to do with friendship. Our antitrust division was

112

logjammed with work, and we needed at least two more senior associates with my experience. It was a terrible time for me to leave, but I didn't care. The firm had eight hundred lawyers. They would find the bodies they needed.

The year before I had billed just under seven hundred fifty thousand dollars. That was why I was eating breakfast in their fancy little room, and listening to their urgent plans to keep me. It also made sense to take my annual salary, throw it at the homeless or any charity I wished, for that matter, then entice me back after one year.

Once he finished with the idea of the sabbatical, we proceeded to review the most pressing matters in my office. We were listing things to do when Braden Chance sat at a table not far from ours. He didn't see me at first. There were a dozen or so partners eating, most alone, most deep in the morning papers. I tried to ignore him, but I finally looked over and caught him glaring at me.

'Good morning, Braden,' I said loudly, startling him and causing Rudolph to jerk around to see who it was.

Chance nodded, said nothing, and suddenly became involved with some toast.

'You know him?' Rudolph asked, under his breath.

'We've met,' I said. During our brief encounter in his office, Chance had demanded the name of my supervising partner. I'd given him Rudolph's name. It was obvious he had not lodged any complaints.

'An ass,' Rudolph said, barely audible. It was unanimous. He flipped a page, immediately forgot about Chance, and plowed ahead. There was a lot of unfinished work in my office.

I found myself thinking of Chance and the eviction file. He had a soft look, with pale skin, delicate features, a fragile manner. I could not imagine him in the streets, examining abandoned warehouses filled

113

with squatters, actually getting his hands dirty to make sure his work was thorough. Of course he never did that; he had paralegals. Chance sat at his desk and supervised the paperwork, billing several hundred an hour while the Hector Palmas of the firm took care of the nasty details. Chance had lunch and played golf with the executives of RiverOaks; that was his role as a partner.

He probably didn't know the names of the people evicted from the RiverOaks/TAG warehouse, and why should he? They were just squatters, nameless, faceless, homeless. He wasn't there with the cops when they were dragged from their little dwellings and thrown into the streets. But Hector Palma probably saw it happen.

And if Chance didn't know the names of Lontae Burton and family, then he couldn't make the connection between the eviction and their deaths. Or maybe he did know now. Maybe someone had told him.

These questions would have to be answered by Hector Palma, and soon. It was Wednesday. I was leaving on Friday.

Rudolph wrapped up our breakfast at eight, just in time for another meeting in his office with some very important people. I went to my desk and read the *Post*. There was a gut-wrenching photo of the five unopened caskets in the sanctuary, and a thorough review of the service and the march afterward.

There was also an editorial, a well-written challenge to all of us with food and roofs to stop and think about the Lontae Burtons of our city. They were not going away. They could not be swept from the streets and deposited in some hidden place so we didn't have to see them. They were living in cars, squatting in shacks, freezing in makeshift tents, sleeping on park benches, waiting for beds in crowded and sometimes dangerous shelters. We shared the same city; they were a part of our society. If we didn't help them, they would multiply in numbers. And they would continue to die in our streets.

I cut the editorial from the paper, folded it, and placed it in my wallet.

Through the paralegal network, I made contact with Hector Palma. It would not be wise to approach him directly; Chance was probably lurking nearby.

We met in the main library on the third floor, between stacks of books, away from security cameras and anybody else. He was extremely nervous.

'Did you put that file on my desk?' I asked him point-blank. There was little time for games.

'What file?' he asked, cutting his eyes around as if gunmen were tracking us.

'The RiverOaks/TAG eviction. You handled it, right?'

He didn't know how much I knew, or how little. 'Yeah,' he said.

'Where's the file?'

He pulled a book off the shelf and acted as though he were deep in research. 'Chance keeps all the files.'

'In his office?'

'Yes. Locked in a file cabinet.' We were practically whispering. I had not been nervous about the meeting, but I caught myself glancing around. Anybody watching would have immediately known that we were up to something.

'What's in the file?' I asked.

'Bad stuff.'

'Tell me.'

'I have a wife and four kids. I'm not about to get fired.'

'You have my word.'

'You're leaving. What do you care?'

Word traveled fast, but I was not surprised. I often

115

wondered who gossiped more, the lawyers or their secretaries. Probably the paralegals.

'Why did you put that file on my desk?' I asked.

He reached for another book, his right hand literally shaking. 'I don't know what you're talking about.'

He flipped a few pages, then walked to the end of the row. I followed along, certain no one was anywhere near us. He stopped and found another book; he still wanted to talk.

'I need that file,' I said.

'I don't have it.'

'Then how can I get it?'

'You'll have to steal it.'

'Fine. Where do I get a key?'

He studied my face for a moment, trying to decide how serious I was. 'I don't have a key,' he said.

'How'd you get the list of evictees?'

'I don't know what you're talking about.'

'Yes you do. You put it on my desk.'

'You're as crazy as hell,' he said, and walked away. I waited for him to stop, but he kept going, past the rows of shelves, past the stacked tiers, past the front desk, and out of the library.

I had no intention of busting my ass my last three days at the firm, regardless of what I'd led Rudolph to believe. Instead, I covered my desk with antitrust litter, shut the door, stared at the walls, and smiled at all the things I was leaving behind. The pressure was lifting with every breath. No more labor with a time clock wrapped around my throat. No more eighty-hour weeks because my ambitious colleagues might be doing eighty-five. No more brown-nosing those above me. No more nightmares about getting the partnership door slammed in my face.

I called Mordecai and formally accepted the job. He laughed, and joked about finding a way to pay me. I would start Monday, but he wanted me to stop by earlier for a brief orientation. I pictured the interior of the 14th Street Legal Clinic, and wondered which of the empty, cluttered offices I would be assigned. As if it mattered.

By late afternoon, I was spending most of my time accepting grave farewells from friends and colleagues convinced I had truly lost my mind.

I took it well. After all, I was approaching sainthood.

Meanwhile, my wife was visiting a divorce lawyer, a female one with the reputation of being a merciless ball-squeezer.

Claire was waiting for me when I arrived home at six, rather early. The kitchen table was covered with notes and computer spreadsheets. A calculator sat ready. She was icy, and well prepared. This time, I walked into the ambush.

'I suggest we get a divorce, on the grounds of irreconcilable differences,' she began pleasantly. 'We don't fight. We don't point fingers. We admit what we have been unable to say – the marriage is over.'

She stopped and waited for me to say something. I couldn't act surprised. Her mind was made up; what good would it do to object? I had to seem as cold-blooded as she. 'Sure,' I said, trying to be as nonchalant as possible. There was an element of relief in finally being honest. But it did bother me that she wanted the divorce more than I did.

To keep the upper hand, she then mentioned her meeting with Jacqueline Hume, her new divorce lawyer, dropping the name as if it were a mortar round, then relaying for my benefit the self-serving opinions her mouthpiece had delivered.

'Why did you hire a lawyer?' I asked, interrupting.

'I want to make sure I'm protected.'

'And you think I would take advantage of you?'

'You're a lawyer. I want a lawyer. It's that simple.'

'You could've saved a lot of money by not hiring her,' I said, trying to be a little contentious. After all, this was a divorce.

'But I feel much better now that I have.'

She handed me Exhibit A, a worksheet of our assets and liabilities. Exhibit B was a proposed split of these. Not surprisingly, she intended to get the majority. We had cash of twelve thousand dollars, and she wanted to use half of it to pay off the bank lien on her car. I would get twenty-five hundred of the remainder. No mention of paying off the sixteen thousand owed on my Lexus. She wanted forty thousand of the fifty-one thousand dollars we had in mutual funds. I got to keep my 401K.

'Not exactly an even split,' I said.

'It's not going to be equal,' she said with all the confidence of one who had just hired a pit bull.

'Why not?'

'Because I'm not the one going through a midlife crisis.'

'So it's my fault?'

'We're not assigning fault. We're dividing the assets. For reasons known only to you, you've decided to take a cut in pay of ninety thousand dollars a year. Why should I suffer the consequences? My lawyer is confident she can convince a judge that your actions have wrecked us financially. You want to go crazy, fine. But don't expect me to starve.'

'Small chance of that.'

'I'm not going to bicker.'

'I wouldn't either if I were getting everything.' I felt compelled to cause some measure of trouble. We couldn't scream and throw things. We damned sure weren't going to cry. We couldn't make nasty accusations about affairs or chemical addictions. What kind of divorce was this?

A very sterile one. She ignored me and continued down her list of notes, one no doubt prepared by the mouthpiece. 'The apartment lease is up June thirtieth, and I'll stay here until then. That's ten thousand in rent.'

'When would you like me to leave?'

'As soon as you'd like.'

'Fine.' If she wanted me out, I wasn't about to beg to stay. It was an exercise in one-upsmanship. Which side of the table could show more disdain than the other?

I almost said something stupid, like, 'You got someone else moving in?' I wanted to rattle her, to watch her do an instant thaw.

Instead, I kept my cool. 'I'll be gone by the weekend,' I said. She had no response, but she didn't frown.

'Why do you think you're entitled to eighty percent of the mutual funds?' I asked.

'I'm not getting eighty percent. I'll spend ten thousand in rent, another three thousand in utilities, two thousand to pay off our joint credit cards, and we'll owe about six thousand in taxes incurred together. That's a total of twenty-one thousand.'

Exhibit C was a thorough list of the personal property, beginning with the den and ending in the empty bedroom. Neither of us would dare fall into a squabble over pots and pans, so the division was quite amicable. 'Take what you want,' I said several times, especially when addressing items such as towels and bed linens. We traded a few things, doing it with finesse. My position on several assets was driven more by a reluctance to physically move them than by any pride of ownership.

I wanted a television and some dishes. Bachelorhood had been sprung suddenly upon me, and I had trouble contemplating the furnishing of a new place.

She, on the other hand, had spent hours living in the future.

But she was fair. We finished the drudgery of Exhibit C, and declared ourselves to be equitably divided. We would sign a separation agreement, wait six months, then go to court together and legally dissolve our union.

Neither of us wanted any postgame chat. I found my overcoat, and went for a long walk through the streets of Georgetown, wondering how life had changed so dramatically.

The erosion of the marriage had been slow, but certain. The change in careers had hit like a bullet. Things were moving much too fast, but I was unable to stop them.

FOURTEEN

The sabbatical concept was killed in the executive committee. While no one was supposed to know what that group did in its private meetings, it was reported to me by a very somber Rudolph that a bad precedent could be set. With a firm so large, granting a year's leave to one associate might trigger all sorts of requests from other malcontents.

There would be no safety net. The door would slam when I walked through it.

'Are you sure you know what you're doing?' he asked, standing before my desk. There were two large storage boxes on the floor next to him. Polly was already packing my junk.

'I'm sure,' I said with a smile. 'Don't worry about me.'

'I tried.'

'Thanks, Rudolph.' He left, shaking his head.

After Claire's blindside the night before, I had not been able to think about the sabbatical. More urgent thoughts cluttered my brain. I was about to be divorced, and single, and homeless myself.

Suddenly I was concerned with a new apartment, not to mention a new job and office and career. I closed the door, and scanned the real estate section of the classifieds.

I would sell the car and get rid of the four-hundred-eighty-dollar-a-month payment. I'd buy a clunker, insure it heavily, and wait for it to disappear into the darkness of my new neighborhoods. If I wanted a decent apartment in the District, it became apparent that most of my new salary would go for rent.

I left early for lunch, and spent two hours racing around Central Washington looking at lofts. The cheapest was a dump for eleven hundred a month, much too much for a street lawyer.

Another file awaited me upon my return from lunch; another plain manila legal-sized one, with no writing on the outside of it. Same spot on my desk. Inside, two keys were taped to the left side, a typed note was stapled to the right. It read:

Top key is to Chance's door. Bottom key is to file drawer under window. Copy and return. Careful, Chance is very suspicious. Lose the keys.

Polly appeared instantly, as she so often did; no knock, not a sound, just a sudden ghostlike presence in the room. She was pouting and ignoring me. We'd been together for four years, and she claimed to be devastated by my departure. We weren't really that close. She'd be reassigned in days. She was a very nice person, but the least of my worries.

I quickly closed the file, not knowing if she had seen it. I waited for a moment as she busied herself with my storage boxes. She didn't mention it – strong evidence that she was unaware of it. But since she saw everything in the hallway around my office, I couldn't imagine how Hector or anyone else could enter and leave without being seen.

Barry Nuzzo, fellow hostage and friend, dropped by to have a serious talk. He shut the door and stepped around the boxes. I didn't want to discuss my leaving, so I told him about Claire. His wife and Claire were both from Providence, a fact that seemed oddly significant in Washington. We had socialized with them a few times over the years, but the group friendship had gone the way of the marriage.

He was surprised, then saddened, then seemed to shake it off quite well. 'You're having a bad month,' he said. 'I'm sorry.'

'It's been a long slide,' I said.

We talked about the old days, the guys who had come and gone. We had not bothered to replay the Mister affair over a beer, and that struck me as strange. Two friends face death together, walk away from it, then get too busy to help each other with the aftermath.

We eventually got around to it; it was difficult to avoid with the storage boxes in the middle of the floor. I realized that the incident was the reason for our conversation.

'I'm sorry I let you down,' he said.

'Come on, Barry.'

'No, really. I should've been here.'

'Why?'

'Because it's obvious you've lost your mind,' he said with a laugh.

I tried to enjoy his humor. 'Yeah, I'm a little crazy now, I guess, but I'll get over it.'

'No, seriously, I heard you were having trouble. I tried to find you last week but you were gone. I was worried about you, but I've been in trial, you know, the usual.'

'I know.'

'I really feel bad for not being here, Mike. I'm sorry.'

'Come on. Stop it.'

'We all got the hell scared out of us, but you could've been hit.'

'He could've killed all of us, Barry. Real dynamite, a missed shot, boom. Let's not replay it.'

'The last thing I saw as we were scrambling out the door was you, covered with blood, screaming. I thought you were hit. We got outside, in a pile, with people grabbing us, yelling, and I was waiting for the blast. I thought, Mike's still in there, and he's hurt. We stopped by the elevators. Somebody cut the ropes from our wrists, and I glanced back just in time to see you as the cops grabbed you. I remember the blood. All that damned blood.'

I didn't say anything. He needed this. Somehow it would ease his mind. He could report to Rudolph and the others that he had at least tried to talk me out of it.

'All the way down, I kept asking, "Did Mike get hit? Did Mike get hit?" No one could answer. It seemed like an hour passed before they said you were okay. I was going to call you when I got home, but the kids wouldn't leave me alone. I should have.'

'Forget it.'

'I'm sorry, Mike.'

'Please don't say that again. It's over, done with. We could've talked about it for days, and nothing would've changed.'

'When did you realize you were leaving?'

I had to think about this for a moment. The truthful answer was at the point Sunday when Bill yanked the sheets back and I saw my little pal Ontario finally at peace. It was then and there, at that moment, in the city morgue, that I became someone else.

'Over the weekend,' I said, with no further explanation. He didn't need one.

He shook his head, as if the storage boxes were primarily his fault. I decided to help him through it. 'You couldn't have stopped me, Barry. No one could.'

Then he began nodding, in agreement because he understood somehow. A gun in your face, the clock stops, priorities emerge at once – God, family, friends. Money falls to the bottom. The Firm and the Career vanish as each awful second ticks by and you realize this could be the last day of your life.

'How about you?' I asked. 'How are you doing?'

The Firm and the Career stay on the bottom for a few short hours.

'We started a trial on Thursday. In fact, we were preparing for it when Mister interrupted us. We couldn't ask the Judge for a continuance because the client had been waiting four years for a trial date. And we weren't injured, you know. Not physically, anyway. So we kicked into high gear, started the trial, and never slowed down. The trial saved us.'

Of course it did. Work is therapy, even salvation at Drake & Sweeney. I wanted to scream at him, because two weeks ago I would have said the same thing.

'Good,' I said. How nice. 'So you're okay?'

'Sure.' He was a litigator, a macho player with Teflon skin. He also had three kids, so the luxury of a thirtysomething detour was out of the question.

The clock suddenly called him. We shook hands, embraced, and made all the usual promises to keep in touch.

I kept the door closed so I could stare at the file and decide what to do. Before long I'd made a few assumptions. One, the keys worked. Two, it was not a setup; I had no known enemies and I was leaving anyway. Three, the file was really in the office, in the drawer under the window. Four, it was possible to get it without being caught. Five, it could be copied in a short period of time. Six, it could then be returned as if nothing had happened. Seven, and the biggest of all, it actually contained damning evidence.

I wrote these down on a legal pad. Taking the file would be grounds for instant dismissal, but I didn't care about that. Same for getting caught in Chance's office with an unauthorized key.

Copying it would be the challenge. Since no file at the firm was less than an inch thick, there would probably be a hundred pages to Xerox, assuming I copied everything. I would have to stand in front of a machine for several minutes, exposed. That would be too dangerous. Secretaries and clerks did the copying, not lawyers. The machines were high-tech, complicated, and no doubt just waiting to jam the instant I pushed a button. They were also coded – buttons had to be pushed so that every copy could be billed to a client. And they were in open areas. I couldn't think of a single copier in a corner. Perhaps I could find one in another section of the firm, but my presence there would be suspicious.

I would have to leave the building with it, and that would border on being a criminal act. I wouldn't steal the file, though, just borrow it.

At four, I walked through the real estate section with my sleeves rolled up, holding a stack of files as if I had serious business there. Hector was not at his desk. Braden Chance was in his office, with his door cracked, his bitchy voice on the phone. A secretary smiled at me as I strolled by. I saw no security cameras peeking down from above. Some floors had them; others didn't. Who'd want to breach security in real estate?

I left at five. I bought sandwiches at a deli and drove to my new office.

My partners were still there, waiting for me. Sofia actually smiled as we shook hands, but only for an instant.

'Welcome aboard,' Abraham said gravely, as if I were climbing onto a sinking ship. Mordecai waved his arms at a small room next to his.

126

'How about this?' he said. 'Suite E.'

'Beautiful,' I said, stepping into my new office. It was about half the size of the one I'd just left. My desk at the firm wouldn't fit in it. There were four file cabinets on one wall, each a different color. The light was a bare bulb hanging from the ceiling. I didn't see a phone.

'I like it,' I said, and I wasn't lying.

'We'll get you a phone tomorrow,' he said, pulling the shades down over a window AC unit. 'This was last used by a young lawyer named Banebridge.'

'What happened to him?'

'Couldn't handle the money.'

It was getting dark, and Sofia seemed anxious to leave. Abraham retreated to his office. Mordecai and I ate dinner at his desk – the sandwiches I'd brought with the bad coffee he'd brewed.

The copier was a bulky one of eighties' vintage, free of code panels and the other bells and whistles favored by my former firm. It sat in a corner of the main room, near one of the four desks covered with old files.

'What time are you leaving tonight?' I asked Mordecai between bites.

'I don't know. In an hour I guess. Why?'

'Just curious. I'm going back to Drake & Sweeney for a couple of hours, last-minute stuff they want me to finish. Then I'd like to bring a load of my office junk here, tonight. Would that be possible?'

He was chewing his food. He reached into a drawer, pulled out a ring with three keys on it, and tossed it to me. 'Come and go as you please,' he said.

'Will it be safe?'

'No. So be careful. Park right out there, as close to the door as you can. Walk fast. Then lock yourself in.'

He must have seen the fear in my eyes, because he said, 'Get used to it. Be smart.'

I walked fast and smart to my car at six-thirty. The

sidewalk was empty; no hoodlums, no gunfire, not a scratch on my Lexus. I felt proud as I unlocked it and drove away. Maybe I could survive on the streets.

The drive back to Drake & Sweeney took eleven minutes. If it took thirty minutes to copy Chance's file, then it would be out of his office for about an hour. Assuming all went well. And he would never know. I waited until eight, then walked casually down to real estate, my sleeves rolled up again as if I were hard at work.

The hallways were deserted. I knocked on Chance's door, no answer. It was locked. I then checked every office, knocking softly at first, then harder, then turning the knob. About half were locked. Around each corner, I checked for security cameras. I looked in conference rooms and typing pools. Not a soul.

The key to his door was just like mine, same color and size. It worked perfectly, and I was suddenly inside a dark office and faced with the decision of whether or not to turn on the lights. A person driving by couldn't tell which office was suddenly lit, and I doubted if anyone in the hallway could see a ray of light at the bottom of the door. Plus, it was very dark, and I didn't have a flashlight. I locked the door, turned on the lights, went straight to the file drawer under the window, and unlocked it with the second key. On my knees, I quietly pulled the drawer out.

There were dozens of files, all relating to RiverOaks, all arranged neatly according to some method. Chance and his secretary were well organized, a trait our firm cherished. A thick one was labeled RiverOaks/TAG, Inc. I gently removed it, and began to flip through it. I wanted to make sure it was the right file.

A male voice yelled 'Hey!' in the hallway, and I jumped out of my skin.

Another male voice answered from a few doors

down, and the two struck up a conversation some-where very near Chance's door. Basketball talk. Bullets and Knicks.

With rubbery knees, I walked to the door. I turned off the lights, listening to their talk. Then I sat on Braden's fine leather sofa for ten minutes. If I was seen leaving the office empty-handed, nothing would be done. Tomorrow was my last day anyway. Of course I wouldn't have the file either.

What if someone spotted me leaving with the file? If they confronted me, I would be dead.

I pondered the situation furiously, getting caught in every scenario. Be patient, I kept telling myself. They'll go away. Basketball was followed by girls, neither sounded married, probably a couple of clerks from Georgetown's law school, working nights. Their voices soon faded.

I locked the drawer in the dark and took the file. Five minutes, six, seven, eight. I quietly opened the door, slowly placed my head in the crack, and looked up and down the hall. No one. I scooted out, past Hector's desk, and headed for the reception area, walking briskly while trying to appear casual.

'Hey!' someone yelled from behind. I turned a corner, and glanced back just quickly enough to see a guy coming after me. The nearest door was to a small library. I ducked inside; luckily it was dark. I moved between tiers of books until I found another door on the other side. I opened it, and at the end of a short hallway I saw an exit sign above a door. I ran through it. Figuring I could run faster down the stairs than up them, I bounded down, even though my office was two floors above. If by chance he recognized me, he might go there looking for me.

I emerged on the ground floor, out of breath, without a coat, not wanting to be seen by anyone, especially the security person guarding the elevators to keep out any more street people. I went to a side exit, the same one Polly and I had used to avoid the reporters the night Mister got shot. It was freezing and a light rain was falling as I ran to my car.

The thoughts of a bungling first-time thief. It was a stupid thing to do. Very stupid. Did I get caught? No one saw me leave Chance's office. No one knew I had a file that wasn't mine.

I shouldn't have run. When he yelled, I should've stopped, chatted him up, acted as if everything were fine, and if he wanted to see the file, I'd rebuke him and send him away. He was probably just one of the lowly clerks I had heard earlier.

But why had he yelled like that? If he didn't know me, why was he trying to stop me from the other end of the hallway? I drove onto Massachusetts, in a hurry to get the copying done and somehow get the file back where it belonged. I had pulled all-nighters before, and if I had to wait until 3 A.M. to sneak back to Chance's office, then I would do so.

I relaxed a little. The heater was blowing at full speed.

There was no way to know that a drug bust had gone bad, a cop had been shot, a Jaguar owned by a dealer was speeding down Eighteenth Street. I had the green light on New Hampshire, but the boys who shot the cop weren't concerned with the rules of the road. The Jaguar was a blur to my left, then the air bag exploded in my face.

When I came to, the driver's door was pinching my left shoulder. Black faces were staring in at me through the shattered window. I heard sirens, then drifted away again.

One of the paramedics unlatched my seat belt, and they pulled me over the console and through the passenger door. 'I don't see any blood,' someone said.

130

'Can you walk?' a paramedic asked. My shoulder and ribs were hurting. I tried to stand, but my legs wouldn't work.

'I'm okay,' I said, sitting on the edge of a stretcher. There was a racket behind me, but I couldn't turn around. They strapped me down, and as I entered the ambulance I saw the Jaguar, upside down and surrounded by cops and medics.

I kept saying, 'I'm okay, I'm okay,' as they checked my blood pressure. We were moving; the siren faded.

They took me to the emergency room at George Washington University Medical Center. X-rays revealed no breaks of any type. I was bruised and in terrible pain. They filled me with pain-killers and rolled me up to a private room.

I awoke sometime in the night. Claire was sleeping in a chair next to my bed.

FIFTEEN

She left before dawn. A sweet note on the table told me that she had to make her rounds, and that she would return mid-morning. She had talked to my doctors, and it was likely that I would not die.

We seemed perfectly normal and happy, a cute couple devoted to each other. I drifted off wondering why, exactly, we were going through the process of a divorce.

A nurse woke me at seven and handed me the note. I read it again as she rattled on about the weather – sleet and snow – and took my blood pressure. I asked her for a newspaper. She brought it thirty minutes later with my cereal. The story was front page, Metro. The narc was shot several times in a gun battle; his condition was critical. He'd killed one dealer. The second dealer was the Jaguar driver, who died at the scene of the crash under circumstances still to be investigated. I was not mentioned, which was fine.

Had I not been involved, the story would have been an everyday shootout between cops and crack dealers, ignored and unread by me. Welcome to the streets. I tried to convince myself it could've happened to any D.C. professional, but it was a hard sell. To be in that part of town after dark was to ask for trouble.

My upper left arm was swollen and already turning blue – the left shoulder and collarbone stiff and tender to the touch. My ribs were sore to the point of keeping me perfectly still. They hurt only when I breathed. I made it to the bathroom where I relieved myself and looked at my face. An air bag is a small bomb. The impact stuns the face and chest. But the damage was minimal: slightly swollen nose and eyes, an upper lip that had a new shape. Nothing that wouldn't disappear over the weekend.

The nurse was back with more pills. I made her identify each one, then I said no to the entire collection. They were for pain and stiffness, and I wanted a clear head. The doc popped in at seven-thirty for a quick going-over. With nothing broken or ripped, my hours as a patient were numbered. He suggested another round of X-rays, to be safe. I tried to say no, but he had already discussed the matter with my wife.

So I limped around my room for an eternity, testing my wounded body parts, watching the morning news-babble, hoping no one I knew would suddenly enter and see me in my yellow paisley gown.

Finding a wrecked car in the District is a baffling chore, especially when initiated so soon after the accident. I started with the phone book, my only source, and half the numbers in Traffic went unanswered. The other half were answered with great indifference. It was early, the weather was bad. It was Friday, why get involved?

Most wrecked cars were taken to a city lot on Rasco Road, up in Northeast. I learned this from a secretary at the Central Precinct. She worked in Animal Control; I was dialing police extensions at random. Other cars were sometimes taken to other lots, and there was a good chance mine could still be attached to the wrecker. The wreckers were privately owned, she explained, and this had always caused trouble. She once worked in Traffic, but hated it over there.

I thought of Mordecai, my new source for all information related to the street. I waited until nine to call him. I told him the story, assured him I was in great shape in spite of being in a hospital, and asked him if he knew how to find a wrecked car. He had some ideas.

I called Polly with the same story.

'You're not coming in?' she asked, her voice faltering.

'I'm in the hospital, Polly. Are you listening to me?'

There was hesitation on her end, confirming what I feared. I could envision a cake with a punch bowl next to it, probably in a conference room, on the table, with fifty people standing around it proposing toasts and making short speeches about how wonderful I was. I had been to a couple of those parties myself. They were awful. I was determined to avoid my own send-off.

'When are you getting out?' she asked.

'Don't know. Maybe tomorrow.' It was a lie; I was leaving before noon, with or without my medical team's approval.

More hesitation. The cake, the punch, the important speeches from busy people, maybe even a gift or two. How would she handle it?

'I'm sorry,' she said.

'Me too. Is anybody looking for me?'

'No. Not yet.'

'Good. Please tell Rudolph about the accident, and I'll call him later. Gotta go. They want more tests.'

And so my once promising career at Drake & Sweeney sputtered to an end. I skipped my own retirement party. At the age of thirty-two I was freed from the shackles of corporate servitude, and the money. I was left to follow my conscience. I would've felt great if not for the knife sticking through my ribs every time I moved.

Claire arrived after eleven. She huddled with my doctor in the hall. I could hear them out there, speaking their language. They stepped into my room, jointly announced my release, and I changed into clean clothes she had brought from home. She drove me there, a short trip during which little was said. There was no chance at reconciliation. Why should a simple car wreck change anything? She was there as a friend and a doctor, not a wife.

She fixed tomato soup and tucked me into the sofa. She lined up my pills on the kitchen counter, gave me my instructions, and left.

I was still for ten minutes, long enough to eat half the soup and a few of the saltines, then I was on the phone. Mordecai had found nothing.

Working from the classifieds, I began calling Realtors and apartment locating services. Then I called for a sedan from a car service. I took a long, hot shower to loosen my bruised body.

My driver was Leon. I sat in the front with him, trying not to grimace and groan with each pothole he hit.

I couldn't afford a nice apartment, but at the least I wanted one that was safe. Leon had some ideas. We stopped at a news-stand and I picked up two free brochures on District real estate.

In Leon's opinion, a good place to live right now, but this could change in six months, he warned me, was Adams-Morgan, north of Dupont Circle. It was a well-known district, one I had been through many times, never with any desire to stop and browse. The streets were lined with turn-of-the-century rowhouses, all of which were still inhabited, which, in D.C., meant a vibrant neighborhood. The bars and clubs were hot at the moment, according to Leon, and the best new restaurants were there. The seedy sections were just around the corner, and of course one had to be extremely careful. If important people like senators got themselves mugged on Capitol Hill, then no one was safe.

Driving toward Adams-Morgan, Leon was suddenly confronted with a pothole larger than his car. We bounced through it, getting airborne for what seemed to be ten seconds, then landing very hard. I couldn't help but scream as the entire left side of my torso collapsed in pain.

Leon was horrified. I had to tell him the truth, where I'd slept last night. He slowed down considerably, and became my Realtor. He helped me up the stairs at my first prospect, a run-down flat with the unmistakable smell of cat urine emanating from the carpet. In no uncertain terms, Leon told the landlord she should be ashamed showing the place in such condition.

The second stop was a loft five floors above the street, and I almost didn't make it up the stairs. No elevator. And not much heating. Leon politely thanked the manager.

The next loft was four floors up, but with a nice, clean elevator. The rowhouse was on Wyoming, a pretty shaded street just off Connecticut. The rent was five hundred and fifty a month, and I had already said yes before I saw the place. I was sinking fast, thinking more and more about the pain pills I'd left on the counter, and ready to rent anything.

Three tiny rooms in an attic with sloping ceilings, a bathroom with plumbing that seemed to be working, clean floors, and something of a view over the street.

'We'll take it,' Leon said to the landlord. I was leaning on a door frame, ready to collapse. In a small office in the basement, I hurriedly read the lease, signed it, and wrote a check for the deposit and first month's rent.

I'd told Claire I'd be out by the weekend. I was determined to make it happen.

If Leon was curious about my move from the swankiness of Georgetown to a three-room pigeonhole in Adams-Morgan, he didn't ask. He was too much of a professional. He returned me to our apartment, and he waited in the car while I swallowed my pills and took a quick nap.

A phone was ringing somewhere in the midst of my chemical-induced fog. I stumbled forth, found it, managed to say, 'Hello.'

Rudolph said, 'Thought you were in the hospital.'

I heard his voice, and recognized it, but the fog was still clearing. 'I was,' I said, thick-tongued. 'Now I'm not. What do you want?'

'We missed you this afternoon.'

Ah yes. The punch and cake show. 'I didn't plan to be in a car wreck, Rudolph. Please forgive me.'

'A lot of people wanted to say good-bye.'

'They can drop me a line. Tell them to just fax it over.'

'You feel lousy, don't you?'

'Yes, Rudolph. I feel like I've just been hit by a car.'

'Are you on medication?'

'Why do you care?'

'Sorry. Look, Braden Chance was in my office an hour ago. He's quite anxious to see you. Odd, don't you think?'

The fog lifted and my head was much clearer. 'See me about what?'

'He wouldn't say. But he's looking for you.'

'Tell him I've left.'

'I did. Sorry to bother you. Stop by if you get a minute. You still have friends here.'

'Thanks, Rudolph.'

I stuffed the pills in my pockets. Leon was napping in the car. As we sped away, I called Mordecai. He'd found the accident report; it listed a Hundley Towing as the wrecker service. Hundley Towing used an answering machine for most of its calls. The streets were slick, lots of accidents, a busy time for people who owned tow trucks. A mechanic had finally answered the phone around three, but proved to be completely useless.

Leon found the Hundley place on Rhode Island near Seventh. In better days it had been a full-service gas station, now it was a garage, towing service, used-car lot, and U-Haul trailer rental. Every window was adorned with black bars. Leon maneuvered as close as possible to the front door. 'Cover me,' I said, as I got out and dashed inside. The door kicked back when I walked through, hitting me on my left arm. I doubled over in pain. A mechanic wearing overalls and grease rounded a corner and glared at me.

I explained why I was there. He found a clipboard and studied papers stuck to it. In the rear, I could hear men talking and cursing – no doubt they were back there shooting dice, drinking whiskey, probably selling crack.

'The police have it,' he said, still looking at the papers.

'Any idea why?'

'Not really. Was there a crime or something?'

'Yeah, but my car wasn't involved with the crime.'

He gave me a blank look. He had his own problems.

'Any idea where it might be?' I asked, trying to be pleasant.

'When they impound them, they usually take them to a lot up on Georgia, north of Howard.'

'How many lots does the city have?'

He shrugged and began walking away. 'More than one,' he said, and disappeared.

I managed the door with care, then bolted for Leon's car.

It was dark when we found the lot, half a city block lined with chain link and razor wire. Inside were hundreds of wrecked cars, arranged haphazardly, some stacked on top of others.

Leon stood with me on the sidewalk, peering through the chain link. 'Over there,' I said, pointing. The Lexus was parked near a shed, facing us. The impact had demolished the left front. The fender was gone; the engine exposed and crushed.

'You're a very lucky man,' Leon said.

Next to it was the Jaguar, its roof flattened, all windows missing.

There was an office of some type in the shed, but it was closed and dark. The gates were locked with heavy chains. The razor wire glistened in the rain. There were tough guys hanging around a corner, not far away. I could feel them watching us.

'Let's get out of here,' I said.

Leon drove me to National Airport, the only place I knew to rent a car.

The table was set; carryout Chinese was on the stove. Claire was waiting, and worried to some degree, though it was impossible to tell how much. I told her I had to go rent a car, pursuant to instructions from my insurance company. She examined me like a good doctor, and made me take a pill.

'I thought you were going to rest,' she said.

'I tried. It didn't work. I'm starving.'

It would be our last meal together as husband and wife, ending the same way we'd begun, with something fast and prepared elsewhere.

'Do you know someone named Hector Palma?' she asked, halfway through dinner.

I swallowed hard. 'Yes.'

'He called an hour ago. Said it was important that he talk to you. Who is he?'

'A paralegal with the firm. I was supposed to spend the morning with him going over one of my cases. He's in a tight spot.'

'Must be. He wants to meet with you at nine tonight, at Nathan's on M.'

'Why a bar?' I mused.

'He didn't say. Sounded suspicious.'

My appetite vanished, but I kept eating to appear unmoved. Not that it was necessary. She couldn't have cared less.

I walked to M Street, in a light rain that was turning to sleet, and in significant pain. Parking would've been impossible on Friday night. And I hoped to stretch my muscles some, and clear my head.

The meeting could be nothing but trouble, and I prepped for it as I walked. I thought of lies to cover my trail, and more lies to cover the first set. Now that I had stolen, the lying didn't seem like such a big deal. Hector might be working for the firm; there was a chance he could be wired. I would listen carefully, and say little.

Nathan's was only half-full. I was ten minutes early, but he was there, waiting for me in a small booth. As I approached he suddenly jumped from his seat and thrust a hand at me. 'You must be Michael. I'm Hector Palma, from real estate. Nice to meet you.'

It was an assault, a burst of personality that put me on my heels. I shook hands, reeling, and said something like, 'Nice to meet you.'

He pointed to the booth. 'Here, have a seat,' he

140

said, all warmth and smiles. I delicately bent and squeezed my way into the booth.

'What happened to your face?' he asked.

'I kissed an air bag.'

'Yeah, I heard about the accident,' he said quickly. Very quickly. 'Are you okay? Any broken bones?'

'No,' I said slowly, trying to read him.

'Heard the other guy got killed,' he said, a split second after I'd spoken. He was in charge of this conversation. I was supposed to follow along.

'Yeah, some drug dealer.'

'This city,' he said, as the waiter appeared. 'What'll you have?' Hector asked me.

'Black coffee,' I said. At that moment, as he pondered his choice of drinks, one of his feet began tapping me on the leg.

'What kind of beer do you have?' he asked the waiter, a question they hated. The waiter looked straight ahead and began rattling off brands.

The tapping brought our eyes together. His hands were together on the table. Using the waiter as a shield, he barely curled his right index finger and pointed to his chest.

'Molson,' he announced suddenly, and the waiter left.

He was wired, and they were watching. Wherever they were, they couldn't see through the waiter. Instinctively, I wanted to turn and examine the other people in the bar. But I withstood the temptation, thanks in no small part to a neck as pliable as a board.

That explained the hearty hello, as if we'd never met. Hector had been grilled all day, and he was denying everything.

'I'm a paralegal in real estate,' he explained. 'You've met Braden Chance, one of our partners.'

'Yes.' Since my words were being recorded, I would offer little.

'I work primarily for him. You and I spoke briefly one day last week when you visited his office.'

'If you say so. I don't remember seeing you.'

I caught a very faint smile, a relaxing around the eyes, nothing a surveillance camera could catch. Under the table, I tapped his leg with my foot. Hopefully we were dancing to the same tune.

'Look, the reason I asked you to meet me is because a file is missing from Braden's office.'

'Am I the accused?'

'Well, no, but you're a possible suspect. It was the file you asked for when you sort of barged into his office last week.'

'Then I *am* being accused,' I said hotly.

'Not yet. Relax. The firm is doing a thorough investigation of the matter, and we're simply talking to everyone we can think of. Since I heard you ask Braden for the file, the firm instructed me to talk to you. It's that simple.'

'I don't know what you're talking about. It's that simple.'

'You know nothing about the file?'

'Of course not. Why would I take a file from a partner's office?'

'Would you take a polygraph?'

'Certainly,' I said firmly, even indignantly. There was no way in hell I would take a polygraph.

'Good. They're asking all of us to do it. Everybody remotely near the file.'

The beer and coffee arrived, giving us a brief pause to evaluate and reposition. Hector had just told me he was in deep trouble. A polygraph would kill him. Did you meet Michael Brock before he left the firm? Did you discuss the missing file? Did you give him copies of anything taken from the file? Did you assist him in obtaining the missing file? Yes or no. Hard questions with simple answers. There was no way he could lie and survive the test.

'They're fingerprinting too,' he said. He said this in a lower voice, not in an effort to avoid the hidden mike, but rather to soften the blow.

It didn't work. The thought of leaving prints had never occurred to me, neither before the theft, nor since. 'Good for them,' I said.

'In fact, they lifted prints all afternoon. From the door, the light switch, the file cabinet. Lots of prints.'

'Hope they find their man.'

'It's really coincidental, you know. Braden had a hundred active files in his office, and the only one missing is the one you were quite anxious to see.'

'Are you trying to say something?'

'I just said it. A real coincidence.' He was doing this for the benefit of our listeners.

I thought perhaps I should perform too. 'I don't like the way you said it,' I practically yelled at him. 'If you want to accuse me of something, then go to the cops, get a warrant, and get me picked up. Otherwise, keep your stupid opinions to yourself.'

'The cops are already involved,' he said, very coolly, and my contrived temper melted. 'It's a theft.'

'Of course it's a theft. Go catch your thief and stop wasting your time with me.'

He took a long drink. 'Did someone give you a set of keys to Braden's office?'

'Of course not.'

'Well, they found this empty file on your desk, with a note about the two keys. One to the door, the other to a file cabinet.'

'I know nothing about it,' I said, as arrogantly as possible while trying to remember the last place I'd put the empty file. My trail was widening. I'd been trained to think like a lawyer, not a criminal.

143

Another long drink by Hector, another sip of coffee by me.

Enough had been said. The messages had been delivered, one by the firm, the other by Hector himself. The firm wanted the file back, with its contents uncompromised. Hector wanted me to know that his involvement could cost him his job.

It was up to me to save him. I could return the file, confess, promise to keep it sealed, and the firm would probably forgive me. There would be no harm. Protecting Hector's job could be a condition of the return.

'Anything else?' I asked, suddenly ready to leave.

'Nothing. When can you do the polygraph?'

'I'll give you a call.'

I picked up my coat and left.

SIXTEEN

For reasons that I would soon understand, Mordecai had an intense dislike for District cops, even though most were black. In his opinion, they were rough on the homeless, and that was the standard he invariably used to measure good and bad.

But he knew a few. One was Sergeant Peeler, a man described by Mordecai as 'from the streets.' Peeler worked with troubled kids in a community center near the legal clinic, and he and Mordecai belonged to the same church. Peeler had contacts, and could pull enough strings to get me to my car.

He walked into the clinic shortly after nine Saturday morning. Mordecai and I were drinking coffee and trying to stay warm. Peeler didn't work Saturdays. I got the impression he would have rather stayed in bed.

With Mordecai doing the driving and talking, and with me in the back, we rode through the slick streets into Northeast. The snow they had forecast was instead a cold rain. Traffic was light. It was another raw February morning; only the hearty ventured onto the sidewalks.

We parked at the curb near the padlocked gates to the city lot just off Georgia Avenue. Peeler said, 'Wait here.' I could see the remains of my Lexus.

He walked to the gates, pushed a button on a pole, and the door to the office shed opened. A small, thin

145

uniformed policeman with an umbrella came over, and he and Peeler exchanged a few words.

Peeler returned to the car, slamming the door and shaking the water off his shoulders. 'He's waiting for you,' he said.

I stepped into the rain, raised my umbrella, and walked quickly to the gates where Officer Winkle was waiting without the slightest trace of humor or goodwill. He produced keys by the dozens, somehow found the three that fit the heavy padlocks, and said to me, 'Over here,' as he opened the gates. I followed him through the gravel lot, avoiding when possible the potholes filled with brown water and mud. My entire body ached with every move, so my hopping and dodging were restricted. He went straight to my car.

I went right to the front seat. No file. After a moment of panic, I found it behind the driver's seat, on the floor, intact. I grabbed it, and was ready to go. I was in no mood to survey the damage I'd walked away from. I had survived in one piece, and that was all that mattered. I'd haggle with the insurance company next week.

'Is that it?' Winkle asked.

'Yes,' I said, ready to bolt.

'Follow me.'

We entered the shed where a butane heater roared in a corner, blasting us with hot air. He selected one of ten clipboards from the wall, and began staring at the file I was holding. 'Brown manila file,' he said as he wrote. 'About two inches thick.' I stood there clutching it as if it were gold. 'Is there a name on it?'

I was in no position to protest. One smart-ass remark, and they would never find me. 'Why do you need it?' I asked.

'Put it on the table,' he said.

On the table it went. 'RiverOaks slash TAG, Inc.,'

146

he said, still writing. 'File number TBC-96–3381.' My trail widened even more.

'Do you own this?' he asked, pointing, with no small amount of suspicion.

'Yes.'

'Okay. You can go now.'

I thanked him, and got no response. I wanted to jog across the lot, but walking was enough of a challenge. He locked the gates behind me.

Mordecai and Peeler both turned around and looked at the file once I was inside. Neither had a clue. I had told Mordecai only that the file was very important. I needed to retrieve it before it was destroyed.

All that effort for one plain manila file?

I was tempted to flip through it as we drove back to the clinic. But I didn't.

I thanked Peeler, said good-bye to Mordecai, and drove, cautiously, to my new loft.

The source of the money was the federal government, no surprise in D.C. The Postal Service planned to construct a twenty-million-dollar bulk-mail facility in the city, and RiverOaks was one of several aggressive real estate companies hoping to build, lease, and manage it. Several sites had been considered, all in rough and decaying sections of the city. A short list of three had been announced the previous December. RiverOaks had begun snapping up all the cheap real estate it might need.

TAG was a duly registered corporation whose sole stock-holder was Tillman Gantry, described in a file memo as a former pimp, small-time hustler, and twice-convicted felon. One of many such characters in the city. After crime, Gantry had discovered used cars and real estate. He purchased abandoned buildings, sometimes doing quickie renovations and reselling,

147

sometimes offering space for rent. Fourteen TAG properties were listed in a file summary. Gantry's path crossed that of RiverOaks' when the U.S. Postal Service needed more space.

On January 6, the Postal Service informed River-Oaks by registered mail that the company had been chosen to be the contractor/owner/landlord of the new bulk facility. A memorandum of agreement provided for annual rental payments of $1.5 million, for a guaranteed period of twenty years. The letter also said, with nongovernmental-like haste, that a final agreement between RiverOaks and the Postal Service would have to be signed no later than March 1, or the deal was off. After seven years of contemplating and planning, the Feds wanted it built overnight.

RiverOaks, and its lawyers and Realtors, went to work. In January, the company purchased four properties on Florida near the warehouse where the eviction took place. The file had two maps of the area, with shaded colors indicating lots purchased and lots under negotiation.

March 1 was only seven days away. Small wonder Chance missed the file so quickly. He was working with it every day.

The warehouse on Florida Avenue had been purchased by TAG the previous July for a sum not revealed in the file. RiverOaks bought it for two hundred thousand dollars on January 31, four days before the eviction that sent DeVon Hardy and the Burton family into the streets.

On the bare wooden floor of what would become my living room, I carefully removed each sheet of paper from the file, examined it, then described it in detail on a legal pad so that I could put it back together in perfect order. There was the usual collection of papers I assumed to be in every real estate file: tax records for prior years, a chain of title, previous deeds, an agreement for the purchase and sale of the property, correspondence with the Realtor, closing papers. It was a cash deal, so no bank was involved.

On the left inside flap of the file was the journal, a preprinted form used to log each entry by date and brief description. You could judge the organizational capacity of a Drake & Sweeney secretary by the level of detail in a file's journal. Every piece of paper, map, photo, or chart – anything and everything that was punched into a file was supposed to be recorded in the journal. This had been drilled into our heads during boot camp. Most of us had learned the hard way – there was nothing more frustrating than flipping through a thick file in search of something that had not been logged in with sufficient detail. If you can't find it in thirty seconds, the axiom said, it's useless.

Chance's file was meticulous; his secretary was a woman of details. But there had been tampering.

On January 22, Hector Palma went to the warehouse, alone, for a routine, prepurchase inspection. As he was entering a designated door, he was mugged by two street punks who hit him over the head with a stick of some sort, and took his wallet and cash at knifepoint. He stayed at home on January 23, and prepared a memo to the file describing the assault. The last sentence read: 'Will return on Monday, January 27, with guard, to inspect.' The memo was properly logged into the file.

But there was no memo from his second visit. A January 27 entry into the journal said: HP memo – site visit, inspection of premises.

Hector went to the warehouse on the twenty-seventh, with a guard, inspected the place, no doubt found that serious squatting was under way, and prepared a memo, which, judging by his other paperwork, was probably quite thorough.

The memo had been removed from the file. Certainly no crime, and I had taken things from files all the time without making a note in the journal. But I damned sure put them back. If an item was logged in, it was supposed to be in the file.

The closing took place on January 31, a Friday. The following Tuesday, Hector returned to the warehouse to remove the squatters. He was assisted by a guard from a private security firm, a District cop, and four roughnecks from an eviction company. It took three hours, according to his memo, which ran for two pages. Though he tried to mask his emotions, Hector didn't have the stomach for evictions.

My heart stopped when I read the following: 'The mother had four children, one an infant. She lived in a two-room apartment with no plumbing. They slept on two mattresses on the floor. She fought with the policeman while her children watched. She was eventually removed.'

So Ontario watched while his mother fought.

There was a list of those evicted, seventeen in all, with children excluded, the same list someone had placed on my desk Monday morning with a copy of the *Post* story.

In the back of the file, lying loose without the benefit of a journal entry, were eviction notices for the seventeen. They had not been used. Squatters have no rights, including the right to be notified. The notices had been prepared as an afterthought, an effort to cover the trail. They had probably been stuck in after the Mister episode by Chance himself, just in case he might need them.

The tampering was obvious, and foolish. But then Chance was a partner. It was virtually unheard of for a partner to surrender a file.

It hadn't been surrendered; it had been stolen. An

act of larceny, a crime for which evidence was now being gathered. The thief was an idiot.

As part of my preemployment ritual seven years earlier, I had been fingerprinted by private investigators. It would be a simple matter to match those prints with the ones lifted from Chance's file cabinet. It would take only minutes. I was certain it had already been done. Could there be a warrant for my arrest? It was inevitable.

Most of the floor was covered when I finished, three hours after I started. I carefully reassembled the file, then drove to the clinic and copied it.

She was shopping, her note said. We had nice luggage, an item we failed to mention when we split the assets. She would be traveling more than I in the near future, so I took the cheap stuff – duffel and gym bags. I didn't want to get caught, so I threw the basics into a pile on the bed – socks, underwear, tee shirts, toiletries, shoes, but only the ones I had worn in the past year. She could discard the others. I hurriedly cleaned out my drawers and my side of the medicine cabinet. Wounded and aching, physically and otherwise, I hauled the bags down two flights of stairs to my rental car, then went back up for a load of suits and dress clothes. I found my old sleeping bag, unused for at least the last five years, and carried it down, along with a quilt and a pillow. I was entitled to my alarm clock, radio, portable CD player with a few CD's, thirteen-inch color TV on the kitchen counter, one coffeepot, hair dryer, and the set of blue towels.

When the car was full, I left a note telling her I was gone. I placed it next to the one she'd left, and refused to stare at it. My emotions were mixed and just under the skin, and I was not equipped to deal with them. I'd never moved out before; I wasn't sure how it was done.

I locked the door and walked down the stairs. I knew I would be back in a couple of days to get the rest of my things, but the trip down felt like the last time.

She would read the note, check the drawers and closets to see what I had taken, and when she realized I had indeed moved out, she would sit in the den for a quick tear. Maybe a good cry. But it would be over before long. She would easily move to the next phase.

As I drove away, there was no feeling of liberation. It wasn't a thrill to be single again. Claire and I had both lost.

SEVENTEEN

I locked myself inside the office. The clinic was colder Sunday than it had been on Saturday. I wore a heavy sweater, corduroy pants, thermal socks, and I read the paper at my desk with two steaming cups of coffee in front of me. The building had a heating system, but I wasn't about to meddle with it.

I missed my chair, my leather executive swivel that rocked and reclined and rolled at my command. My new one was a small step above a folding job you'd rent for a wedding. It promised to be uncomfortable on good days; in my pummeled condition at that moment, it was a torture device.

The desk was a battered hand-me-down, probably from an abandoned school; square and boxlike, with three drawers down each side, all of which actually opened, but not without a struggle. The two clients' chairs on the other side were indeed folding types – one black, the other a greenish color I'd never seen before.

The walls were plaster, painted decades ago and allowed to fade into a shade of pale lemon. The plaster was cracked; the spiders had taken over the corners at the ceiling. The only decoration was a framed placard advertising a March for Justice on the Mall in July of 1988.

The floor was ancient oak, the planks rounded at

the edges, evidence of heavy use in prior years. It had been swept recently, the broom still standing in a corner with a dustpan, a gentle cue that if I wanted the dirt cleared again, then it was up to me.

Oh how the mighty had fallen! If my dear brother Warner could've seen me sitting there on Sunday, shivering at my sad little desk, staring at the cracks in the plaster, locked in so that my potential clients couldn't mug me, he would've hurled insults so rich and colorful that I would've been compelled to write them down.

I couldn't comprehend my parents' reaction. I would be forced to call them soon, and deliver the double shock of my changes of address.

A loud bang at the door scared the hell out of me. I bolted upright, unsure of what to do. Were the street punks coming after me? Another knock as I moved toward the front, and I could see a figure trying to look through the bars and thick glass of the front door.

It was Barry Nuzzo, shivering and anxious to get to safety. I got things unlocked, and let him in.

'What a slumhole!' he began pleasantly, looking around the front room as I relocked the door.

'Quaint, isn't it?' I said, reeling from his presence and trying to figure out what it meant.

'What a dump!' He was amused by the place. He walked around Sofia's desk, slowly taking off his gloves, afraid to touch anything for fear of starting an avalanche of files.

'We keep the overhead low, so we can take all the money home,' I said. It was an old joke around Drake & Sweeney. The partners were constantly bitching about the overhead, while at the same time most were concerned about redecorating their offices.

'So you're here for the money?' he asked, still amused.

'Of course.'

154

'You've lost your mind.'

'I've found a calling.'

'Yeah, you're hearing voices.'

'Is that why you're here? To tell me I'm crazy?'

'I called Claire.'

'And what did she say?'

'Said you had moved out.'

'That's true. We're getting a divorce.'

'What's wrong with your face?'

'Air bag.'

'Oh, yeah. I forgot. I heard it was just a fender bender.'

'It was. The fenders got bent.'

He draped his coat over a chair, then hurriedly put it back on. 'Does low overhead mean you don't pay your heating bill?'

'Now and then we skip a month.'

He walked around some more, peeking into the small offices to the side. 'Who pays for this operation?' he asked.

'A trust.'

'A declining trust?'

'Yes, a rapidly declining trust.'

'How'd you find it?'

'Mister hung out here. These were his lawyers.'

'Good old Mister,' he said. He stopped his examination for a moment, and stared at a wall. 'Do you think he would've killed us?'

'No. Nobody was listening to him. He was just another homeless guy. He wanted to be heard.'

'Did you ever consider jumping him?'

'No, but I thought about grabbing his gun and shooting Rafter.'

'I wish you had.'

'Maybe next time.'

'Got any coffee?'

'Sure. Have a seat.'

155

I didn't want Barry to follow me into the kitchen, because it left much to be desired. I found a cup, washed it quickly, and filled it with coffee. I invited him into my office.

'Nice,' he said, looking around.

'This is where all the long balls are hit,' I said proudly. We took positions across the desk, both chairs squeaking and on the verge of collapse.

'Is this what you dreamed about in law school?' he asked.

'I don't remember law school. I've billed too many hours since then.'

He finally looked at me, without a smirk or a smile, and the kidding was set aside. As bad as the thought was, I couldn't help but wonder if Barry was wired. They had sent Hector into the fray with a bug under his shirt; they would do the same with Barry. He wouldn't volunteer, but they could apply the pressure. I was the enemy.

'So you came here searching for Mister?' he said.

'I guess.'

'What did you find?'

'Are you playing dumb, Barry? What's happening at the firm? Have you guys circled the wagons? Are you coming after me?'

He weighed this carefully, while taking quick sips from his mug. 'This coffee is awful,' he said, ready to spit.

'At least it's hot.'

'I'm sorry about Claire.'

'Thanks, but I'd rather not talk about it.'

'There's a file missing, Michael. Everyone's pointing at you.'

'Who knows you're here?'

'My wife.'

'The firm send you?'

'Absolutely not.'

I believed him. He'd been a friend for seven years, close at times. More often than not, though, we'd been too busy for friendship.

'Why are they pointing at me?'

'The file has something to do with Mister. You went to Braden Chance and demanded to see it. You were seen near his office the night it disappeared. There is evidence someone gave you some keys that perhaps you shouldn't have had.'

'Is that all?'

'That, and the fingerprints.'

'Fingerprints?' I asked, trying to appear surprised.

'All over the place. The door, the light switch, the file cabinet itself. Perfect matches. You were there, Michael. You took the file. Now what will you do with it?'

'How much do you know about the file?'

'Mister got evicted by one of our real estate clients. He was a squatter. He went nuts, scared the hell out of us, you almost got hit. You cracked up.'

'Is that all?'

'That's all they've told us.'

'They being?'

'They being the big dogs. We got memos late Friday – the entire firm, lawyers, secretaries, paralegals, everybody – informing us that a file had been taken, you were the suspect, and that no member of the firm should have any contact with you. I am forbidden to be here right now.'

'I won't tell.'

'Thanks.'

If Braden Chance had made the connection between the eviction and Lontae Burton, he was not the type who would admit this to anyone. Not even his fellow partners. Barry was being truthful. He probably thought my only interest in the file was DeVon Hardy.

'Then why are you here?'

157

'I'm your friend. Things are crazy right now. My God we had cops in the office on Friday, can you believe that? Last week it was the SWAT team, and we were hostages. Now you've jumped off a cliff. And the thing with Claire. Why don't we take a break? Let's go somewhere for a couple of weeks. Take our wives.'

'Where?'

'I don't know. Who cares. The islands.'

'What would that accomplish?'

'We could thaw out for one thing. Play some tennis. Sleep. Get recharged.'

'Paid for by the firm?'

'Paid for by me.'

'Forget about Claire. It's over, Barry. It took a long time, but it's over.'

'Okay. The two of us will go.'

'But you're not supposed to have any contact with me.'

'I have an idea. I think I can go to Arthur and have a long chat. We can unwind this thing. You bring back the file, forget whatever is in it, the firm forgives and forgets too, you and I go play tennis for two weeks on Maui, then when we return you go back to your plush office where you belong.'

'They sent you, didn't they?'

'No. I swear.'

'It won't work, Barry.'

'Give me a good reason. Please.'

'There's more to being a lawyer than billing hours and making money. Why do we want to become corporate whores? I'm tired of it, Barry. I want to make a difference.'

'You sound like a first-year law student.'

'Exactly. We got into this business because we thought the law was a higher calling. We could fight injustice and social ills, and do all sorts of great things

158

because we were lawyers. We were idealistic once. Why can't we do it again?'

'Mortgages.'

'I'm not trying to recruit. You have three kids; luckily Claire and I have none. I can afford to go a little nuts.'

A radiator in a corner, one I had not yet noticed, began to rattle and hiss. We watched it and waited hopefully for a little heat. A minute passed. Then two.

'They're gonna come after you, Michael,' he said, still looking at the radiator, but not seeing.

'They? You mean we?'

'Right. The firm. You can't steal a file. Think about the client. The client has a right to expect confidentiality. If a file walks out, the firm has no choice but to go after it.'

'Criminal charges?'

'Probably. They're mad as hell, Michael. You can't blame them. There's also talk of a disciplinary action with the bar association. An injunction is likely. Rafter is already working on it.'

'Why couldn't Mister have aimed a little lower?'

'They're coming hard.'

'The firm has more to lose than I do.'

He studied me. He did not know what was in the file. 'There's more than Mister?' he asked.

'A lot more. The firm has tremendous exposure. If they come after me, I go after the firm.'

'You can't use a stolen file. No court in the country will allow it into evidence. You don't understand litigation.'

'I'm learning. Tell them to back off. Remember, I've got the file, and the file's got the dirt.'

'They were just a bunch of squatters, Michael.'

'It's much more complicated than that. Someone needs to sit down with Braden Chance and get the truth. Tell Rafter to do his homework before he pulls

159

some harebrained stunt. Believe me, Barry, this is front-page stuff. You guys will be afraid to leave your homes.'

'So you're proposing a truce? You keep the file, we leave you alone.'

'For now anyway. I don't know about next week or the week after.'

'Why can't you talk to Arthur? I'll referee. The three of us will get in a room, lock the door, work this thing out. What do you say?'

'It's too late. People are dead.'

'Mister got himself killed.'

'There are others.' And with that, I had said enough. Though he was my friend, he would repeat most of our conversation to his bosses.

'Would you like to explain?' he said.

'I can't. It's confidential.'

'That has a phony sound to it, coming from a lawyer who steals files.'

The radiator gurgled and burped, and it was easier to watch it than to talk for a while. Neither of us wanted to say things we would later regret.

He asked about the other employees of the clinic. I gave him a quick tour. 'Unbelievable,' he mumbled, more than once.

'Can we keep in touch?' he said at the door.

'Sure.'

EIGHTEEN

My orientation lasted about thirty minutes, the time it took us to drive from the clinic to the Samaritan House in Petworth, in Northeast. Mordecai handled the driving and the talking; I sat quietly, holding my briefcase, as nervous as any rookie about to be fed to the wolves. I wore jeans, a white shirt and tie, an old navy blazer, and on my feet I had well-worn Nike tennis shoes and white socks. I had stopped shaving. I was a street lawyer, and I could dress any way I wanted.

Mordecai, of course, had instantly noted the change in style when I walked into his office and announced I was ready for work. He didn't say anything, but his glance lingered on the Nikes. He had seen it all before – big-firm types coming down from the towers to spend a few hours with the poor. For some reason, they felt compelled to grow whiskers and wear denim.

'Your clientele will be a mixture of thirds,' he said, driving badly with one hand, holding coffee with another, oblivious to any of the other vehicles crowded around us. 'About a third are employed, a third are families with children, a third are mentally disabled, a third are veterans. And about a third of those eligible for low-income housing receive it. In the past fifteen years, two and a half million low-cost housing units

have been eliminated, and the federal housing programs have been cut seventy percent. Small wonder
people are living on the streets. Governments are
balancing budgets on the backs of the poor.'

The statistics flowed forth with no effort whatsoever. This was his life and his profession. As a lawyer
trained to keep meticulous notes, I fought the compul-
sion to rip open my briefcase and begin scribbling. I
just listened.

'These people have minimum-wage jobs, so private
housing is not even considered. They don't even
dream about it. And their earned income has not kept
pace with housing costs. So they fall farther and
farther behind, and at the same time assistance
programs take more and more hits. Get this: Only
fourteen percent of disabled homeless people receive
disability benefits. Fourteen percent! You'll see a lot of
these cases.'

We squealed to a stop at a red light, his car partially
blocking the intersection. Horns erupted all around
us. I slid lower in the seat, waiting for another
collision. Mordecai hadn't the slightest clue that his
car was impeding rush-hour traffic. He stared blankly
ahead, in another world.

'The frightening part of homelessness is what you
don't see on the street. About half of all poor people
spend seventy percent of their income trying to keep
the housing they have. HUD says they should spend a
third. There are tens of thousands of people in this city
who are clinging to their roofs; one missed paycheck,
one unexpected hospital visit, one unseen emergency,
and they lose their housing.'

'Where do they go?'

'They rarely go straight to the shelters. At first,
they'll go to their families, then friends. The strain is
enormous because their families and friends also have

subsidized housing, and their leases restrict the number of people who can live in one unit. They're forced to violate their leases, which can lead to eviction. They move around, sometimes they leave a kid with this sister and a kid with that friend. Things go from bad to worse. A lot of homeless people are afraid of the shelters, and they are desperate to avoid them.'

He paused long enough to drink his coffee. 'Why?' I asked.

'Not all shelters are good. There have been assaults, robberies, even rapes.'

And this was where I was expected to spend the rest of my legal career. 'I forgot my gun,' I said.

'You'll be okay. There are hundreds of pro bono volunteers in this city. I've never heard of one getting hurt.'

'That's good to hear.' We were moving again, somewhat safer.

'About half of the people have some type of substance abuse problem, like your pal DeVon Hardy. It's very common.'

'What can you do for them?'

'Not much, I'm afraid. There are a few programs left, but it's hard to find a bed. We were successful in placing Hardy in a recovery unit for veterans, but he walked away. The addict decides when he wants to get sober.'

'What's the drug of choice?'

'Alcohol. It's the most affordable. A lot of crack because it's cheap too. You'll see everything, but the designer drugs are too expensive.'

'What will my first five cases be?'

'Anxious, aren't you?'

'Yeah, and I don't have a clue.'

'Relax. The work is not complicated; it takes patience. You'll see a person who's not getting benefits, probably food stamps. A divorce. Someone with a complaint against a landlord. An employment dispute. You're guaranteed a criminal case.'

'What type of criminal case?'

'Small stuff. The trend in urban America is to criminalize homelessness. The big cities have passed all sorts of laws designed to persecute those who live on the streets. Can't beg, can't sleep on a bench, can't camp under a bridge, can't store personal items in a public park, can't sit on a sidewalk, can't eat in public. Many of these have been struck down by the courts. Abraham has done some beautiful work convincing federal judges that these bad laws infringe on First Amendment rights. So the cities selectively enforce general laws, such as loitering, vagrancy, public drunkenness. They target the homeless. Some guy with a nice suit gets drunk in a bar and pees in an alley, no big deal. A homeless guy pees in the same alley, and he's arrested for urinating in public. Sweeps are common.'

'Sweeps?'

'Yes. They'll target one area of the city, shovel up all the homeless, dump them somewhere else. Atlanta did it before the Olympics – couldn't have all those poor people begging and sleeping on park benches with the world watching – so they sent in the S.S. troops and eliminated the problem. Then the city bragged about how pretty everything looked.'

'Where did they put them?'

'They damned sure didn't take them to shelters because they don't have any. They simply moved them around; dumped them in other parts of the city like manure.' A quick sip of coffee as he adjusted the heater – no hands on the wheel for five seconds. 'Remember, Michael, everybody has to be somewhere. These people have no alternatives. If you're hungry, you beg for food. If you're tired, then you sleep wherever you can find a spot. If you're homeless, you have to live somewhere.'

'Do they arrest them?'

'Every day, and it's stupid public policy. Take a guy living on the streets, in and out of shelters, working somewhere for minimum wage, trying his best to step up and become self-sufficient. Then he gets arrested for sleeping under a bridge. He doesn't want to be sleeping under a bridge, but everybody's got to sleep somewhere. He's guilty because the city council, in its brilliance, has made it a crime to be homeless. He has to pay thirty bucks just to get out of jail, and another thirty for his fine. Sixty bucks out of a very shallow pocket. So the guy gets kicked down another notch. He's been arrested, humiliated, fined, punished, and he's supposed to see the error of his ways and go find a home. Get off the damned streets. It's happening in most of our cities.'

'Wouldn't he be better off in jail?'

'Have you been to jail lately?'

'No.'

'Don't go. Cops are not trained to deal with the homeless, especially the mentally ill and the addicts. The jails are overcrowded. The criminal justice system is a nightmare to begin with, and persecuting the homeless only clogs it more. And here's the asinine part: It costs twenty-five percent more per day to keep a person in jail than to provide shelter, food, transportation, and counseling services. These, of course, would have a long-term benefit. These, of course, would make more sense. Twenty-five percent. And that doesn't include the costs of arrests and processing. Most of the cities are broke anyway, especially D.C. – that's why they're closing shelters, remember – yet they waste money by making criminals out of the homeless.'

'Seems ripe for litigation,' I said, though he needed no prompting.

'We're suing like crazy. Advocates all over the country are attacking these laws. Damned cities are spending more on legal fees than on building shelters for the homeless. You gotta love this country. New York, richest city in the world, can't house its people, so they sleep on the streets and panhandle on Fifth Avenue, and this upsets the sensitive New Yorkers, so they elect Rudy WhatsHisFace who promises to clean up the streets, and he gets his blue ribbon city council to outlaw homelessness, just like that – can't beg, can't sit on the sidewalk, can't be homeless – and they cut budgets like hell, close shelters and cut assistance, and at the same time they spend a bloody fortune paying New York lawyers to defend them for trying to eliminate poor people.'

'How bad is Washington?'

'Not as bad as New York, but not much better, I'm afraid.' We were in a part of town I would not have driven through in broad daylight in an armored vehicle two weeks ago. The storefronts were laden with black iron bars; the apartment buildings were tall, lifeless structures with laundry hanging over the railings. Each was gray-bricked, each stamped with the architectural blandness of hurried federal money.

'Washington is a black city,' he continued, 'with a large welfare class. It attracts a lot of people who want change, a lot of activists and radicals. People like you.'

'I'm hardly an activist or a radical.'

'It's Monday morning. Think of where you've been every Monday morning for the past seven years.'

'At my desk.'

'A very nice desk.'

'Yes.'

'In your elegantly appointed office.'

'Yes.'

166

He offered me a large grin, and said, 'You are now a radical.'

And with that, orientation ended.

Ahead on the right was a group of heavily clad men, huddled over a portable butane burner on a street corner. We turned beside them, and parked at the curb. The building was once a department store, many years in the past. A hand-painted sign read: Samaritan House.

'It's a private shelter,' Mordecai said. 'Ninety beds, decent food, funded by a coalition of churches in Arlington. We've been coming here for six years.'

A van from a food bank was parked by the door; volunteers unloaded boxes of vegetables and fruit. Mordecai spoke to an elderly gentleman who worked the door, and we were allowed inside.

'I'll give you a quick tour,' Mordecai said. I stayed close to him as we walked through the main floor. It was a maze of short hallways, each lined with small square rooms made of unpainted Sheetrock. Each room had a door, with a lock. One was open. Mordecai looked inside and said, 'Good morning.'

A tiny man with wild eyes sat on the edge of a cot, looking at us but saying nothing. 'This is a good room,' Mordecai said to me. 'It has privacy, a nice bed, room to store things, and electricity.' He flipped a switch by the door and the bulb of a small lamp went out. The room was darker for a second, then he flipped the switch again. The wild eyes never moved.

There was no ceiling for the room; the aging panels of the old store were thirty feet above.

'What about a bathroom?' I asked.

'They're in the back. Few shelters provide individual baths. Have a nice day,' he said to the resident, who nodded.

Radios were on, some with music, some with news

167

talk. People were moving about. It was Monday morning; they had jobs and places to be.

'Is it hard to get a room here?' I asked, certain of the answer.

'Nearly impossible. There's a waiting list a mile long, and the shelter can screen who gets in.'

'How long do they stay here?'

'It varies. Three months is probably a good average. This is one of the nicer shelters, so they're safe here. As soon as they get stable, the shelter starts trying to relocate them into affordable housing.'

He introduced me to a young woman in black combat boots who ran the place. 'Our new lawyer,' was my description. She welcomed me to the shelter. They talked about a client who'd disappeared, and I drifted along the hallway until I found the family section. I heard a baby cry and walked to an open door. The room was slightly larger, and divided into cubicles. A stout woman of no more than twenty-five was sitting in a chair, naked from the waist up, breast-feeding an infant, thoroughly unfazed by my gawking ten feet away. Two small children were tumbling over a bed. Rap came from a radio.

With her right hand, the woman cupped her unused breast and offered it to me. I bolted down the hall and found Mordecai.

Clients awaited us. Our office was in a corner of the dining hall, near the kitchen. Our desk was a folding table we borrowed from the cook. Mordecai unlocked a file cabinet in the corner, and we were in business. Six people sat in a row of chairs along the wall.

'Who's first?' he announced, and a woman came forward with her chair. She sat across from her lawyers, both ready with pen and legal pad, one a seasoned veteran of street law, the other clueless.

Her name was Waylene, age twenty-seven, two children, no husband.

168

'Half will come from the shelter,' Mordecai said to me as we took notes. 'The other half come from the streets.'

'We take anybody?'

'Anybody who's homeless.'

Waylene's problem was not complicated. She had worked in a fast-food restaurant before quitting for some reason Mordecai deemed irrelevant, and she was owed her last two paychecks. Because she had no permanent address, the employer had sent the checks to the wrong place. The checks had disappeared; the employer was unconcerned.

'Where will you be staying next week?' Mordecai asked her.

She wasn't sure. Maybe here, maybe there. She was looking for a job, and if she found one, then other events might occur, and she could possibly move in with so and so. Or get a place of her own.

'I'll get your money, and I'll have the checks sent to my office.' He handed her a business card. 'Phone me at this number in a week.'

She took the card, thanked us, and hurried away.

'Call the taco place, identify yourself as her attorney, be nice at first, then raise hell if they don't cooperate. If necessary, stop by and pick up the checks yourself.'

I wrote down these instructions as if they were complicated. Waylene was owed two hundred ten dollars. The last case I worked on at Drake & Sweeney was an antitrust dispute with nine hundred million dollars at stake.

The second client was unable to articulate a specific legal problem. He just wanted to talk to someone. He was drunk or mentally ill, probably both, and Mordecai walked him to the kitchen and poured him coffee.

'Some of these poor folks can't resist getting in a line,' he said.

Number three was a resident of the shelter, had been for two months, so the address challenge was simpler. She was fifty-eight, clean and neat, and the widow of a veteran. According to the stack of paperwork I rummaged through while my co-counsel talked to her, she was entitled to veteran's benefits. But the checks were being sent to a bank account in Maryland, one she could not access. She explained this. Her paperwork verified it. Mordecai said, 'VA is a good agency. We'll get the checks sent here.'

The line grew as we efficiently worked the clients. Mordecai had seen it all before: food stamps disrupted for lack of a permanent address; a landlord's refusal to refund a security deposit; unpaid child support; an arrest warrant for writing bad checks; a claim for Social Security disability benefits. After two hours and ten clients, I moved to the end of the table and began interviewing them myself. During my first full day as a poverty lawyer, I was on my own, taking notes and acting just as important as my co-counsel.

Marvis was my first solo client. He needed a divorce. So did I. After listening to his tale of sorrow, I felt like racing home to Claire and kissing her feet. Marvis' wife was a prostitute, who at one time had been a decent sort until she discovered crack. The crack led her to a pusher, then to a pimp, then to life on the streets. Along the way, she stole and sold everything they owned and racked up debts he got stuck with. He filed for bankruptcy. She took both kids and moved in with her pimp.

He had a few general questions about the mechanics of divorce, and since I knew only the basics I winged it as best I could. In the midst of my note-taking, I was struck by a vision of Claire sitting in her lawyer's fine office, at that very moment, finalizing plans to dissolve our union.

'How long will it take?' he asked, bringing me out of my brief daydream.

'Six months,' I answered. 'Do you think she will contest it?'

'What do you mean?'

'Will she agree to the divorce?'

'We ain't talked about it.'

The woman had moved out a year earlier, and that sounded like a good case of abandonment to me. Throw in the adultery, and I figured the case was a cinch.

Marvis had been at the shelter for a week. He was clean, sober, and looking for work. I enjoyed the half hour I spent with him, and I vowed to get his divorce.

The morning passed quickly; my nervousness vanished. I was reaching out to help real people with real problems, little people with no other place to go for legal representation. They were intimidated not only by me but also by the vast world of laws and regulations and courts and bureaucracies. I learned to smile, and make them feel welcome. Some apologized for not being able to pay me. Money was not important, I told them. Money was not important.

At twelve, we surrendered our table so lunch could be served. The dining area was crowded; the soup was ready.

Since we were in the neighborhood, we stopped for soul food at the Florida Avenue Grill. Mine was the only white face in the crowded restaurant, but I was coming to terms with my whiteness. No one had tried to murder me yet. No one seemed to care.

Sofia found a phone that happened to be working. It was under a stack of files on the desk nearest the door. I thanked her, and retreated to the privacy of my office. I counted eight people sitting quietly and waiting for Sofia, the nonlawyer, to dispense advice.

Mordecai suggested that I spend the afternoon work-ing on the cases we had taken in during the morning at Samaritan. There was a total of nineteen. He also implied that I should work diligently so that I could help Sofia with the traffic.

If I thought the pace would be slower on the street, I was wrong. I was suddenly up to my ears with other people's problems. Fortunately, with my background as a self-absorbed workaholic, I was up to the task.

My first phone call, however, went to Drake & Sweeney. I asked for Hector Palma in real estate, and was put on hold. I hung up after five minutes, then called again. A secretary finally answered, then put me on hold again. The abrasive voice of Braden Chance was suddenly barking in my ear, 'Can I help you?'

I swallowed hard, and said, 'Yes, I was holding for Hector Palma.' I tried to raise my voice and clip my words.

'Who is this?' he demanded.

'Rick Hamilton, an old friend from school.'

'He doesn't work here anymore. Sorry.' He hung up, and I stared at the phone. I thought about calling Polly, and asking her to check around, see what had happened to Hector. It wouldn't take her long. Or maybe Rudolph, or Barry Nuzzo, or my own favorite paralegal. Then I realized that they were no longer my friends. I was gone. I was off-limits. I was the enemy. I was trouble and the powers above had forbidden them to talk to me.

There were three Hector Palmas in the phone book. I was going to call them, but the phone lines were taken. The clinic had two lines, and four advocates.

NINETEEN

I was in no hurry to leave the clinic at the end of my first day. Home was an empty attic, not much larger than any three of the cubbyholes at the Samaritan House. Home was a bedroom with no bed, a living room with cableless TV, a kitchen with a card table and no fridge. I had vague, distant plans to furnish and decorate.

Sofia left promptly at five, her standard hour. Her neighborhood was rough, and she preferred to be home with the doors locked at dark. Mordecai left around six, after spending thirty minutes with me discussing the day. Don't stay too late, he warned, and try to leave in pairs. He had checked with Abraham Lebow, who planned to work until nine, and suggested we leave together. Park close. Walk fast. Watch everything.

'So what do you think?' he asked, pausing by the door on the way out.

'I think it's fascinating work. The human contact is inspiring.'

'It'll break your heart at times.'

'It already has.'

'That's good. If you reach the point where it doesn't hurt, then it's time to quit.'

'I just started.'

'I know, and it's good to have you. We've needed a WASP around here.'

'Then I'm just happy to be a token.'

He left, and I closed the door again. I had detected an unspoken, open-door policy; Sofia worked out in the open, and I had been amused throughout the afternoon as I heard her berate one bureaucrat after another over the phone while the entire clinic listened. Mordecai was an animal on the phone, his deep gravel voice roaring through the air, making all sorts of demands and vile threats. Abraham was much quieter, but his door was always open.

Since I didn't yet know what I was doing, I preferred to keep mine closed. I was sure they would be patient.

I called the three Hector Palmas in the phone book. The first was not the Hector I wanted. The second number was not answered. The third was voice mail for the real Hector Palma; the message was brusque: We're not home. Leave message. We'll return your call.

It was his voice.

With infinite resources, the firm had many ways and places to hide Hector Palma. Eight hundred lawyers, 170 paralegals, offices in Washington, New York, Chicago, L.A., Portland, Palm Beach, London, and Hong Kong. They were too smart to fire him because he knew too much. So they would double his pay, promote him, move him to a different office in a new city with a larger apartment.

I wrote down his address from the phone book. If the voice mail was still working, perhaps he hadn't yet moved. With my newly acquired street savvy, I was sure I could track him down.

There was a slight knock on the door, which opened as it was being tapped. The bolt and knob were worn and wobbly, and the door would shut but it wouldn't catch. It was Abraham. 'Got a minute?' he said, sitting down.

It was his courtesy call, his hello. He was a quiet, distant man with an intense, brainy aura that would have been intimidating except for the fact that I had spent the past seven years in a building with four hundred lawyers of all stripes and sorts. I had met and known a dozen Abrahams, aloof and earnest types with little regard for social skills.

'I wanted to welcome you,' he said, then immediately launched into a passionate justification for public interest law. He was a middle-class kid from Brooklyn, law school at Columbia, three horrible years with a Wall Street firm, four years in Atlanta with an anti-death-penalty group, two frustrating years on Capitol Hill, then an ad in a lawyer's magazine for an advocate's position with the 14th Street Legal Clinic had caught his attention.

'The law is a higher calling,' he said. 'It's more than making money.' Then he delivered another speech, a tirade against big firms and lawyers who rake in millions in fees. A friend of his from Brooklyn was making ten million a year suing breast implant companies from coast to coast. 'Ten million dollars a year! You could house and feed every homeless person in the District!'

Anyway, he was delighted I had seen the light, and sorry about the episode with Mister.

'What, specifically, do you do?' I asked. I was enjoying our talk. He was fiery and bright, with a vast vocabulary that kept me reeling.

'Two things. Policy. I work with other advocates to shape legislation. And I direct litigation, usually class actions. We've sued the Commerce Department because the homeless were grossly underrepresented in the ninety census. We've sued the District school system for refusing to admit homeless children. We've

175

sued as a class because the District wrongfully terminated several thousand housing grants without due
process. We've attacked many of the statutes designed
to criminalize homelessness. We'll sue for almost
anything if the homeless are getting screwed.'

'That's complicated litigation.'

'It is, but, fortunately, here in D.C. we have lots of
very good lawyers willing to donate their time. I'm the
coach. I devise the game plan, put the team together,
then call the plays.'

'You don't see clients?'

'Occasionally. But I work best when I'm in my little
room over there, alone. That's the reason I'm glad
you're here. We need help with the traffic.'

He jumped to his feet; the conversation was over.
We planned our getaway at precisely nine, and he was
gone. In the midst of one of his speeches, I had
noticed he did not have a wedding band.

The law was his life. The old adage that the law was
a jealous mistress had been taken to a new level by
people like Abraham and myself.

The law was all we had.

The district police waited until almost 1 A.M., then
struck like commandos. They rang the doorbell, then
immediately started hitting the door with their fists. By
the time Claire could collect her wits, get out of bed,
and pull something on over her pajamas, they were
kicking the door, ready to smash it in. 'Police!' they
announced after her terrified inquiry. She slowly
opened the door, then stepped back in horror as four
men – two in uniforms and two in suits – rushed in as
if lives were in danger.

'Stand back!' one demanded. She was unable to
speak.

'Stand back!' he screamed at her.

They slammed the door behind them. The leader,

Lieutenant Gasko, in a cheap tight suit, stepped forward and jerked from his pocket some folded papers. 'Are you Claire Brock?' he asked, in his worst Columbo impersonation.

She nodded, mouth open.

'I'm Lieutenant Gasko. Where's Michael Brock?'

'He doesn't live here anymore,' she managed to utter. The other three hovered nearby, ready to pounce on something.

There was no way Gasko could believe this. But he didn't have a warrant for arrest, just one authorizing a search. 'I have a search warrant for this apartment, signed by Judge Kisner at five P.M. this afternoon.' He unfolded the papers and held them open for her to see, as if the fine print could be read and appreciated at that moment.

'Please stand aside,' he said. Claire backed up even farther.

'What are you looking for?' she asked.

'It's in the papers,' Gasko said, tossing them onto the kitchen counter. The four fanned out through the apartment.

The cell phone was next to my head, which was resting on a pillow on the floor at the opening of my sleeping bag. It was the third night I'd slept on the floor, part of my effort to identify with my new clients. I was eating little, sleeping even less, trying to acquire an appreciation for park benches and sidewalks. The left side of my body was purple down to the knee, extremely sore and painful, and so I slept on my right side.

It was a small price to pay. I had a roof, heat, a locked door, a job, the security of food tomorrow, the future.

I found the cell phone and said, 'Hello.'

'Michael!' Claire hissed in a low voice. 'The cops are searching the apartment.'

'What?'

'They're here now. Four of them, with a search warrant.'

'What do they want?'

'They're looking for a file.'

'I'll be there in ten minutes.'

'Please hurry.'

I roared into the apartment like a man possessed. Gasko happened to be the first cop I encountered. 'I'm Michael Brock. Who the hell are you?'

'Lieutenant Gasko,' he said with a sneer.

'Let me see some identification.' I turned to Claire, who was leaning on the refrigerator holding a cup of coffee. 'Get me a piece of paper,' I said.

Gasko pulled his badge from his coat pocket, and held it high for me to see.

'Larry Gasko,' I said. 'You'll be the first person I sue, at nine o'clock this morning. Now, who's with you?'

'There are three others,' Claire said, handing me a sheet of paper. 'I think they're in the bedrooms.'

I walked to the rear of the apartment, Gasko behind me, Claire somewhere behind him. I saw a plain-clothes cop in the guest bedroom on all fours peeking under the bed. 'Let me see some identification,' I yelled at him. He scrambled to his feet, ready to fight. I took a step closer, gritted my teeth, and said, 'ID, asshole.'

'Who are you?' he asked, taking a step back, looking at Gasko.

'Michael Brock. Who are you?'

He flipped out a badge. 'Darrell Clark,' I announced loudly as I scribbled it down. 'Defendant number two.'

'You can't sue me,' he said.

'Watch me, big boy. In eight hours, in federal court,

I will sue you for a million bucks for an illegal search. And I'll win, and get a judgment, then I'll hound your ass until you file for bankruptcy.'

The other two cops appeared from my old bedroom, and I was surrounded by them.

'Claire,' I said. 'Get the video camera please. I want this recorded.' She disappeared into the living room.

'We have a warrant signed by a judge,' Gasko said, somewhat defensively. The other three took a step forward to tighten the circle.

'The search is illegal,' I said bitterly. 'The people who signed the warrant will be sued. Each of you will be sued. You will be placed on leave, probably without pay, and you will face a civil lawsuit.'

'We have immunity,' Gasko said, glancing at his buddies.

'Like hell you do.'

Claire was back with the camera. 'Did you tell them I didn't live here?' I asked her.

'I did,' she said, and raised the camera to her eye.

'Yet you boys continued the search. At that point it became illegal. You should've known to stop, but of course that wouldn't be any fun, would it? It's much more fun to pilfer through the private things of others. You had a chance, boys, and you blew it. Now you'll have to pay the consequences.'

'You're nuts,' Gasko said. They tried not to show fear – but they knew I was a lawyer. They had not found me in the apartment, so maybe I knew what I was talking about. I did not. But at that moment, it sounded good.

The legal ice upon which I was skating was very thin.

I ignored him. 'Your names please,' I said to the two uniformed cops. They produced badges. Ralph Lilly and Robert Blower. 'Thanks,' I said like a real smart-ass. 'You will be defendants number three and four. Now, why don't you leave.'

'Where's the file?' Gasko asked.

'The file is not here because I don't live here. That's why you're going to get sued, Officer Gasko.'

'Get sued all the time, no big deal.'

'Great. Who's your attorney?'

He couldn't pull forth the name of one in the crucial split-second that followed. I walked to the den, and they reluctantly followed.

'Leave,' I said. 'The file is not here.'

Claire was nailing them with the video, and that kept their bitching to a minimum. Blower mumbled something about lawyers as they shuffled toward the door.

I read the warrant after they were gone. Claire watched me, sipping coffee at the kitchen table. The shock of the search had worn off; she was once again subdued, even icy. She would not admit to being frightened, would not dare seem the least bit vulnerable, and she certainly wasn't about to give the impression that she needed me in any way.

'What's in the file?' she asked.

She didn't really want to know. What Claire wanted was some assurance that it wouldn't happen again.

'It's a long story.' In other words, don't ask. She understood that.

'Are you really going to sue them?'

'No. There are no grounds for a suit. I just wanted to get rid of them.'

'It worked. Can they come back?'

'No.'

'That's good to hear.'

I folded the search warrant and stuck it in a pocket. It covered only one item – the RiverOaks/TAG file, which at the moment was well hidden in the walls of my new apartment along with a copy of it.

180

'Did you tell them where I live?' I asked.

'I don't know where you live,' she answered. Then there was a space of time during which it would have been appropriate for her to ask where, in fact, I did live. She did not.

'I'm very sorry this happened, Claire.'

'It's okay. Just promise it won't happen again.'

'I promise.'

I left without a hug, a kiss, a touching of any kind. I simply said good night and walked through the door. That was precisely what she wanted.

TWENTY

Tuesday was an intake day at the Community for Creative Non-Violence, or CCNV, by far the largest shelter in the District. Once again Mordecai handled the driving. His plan was to accompany me for the first week, then turn me loose on the city.

My threats and warnings to Barry Nuzzo had fallen on deaf ears. Drake & Sweeney would play hardball, and I wasn't surprised. The predawn raid of my former apartment was a rude warning of what was to come. I had to tell Mordecai the truth about what I'd done.

As soon as we were in the car and moving, I said, 'My wife and I have separated. I've moved out.'

The poor guy was not prepared for such dour news at eight in the morning. 'I'm sorry,' he said, looking at me and almost hitting a jaywalker.

'Don't be. Early this morning, the cops raided the apartment where I used to live, looking for me, and, specifically, a file I took when I left the firm.'

'What kind of file?'

'The DeVon Hardy and Lontae Burton file.'

'I'm listening.'

'As we now know, DeVon Hardy took hostages and got himself killed because Drake & Sweeney evicted him from his home. Evicted with him were sixteen others, and some children. Lontae and her little family were in the group.'

He mulled this over, then said, 'This is a very small city.'

'The abandoned warehouse happened to be on land RiverOaks planned to use for a postal facility. It's a twenty-million-dollar project.'

'I know the building. It's always been used by squatters.'

'Except they weren't squatters, at least I don't think so.'

'Are you guessing? Or do you know for sure?'

'For now, I'm guessing. The file has been tampered with; papers taken, papers added. A paralegal named Hector Palma handled the dirty work, the site visits, and the actual eviction, and he's become my deep throat. He sent an anonymous note informing me that the evictions were wrongful. He provided me with a set of keys to get the file. As of yesterday, he no longer works at the office here in the District.'

'Where is he?'

'I'd love to know.'

'He gave you keys?'

'He didn't hand them to me. He left them on my desk, with instructions.'

'And you used them?'

'Yes.'

'To steal a file?'

'I didn't plan to steal it. I was on my way to the clinic to copy it when some fool ran a red light and sent me to the hospital.'

'That's the file we retrieved from your car?'

'That's it. I was going to copy it, take it back to its little spot at Drake & Sweeney, and no one would have ever known.'

'I question the wisdom of that.' He wanted to call me a dumb-ass, but our relationship was still new.

'What's missing from it?' he asked.

I summarized the history of RiverOaks and its race to build the mail facility. 'The pressure was on to grab the land fast. Palma went to the warehouse the first time, and got mugged. Memo to the file. He went again, the second time with a guard, and that memo is missing. It was properly logged into the file, then removed, probably by Braden Chance.'

'So what's in the memo?'

'Don't know. But I have a hunch that Hector inspected the warehouse, found the squatters in their makeshift apartments, talked to them, and learned that they were in fact paying rent to Tillman Gantry. They were not squatters, but tenants, entitled to all the protections under landlord-tenant law. By then, the wrecking ball was on its way, the closing had to take place, Gantry was about to make a killing on the deal, so the memo was ignored and the eviction took place.'

'There were seventeen people.'

'Yes, and some children.'

'Do you know the names of the others?'

'Yes. Someone, Palma I suspect, gave me a list. Placed it on my desk. If we can find those people, then we have witnesses.'

'Maybe. It's more likely, though, that Gantry has put the fear of hell in them. He's a big man with a big gun, fancies himself as a godfather type. When he tells people to shut up, they do so or you find them in a river.'

'But you're not afraid of him, are you, Mordecai? Let's go find him, push him around some; he'll break down and tell all.'

'Spent a lot of time on the streets, have you? I've hired a dumb-ass.'

'He'll run when he sees us.'

The humor wasn't working at that hour. Neither

was his heater, though the fan was blowing at full speed. The car was freezing.

'How much did Gantry get for the building?' he asked.

'Two hundred thousand. He'd bought it six months earlier; there's no record in the file indicating how much he paid for it.'

'Who'd he buy it from?'

'The city. It was abandoned.'

'He probably paid five thousand for it. Ten at the most.'

'Not a bad return.'

'Not bad. It's a step up for Gantry. He's been a nickel and dimer – duplexes and car washes and quick-shop groceries, small ventures.'

'Why would he buy the warehouse and rent space for cheap apartments?'

'Cash. Let's say he pays five thousand for it, then spends another thousand throwing up a few walls and installing a couple of toilets. He gets the lights turned on, and he's in business. Word gets out; renters show up; he charges them a hundred bucks a month, payable only in cash. His clients are not concerned with paperwork anyway. He keeps the place looking like a dump, so if the city comes in he says they're just a bunch of squatters. He promises to kick them out, but he has no plans to. It happens all the time around here. Unregulated housing.'

I almost asked why the city didn't intervene and enforce its laws, but fortunately I caught myself. The answer was in the potholes too numerous to count or avoid; and the fleet of police cars, a third of which were too dangerous to drive; and the schools with roofs caving in; and the hospitals with patients stuffed in closets; and the five hundred homeless mothers and children unable to find a shelter. The city simply didn't work.

And a renegade landlord, one actually getting people off the streets, did not seem like a priority.

'How do you find Hector Palma?' he asked.

'I'm assuming the firm would be smart enough not to fire him. They have seven other offices, so I figure they've got him tucked away somewhere. I'll find him.'

We were downtown. He pointed, and said, 'See those trailers stacked on top of each other. That's Mount Vernon Square.'

It was half a city block, fenced high to hinder a view from the outside. The trailers were different shapes and lengths, some dilapidated, all grungy.

'It's the worst shelter in the city. Those are old postal trailers the government gave to the District, which in turn had the brilliant idea of filling them with homeless. They're packed in those trailers like sardines in a can.'

At Second and D, he pointed to a long, three-story building – home to thirteen hundred people.

The CCNV was founded in the early seventies by a group of war protestors who had assembled in Washington to torment the government. They lived together in a house in Northwest. During their protests around the Capitol, they met homeless veterans of Vietnam, and began taking them in. They moved to larger quarters, various places around the city, and their number grew. After the war, they turned their attention to the plight of the D.C. homeless. In the early eighties, an activist named Mitch Snyder appeared on the scene, and quickly became a passionate and noisy voice for street people.

CCNV found an abandoned junior college, one built with federal money and still owned by the government, and invaded it with six hundred squatters. It became their headquarters, and their home. Various efforts were made to displace them, all to no

186

avail. In 1984, Snyder endured a fifty-one-day hunger strike to call attention to the neglect of the homeless. With his reelection a month away, President Reagan boldly announced his plans to turn the building into a model shelter for the homeless. Snyder ended his strike. Everyone was happy. After the election, Reagan reneged on his promise, and all sorts of nasty litigation ensued.

In 1989, the city built a shelter in Southeast, far away from downtown, and began planning the removal of the homeless from the CCNV. But the city found the homeless to be an ornery lot. They had no desire to leave. Snyder announced that they were boarding up windows and preparing for a siege. Rumors were rampant – eight hundred street people were in there; weapons were stockpiled; it would be a war.

The city backed away from its deadlines, and managed to make peace. The CCNV grew to thirteen hundred beds. Mitch Snyder committed suicide in 1990, and the city named a street after him.

It was almost eight-thirty when we arrived, time for the residents to leave. Many had jobs, most wanted to leave for the day. A hundred men loitered around the front entrance, smoking cigarettes and talking the happy talk of a cold morning after a warm night's rest.

Inside the door on the first level, Mordecai spoke to a supervisor in the 'bubble.' He signed his name and we walked across the lobby, weaving through and around a swarm of men leaving in a hurry. I tried hard not to notice my whiteness, but it was impossible. I was reasonably well dressed, with a jacket and tie. I had known affluence for my entire life, and I was adrift in a sea of black – young tough street men, most of whom had criminal records, few of whom had three dollars in their pockets. Surely one of them would break my neck and take my wallet. I avoided eye contact and frowned at the floor. We waited by the intake room.

'Weapons and drugs are automatic lifetime bans,' Mordecai said, as we watched the men stream down the stairway. I felt somewhat safer.

'Do you ever get nervous in here?' I asked.

'You get used to it.' Easy for him to say. He spoke the language.

On a clipboard next to the door was a sign-up sheet for the legal clinic. Mordecai took it and we studied the names of our clients. Thirteen so far. 'A little below average,' he said. While we waited for the key, he filled me in. 'That's the post office over there. One of the frustrating parts of this work is keeping up with our clients. Addresses are slippery. The good shelters allow their people to send and receive mail.' He pointed to another nearby door. 'That's the clothes room. They take in between thirty and forty new people a week. The first step is a medical exam; tuberculosis is the current scare. Second step is a visit there for three sets of clothes – underwear, socks, everything. Once a month, a client can come back for another suit, so by the end of the year he has a decent wardrobe. This is not junk. They get more clothing donated than they can ever use.'

'One year?'

'That's it. They boot them after one year, which at first may seem harsh. But it isn't. The goal is self-sufficiency. When a guy checks in, he knows he has twelve months to clean up, get sober, acquire some skills, and find a job. Most are gone in less than a year. A few would like to stay forever.'

A man named Ernie arrived with an impressive ring of keys. He unlocked the door to the intake room, and disappeared. We set up our clinic, and were ready to dispense advice. Mordecai walked to the door with the clipboard, and called out the first name: 'Luther Williams.'

Luther barely fit through the door, and the chair popped as he fell into it across from us. He wore a green work uniform, white socks, and orange rubber shower sandals. He worked nights at a boiler room under the Pentagon. A girlfriend had moved out and taken everything, then run up bills. He lost his apartment, and was ashamed to be in the shelter. 'I just need a break,' he said, and I felt sorry for him.

He had a lot of bills. Credit agencies were hounding him. For the moment, he was hiding at CCNV.

'Let's do a bankruptcy,' Mordecai said to me. I had no idea how to do a bankruptcy. I nodded with a frown. Luther seemed pleased. We filled out forms for twenty minutes, and he left a happy man.

The next client was Tommy, who slid gracefully into the room and extended a hand upon which the fingernails had been painted bright red. I shook it; Mordecai did not. Tommy was in drug rehab full-time – crack and heroin – and he owed back taxes. He had not filed a tax return for three years, and the IRS had suddenly discovered his oversights. He also hadn't paid a couple of thousand in back child support. I was somewhat relieved to learn he was a father, of some sort. The rehab was intense – seven days a week – and prevented full-time employment.

'You can't bankrupt the child support, nor the taxes,' Mordecai said.

'Well, I can't work because of the rehab, and if I drop out of rehab then I'll get on drugs again. So if I can't work and can't go bankrupt, then what can I do?'

'Nothing. Don't worry about it until you finish rehab and get a job. Then call Michael Brock here.'

Tommy smiled and winked at me, then floated out of the room.

'I think he likes you,' Mordecai said.

189

Ernie brought another sign-up sheet with eleven names on it. There was a line outside the door. We embraced the strategy of separation; I went to the far end of the room, Mordecai stayed where he was, and we began interviewing clients two at a time.

The first one for me was a young man facing a drug charge. I wrote down everything so I could replay it to Mordecai at the clinic.

Next was a sight that shocked me: a white man, about forty, with no tattoos, facial scars, chipped teeth, earrings, bloodshot eyes, or red nose. His beard was a week old and his head had been shaved about a month earlier. When we shook hands I noticed his were soft and moist. Paul Pelham was his name, a three-month resident of the shelter. He had once been a doctor.

Drugs, divorce, bankruptcy, and the revocation of his license were all water under his bridge, recent memories but fading fast. He just wanted someone to talk to, preferably someone with a white face. Occasionally, he glanced fearfully down the table at Mordecai.

Pelham had been a prominent gynecologist in Scranton, Pennsylvania – big house, Mercedes, pretty wife, couple of kids. First he abused Valium, then got addicted to harder stuff. He also began sampling the delights of cocaine and the flesh of various nurses in his clinic. On the side, he was a real estate swinger with developments and lots of bank financing. Then he dropped a baby during a routine delivery. It died. Its father, a well-respected minister, witnessed the accident. The humiliation of a lawsuit, more drugs, more nurses, and everything collapsed. He caught herpes from a patient, gave it to his wife, she got everything and moved to Florida.

I was spellbound by his story. With every client I had met so far during my brief career as a homeless lawyer, I had wanted to hear the sad details of how each ended up on the streets. I wanted reassurance that it couldn't happen to me; that folks in my class needn't worry about such misfortune.

Pelham was fascinating because for the first time I could look at a client and say, yes, perhaps that could be me. Life could conspire to knock down just about anyone. And he was quite willing to talk about it.

He hinted that perhaps his trail was not cold. I had listened long enough and was about to ask why, exactly, did he need a lawyer when he said, 'I hid some things in my bankruptcy.'

Mordecai was shuffling clients in and out while the two white boys chatted, so I began taking notes again. 'What kind of things?'

His bankruptcy lawyer had been crooked, he said, then he launched into a windy narrative about how the banks had foreclosed too early and ruined him. His words were soft and low, and each time Mordecai glanced down at us Pelham stopped.

'And there's more,' he said.

'What?' I asked.

'This is confidential, isn't it? I mean, I've used lots of lawyers, but I've always paid them. God knows how I've paid them.'

'It's extremely confidential,' I said earnestly. I may have been working for free, but the payment or nonpayment of fees did not affect the attorney-client privilege.

'You can't tell a soul.'

'Not a word.' It dawned on me that living in a homeless shelter in downtown D.C. with thirteen hundred others would be a wonderful way to hide.

This seemed to satisfy him. 'When I was rolling,' he said, even quieter, 'I found out that my wife was seeing another man. One of my patients told me. When you examine naked women, they'll tell you everything. I was devastated. I hired a private detective, and sure enough, it was true. The other man, well, let's say that he just disappeared one day.' He stopped, and waited for me to respond.

'Disappeared?'

'Yep. Has never been seen since.'

'Is he dead?' I asked, stunned.

He nodded slightly.

'Do you know where he is?'

Another nod.

'How long ago was this?'

'Four years.'

My hand shook as I tried to write down everything.

He leaned forward, and whispered, 'He was an FBI agent. An old boyfriend from college – Penn State.'

'Come on,' I said, completely uncertain if he were telling the truth.

'They're after me.'

'Who?'

'The FBI. They've been chasing me for four years.'

'What do you want me to do?'

'I don't know. Maybe cut a deal. I'm tired of being stalked.' I analyzed this for a moment as Mordecai finished with a client and called for another. Pelham watched every move he made.

'I'll need some information,' I said. 'Do you know the agent's name?'

'Yep. I know when and where he was born.'

'And when and where he died.'

'Yep.'

He had no notes or papers with him.

'Why don't you come to my office? Bring the information. We can talk there.'

'Let me think about it,' he said, looking at his watch. He explained that he worked part-time as a janitor in a church, and he was late. We shook hands, and he left.

I was rapidly learning that one of the challenges of being a street lawyer was to be able to listen. Many of my clients just wanted to talk to someone. All had been kicked and beaten down in some manner, and since free legal advice was available, why not unload on the lawyers? Mordecai was a master at gently poking through the narratives and determining if there was an issue for him to pursue. I was still awed by the fact that people could be so poor.

I was also learning that the best case was one that could be handled on the spot, with no follow-up. I had a notebook filled with applications for food stamps, housing assistance, Medicare, Social Security cards, even driver's licenses. When in doubt, we filled out a form.

Twenty-six clients passed through our session before noon. We left exhausted.

'Let's take a walk,' Mordecai said when we were outside the building. The sky was clear, the air cold and windy and refreshing after three hours in a stuffy room with no windows. Across the street was the U.S. Tax Court, a handsome modern building. In fact, the CCNV was surrounded by much nicer structures of more recent construction. We stopped at the corner of Second and D, and looked at the shelter.

'Their lease expires in four years,' Mordecai said. 'The real estate vultures are already circling. A new convention center is planned two blocks over.'

'That'll be a nasty fight.'

'It'll be a war.'

We crossed the street and strolled toward the Capitol.

'That white guy. What's his story?' Mordecai asked.

Pelham had been the only white guy. 'Amazing,' I said, not sure where to start. 'He was once a doctor, up in Pennsylvania.'

'Who's chasing him now?'

193

'What?'

'Who's chasing him now?'

'FBI.'

'That's nice. Last time it was the CIA.'

My feet stopped moving; his did not. 'You've seen him before?'

'Yeah, he makes the rounds. Peter something or other.'

'Paul Pelham.'

'That changes too,' he said, over his shoulder. 'Tells a great story, doesn't he?'

I couldn't speak. I stood there, watching Mordecai walk away, hands deep in his trench coat, his shoulders shaking because he was laughing so hard.

TWENTY-ONE

When I mustered the courage to explain to Mordecai that I needed the afternoon off, he very brusquely informed me that my standing was equal to the rest, that no one monitored my hours, and that if I needed time off, then I should damned well take it. I left the office in a hurry. Only Sofia seemed to notice.

I spent an hour with the claims adjuster. The Lexus was a total wreck; my company was offering $21,480, with a release so it could then go after the insurer of the Jaguar. I owed the bank $16,000, so I left with a check for $5,000 and change, certainly enough to buy a suitable vehicle, one appropriate to my new position as a poverty lawyer, and one that wouldn't tempt car thieves.

Another hour was wasted in the reception area of my doctor. As a busy attorney with a cell phone and many clients, I stewed as I sat among the magazines and listened to the clock tick.

A nurse made me strip to my boxers, and I sat for twenty minutes on a cold table. The bruises were turning dark brown. The doctor poked and made things worse, then pronounced me good for another two weeks.

I arrived at Claire's lawyer's office promptly at four, and was met by an unsmiling receptionist dressed like a man. Bitchiness resonated from every corner of the place. Every sound was anti-male: the abrupt, husky voice of the gal answering the phone; the sounds of some female country crooner wafting through the speakers; the occasional shrill voice from down the hall. The colors were soft pastel: lavender and pink and beige. The magazines on the coffee table were there to make a statement: hard-hitting female issues, nothing glamorous or gossipy. They were to be admired by the visitors, not read.

Jacqueline Hume had first made a ton of money cleaning out wayward doctors, then had created a fierce reputation by destroying a couple of philandering senators. Her name struck fear into every unhappily married D.C. male with a nice income. I was anxious to sign the papers and leave.

Instead, I was allowed to wait for thirty minutes, and was on the verge of creating a nasty scene when an associate fetched me and led me to an office down the hall. She handed me the separation agreement, and for the first time I saw the reality. The heading was: Claire Addison Brock versus Michael Nelson Brock.

The law required us to be separated for six months before we could be divorced. I read the agreement carefully, signed it, and left. By Thanksgiving I would be officially single again.

My fourth stop of the afternoon was the parking lot of Drake & Sweeney, where Polly met me at precisely five with two storage boxes filled with the remaining souvenirs from my office. She was polite and efficient, but tight-lipped and of course in a hurry. They probably had her wired.

I walked several blocks and stopped at a busy corner. Leaning on a building, I dialed Barry Nuzzo's number. He was in a meeting, as usual. I gave my name, said it was an emergency, and within thirty seconds Barry was on the phone.

'Can we talk?' I asked. I assumed the call was being recorded.

'Sure.'

'I'm just down the street, at the corner of K and Connecticut. Let's have coffee.'

'I can be there in an hour.'

'No. It's right now, or forget it.' I didn't want the boys to be able to plot and scheme. No time for wires either.

'Okay, let's see. Yeah, all right. I can do it.'

'I'm at a Bingler's Coffee.'

'I know it.'

'I'm waiting. And come alone.'

'You've been watching too many movies, Mike.'

Ten minutes later, we were sitting in front of the window of a crowded little shop, holding hot coffee and watching the foot traffic on Connecticut.

'Why the search warrant?' I asked.

'It's our file. You have it, we want it back. Very simple.'

'You're not going to find it, okay. So stop the damned searches.'

'Where do you live now?'

I grunted and gave him my best smart-ass laugh. 'The arrest warrant usually follows the search warrant,' I said. 'Is that the way it's going to happen?'

'I'm not at liberty to say.'

'Thanks, pal.'

'Look, Michael, let's start with the premise that you're wrong. You've taken something that's not yours. That's stealing, plain and simple. And in doing so, you've become an adversary of the firm's. I, your friend, still work for the firm. You can't expect me to help you when your actions may be damaging to the firm. You created this mess, not me.'

'Braden Chance is not telling everything. The guy's

a worm, an arrogant little jerk who committed malpractice, and now he's trying to cover his ass. He
wants you to think it's a simple matter of a stolen file
and that it's safe to come after me. But the file can
humiliate the firm.'

'So what's your point?'

'Lay off. Don't do anything stupid.'

'Like get you arrested?'

'Yeah, for starters. I've been looking over my
shoulder all day, and it's no fun.'

'You shouldn't steal.'

'I didn't plan to steal, okay? I borrowed the file. I
planned to copy and return it, but I never made it.'

'So you finally admit you have it.'

'Yeah. But I can deny it too.'

'You're playing, Michael, and this is not a game.
You're gonna get yourself hurt.'

'Not if you guys lay off. Just for now. Let's have a
truce for a week. No more search warrants. No
arrests.'

'Okay, and what are you offering?'

'I won't embarrass the firm with the file.'

Barry shook his head and gulped hot coffee. 'I'm not
in a position to make deals. I'm just a lowly associate.'

'Is Arthur calling the shots?'

'Of course.'

'Then tell Arthur I'm talking only to you.'

'You're assuming too much, Michael. You're
assuming the firm wants to talk to you. Frankly, they
don't. They are highly agitated by the theft of the file,
and by your refusal to return it. You can't blame
them.'

'Get their attention, Barry. This file is front-page
news; big bold headlines with noisy journalists following up with a dozen stories. If I get arrested, I'll go
straight to the *Post*.'

'You've lost your mind.'

198

'Probably so. Chance had a paralegal named Hector Palma. Have you heard of him?'

'No.'

'You're out of the loop.'

'I never claimed to be in.'

'Palma knows too much about the file. As of yesterday, he no longer works where he worked last week. I don't know where he is, but it would be interesting to find out. Ask Arthur.'

'Just give the file back, Michael. I don't know what you're planning to do with it, but you can't use it in court.'

I took my coffee and stepped off the stool. 'A truce for one week,' I said, walking away. 'And tell Arthur to put you in the loop.'

'Arthur doesn't take orders from you,' he snapped at me.

I left quickly, darting through people on the sidewalk, practically running toward Dupont Circle, anxious to leave Barry behind and anyone else they'd sent along to spy.

The Palmas' address, according to the phone book, was an apartment building in Bethesda. Since I was in no hurry and needed to think, I circled the city on the Beltway, bumper to bumper with a million others.

I gave myself fifty-fifty odds of being arrested within the week. The firm had no choice but to come after me, and if Braden Chance was in fact hiding the truth from Arthur and the executive committee, then why not play hardball? There was enough circumstantial evidence of my theft to convince a magistrate to issue an arrest warrant.

The Mister episode had rattled the firm. Chance had been called onto the carpet, grilled at length by the brass, and it was inconceivable that he admitted any deliberate wrongdoing. He lied, and he did so with the hope that he could doctor the file and somehow survive. His victims, after all, were only a bunch of homeless squatters.

How, then, was he able to dispose of Hector so quickly? Money was no object – Chance was a partner. If I had been Chance, I would've offered cash to Hector, cash on one hand with the threat of immediate termination on the other. And I would've called a partner buddy in, say, Denver, and asked for a favor – a quick transfer for a paralegal. It would not have been difficult.

Hector was away, hiding from me and anyone else who came with questions. He was still employed, probably at a higher salary.

Then what about the polygraph? Had it been simply a threat used by the firm against both Hector and myself? Could he have taken the test and passed? I doubted it.

Chance needed Hector to keep the truth hidden. Hector needed Chance to protect his job. At some point, the partner blocked any notion of a polygraph, if in fact it had been seriously considered.

The apartment complex was long and rambling, new sections added as the sprawl moved northward away from the city. The streets around it were packed with fast food, fast gas, video rentals, everything hurried commuters needed to save time.

I parked next to some tennis courts, and began a tour of the various units. I took my time; there was no place to go after this adventure. District cops could be lurking anywhere with a warrant and handcuffs. I tried not to think of the horror stories I'd heard about the city jail.

But one stuck like a cattle brand seared into my memory. Several years earlier, a young Drake & Sweeney associate spent several hours after work on Friday drinking in a bar in Georgetown. As he was trying to get to Virginia, he was arrested on suspicion of driving under the influence. At the police station, he refused a breath test, and was immediately thrown into the drunk tank. The cell was overcrowded; he was the only guy with a suit, the only guy with a nice watch, fine loafers, white face. He accidentally stepped on the foot of a fellow inmate, and he was then beaten to a bloody mess. He spent three months in a hospital getting his face rebuilt, then went home to Wilmington, where his family took care of him. The brain damage was slight, but enough to disqualify him for the rigors of a big firm.

The first office was closed. I trudged along a sidewalk in search of another. The phone address did not list an apartment number. It was a safe complex. There were bikes and plastic toys on the small patios. Through the windows I could see families eating and watching television. The windows were not defended by rows of bars. The cars crammed into the parking lots were of the midsized commuter variety, mostly clean and with all four hubcaps.

A security guard stopped me. Once he determined that I posed no threat, he pointed in the direction of the main office, at least a quarter of a mile away.

'How many units are in this place?' I asked.

'A lot,' he answered. Why should he know the number?

The night manager was a student eating a sandwich, a physics textbook opened before him. But he was watching the Bullets-Knicks game on a small TV. I asked about Hector Palma, and he pecked away on a keyboard. G-134 was the number.

'But they've moved,' he said with a mouthful of food.

'Yeah, I know,' I said. 'I worked with Hector. Friday was his last day. I'm looking for an apartment, and I was wondering if I could see his.'

He was shaking his head no before I finished. 'Only on Saturdays, man. We have nine hundred units. And there's a waiting list.'

'I'm gone on Saturday.'

'Sorry,' he said, taking another bite and glancing at the game.

I removed my wallet. 'How many bedrooms?' I asked.

He glanced at the monitor. 'Two.'

Hector had four children. I was sure his new digs were more spacious.

'How much a month?'

'Seven-fifty.'

I took out a one-hundred-dollar bill, which he immediately saw. 'Here's the deal. Give me the key. I'll take a look at the place and be back in ten minutes. No one will ever know.'

'We have a waiting list,' he said again, dropping the sandwich onto a paper plate.

'Is it there in that computer?' I asked, pointing.

'Yeah,' he said, wiping his mouth.

'Then it would be easy to shuffle.'

He found the key in a locked drawer, and grabbed the money. 'Ten minutes,' he said.

The apartment was nearby, on the ground floor of a three-story building. The key worked. The smell of fresh paint escaped through the door before I went inside. In fact, the painting was still in progress; in the living room there was a ladder, drop-cloths, white buckets.

A team of fingerprinters could not have found a trace of the Palma clan. All drawers, cabinets, and closets were bare; all carpets and padding ripped up and gone. Even the tub and toilet bowl stains had been removed. No dust, cobwebs, dirt under the kitchen sink. The place was sterile. Every room had a fresh coat of dull white, except the living room, which was half-finished.

I returned to the office and tossed the key on the counter.

'How about it?' he asked.

'Too small,' I said. 'But thanks anyway.'

'You want your money back?'

'Are you in school?'

'Yes.'

'Then keep it.'

'Thanks.'

I stopped at the door, and asked, 'Did Palma leave a forwarding address?'

'I thought you worked with him,' he said.

'Right,' I said, and quickly closed the door behind me.

TWENTY-TWO

The little woman was sitting against our door when I arrived for work Wednesday morning. It was almost eight; the office was locked; the temperature was below freezing. At first I thought she had parked herself there for the night, using our doorway to battle the wind. But when she saw me approach, she immediately jumped to her feet and said, 'Good morning.'

I smiled, said hello, and started fumbling keys.

'Are you a lawyer?' she asked.

'Yes I am.'

'For people like me?'

I assumed she was homeless, and that was all we asked of our clients. 'Sure. Be my guest,' I said as I opened the door. It was colder inside than out. I adjusted a thermostat, one that, as far as I had been able to determine, was connected to nothing. I made coffee and found some stale doughnuts in the kitchen. I offered them to her, and she quickly ate one.

'What's your name?' I asked. We were sitting in the front, next to Sofia's desk, waiting for the coffee and praying for the radiators.

'Ruby.'

'I'm Michael. Where do you live, Ruby?'

'Here and there.' She was dressed in a gray Georgetown Hoya sweat suit, thick brown socks, dirty white sneakers with no brand name. She was between thirty and forty, rail-thin, and slightly cockeyed.

'Come on,' I said with a smile. 'I need to know where you live. Is it a shelter?'

'Used to live in a shelter, but had to leave. Almost got raped. I got a car.'

I had seen no vehicles parked near the office when I arrived. 'You have a car?'

'Yes.'

'Do you drive it?'

'It don't drive. I sleep in the back.'

I was asking questions without a legal pad, something I was not trained to do. I poured two large paper cups of coffee, and we retreated to my office, where, mercifully, the radiator was alive and gurgling. I closed the door. Mordecai would arrive shortly, and he had never learned the art of a quiet entry.

Ruby sat on the edge of my brown folding client's chair, her shoulders slumped, her entire upper body wrapped around the cup of coffee, as if it might be the last warm thing in life.

'What can I do for you?' I asked, armed with a full assortment of legal pads.

'It's my son, Terrence. He's sixteen, and they've taken him away.'

'Who took him?'

'The city, the foster people.'

'Where is he now?'

'They got him.'

Her answers were short, nervous bursts, quick on the heels of each question. 'Why don't you relax and tell me about Terrence?' I said.

And she did. With no effort at eye contact, and with both hands on the coffee cup, she zipped through her narrative. Several years earlier, she couldn't remember how long, but Terrence was around ten, they were living alone in a small apartment. She was arrested for selling drugs. She went to jail for four months. Terrence went to live with her sister. Upon her release, she collected Terrence, and they began a nightmare existence living on the streets. They slept in cars, squatted in empty buildings, slept under bridges in warm weather, and retreated to the shelters when it was cold. Somehow, she kept him in school. She begged on the sidewalks; she sold her body – 'tricking' as she called it; she peddled a little crack. She did whatever it took to keep Terrence fed, in decent clothes, and in school.

But she was an addict, and couldn't kick the crack. She became pregnant, and when the child was born the city took it immediately. It was a crack baby.

She seemed to have no affection for the baby; only for Terrence. The city began asking questions about him, and mother and child slid deeper into the shadows of the homeless. Out of desperation, she went to a family she had once worked for as a maid, the Rowlands, a couple whose children were grown and away from home. They had a warm little house near Howard University. She offered to pay them fifty dollars a month if Terrence could live with them. There was a small bedroom above the back porch, one she'd cleaned many times, and it would be perfect for Terrence. The Rowlands hesitated at first, but finally agreed. They were good people, back then. Ruby was allowed to visit Terrence for an hour each night. His grades improved; he was clean and safe, and Ruby was pleased with herself.

She rearranged her life around his: new soup kitchens and dinner programs closer to the Rowlands; different shelters for emergencies; different alleys and parks and abandoned cars. She scraped together the money each month, and never missed a nightly visit with her son.

Until she was arrested again. The first arrest was for

206

prostitution; the second was for sleeping on a park bench in Farragut Square. Maybe there was a third one, but she couldn't remember.

She was rushed to D.C. General once when someone found her lying in a street, unconscious. She was placed in a dry-out tank for addicts, but walked out after three days because she missed Terrence.

She was with him one night in his room when he stared at her stomach and asked if she was pregnant again. She said she thought so. Who was the father? he demanded. She had no idea. He cursed her and yelled so much that the Rowlands asked her to leave.

While she was pregnant, Terrence had little to do with her. It was heartbreaking – sleeping in cars, begging for coins, counting the hours until she could see him, then being ignored for an hour while she sat in a corner of his room watching him do his homework.

Ruby began crying at that point in her story. I made some notes, and listened as Mordecai stomped around the front room, trying to pick a fight with Sofia.

Her third delivery, only a year before, produced another crack baby, one immediately taken by the city. She didn't see Terrence for four days while she was in the hospital recovering from the birth. When she was released, she returned to the only life she knew.

Terrence was an A student, excellent in math and Spanish, a trombone player and an actor in school dramas. He was dreaming of the Naval Academy. Mr. Rowland had served in the military.

Ruby arrived one night for a visit in bad shape. A fight started in the kitchen when Mrs. Rowland confronted her. Harsh words were exchanged; ultimatums thrown down. Terrence was in the middle of it; three against one. Either she got help, or she would be banned from the house. Ruby declared that she would simply take her boy and leave. Terrence said he wasn't going anywhere.

The next night, a social worker from the city was waiting for her with paperwork. Someone had already been to court. Terrence was being taken into foster care. The Rowlands would be his new parents. He had already lived with them for three years. Visitation would be terminated until she underwent rehab and was clean for a period of sixty days.

Three weeks had passed.

'I want to see my son,' she said. 'I miss him so bad.'

'Are you in rehab?' I asked.

She shook her head quickly and closed her eyes.

'Why not?' I asked.

'Can't get in.'

I had no idea how a crack addict off the street got admitted to a recovery unit, but it was time to find out. I pictured Terrence in his warm room, well fed, well dressed, safe, clean, sober, doing his homework under the strict supervision of Mr. and Mrs. Rowland, who had grown to love him almost as much as Ruby did. I could see him eating breakfast at the family table, reciting vocabulary lists over hot cereal as Mr. Rowland ignored the morning paper and grilled him on his Spanish. Terrence was stable and normal, unlike my poor little client, who lived in hell.

And she wanted me to handle their reunion.

'This will take some time, okay,' I said, thoroughly clueless about how long anything would take. In a city where five hundred families waited for a small space in an emergency shelter, there couldn't be many beds available for drug addicts.

'You won't see Terrence until you're drug-free,' I said, trying not to sound pious.

Her eyes watered and she said nothing.

I realized just how little I knew about addiction. Where did she get her drugs? How much did they cost? How many hits and highs each day? How long would it take to dry her out? Then to cure her? What were her chances of kicking a habit she'd had for over a decade?

And what did the city do with all those crack babies?

She had no paperwork, no address, no identification, nothing but a heartbreaking story. She seemed perfectly content sitting in my chair, and I began to wonder how I might ask her to leave. The coffee was gone.

Sofia's shrill voice brought back reality. There were sharp voices around her. As I raced for the door, my first thought was that another nut like Mister had walked in with a gun.

But there were other guns. Lieutenant Gasko was back, again with plenty of help. Three uniformed cops were approaching Sofia, who was bitching unmercifully but to no avail. Two in jeans and sweatshirts were waiting for action. As I walked out of my office, Mordecai walked out of his.

'Hello, Mikey,' Gasko said to me.

'What the hell is this!' Mordecai growled and the walls shook. One of the uniformed cops actually reached for his service revolver.

Gasko went straight for Mordecai. 'It's a search,' he said, pulling out the required papers and flinging them at Mordecai. 'Are you Mr. Green?'

'I am,' he answered, snatching the papers.

'What are you looking for?' I yelled at Gasko.

'Same thing,' he yelled back. 'Give it to us, and we'll be happy to stop.'

'It's not here.'

'What file?' Mordecai asked, looking at the search warrant.

'The eviction file,' I replied.

'Haven't seen your lawsuit,' Gasko said to me. I

209

recognized two of the uniformed cops as Lilly and Blower. 'A lotta big talk,' Gasko said.

'Get the hell outta here!' Sofia barked at Blower as he inched toward her desk.

Gasko was very much in charge. 'Listen, lady,' he said, with his usual sneer. 'We can do this two ways. First, you put your ass in that chair and shut up. Second, we put the cuffs on you and you sit in the back of a car for the next two hours.'

One cop was poking his head into each of the side offices. I felt Ruby ease behind me.

'Relax,' Mordecai said to Sofia. 'Just relax.'

'What's upstairs?' Gasko asked me.

'Storage,' Mordecai replied.

'Your storage?'

'Yes.'

'It's not there,' I said. 'You're wasting your time.'

'Then we'll have to waste it, won't we?'

A prospective client opened the front door, startling those of us inside. His eyes darted quickly around the room, then settled on the three men in uniform. He made a hasty retreat into the safety of the streets.

I asked Ruby to leave too. Then I stepped into Mordecai's office and closed the door.

'Where's the file?' he asked in a low voice.

'It's not here, I swear. This is just harassment.'

'The warrant looks valid. There's been a theft; it's reasonable to assume the file would be with the attorney who stole it.'

I tried to say something lawyerly and bright, some piercing legal nugget that would stop the search cold and send the cops running. But words failed me. Instead, I was embarrassed at having brought the police to nose through the clinic.

'Do you have a copy of the file?' he asked.

'Yes.'

'Have you thought about giving them their original?'

'I can't. That would be an admission of guilt. They don't know for a fact that I have the file. And even if I gave it back, they would know that I had copied it.'

He rubbed his beard and agreed with me. We stepped out of his office just as Lilly missed a step near the unused desk next to Sofia's. An avalanche of files slid onto the floor. Sofia yelled at him; Gasko yelled at her. The tension was quickly moving away from words and in the direction of physical conflict.

I locked the front door so our clients wouldn't see the search. 'Here's the way we'll do it,' Mordecai announced. The cops glared, but they were anxious for some direction. Searching a law office was quite unlike raiding a bar filled with minors.

'The file isn't here, okay. We'll start with that promise. You can look at all the files you want, but you can't open them. That would violate client confidentiality. Agreed?'

The other cops looked at Gasko, who shrugged as if that was acceptable.

We started in my office; all six cops, me, and Mordecai crammed into the tiny room, working hard at avoiding contact. I opened each drawer of my desk, none of which would open unless yanked viciously. At one point I heard Gasko whisper to himself, 'Nice office.'

I removed each file from my cabinets, waved them under Gasko's nose, and returned them to their place. I'd only been there since Monday, so there wasn't much to search.

Mordecai slipped from the room and went to Sofia's desk, where he used the phone. When Gasko declared my office to be officially searched, we left it, just in time to hear Mordecai say into the receiver, 'Yes, Judge, thank you. He's right here.'

His smile showed every tooth as he thrust the phone at Gasko. 'This is Judge Kisner, the gentleman who signed the search warrant. He would like to speak to you.'

Gasko took the phone as if it were owned by a leper. 'This is Gasko,' he said, holding it inches from his head.

Mordecai turned to the other cops. 'Gentlemen, you may search this room, and that's it. You cannot go into the private offices to the sides. Judge's orders.'

Gasko mumbled, 'Yes sir,' and hung up.

We monitored their movements for an hour, as they went from desk to desk – four of them in all, including Sofia's. After a few minutes, they realized the search was futile, and so they prolonged it by moving as slowly as possible. Each desk was covered with files long since closed. The books and legal publications had last been looked at years earlier. Some stacks were covered with dust. A few cobwebs had to be dealt with.

Each file was tabbed, with the case name either typed or hand-printed. Two of the cops wrote down the names of the files as they were called out by Gasko and the others. It was tedious, and utterly hopeless.

They saved Sofia's desk for last. She handled things herself, calling off the name of each file, spelling the simpler ones like Jones, Smith, Williams. The cops kept their distance. She opened drawers just wide enough for a quick peek. She had a personal drawer, which no one wanted to see. I was sure there were weapons in there.

They left without saying good-bye. I apologized to Sofia and Mordecai for the intrusion, and retreated to the safety of my office.

TWENTY-THREE

Number five on the list of evictees was Kelvin Lam, a name vaguely familiar to Mordecai. He once estimated the number of homeless in the District to be around ten thousand. There were at least that many files scattered throughout the 14th Street Legal Clinic. Every name rang a bell with Mordecai.

He worked the circuits, the kitchens and shelters and service providers, the preachers and cops and other street lawyers. After dark we drove downtown to a church wedged between high-priced office buildings and ritzy hotels. In a large basement two levels below, the Five Loaves dinner program was in full swing. The room was lined with folding tables, all surrounded by hungry folks eating and talking. It was not a soup kitchen; the plates were filled with corn, potatoes, a slice of something that was either turkey or chicken, fruit salad, bread. I had not eaten dinner, and the aroma made me hungry.

'I haven't been here in years,' Mordecai said as we stood by the entrance looking down at the dining area. 'They feed three hundred a day. Isn't it wonderful?'

'Where does the food come from?'

'D.C. Central Kitchen, an outfit in the basement of the CCNV. They've developed this amazing system of collecting excess food from local restaurants, not leftovers, but uncooked food that will simply go bad if not used immediately. They have a fleet of refrigerated trucks, and they run all over the city collecting food which they take to the kitchen and prepare, frozen dinners. Over two thousand a day.'

'It looks tasty.'

'It's really quite good.'

A young lady named Liza found us. She was new at Five Loaves. Mordecai had known her predecessor, whom they talked about briefly as I watched the people eat.

I noticed something I should have seen before. There were different levels of homelessness, distinct rungs on the socioeconomic ladder. At one table, six men ate and talked happily about a basketball game they had seen on television. They were reasonably well dressed. One wore gloves while he ate, and except for that, the group could've been sitting in any working-class bar in the city without being immediately branded as homeless. Behind them, a hulking figure with thick sunglasses ate alone, handling the chicken with his fingers. He had rubber boots similar to the ones Mister wore at the time of his death. His coat was dirty and frayed. He was oblivious to his surroundings. His life was noticeably harder than the lives of the men laughing at the next table. They had access to warm water and soap; he couldn't have cared less. They slept in shelters. He slept in parks with the pigeons. But they were all homeless.

Liza did not know Kelvin Lam, but she would ask around. We watched her as she moved through the crowd, speaking to the people, pointing to the waste-baskets in one corner, fussing over an elderly lady. She sat between two men, neither of whom looked at her as they talked. She went to another table, then another.

Most surprisingly, a lawyer appeared, a young associate from a large firm, a pro bono volunteer with the Washington Legal Clinic for the Homeless. He recognized Mordecai from a fund-raiser the year before. We did law talk for a few minutes, then he disappeared into a back room to begin three hours of intake.

'The Washington Legal Clinic has a hundred and fifty volunteers,' Mordecai said.

'Is that enough?' I asked.

'It's never enough. I think we should revive our pro bono volunteer program. Maybe you'd like to take charge and supervise it. Abraham likes the idea.'

It was nice to know that Mordecai and Abraham, and no doubt Sofia too, had been discussing a program for me to run.

'It will expand our base, make us more visible in the legal community, and help with raising money.'

'Sure,' I said, without conviction.

Liza was back. 'Kelvin Lam is in the rear,' she said, nodding. 'Second table from the back. Wearing the Redskins cap.'

'Did you talk to him?' Mordecai asked.

'Yes. He's sober, pretty sharp, said he's been staying at CCNV, works part-time on a garbage truck.'

'Is there a small room we can use?'

'Sure.'

'Tell Lam a homeless lawyer needs to talk to him.'

Lam didn't say hello or offer to shake hands. Mordecai sat at a table. I stood in a corner. Lam took the only available chair, and gave me a look that made my skin crawl.

'Nothing's wrong,' Mordecai said in his best sooth-ing tone. 'We need to ask you a few questions, that's all.'

Not a peep out of Lam. He was dressed like a resident of a shelter – jeans, sweatshirt, sneakers, wool jacket – as opposed to the pungent multilayered garb of one sleeping under a bridge.

'Do you know a woman named Lontae Burton?' Mordecai asked. He would do the talking for us lawyers.

Lam shook his head no.

'DeVon Hardy?'

Another no.

'Last month, were you living in an abandoned warehouse?'

'Yep.'

'At the corner of New York and Florida?'

'Uh-huh.'

'Were you paying rent?'

'Yep.'

'A hundred dollars a month?'

'Yep.'

'To Tillman Gantry?'

Lam froze, and closed his eyes to ponder the question. 'Who?' he asked.

'Who owned the warehouse?'

'I paid rent to some dude named Johnny.'

'Who did Johnny work for?'

'Don't know. Don't care. Didn't ask.'

'How long did you live there?'

''Bout four months.'

'Why did you leave?'

'Got evicted.'

'Who evicted you?'

'I don't know. The cops showed up one day with some other dudes. They yanked us and threw us on the sidewalk. Couple of days later, they bulldozed the warehouse.'

'Did you explain to the cops that you were paying rent to live there?'

'A lot of people were saying that. This one woman with little kids tried to fight with the police, but didn't

216

do no good. Me, I don't fight with cops. It was a bad scene, man.'

'Were you given any paperwork before the eviction?'

'No.'

'Any notice to get out?'

'No. Nothing. They just showed up.'

'Nothing in writing?'

'Nothing. Cops said we were just squatters; had to get out right then.'

'So you moved in last fall, sometime around October.'

'Something like that.'

'How did you find the place?'

'I don't know. Somebody said they were renting little apartments in the warehouse. Cheap rent, you know. So I went over to check it out. They were putting up some boards and walls and things. There was a roof up there, a toilet not far away, running water. It wasn't a bad deal.'

'So you moved in?'

'Right.'

'Did you sign a lease?'

'No. Dude told me that the apartment was illegal, so nothing was in writing. Told me to say I was squatting in case anybody asked.'

'And he wanted cash?'

'Only cash.'

'Did you pay every month?'

'Tried to. He came around on the fifteenth to collect.'

'Were you behind on your rent when you were evicted?'

'A little.'

'How much?'

'Maybe one month.'

'Was that the reason you were evicted?'

'I don't know. They didn't give no reason. They just evicted everybody, all at once.'

'Did you know the other people in the warehouse?'

'I knew a couple. But we kept to ourselves. Each apartment had a good door, one that would lock.'

'This mother you mentioned, the one who fought with the police, did you know her?'

'No. I'd maybe seen her once or twice. She lived on the other end.'

'The other end?'

'Right. There was no plumbing in the middle of the warehouse, so they built the apartments on each end.'

'Could you see her apartment from yours?'

'No. It was a big warehouse.'

'How big was your apartment?'

'Two rooms, I don't know how big.'

'Electricity?'

'Yeah, they ran some wires in. We could plug in radios and things like that. We had lights. There was running water, but you had to use a community toilet.'

'What about heating?'

'Not much. It got cold, but not nearly as cold as sleeping on the street.'

'So you were happy with the place?'

'It was okay. I mean, for a hundred bucks a month it wasn't bad.'

'You said you knew two other people. What are their names?'

'Herman Harris and Shine somebody.'

'Where are they now?'

'I haven't seen them.'

'Where are you staying?'

'CCNV.'

Mordecai pulled a business card from his pocket and handed it to Lam. 'How long will you be there?' he asked.

'I don't know.'

'Can you keep in touch with me?'

'Why?'

'You might need a lawyer. Just call me if you change shelters or find a place of your own.'

Lam took the card without a word. We thanked Liza and returned to the office.

As with any lawsuit, there were a number of ways to proceed with our action against the defendants. There were three of them – RiverOaks, Drake & Sweeney, and TAG, and we did not expect to add more.

The first method was the ambush. The other was the serve and volley.

With the ambush, we would prepare the skeletal framework of our allegations, run to the courthouse, file the suit, leak it to the press, and hope we could prove what we thought we knew. The advantage was surprise, and embarrassment for the defendants, and, hopefully, public opinion. The downside was the legal equivalent of jumping off a cliff with the strong, but unconfirmed, belief that there was a net down there somewhere.

The serve and volley would begin with a letter to the defendants, in which we made the same allegations, but rather than sue we would invite them to discuss the matter. The letters would go back and forth with each side generally able to predict what the other might do. If liability could be proved, then a quiet settlement would probably occur. Litigation could be avoided.

The ambush appealed to Mordecai and myself for two reasons. The firm had shown no interest in leaving me alone; the two searches were clear proof that Arthur on the top floor and Rafter and his band of hard-asses in litigation were coming after me. My arrest would make a nice news story, one they would undoubtedly leak to humiliate me and build pressure. We had to be ready with our own assault.

The second reason went to the heart of our case. Hector and the other witnesses could not be compelled to testify until we filed suit and forced them to give their depositions. During the discovery period that followed the initial filing, we would have the opportunity to ask all sorts of questions of the defendants, and they would be required to answer under oath. We would also be allowed to depose anybody we wanted. If we found Hector Palma, we could grill him under oath. If we tracked down the other evictees, we could force them to tell what happened.

We had to find out what everyone knew, and there was no way to do this without using court-sanctioned discovery.

In theory, our case was really quite simple: The warehouse squatters had been paying rent, in cash with no records, to Tillman Gantry or someone working on his behalf. Gantry had an opportunity to sell the property to RiverOaks, but it had to be done quickly. Gantry lied to RiverOaks and its lawyers about the squatters. Drake & Sweeney, exercising diligence, had sent Hector Palma to inspect the property prior to closing. Hector was mugged on the first visit, took a guard with him on the second, and upon inspecting the premises learned that the residents were, in fact, not squatters, but tenants. He reported this in a memo to Braden Chance, who made the ill-fated decision to disregard it and proceed with the closing. The tenants were summarily evicted as squatters, without due process.

A formal eviction would have taken at least thirty more days, time none of the participants wanted to waste. Thirty days and the worst of winter would be gone; the threat of snowstorms or sub-zero nights would be diminished, along with the need to sleep in a car with the heater running.

They were just street people, with no records, no rent receipts, and no trail to be followed.

It was not a complicated case, in theory. But the hurdles were enormous. Locking in testimony of homeless people could be treacherous, especially if Mr. Gantry decided to assert himself. He ruled the streets, an arena I was not eager to fight in. Mordecai had a vast network built on favors and whispers, but he was no match for Gantry's artillery. We spent an hour discussing various ways to avoid naming TAG, Inc., as a defendant. For obvious reasons, the lawsuit would be far messier and more dangerous with Gantry as a party. We could sue without him, and leave it to his co-defendants – RiverOaks and Drake & Sweeney – to haul him in as a third party.

But Gantry was a contributing cause in our theory of liability, and to ignore him as a defendant would be to ask for trouble as the case progressed.

Hector Palma had to be found. And once we found him, we somehow had to convince him to either produce the hidden memo, or to tell us what was in it. Finding him would be the easy part; getting him to talk might be impossible. He quite likely wouldn't want to, since he needed to keep his job. He'd been quick to tell me he had a wife and four kids.

There were other problems with the lawsuit, the first of which was purely procedural. We, as lawyers, did not have the authority to file suit on behalf of the heirs of Lontae Burton and her four children. We had to be employed by her family, such as it was. With her mother and two brothers in prison, and her father's identity yet to be revealed, Mordecai was of the opinion we should petition the Family Court for the appointment of a trustee to handle the affairs of Lontae's estate. In doing so, we could bypass her family, at least initially. In the event we recovered damages, the family would be a nightmare. It was safe to assume that the four children had two or more different fathers, and each one of those tomcats would have to be notified if money changed hands.

'We'll worry about that later,' Mordecai said. 'We have to win first.' We were in the front, at the desk next to Sofia's where the aging computer worked most of the time. I was typing, Mordecai pacing and dictating.

We plotted until midnight, drafting and redrafting the lawsuit, arguing theories, discussing procedure, dreaming of ways to haul RiverOaks and my old firm into court for a noisy trial. Mordecai saw it as a watershed, a pivotal moment to reverse the decline in public sympathy for the homeless. I saw it simply as a way to correct a wrong.

TWENTY-FOUR

Coffee again with Ruby. She was waiting by the front
door when I arrived at seven forty-five, happy to see
me. How could anyone be so cheerful after spending
eight hours trying to sleep in the backseat of an
abandoned car?

'Got any doughnuts?' she asked as I was flipping on
the light switches.

It was already a habit.

'I'll see. You have a seat, and I'll make us some
coffee.' I rattled around the kitchen, cleaning the
coffeepot, looking for something to eat. Yesterday's
stale doughnuts were even firmer, but there was
nothing else. I made a mental note to buy fresh ones
tomorrow, just in case Ruby arrived for the third day
in a row. Something told me she would.

She ate one doughnut, nibbling around the hard
edges, trying to be polite.

'Where do you eat breakfast?' I asked.

'Don't usually.'

'How about lunch and dinner?'

'Lunch is at Naomi's on Tenth Street. For dinner I
go to Calvary Mission over on Fifteenth.'

'What do you do during the day?'

She was curled around her paper cup again, trying
to keep her frail body warm.

'Most of the time I stay at Naomi's,' she said.

'How many women are there?'

'Don't know. A lot. They take good care of us, but it's just for the day.'

'Is it only for homeless women?'

'Yeah, that's right. They close at four. Most of the women live in shelters, some on the street. Me, I got a car.'

'Do they know you're using crack?'

'I think so. They want me to go to meetings for drunks and people on dope. I'm not the only one. Lots of the women do it too, you know.'

'Did you get high last night?' I asked. The words echoed in my ears. I found it hard to believe I was asking such questions.

Her chin fell to her chest; her eyes closed.

'Tell me the truth,' I said.

'I had to. I do it every night.'

I wasn't about to scold her. I had done nothing since the day before to help her find treatment. It suddenly became my priority.

She asked for another doughnut. I wrapped the last one in foil and topped off her coffee. She was late for something at Naomi's, and off she went.

The march began at the District Building with a rally for justice. Since Mordecai was a Who's Who in the world of the homeless, he left me in the crowd and went to his spot on the platform.

A church choir robed in burgundy and gold got organized on the steps and began flooding the area with lively hymns. Hundreds of police loitered in loose formation up and down the street, their barricades stopping traffic.

The CCNV had promised a thousand of its foot soldiers, and they arrived in a group – one long, impressive, disorganized column of men homeless and proud of it. I heard them coming before I saw them, their well-rehearsed marching yells clear from blocks away. When they rounded the corner, the TV cameras scrambled to greet them.

They gathered intact before the steps of the District Building and began waving their placards, most of which were of the homemade, hand-painted variety. STOP THE KILLINGS; SAVE THE SHELTERS; I HAVE THE RIGHT TO A HOME; JOBS, JOBS, JOBS. The signs were hoisted above their heads, where they danced with the rhythm of the hymns and the cadence of each noisy chant.

Church buses stopped at the barricades and unloaded hundreds of people, many of whom did not appear to be living on the streets. They were nicely dressed church folk, almost all women. The crowd swelled, the space around me shrunk. I did not know a single person, other than Mordecai. Sofia and Abraham were somewhere in the crowd, but I didn't see them. It was billed as the largest homeless march in the past ten years – Lontae's Rally.

A photo of Lontae Burton had been enlarged and mass-produced on large placards, trimmed in black, and under her face were the ominous words: WHO KILLED LONTAE? These were dispersed through the crowd, and quickly became the placard of choice, even among the men from the CCNV who'd brought their own protest banners. Lontae's face bobbed and weaved above the mass of people.

A lone siren wailed in the distance, then grew closer. A funeral van with a police escort was allowed through the barricades and stopped directly in front of the District Building, in the midst of the throng. The rear doors opened; a mock casket, painted black, was removed by the pallbearers – six homeless men who lifted it onto their shoulders and stood ready to begin the procession. Four more caskets, same color and

225

make but much smaller, were removed by more pallbearers.

The sea parted; the procession moved slowly toward the steps as the choir launched into a soulful requiem that almost brought tears to my eyes. It was a death march. One of those little caskets represented Ontario.

Then the crowd pressed together. Hands reached upward and touched the caskets so that they floated along, rocking gently side to side, end to end.

It was high drama, and the cameras packed near the platform recorded every solemn movement of the procession. We would see it replayed on TV for the next forty-eight hours.

The caskets were placed side by side, with Lontae's in the middle, on a small plywood ledge in the center of the steps, a few feet below the platform where Mordecai stood. They were filmed and photographed at length, then the speeches started.

The moderator was an activist who began by thanking all the groups that had helped organize the march. It was an impressive list, at least in quantity. As he rattled off the names, I was pleasantly surprised at the sheer number of shelters, missions, kitchens, coalitions, medical clinics, legal clinics, churches, centers, outreach groups, job-training programs, substance-abuse programs, even a few elected officials – all responsible to some degree for the event.

With so much support, how could there be a homeless problem?

The next six speakers answered that question. Lack of adequate funding to begin with, then budget cuts, a deaf ear by the federal government, a blind eye by the city, a lack of compassion from those with means, a court system grown much too conservative, the list went on and on. And on and on.

The same themes were repeated by each speaker, except for Mordecai, who spoke fifth and silenced the crowd with his story of the last hours of the Burton family. When he told of changing the baby's diaper, probably its last one, there wasn't a sound in the crowd. Not a cough or a whisper. I looked at the caskets as if one actually held the baby.

Then the family left the shelter, he explained, his voice slow, deep, resonating. They went back into the streets, into the snowstorm where Lontae and her children survived only a few more hours. Mordecai took great license with the facts at that point, because no one knew exactly what had happened. I knew this, but I didn't care. The rest of the crowd was equally mesmerized by his story.

When he described the last moments, as the family huddled together in a futile effort to stay warm, I heard women crying around me.

My thoughts turned selfish. If this man, my friend and fellow lawyer, could captivate a crowd of thousands from an elevated platform a hundred feet away, what could he do with twelve people in a jury box close enough to touch?

I realized at that moment that the Burton lawsuit would never get that far. No defense team in its right mind would allow Mordecai Green to preach to a black jury in this city. If our assumptions were correct, and if we could prove them, there would never be a trial.

After an hour and a half of speeches, the crowd was restless and ready to walk. The choir began again, and the caskets were lifted by the pallbearers, who led the procession away from the building. Behind the caskets were the leaders, including Mordecai. The rest of us followed. Someone handed me a Lontae placard, and I held it as high as anyone else.

Privileged people don't march and protest; their world is safe and clean and governed by laws designed to keep them happy. I had never taken to the streets

227

before; why bother? And for the first block or two I felt odd, walking in a mass of people, holding a stick with a placard bearing the face of a twenty-two-year-old black mother who bore four illegitimate children.

But I was no longer the same person I'd been a few weeks earlier. Nor could I go back, even if I'd wanted to. My past had been about money and possessions and status, afflictions that now disturbed me.

And so I relaxed and enjoyed the walk. I chanted with the homeless, rolled and pitched my placard in perfect unison with the others, and even tried to sing hymns foreign to me. I savored my first exercise in civil protest. It wouldn't be my last.

The barricades protected us as we inched toward Capitol Hill. The march had been well planned, and because of its size it attracted attention along the way. The caskets were placed on the steps of the Capitol. We congregated in a mass around them, then listened to another series of fiery speeches from civil rights activists and two members of Congress.

The speeches grew old; I'd heard enough. My homeless brethren had little to do; I had opened thirty-one files since beginning my new career on Monday. Thirty-one real people were waiting for me to get food stamps, locate housing, file divorces, defend criminal charges, obtain disputed wages, stop evictions, help with their addictions, and in some way snap my fingers and find justice. As an antitrust lawyer, I rarely had to face the clients. Things were different on the street.

I bought a cheap cigar from a sidewalk vendor, and went for a short walk on the Mall.

TWENTY-FIVE

I knocked on the door next to where the Palmas had lived, and a woman's voice asked, 'Who's there?' There was no effort to unbolt and open. I had thought long and hard about my ploy. I'd even rehearsed it driving to Bethesda. But I was not convinced I could be convincing.

'Bob Stevens,' I said, cringing. 'I'm looking for Hector Palma.'

'Who?' she asked.

'Hector Palma. He used to live next door to you.'

'What do you want?'

'I owe him some money. I'm trying to find him, that's all.'

If I were collecting money, or had some other unpleasant mission, then the neighbors would naturally be defensive. I thought this was a nifty little ruse.

'He's gone,' she said flatly.

'I know he's gone. Do you know where he went?'

'No.'

'Did he leave this area?'

'Don't know.'

'Did you see them move?'

Of course the answer was yes; there was no way around it. But instead of being helpful, she withdrew into the depths of her apartment and probably called security. I repeated the question, then rang the doorbell again. Nothing.

So I went to the door on the other side of Hector's last-known address. Two rings, it opened slightly until the chain caught, and a man my age with mayonnaise in the corner of his mouth said, 'What do you want?'

I repeated the Bob Stevens plot. He listened carefully while his kids romped through the living room behind him, a television blasting away. It was after eight, dark and cold, and I'd interrupted a late dinner.

But he was not unpleasant. 'I never knew him,' he said.

'What about his wife?'

'Nope. I travel a lot. Gone most of the time.'

'Did your wife know them?'

'No.' He said this too quickly.

'Did you or your wife see them move?'

'We weren't here last weekend.'

'And you have no idea where they went?'

'None.'

I thanked him, then turned around to meet a beefy security guard, in uniform, holding a billy club with his right hand and tapping it on his left palm, like a street cop in a movie. 'What are you doing?' he snarled.

'Looking for someone,' I said. 'Put that thing away.'

'We don't allow solicitation.'

'Are you deaf? I'm looking for someone, not soliciting.' I walked past him, toward the parking lot.

'We've had a complaint,' he said to my back. 'You need to leave.'

'I'm leaving.'

Dinner was a taco and a beer in a corporate bar not far away. I felt safer eating in the suburbs. The restaurant was of the cookie-cutter variety, a national chain getting rich with shiny new neighborhood watering holes. The crowd was dominated by young government workers, still trying to get home, all talking policy and politics while drinking draft beer and yelling at a game.

Loneliness was an adjustment. My wife and friends had been left behind. Seven years in the sweatshop of Drake & Sweeney had not been conducive to nurturing friendships; or a marriage either, for that matter. At the age of thirty-two, I was ill-prepared for the single life. As I watched the game, and the women, I asked myself if I were expected to return to the bar and nightclub scene to find companionship. Surely there was some other place and method.

I got dejected and left.

I drove slowly into the city, not anxious to arrive at my apartment. My name was on a lease, in a computer somewhere, and I figured the police could find my loft without too much trouble. If they were planning an arrest, I was certain it would happen at night. They would enjoy terrifying me with a midnight knock on the door, a little roughing up as they frisked me and slapped on the cuffs, a shove out the door, down the elevator with death grips under my arms, a push into the rear seat of a squad car for the ride to the city jail where I would be the only young white professional arrested that night. They would like nothing better than to throw me into a holding cell with the usual assortment of thugs, and leave me there to fend for myself.

I carried with me two things, regardless of what I was doing. One was a cell phone, with which to call Mordecai as soon as I was arrested. The other was a folded stack of bills – twenty hundred-dollar bills – to use to make bail and hopefully spring myself before I got near the holding cell.

I parked two blocks away from my building, and

watched every empty car for suspicious characters. I made it to the loft, untouched, unapprehended.

My living room was now furnished with two lawn chairs and a plastic storage box used as a coffee table/footstool. The television was on a matching storage box. I was amused at the sparse furnishings and determined to keep the place to myself. No one would see how I was living.

My mother had called. I listened to her recording. She and Dad were worried about me, and wanted to come for a visit. They had discussed things with brother Warner, and he might make the trip too. I could almost hear their analysis of my new life. Somebody had to talk some sense into me.

The rally for Lontae was the lead story at eleven. There were close-ups of the five black caskets lying on the steps of the District Building, and later as they were marched down the street. Mordecai was featured preaching to the masses. The crowd appeared larger than I had realized – the estimate was five thousand. The mayor had no comment.

I turned off the television, and punched Claire's number on the phone. We had not talked in four days, and I thought I would show some civility and break the ice. Technically we were still married. It would be nice to have dinner in a week or so.

After the third ring, a strange voice reluctantly said, 'Hello.' It was that of a male.

For a second, I was too stunned to speak. It was eleven-thirty on a Thursday night. Claire had a man over. I had been gone for less than a week. I almost hung up, but then collected myself and said, 'Claire, please.'

'Who's calling?' he asked, gruffly.

'Michael, her husband.'

'She's in the shower,' he said, with a trace of satisfaction.

232

'Tell her I called,' I said, and hung up as quickly as possible.

I paced the three rooms until midnight, then dressed again and went for a walk in the cold. When a marriage crumbles, you ponder all scenarios. Was it a simple matter of growing apart, or was it much more complicated than that? Had I missed the signals? Was he a casual one-nighter, or had they been seeing each other for years? Was he some overheated doctor, married with children, or a young virile med student giving her what she'd missed from me?

I kept telling myself it didn't matter. We weren't divorcing because of infidelities. It was too late to worry if she'd been sleeping around.

The marriage was over, plain and simple. For whatever reason. She could go to hell for all I cared. She was done, dismissed, forgotten. If I was free to chase the ladies, then the same rules applied to her.

Yeah, right.

At 2 A.M., I found myself at Dupont Circle, ignoring catcalls from the queers and stepping around men bundled in layers and quilts and sleeping on benches. It was dangerous, but I didn't care.

A few hours later, I bought a box of a dozen assorted at a Krispy Kreme, with two tall coffees and a newspaper. Ruby was waiting faithfully at the door, shivering from the cold. Her eyes were redder than usual, her smile was not as quick.

Our spot was a desk in the front, the one with the fewest stacks of long-forgotten files. I cleared the top of the desk, and served the coffee and doughnuts. She didn't like chocolate, but instead preferred the ones with the fruit filling.

'Do you read the newspaper?' I asked as I unfolded it.

'No.'

'How well do you read?'

'Not good.'

So I read it to her. We started with the front page, primarily because it had a large photo of the five caskets seemingly adrift above the mass of people. The story was headlined across the bottom half, and I read every word of it to Ruby, who listened intently. She had heard stories about the deaths of the Burton family; the details fascinated her.

'Could I die like that?' she asked.

'No. Not unless your car has an engine and you run the heater.'

'I wish it had a heater.'

'You could die from exposure.'

'What's that?'

'Freezing to death.'

She wiped her mouth with a napkin, and sipped her coffee. The temperature had been eleven degrees the night Ontario and his family died. How had Ruby survived?

'Where do you go when it gets real cold?' I asked.

'Don't go nowhere.'

'You stay in the car?'

'Yes.'

'How do you keep from freezing?'

'I got plenty of blankets. I just bury down in them.'

'You never go to a shelter?'

'Never.'

'Would you go to a shelter if it would help you see Terrence?'

She rolled her head to one side, and gave me a strange look. 'Say it again,' she said.

'You want to see Terrence, right?'

'Right.'

'Then you have to get clean. Right?'

'Right.'

'To get clean, you'll have to live in a detox center for a while. Is that something you're willing to do?'

'Maybe,' she said. 'Just maybe.'

It was a small step, but not an insignificant one.

'I can help you see Terrence again, and you can be a part of his life. But you have to get clean, and stay clean.'

'How do I do it?' she asked, her eyes unable to meet mine. She cradled her coffee, the steam rising to her face.

'Are you going to Naomi's today?'

'Yes.'

'I talked to the director over there. They have two meetings today, alcoholics and drug addicts together. They're called AA/NA. I want you to attend both of them. The director will call me.'

She nodded like a scolded child. I would push no further, not at that moment. She nibbled her doughnuts, sipped her coffee, and listened with rapt attention as I read one news story after another. She cared little for foreign affairs and sports, but the city news fascinated her. She had voted at one time, many years ago, and the politics of the District were easily digested. She understood the crime stories.

A long editorial blistered Congress and the city for their failure to fund services for the homeless. Other Lontaes would follow, it warned. Other children would die in our streets, in the shadows of the U.S. Capitol. I paraphrased this for Ruby, who concurred with every phrase.

A soft, freezing rain began falling, so I drove Ruby to her next stop for the day. Naomi's Women's Center was a four-level rowhouse on Tenth Street, NW, in a block of similar structures. It opened at seven, closed at four, and during each day provided food, showers, clothing, activities, and counseling for any homeless woman who could find the place. Ruby was a regular, and received a warm greeting from her friends when we entered.

I spoke quietly with the director, a young woman named Megan. We conspired to push Ruby toward sobriety. Half the women there were mentally ill, half were substance abusers, a third were HIV-positive. Ruby, as far as Megan knew, carried no infectious diseases.

When I left, the women were crowded into the main room, singing songs.

I was hard at work at my desk when Sofia knocked on my door and entered before I could answer.

'Mordecai says you're looking for someone,' she said. She held a legal pad, ready to take notes.

I thought for a second, then remembered Hector. 'Oh yes. I am.'

'I can help. Tell me everything you know about the person.' She sat down and began writing as I rattled off his name, address, last known place of employment, physical description, and the fact that he had a wife and four kids.

'Age?'

'Maybe thirty.'

'Approximate salary?'

'Thirty-five thousand.'

'With four kids, it's safe to assume at least one was enrolled in school. With that salary, and living in Bethesda, I doubt if they'd go the private route. He's Hispanic, so he's probably Catholic. Anything else?'

I couldn't think of a thing. She left and returned to her desk where she opened a thick three-ring notebook and flipped pages. I kept my door open so I could watch and listen. The first call went to someone with the Postal Service. The conversation changed instantly to Spanish, and I was lost. One call followed another. She would say hello in English, ask for her contact, then switch to her native tongue. She called the Catholic diocese, which led to another series of rapid calls. I lost interest.

An hour later, she walked to my door and announced, 'They moved to Chicago. Do you need an address?'

'How did you . . . ?' My words trailed off as I stared at her in disbelief.

'Don't ask. A friend of a friend in their church. They moved over the weekend, in a hurry. Do you need their new address?'

'How long will it take?'

'It won't be easy. I can point you in the right direction.'

She had at least six clients sitting along the front window waiting to seek her advice. 'Not now,' I said. 'Maybe later. Thanks.'

'Don't mention it.'

Don't mention it. I'd planned to spend a few more hours after dark knocking on the doors of neighbors, in the cold, dodging security guards, hoping no one shot me. And she worked the phone for an hour and found the missing person.

Drake & Sweeney had more than a hundred lawyers in its Chicago branch. I had been there twice on antitrust cases. The offices were in a skyscraper near the lakefront. The building's foyer was several stories tall, with fountains and shops around the perimeter, escalators zigzagging upward. It was the perfect place to hide and watch for Hector Palma.

TWENTY-SIX

The homeless are close to the streets, to the pavement, the curbs and gutters, the concrete, the litter, the sewer lids and fire hydrants and wastebaskets and bus stops and storefronts. They move slowly over familiar terrain, day after day, stopping to talk to each other because time means little, stopping to watch a stalled car in traffic, a new drug dealer on a corner, a strange face on their turf. They sit on their sidewalks hidden under hats and caps and behind drugstore sunshades, and like sentries they observe every movement. They hear the sounds of the street, they absorb the odors of diesel fumes from city buses and fried grease from cheap diners. The same cab passes twice in an hour, and they know it. A gun is fired in the distance, and they know where it came from. A fine auto with Virginia or Maryland plates is parked at the curb, they'll watch it until it leaves.

A cop with no uniform waits in a car with no markings, and they see it.

'The police are out there,' one of our clients said to Sofia. She walked to the front door, looked southeast on Q, and there she saw what appeared to be an unmarked police car. She waited half an hour, and checked it again. Then she went to Mordecai.

I was oblivious because I was fighting with the food

238

stamp office on one front and the prosecutor's office on another. It was Friday afternoon, and the city bureaucracy, substandard on a good day, was shutting down fast. They delivered the news together.

'I think the cops might be waiting,' Mordecai announced solemnly.

My first reaction was to duck under the desk, but, of course, I did not. I tried to appear calm. 'Where?' I asked, as if it mattered.

'At the corner. They've been watching the building for more than a half hour.'

'Maybe they're coming after you,' I said. Ha-ha. Stone faces all around.

'I've called,' Sofia said. 'And there's a warrant for your arrest. Grand larceny.'

A felony! Prison! A handsome white boy thrown into the pit. I shifted weight from one side to another, and I tried my best to show no fear.

'That's no surprise,' I said. Happened all the time. 'Let's get it over with.'

'I have a call in for a guy at the prosecutor's office,' Mordecai said. 'It would be nice if they allowed you to turn yourself in.'

'That would be nice,' I said as if it didn't really matter. 'But I've been talking to the prosecutor's office all afternoon. No one's listening.'

'They have two hundred lawyers,' he said.

Mordecai did not make friends on that side of the street. Cops and prosecutors were his natural enemies.

A quick game plan was devised. Sofia would call a bail bondsman, who would meet us at the jail. Mordecai would try to find a friendly judge. What was not said was the obvious – it was Friday afternoon. I might not survive a weekend in the city jail.

They left to make their calls, and I sat at my desk, petrified, unable to move or think or do anything but listen for the squeaking of the front door. I didn't have to wait long. At precisely 4 P.M., Lieutenant Gasko entered with a couple of his men behind him.

During my first encounter with Gasko, when he was searching Claire's apartment, when I was ranting and taking names and threatening all sorts of vile litigation against him and his buddies, when every word uttered by him was met with a caustic retort from me, when I was a hard-charging lawyer and he was a lowly cop, it never occurred to me that he one day might have the pleasure of arresting me. But there he was, swaggering like an aging jock, somehow sneering and smiling at the same time, holding yet more papers, folded and just waiting to be slapped against my chest.

'I need to see Mr. Brock,' he said to Sofia, and about that time I walked into the front room, smiling.

'Hello, Gasko,' I said. 'Still looking for that file?'

'Nope. Not today.'

Mordecai appeared from his office. Sofia was standing at her desk. Everybody looked at everybody. 'You got a warrant?' Mordecai asked.

'Yep. For Mr. Brock here,' Gasko said.

I shrugged and said, 'Let's go.' I moved toward Gasko. One of the goons unsnapped a pair of handcuffs from his waist. I was determined to at least look cool.

'I'm his lawyer,' Mordecai said. 'Let me see that.' He took the arrest warrant from Gasko and examined it as I was getting cuffed, hands behind my back, wrists pinched by cold steel. The cuffs were too tight, or at least tighter than they had to be, but I could bear it and I was determined to be nonchalant.

'I'll be happy to take my client to the police station,' Mordecai said.

'Gee thanks,' Gasko said. 'But I'll save you the trouble.'

'Where will he go?'

'Central.'

'I'll follow you there,' Mordecai said to me. Sofia was on the phone, and that was even more comforting than knowing that Mordecai would be somewhere behind me.

Three of our clients saw it all; three harmless street gentlemen in for a quick word with Sofia. They were sitting where the clients always waited, and when I walked by them they watched in disbelief.

One of the goons squeezed my elbow and yanked me through the front door, and I stepped onto the sidewalk anxious to duck into their car: a dirty unmarked white one parked at the corner. The homeless saw it all – the car moving into position, the cops rushing in, the cops coming out with me handcuffed.

'A lawyer got arrested,' they would soon whisper to each other, and the news would race along the streets.

Gasko sat in the rear with me. I stayed low in the seat, eyes watching nothing, the shock settling in.

'What a waste of time,' Gasko said as he relaxed by placing a cowboy boot on a knee. 'We got a hundred and forty unsolved murders in this city, dope on every corner, drug dealers selling in middle schools, and we gotta waste time on you.'

'Are you trying to interrogate me, Gasko?' I asked.

'No.'

'Good.' He hadn't bothered with the Miranda warning, and he didn't have to until he started asking questions.

Goon One was flying south on Fourteenth, no lights or sirens, and certainly no respect for traffic signals and pedestrians.

'Then let me go,' I said.

'If it's up to me, I would. But you really pissed some folks off. The prosecutor tells me he's under pressure to get you.'

'Pressure from who?' I asked. But I knew the

241

answer. Drake & Sweeney wouldn't waste time with the cops; they would rather talk legalspeak with the chief prosecutor.

'The victims,' Gasko said with heavy sarcasm. I agreed with his assessment; it was difficult to picture a bunch of wealthy lawyers as victims of a crime.

Lots of famous people had been arrested. I tried to recall them. Martin Luther King went to jail several times. There were Boesky and Milken and other noted thieves whose names escaped me. And what about all those famous actors and athletes caught driving drunk and picking up prostitutes and possessing coke? They had been thrown into the backseats of police cars and led away like common criminals. There was a judge from Memphis serving life; an acquaintance from college in a halfway house; a former client in the federal pen for tax evasion. All had been arrested, led downtown, booked, fingerprinted, and had their pictures taken with the little number under their chins. And all had survived.

I suspected that even Mordecai Green had felt the cold clasp of handcuffs.

There was an element of relief because it was finally happening. I could stop running, and hiding, and looking to see if anyone was behind me. The waiting was over. And it was not a midnight raid, one that would certainly keep me in jail until morning. Instead, the hour was manageable. With luck, I could get processed and bailed out before the weekend rush hit.

But there was also an element of horror, a fear I had never felt in my life. Many things could go wrong at the city jail. Paperwork might get lost. Delays of a dozen varieties could be created. Bail could be postponed until Saturday, or Sunday, or even Monday. I could be placed in a crowded cell with unfriendly to nasty people.

Word would leak that I had been arrested. My

friends would shake their heads and wonder what else I could do to screw up my life. My parents would be devastated. I wasn't sure about Claire, especially now that the gigolo was keeping her company.

I closed my eyes and tried to get comfortable, which I found impossible to do while sitting on my hands.

The processing was a blur; surreal movements from one point to the next with Gasko leading me like a lost puppy. Eyes on the floor, I kept telling myself. Don't look at these people. Inventory first, everything from the pockets, sign a form. Down the dirty hall to Photos, shoes off, up against the measuring tape, don't have to smile if you don't want to, but please look at the camera. Then a profile. Then to Fingerprinting, which happened to be busy, so Gasko handcuffed me like a mental patient to a chair in the hall while he went to find coffee. Arrestees shuffled past, all in various stages of processing. Cops everywhere. A white face, not a cop but a defendant much like myself – young, male, handsome navy suit, obviously drunk with a bruise on his left cheek. How does one get plastered before 5 P.M. on a Friday? He was loud and threatening, his words garbled and harsh, and ignored by everyone I could see. Then he was gone. Time passed and I began to panic. It was dark outside, the weekend had started, crime would begin and the jail would get busier. Gasko came back, took me into Fingerprinting, and watched as Poindexter efficiently applied the ink and stuck my fingers to the sheets.

No phone calls were needed. My lawyer was somewhere close by, though Gasko hadn't seen him. The doors got heavier as we descended into the jail. We were going in the wrong direction; the street was back behind us.

'Can't I make bail?' I finally asked. I saw bars ahead; bars over windows and busy guards with guns.

'I think your lawyer's working on it,' Gasko said.

He gave me to Sergeant Coffey, who pushed me against a wall, kicked my legs apart, and frisked me as if searching for a dime. Finding none, he pointed and grunted at a metal detector, which I walked through, without offense. A buzzer, a door slid open, a hallway appeared, one with rows of bars on both sides. A door clanged behind me, and my prayer for an easy release vanished.

Hands and arms protruded through the bars, into the narrow hall. The men watched us as we moved past. My gaze returned to my feet. Coffey looked into each cell; I thought he was counting bodies. We stopped at the third one on the right.

My cellmates were black, all much younger than I was. I counted four at first, then saw a fifth lying on the top bunk. There were two beds, for six people. The cell was a small square with three walls of nothing but bars, so I could see the prisoners next door and across the hall. The rear wall was cinder block with a small toilet in one corner.

Coffey slammed the door behind me. The guy on the top bunk sat up and swung his legs over the side, so that they dangled near the face of a guy sitting on the bottom bunk. All five glared at me as I stood by the door, trying to appear calm and unafraid, trying desperately to find a place to sit on the floor so that I wouldn't be in danger of touching any of my cellmates.

Thank God they had no weapons. Thank God someone installed the metal detector. They had no guns and knives; I had no assets, other than clothing. My watch, wallet, cell phone, cash – and everything else I had with me – had been taken and inventoried.

The front of the cell would be safer than the rear. I ignored their eyes and took my spot on the floor, my back resting on the door. Down the hall, someone was yelling for a guard.

A fight broke out two cells away, and through the bars and bunks I could see the drunk guy with the white face and navy suit pinned in a corner by two large black men who were pounding his head. Other voices encouraged them on and the entire wing grew rowdy. It was not a good moment to be white.

A shrill whistle, a door opened, and Coffey was back, nightstick in hand. The fight ended abruptly with the drunk on his stomach and still. Coffey went to the cell, and inquired as to what happened. No one knew; no one had seen a thing.

'Keep it quiet!' he demanded, then left.

Minutes passed. The drunk began to groan; someone was vomiting in the distance. One of my cellmates got to his feet, and walked to where I was sitting. His bare feet barely touched my leg. I glanced up, then away. He glared down, and I knew this was the end.

'Nice jacket,' he said.

'Thanks,' I mumbled, trying not to sound sarcastic, or in any way provocative. The jacket was a navy blazer, an old one that I wore every day with jeans and khakis – my radical attire. It certainly wasn't worth being slaughtered over.

'Nice jacket,' he said again, and he added a slight nudge with his foot. The guy on the top bunk jumped down, and stepped closer for a better look.

'Thanks,' I said again.

He was eighteen or nineteen, lean and tall, not an ounce of fat, probably a gang member who'd spent his life on the streets. He was cocky and anxious to impress the others with his bravado.

Mine would be the easiest ass he'd ever kicked.

'I don't have a jacket that nice,' he said. A firmer nudge with his foot, one intended to provoke.

Shouldn't be a low-life street punk, I thought. He

couldn't steal it because there was no place to run. 'Would you like to borrow it?' I asked, without looking up.

'No.'

I pulled my feet in so that my knees were close to my chin. It was a defensive position. When he kicked or swung, I was not going to fight back. Any resistance would immediately bring in the other four, and they would have a delightful time thrashing the white boy.

'Dude says you got a nice jacket,' said the one from the top bunk.

'And I said thanks.'

'Dude says he ain't got no jacket that nice.'

'So what am I supposed to do?' I asked.

'A gift would be appropriate.'

A third one stepped forward and closed the semi-circle around me. The first one kicked my foot, and all inched closer. They were ready to pounce, each waiting for the other, so I quickly removed my blazer and thrust it forward.

'Is this a gift?' the first one asked, taking it.

'It's whatever you want it to be,' I said. I was looking down, still avoiding eye contact; thus, I didn't see his foot. It was a vicious kick that slapped my left temple and jerked my head backward where it cracked against the bars. 'Shit!' I yelled as I felt the back of my head.

'You can have the damned thing,' I said, bracing for the onslaught.

'Is it a gift?'

'Yes.'

'Thanks, man.'

'Don't mention it,' I said, rubbing my face. My entire head was numb.

They backed away, leaving me curled in a tight ball.

Minutes passed, though I had no concept of time. The drunk white guy two doors down was making an

246

effort to revive himself, and another voice was calling for a guard. The punk with my jacket did not put it on. The cell swallowed it.

My face throbbed, but there was no blood. If I received no further injuries as an inmate, I would consider myself lucky. A comrade down the hall yelled something about trying to sleep, and I began to ponder what the night might bring. Six inmates, two very narrow beds. Were we expected to sleep on the floor, with no blanket and pillow?

The floor was getting cold, and as I sat on it I glanced at my cellmates and speculated as to what crimes they had committed. I, of course, had borrowed a file with every intention of returning it. Yet there I was, low man on the pole among drug dealers, car thieves, rapists, probably even murderers.

I wasn't hungry, but I thought about food. I had no toothbrush. I didn't need the toilet, but what would happen when I did? Where was the drinking water? The basics became crucial.

'Nice shoes,' a voice said, startling me. I looked up to see another one of them standing above me. He wore dirty white socks, no shoes, and his feet were several inches longer than mine.

'Thanks,' I said. The shoes in question were old Nike cross-trainers. They were not basketball shoes, and should not have appealed to my cellmate. For once, I wished I'd been wearing the tasseled loafers from my previous career.

'What size?' he asked.

'Tens.'

The punk who took my jacket walked closer; the message was given and received.

'Same size I wear,' the first one said.

'Would you like to have these?' I said. I immediately began unlacing them. 'Here, I would like to present you with a gift of my shoes.' I quickly kicked them off, and he took them.

What about my jeans and underwear? I wanted to ask.

Mordecai finally broke through around 7 P.M. Coffey fetched me from the cell, and as we made our way toward the front, he asked, 'Where are your shoes?'

'In the cell,' I said. 'They were taken.'

'I'll get them.'

'Thanks. I had a navy blazer too.'

He looked at the left side of my face where the corner of my eye was beginning to swell. 'Are you okay?'

'Wonderful. I'm free.'

My bail was ten thousand dollars. Mordecai was waiting with the bondsman. I paid him a thousand in cash, and signed the paperwork. Coffey brought my shoes and blazer, and my incarceration was over. Sofia waited outside with her car, and they whisked me away.

TWENTY-SEVEN

Strictly in physical terms, I was paying a price for my journey from the tower to the street. The bruises from the car wreck were almost gone, but the soreness in the muscles and joints would take weeks. I was losing weight, for two reasons – I couldn't afford the restaurants I'd once taken for granted; and I'd lost interest in food. My back ached from sleeping on the floor in a sleeping bag, a practice I was determined to pursue in an effort to see if it would ever become tolerable. I had my doubts.

And then a street punk almost cracked my skull with his bare foot. I iced it until late, and every time I awoke during the night it seemed to be expanding.

But I felt lucky to be alive, lucky to be in one piece after descending into hell for a few hours before being rescued. The fear of the unknown had been removed, at least for the present. There were no cops lurking in the shadows.

Grand larceny was nothing to laugh at, especially since I was guilty. The maximum was ten years in prison. I would worry about it later.

I left my apartment just before sunrise, Saturday, in a rush to find the nearest newspaper. My new neighborhood coffee shop was a tiny all-night bakery run by a rowdy family of Pakistanis on Kalorama, in a section of Adams-Morgan that could go from safe to

249

treacherous in one small block. I sidled up to the counter and ordered a large latte. Then I opened the newspaper and found the one little story I'd lost sleep over.

My friends at Drake & Sweeney had planned it well. On page two of Metro, there was my face, in a photo taken a year earlier for a recruiting brochure the firm had developed. Only the firm had the negative.

The story was four paragraphs, brief, to the point, and filled primarily with information fed to the reporter by the firm. I had worked there for seven years, in antitrust, law school at Yale, no prior criminal record. The firm was the fifth-largest in the country – eight hundred lawyers, eight cities, and so on. No one got quoted, because no quotes were necessary. The sole purpose of the story was to humiliate me, and to that end it worked well. LOCAL ATTORNEY ARRESTED FOR GRAND LARCENY read the headline next to my face. 'Items taken' was the description of the stolen loot. Items taken during my recent departure from the firm.

It sounded like a silly little spat – a bunch of lawyers quibbling over nothing but paperwork. Who would care, other than myself and anyone who might know me? The embarrassment would quickly go away; there were too many real stories in the world.

The photo and the background had found a friendly reporter, one willing to process his four paragraphs and wait until my arrest could be confirmed. With no effort whatsoever, I could see Arthur and Rafter and their team spending hours planning my arrest and its aftermath, hours that no doubt would be billed to RiverOaks, only because it happened to be the client nearest the mess.

What a public relations coup! Four paragraphs in the Saturday edition.

The Pakistanis didn't bake fruit-filled doughnuts. I

bought oatmeal cookies instead, and drove to the office.

Ruby was asleep in the doorway, and as I approached I wondered how long she had been there. She was covered with two or three old quilts, and her head rested on a large canvas shopping bag, packed with her belongings. She sprang to her feet after I coughed and made noise.

'Why are you sleeping here?' I asked.

She looked at the paper bag of food, and said, 'I gotta sleep somewhere.'

'I thought you slept in a car.'

'I do. Most of the time.'

Nothing productive would come from a conversation with a homeless person about why she slept here or there. Ruby was hungry. I unlocked the door, turned on lights, and went to make coffee. She, according to our ritual, went straight to what had become her desk and waited.

We had coffee and cookies with the morning news. We alternated stories – I read one I wanted, then one that was of interest to her. I ignored the one about me.

Ruby had walked out of the AA/NA meeting the afternoon before at Naomi's. The morning session had gone without incident, but she had bolted from the second one. Megan, the director, had called me about an hour before Gasko made his appearance.

'How do you feel this morning?' I asked when we finished the paper.

'Fine. And you?'

'Fine. I'm clean. Are you?'

Her chin dropped an inch; her eyes cut to one side, and she paused just long enough for the truth. 'Yes,' she said. 'I'm clean.'

'No you're not. Don't lie to me, Ruby. I'm your friend, and your lawyer, and I'm going to help you see

251

Terrence. But I can't help you if you lie to me. Now, look me in the eyes, and tell me if you're clean.'

She somehow managed to shrink even more, and with her eyes on the floor, she said, 'I'm not clean.'

'Thank you. Why did you walk out of the AA/NA meeting yesterday afternoon?'

'I didn't.'

'The director said you did.'

'I thought they was through.'

I was not going to be sucked into an argument I couldn't win. 'Are you going to Naomi's today?'

'Yes.'

'Good. I'll take you, but you have to promise me you'll go to both meetings.'

'I promise.'

'You have to be the first one in the meetings, and the last one to leave, okay?'

'Okay.'

'And the director will be watching.'

She nodded and took another cookie, her fourth. We talked about Terrence, and rehab and getting clean, and again I began to feel the hopelessness of addiction. She was overwhelmed by the challenge of staying clean for just twenty-four hours.

The drug was crack, as I suspected. Instantly addictive and dirt cheap.

As we drove to Naomi's, Ruby suddenly said, 'You got arrested, didn't you?'

I almost ran a red light. She was sleeping on the office doorstep at sunrise; she was barely literate. How could she have seen the newspaper?

'Yes, I did.'

'Thought so.'

'How did you know?'

'You hear stuff on the street.'

Ah, yes. Forget papers. The homeless carry their own news. That young lawyer down at Mordecai's got himself arrested. Cops hauled him away, just like he was one of us.

'It's a misunderstanding,' I said, as if she cared.

They'd started singing without her; we could hear them as we walked up the steps to Naomi's. Megan unlocked the front door, and invited me to stay for coffee. In the main room on the first level, in what was once a fine parlor, the ladies of Naomi's sang and shared and listened to each other's problems. We watched them for a few minutes. As the only male, I felt like an intruder.

Megan poured coffee in the kitchen, and gave me a quick tour of the place. We whispered, because the ladies were praying not far away. There were rest rooms and showers on the first floor near the kitchen; a small garden out back where those suffering from depression often went to be alone. The second floor was offices, intake centers, and a rectangular room crammed with chairs where the Alcoholics Anonymous/Narcotics Anonymous chapters met together.

As we climbed the narrow stairs, a joyous chorus erupted from below. Megan's office was on the third floor. She invited me in, and as soon as I sat down she tossed a copy of the *Post* into my lap.

'Rough night, huh?' she said with a smile.

I looked at my photo again. 'It wasn't too bad.'

'What's this?' she asked, pointing to her temple.

'My cell partner wanted my shoes. He took them.'

She looked at my well-used Nikes. 'Those?'

'Yes. Handsome, aren't they?'

'How long were you in jail?'

'Couple of hours. Then I got my life together. Made it through rehab. Now I'm a new man.'

She smiled again, a perfect smile, and our eyes lingered for a second, and I thought, Oh boy! No wedding ring on her finger. She was tall and a little too thin. Her hair was dark red and cut short and smart,

253

above the ears like a preppie. Her eyes were light brown, very big and round and quite pleasant to gaze into for a second or two. It struck me that she was very attractive, and it seemed odd that I hadn't noticed it sooner.

Was I being set up? Had I wandered up the stairs for a reason other than the tour? How had I missed the smile and the eyes yesterday?

We swapped bios. Her father was an Episcopal priest in Maryland, and a Redskins fan who loved D.C. As a teenager, she had decided to work with the poor. There was no higher calling.

I had to confess I had never thought about the poor until two weeks earlier. She was captivated by the story of Mister, and its purifying effects on me.

She invited me to return for lunch, to check on Ruby. If the sun was out, we could eat in the garden.

Poverty lawyers are no different from other people. They can find romance in odd places, like a shelter for homeless women.

After a week of driving through D.C.'s roughest sections, and spending hours in shelters, and in general mixing and mingling with the homeless, I no longer felt the need to hide behind Mordecai every time I ventured out. He was a valuable shield, but to survive on the streets I had to jump in the lake and learn to swim.

I had a list of almost thirty shelters and kitchens and centers where the homeless came and went. And I had a list of the names of the seventeen people evicted, including DeVon Hardy and Lontae Burton.

My next stop Saturday morning, after Naomi's, was the Mount Gilead Christian Church near Gallaudet University. According to my map, it was the kitchen nearest the intersection of New York and Florida, where the warehouse had once stood. The director was a young woman named Gloria, who, when I arrived at nine, was alone in the kitchen, chopping celery and fretting over the fact that no volunteers had arrived. After I introduced myself and did a thorough job of convincing her that my credentials were in order, she pointed to a cutting board and asked me to dice the onions. How could a bona fide poverty lawyer say no?

I had done it before, I explained, in Dolly's kitchen back during the snowstorm. She was polite but behind schedule. As I worked the onions and wiped my eyes, I described the case I was working on, and rattled off the names of the people evicted along with DeVon Hardy and Lontae Burton.

'We're not case managers,' she said. 'We just feed them. I don't know many names.'

A volunteer arrived with a sack of potatoes. I made preparations to leave. Gloria thanked me, and took a copy of the names. She promised to listen harder.

My movements were planned; I had many stops to make, and little time. I talked to a doctor at the Capitol Clinic, a privately funded walk-in facility for the homeless. The clinic kept a record of every patient. It was Saturday, and on Monday he would have the secretary check the computer files against my list. If there was a match, the secretary would call.

I drank tea with a Catholic priest at the Redeemer Mission off Rhode Island. He studied the names with great intensity, but no bells went off. 'There are so many,' he said.

The only scare of the morning occurred at the Freedom Coalition, a large gathering hall built by some long-forgotten association and later converted to a community center. At eleven, a lunch line was forming by the front entrance. Since I wasn't there to eat, I simply ignored the line and walked directly to the door. Some of the gentlemen waiting for food thought I was breaking their line, and they threw obscenities at me. They were hungry, and suddenly angry, and the fact that I was white didn't help matters. How could they mistake me for a homeless person? The door was being manned by a volunteer, who also thought I was being an ass. He stiff-armed me rudely, another act of violence against my person.

'I'm not here to eat!' I said angrily. 'I'm a lawyer for the homeless!'

That settled them down; suddenly I was a blue-eyed brother. I was allowed to enter the building without further assault. The director was Reverend Kip, a fiery little guy with a red beret and a black collar. We did not connect. When he realized that (a) I was a lawyer; (b) my clients were the Burtons; (c) I was working on their lawsuit; and (d) there might be a recovery of damages down the road, he began thinking about money. I wasted thirty minutes with him, and left with the vow to send in Mordecai.

I called Megan and begged off lunch. My excuse was that I was on the other side of the city, with a long list of people yet to see. The truth was that I couldn't tell if she was flirting. She was pretty and smart and thoroughly likable, and she was the last thing I needed. I hadn't flirted in almost ten years; I didn't know the rules.

But Megan had great news. Ruby had not only survived the morning session of AA/NA, she had vowed to stay clean for twenty-four hours. It was an emotional scene, and Megan had watched from the rear of the room.

'She needs to stay off the streets tonight,' Megan said. 'She hasn't had a clean day in twelve years.'

I, of course, was of little help. Megan had several ideas.

The afternoon was as fruitless as the morning, though

256

I did learn the location of every shelter in the District. And I met people, made contacts, swapped cards with folks I'd probably see again.

Kelvin Lam remained the sole evictee we'd been able to locate. DeVon Hardy and Lontae Burton were dead. I was left with a total of fourteen people who had fallen through the cracks in the sidewalks.

The hard-core homeless venture into shelters from time to time for a meal, or a pair of shoes, or a blanket, but they leave no trail. They do not want help. They have no desire for human contact. It was hard to believe that the remaining fourteen were hard core. A month earlier, they had been living under a roof and paying rent.

Patience, Mordecai kept telling me. Street lawyers must have patience.

Ruby met me at the door of Naomi's, with a gleaming smile and a fierce hug. She had completed both sessions. Megan had already laid the groundwork for the next twelve hours – Ruby would not be allowed to stay on the streets. Ruby had acquiesced.

Ruby and I left the city and drove west into Virginia. In a suburban shopping center, we bought a toothbrush and toothpaste, soap, shampoo, and enough candy to get through Halloween. We drove farther away from the city, and in the small town of Gainesville I found a shiny new motel advertising single rooms for forty-two dollars a night. I paid with a credit card; surely it would somehow be deductible.

I left her there, with strict instructions to stay in the room with the door locked until I came for her Sunday morning.

TWENTY-EIGHT

Saturday night, the first day of March. Young, single, certainly not as rich as I was not too long ago, but not completely broke, yet. A closet full of nice clothes, which were not being used. A city of one million people with scores of attractive young women drawn to the center of political power, and always ready, it was rumored, for a good time.

I had beer and pizza and watched college basketball, alone in my loft and not unhappy. Any public appearance that night could have ended quickly with the cruel greeting 'Hey, aren't you the guy who got arrested? Saw it in the paper this morning.'

I checked on Ruby. The phone rang eight times before she answered, and I was about to panic. She was enjoying herself immensely, having taken a long shower, eaten a pound of candy, and watched TV nonstop. She had not left the room.

She was twenty miles away, in a small town just off the interstate in the Virginia countryside where neither she nor I knew a soul. There was no way she could find drugs. I patted myself on the back again.

During halftime of the Duke-Carolina game, the cell phone on the plastic storage box next to the pizza squawked and startled me. A very pleasant female voice said, 'Hello, jailbird.'

It was Claire, without the edge.

'Hello,' I said, muting the television.

'You okay?'

'Just doing great. How about you?'

'Fine. I saw your smiling face in the paper this morning, and I was worried about you.' Claire read the Sunday paper only, so if she saw my little story, someone gave it to her. Probably the same hot-blooded doc who'd answered the phone the last time I'd called. Was she alone on Saturday night, like me?

'It was an experience,' I said, then told her the entire story, beginning with Gasko and ending with my release. She wanted to talk, and as the narrative plodded along I decided that she was indeed by herself, probably bored and maybe lonely. And perhaps there was a chance that she was really worried about me.

'How serious are the charges?' she asked.

'Grand larceny carries up to ten years,' I said gravely. I liked the prospect of her being concerned. 'But I'm not worried about that.'

'It's just a file, isn't it?'

'Yes, and it wasn't a theft.' Sure it was, but I was not yet prepared to admit that.

'Could you lose your license to practice?'

'Yes, if I'm convicted of a felony, it would be automatic.'

'That's awful, Mike. What would you do then?'

'Truthfully, I haven't thought about it. It's not going to happen.' I was being completely honest; I had not seriously thought about losing my law license. Perhaps it was an issue requiring consideration, but I had not found the time for it.

We politely inquired about each other's family, and I remembered to ask about her brother James and his Hodgkin's disease. His treatment was under way; the family was optimistic.

I thanked her for calling, and we promised to keep

in touch. When I laid the cell phone next to the pizza, I stared at the muted game and grudgingly admitted to myself that I missed her.

Ruby was showered and shined and wearing the fresh clothing Megan had given her yesterday. Her motel room was on the ground floor with the door facing the parking lot. She was waiting for me. She stepped into the sunlight and hugged me tightly. 'I'm clean!' she said with a huge smile. 'For twenty-four hours I'm clean!' We hugged again.

A couple in their sixties stepped from the room two doors down and stared at us. God knows what they were thinking.

We returned to the city and went to Naomi's, where Megan and her staff were waiting for the news. A small celebration erupted when Ruby made her announcement. Megan had told me that the biggest cheers were always for the first twenty-four hours.

It was Sunday, and a local pastor arrived to conduct a Bible study. The women gathered in the main room for hymns and prayer. Megan and I drank coffee in the garden and worked out the next twenty-four hours. In addition to prayer and worship, Ruby would get two heavy sessions of AA/NA. But our optimism was guarded. Megan lived in the midst of addiction, and she was convinced Ruby would slide as soon as she returned to the streets. She saw it every day.

I could afford the motel strategy for a few days, and I was willing to pay for it. But I would leave for Chicago at four that afternoon, to begin my search for Hector, and I wasn't sure how long I would be away. Ruby liked the motel, in fact she appeared to be quite fond of it.

We decided to take things one day at a time. Megan would drive Ruby to a suburban motel, one I would pay for, and deposit her there for Sunday night. She would retrieve her Monday morning, and we would then worry about what to do next.

Megan would also begin the task of trying to convince Ruby she had to leave the streets. Her first stop would be a detox center, then a transitional women's shelter for six months of structured living, job training, and rehab.

'Twenty-four hours is a big step,' she said. 'But there is still a mountain to climb.'

I left as soon as I could. She invited me to return for lunch. We could eat in her office, just the two of us, and discuss important matters. Her eyes were dancing and daring me to say yes. So I did.

Drake & Sweeney lawyers always flew first-class; they felt as if they deserved it. They stayed in four-star hotels, ate in swanky restaurants, but drew the line at limousines, which were deemed too extravagant. So they rented Lincolns. All travel expenses were billed to the clients, and since the clients were getting the best legal talent in the world, the clients shouldn't complain about the perks.

My seat on the flight to Chicago was in coach, booked at the last minute and therefore in the dreaded middle. The window seat was occupied by a hefty gentleman whose knees were the size of basketballs, and on the aisle was a smelly youngster of eighteen or so with jet-black hair, cut into a perfect Mohawk, and adorned in an amazing collection of black leather and pointed chrome. I squeezed myself together, closed my eyes for two hours, and tried not to think about the pompous asses sitting up there in first-class, where I once rode.

The trip was in direct violation of my bail agreement – I was not to leave the District without permission of the Judge. But Mordecai and I agreed that it was a minor violation, one that would be of no consequence as long as I returned to D.C.

From O'Hare, I took a cab to an inexpensive hotel downtown.

Sofia had been unable to find a new residential address for the Palmas. If I couldn't find Hector at the Drake & Sweeney office, then we were out of luck.

The chicago branch of Drake & Sweeney had one hundred and six lawyers, third highest after Washington and New York. The real estate section was disproportionately large, with eighteen lawyers, more than the Washington office. I assumed that was the reason Hector had been sent to Chicago – there was a place for him. There was plenty of work to do. I vaguely recalled some story of Drake & Sweeney absorbing a prosperous Chicago real estate firm early in my career.

I arrived at the Associated Life Building shortly after seven Monday morning. The day was gray and gloomy, with a vicious wind whipping across Lake Michigan. It was my third visit to Chicago, and the other two times it had been just as raw. I bought coffee to drink and a newspaper to hide behind, and I found a vantage point at a table in a corner of the ground floor's vast atrium. The escalators crisscrossed to the second and third levels where a dozen elevators stood waiting.

By seven-thirty the ground floor was crawling with busy people. At eight, after three cups of coffee, I was wired and expecting the man at any moment. The escalators were packed with hundreds of executives, lawyers, secretaries, all bundled in heavy coats and looking remarkably similar.

At eight-twenty, Hector Palma entered the atrium from the south side of the building, stepping hurriedly inside with a swarm of other commuters. He raked his

262

fingers through his wind-tossed hair and went straight for the escalators. As casually as possible, I walked to another escalator, and eased my way up the steps. I caught a glimpse of him as he turned a corner to wait for an elevator.

It was definitely Hector, and I decided not to press my luck. My assumptions were correct; he had been transferred out of Washington, in the middle of the night, and sent to the Chicago office where he could be monitored, and bribed with more money, and, if necessary, threatened.

I knew where he was, and I knew he wouldn't be leaving for the next eight to ten hours. From the second level of the atrium, with a splendid view of the lake, I phoned Megan. Ruby had survived the night; we were now at forty-eight hours and counting. I called Mordecai to report my finding.

According to last year's Drake & Sweeney handbook, there were three partners in the real estate section of the Chicago office. The building directory in the atrium listed all three on floor number fifty-one. I picked one of them at random: Dick Heile.

I rode the nine o'clock surge upward to the fifty-first floor, and stepped off the elevator into a familiar setting – marble, brass, walnut, recessed lighting, fine rugs.

As I walked casually toward the receptionist, I glanced around in search of rest rooms. I did not see any.

She was answering the phone with a headset. I frowned and tried to look as pained as possible.

'Yes sir,' she said with a bright smile between calls.

I gritted my teeth, sucked in air, said, 'Yes, I have a nine o'clock appointment with Dick Heile, but I'm afraid I'm about to be sick. It must've been something I ate. Can I use your rest room?' I clutched my stomach, folded my knees, and I must have convinced her that I was about to vomit on her desk.

The smile vanished as she jumped to her feet and began pointing. 'Down there, around the corner, to your right.'

I was already moving, bent at the waist as if I might blow up at any second. 'Thanks,' I managed to say.

'Can I get you something?' she asked.

I shook my head, too stricken to say anything else. Around the corner, I ducked into the men's rest room, where I locked myself in a stall, and waited.

At the rate her phone was ringing, she would be too busy to worry about me. I was dressed like a big-firm lawyer, so I did not appear to be suspicious. After ten minutes, I walked out of the men's room, and started down the hall away from the receptionist. At the first empty desk, I grabbed some papers that were stapled together and scribbled as I walked, as if I had important business. My eyes darted in every direction – names on doors, names on desks, secretaries too busy to look up, lawyers with gray hair in shirtsleeves, young lawyers on the phone with their doors cracked, typists pecking away with dictation.

It was so familiar!

Hector had his own office, a small room with no name anywhere in sight. I saw him through his half-open door, and I immediately burst in and slammed it behind me.

He jerked back in his chair with both palms up, as if he were facing a gun. 'What the hell!' he said.

'Hello, Hector.'

No gun, no assault, just a bad memory. His palms fell to his desk, and he actually smiled. 'What the hell?' he said again.

'So how's Chicago?' I asked, resting my butt on the edge of his desk.

'What are you doing here?' he asked, in disbelief.

'I could ask you the same question.'

'I'm working,' he said, scratching his head. Five hundred feet above the street, tucked away in his nondescript little room with no windows, insulated by layers of more important people, Hector had been found by the only person he was running from. 'How'd you find me?' he asked.

'It was very easy, Hector. I'm a street lawyer now, savvy and smart. You run again, I'll find you again.'

'I'm not running anymore,' he said, looking away. It was not entirely for my benefit.

'We're filing suit tomorrow,' I said. 'The defendants will be RiverOaks, TAG, and Drake & Sweeney. There's no place for you to hide.'

'Who are the plaintiffs?'

'Lontae Burton and family. Later, we'll add the other evictees, when we find all of them.'

He closed his eyes and pinched the bridge of his nose.

'You remember Lontae, don't you, Hector? She was the young mother who fought with the cops when you were evicting everyone. You saw it all, and you felt guilty because you knew the truth, you knew she was paying rent to Gantry. You put it all in your memo, the one dated January twenty-seventh, and you made sure the memo was properly indexed into the file. You did this because you knew Braden Chance would remove it at some point. And he did. And that's why I'm here, Hector. I want a copy of the memo. I have the rest of the file, and it's about to be exposed. Now I want the memo.'

'What makes you think I have a copy?'

'Because you're too smart not to copy it. You knew Chance would remove the original to cover his ass. But now he is about to be exposed. Don't go down with him.'

'Then where do I go?'

'Nowhere,' I said. 'You have nowhere to go.'

He knew it. Since he knew the truth about the eviction, he would be forced to testify at some point, and in some manner. His testimony would sink Drake & Sweeney, and he would be terminated. It was a course of events Mordecai and I had talked about. We had a few crumbs to offer.

'If you give me the memo,' I said, 'I will not tell where it came from. And I will not call you as a witness unless I am absolutely forced to.'

He was shaking his head. 'I could lie, you know,' he said.

'Sure you could. But you won't because you'll get nailed. It's easy to prove your memo was logged into the file, then removed. You can't deny writing it. Then we have the testimony of the people you evicted. They'll make great witnesses before an all-black jury in D.C. And we've talked to the guard who was with you on January twenty-seventh.'

Every punch landed flush on the jaw, and Hector was on the ropes. Actually, we had been unable to find the guard; the file did not give his name.

'Forget lying,' I said. 'It will only make things worse.'

Hector was too honest to lie. He was, after all, the person who had slipped me the list of the evictees, and the keys with which to steal the file. He had a soul and a conscience, and he couldn't be happy hiding in Chicago, running from his past.

'Has Chance told them the truth?' I asked.

'I don't know,' he said. 'I doubt it. That would take guts, and Chance is a coward. . . They'll fire me, you know.'

'Maybe, but you'll have a beautiful lawsuit against them. I'll handle it for you. We'll sue them again, and I won't charge you a dime.'

There was a knock on his door. It scared both of us;

266

our conversation had taken us back in time. 'Yes,' he said, and a secretary entered.

'Mr. Peck is waiting,' she said, sizing me up.

'I'll be there in one minute,' Hector said, and she slowly backtracked through the door, leaving it open.

'I have to go,' he said.

'I'm not leaving without a copy of the memo.'

'Meet me at noon by the water fountain in front of the building.'

'I'll be there.'

I winked at the receptionist as I passed through the foyer. 'Thanks,' I said. 'I'm much better.'

'You're welcome,' she said.

From the fountain we went west on Grand Avenue to a crowded Jewish deli. As we waited in line to order a sandwich, Hector handed me an envelope. 'I have four children,' he said. 'Please protect me.'

I took the envelope, and was about to say something when he stepped backward and got lost in the crowd. I saw him squeeze through the door and go past the deli, the flaps of his overcoat around his ears, almost running to get away from me.

I forgot about lunch. I walked four blocks to the hotel, checked out, and threw my things into a cab. Sitting low in the backseat, doors locked, cabbie half-asleep, no one in the world knowing where I was at that moment, I opened the envelope.

The memo was in the typical Drake & Sweeney format, prepared on Hector's PC with the client code, file number, and date in tiny print along the bottom left. It was dated January 27, sent to Braden Chance from Hector Palma, regarding the RiverOaks/TAG eviction, Florida warehouse property. On that day, Hector had gone to the warehouse with an armed guard, Jeff Mackle of Rock Creek Security, arriving at 9:15 A.M. and leaving at 12:30. The warehouse had three levels, and after first noticing squatters on the ground floor, Hector went to the second level, where there was no sign of habitation. On the third level, he saw litter, old clothing, and the remnants of a campfire someone had used many months earlier.

On the west end of the ground level, he found eleven temporary apartments, all hastily assembled from plywood and Sheetrock, unpainted, but obviously built by the same person, at about the same time, with some effort at order. Each apartment was roughly the same size, judging from the outside; Hector couldn't obtain entry to any of them. Every door was the same, a light, hollow, synthetic material, probably plastic, with a doorknob and a dead bolt.

The bathroom was well used and filthy. There had been no recent improvements to it.

Hector encountered a man who identified himself only as Herman, and Herman had no interest in talking. Hector asked how much rent was being charged for the apartments, and Herman said none; said that he was squatting. The sight of an armed guard in a uniform had a chilling effect on the conversation.

On the east end of the building, ten units of similar design and construction were found. A crying child drew Hector to one of the doors, and he asked the guard to stand back in the shadows. A young mother answered his knock; she held a baby, three other children swarmed around her legs. Hector informed her that he was with a law firm, that the building had been sold, and that she would be asked to leave in a few days. She at first said she was squatting, then quickly went on the attack. It was her apartment. She rented it from a man named Johnny, who came around on the fifteenth of each month to collect a hundred dollars. Nothing in writing. She had no idea who owned the building; Johnny was her only contact.

She had been there for three months, couldn't leave because there was no place to go. She worked twenty hours a week at a grocery store.

Hector told her to pack her things and get ready to move. The building would be leveled in ten days. She became frantic. Hector tried to provoke her further. He asked if she had any proof that she was paying rent. She found her purse, under the bed, and handed him a scrap of paper, a tape from a grocery store cash register. On the back someone had scrawled: Recd frm Lontae Burton, Jan 15, $100 rent.

The memo was two pages long. But there was a third page attached to it, a copy of the scarcely readable receipt. Hector had taken it from her, copied it, and attached the original to the memo. The writing was hurried, the spelling flawed, the copying blurred, but it was stunning. I must have made some ecstatic noise because the cabdriver jerked his head and examined me in the mirror.

The memo was a straightforward description of what Hector saw, said, and heard. There were no conclusions, no caveats to his higher-ups. Give them enough rope, he must have said to himself, and see if they'll hang themselves. He was a lowly paralegal, in no position to give advice, or offer opinions, or stand in the way of a deal.

At O'Hare, I faxed it to Mordecai. If my plane crashed, or if I got mugged and someone stole it, I wanted a copy tucked away deep in the files of the 14th Street Legal Clinic.

TWENTY-NINE

Since Lontae Burton's father was a person unknown to us, and probably unknown to the world, and since her mother and all siblings were behind bars, we made the tactical decision to bypass the family and use a trustee as a client. While I was in Chicago Monday morning, Mordecai appeared before a judge in the D.C. Family Court and asked for a temporary trustee to serve as guardian of the estates of Lontae Burton and each of her children. It was a routine matter done in private. The Judge was an acquaintance of Mordecai's. The petition was approved in minutes, and we had ourselves a new client. Her name was Wilma Phelan, a social worker Mordecai knew. Her role in the litigation would be minor, and she would be entitled to a very small fee in the event we recovered anything.

The Cohen Trust may have been ill-managed from a financial standpoint, but it had rules and bylaws covering every conceivable aspect of a nonprofit legal clinic. Leonard Cohen had been a lawyer, obviously one with an appetite for detail. Though discouraged and frowned upon, it was permissible for the clinic to handle an injury or wrongful death case on a contingency-fee basis. But the fee was capped at twenty percent of the recovery, as opposed to the standard one third. Some trial lawyers customarily took forty percent.

Of the twenty percent contingency fee, the clinic could keep half; the other ten percent went to the trust. In fourteen years, Mordecai had handled two cases on a contingency basis. The first he'd lost with a bad jury. The second involved a homeless woman hit by a city bus. He'd settled it for one hundred thousand dollars, netting the clinic a grand total of ten thousand dollars, from which he purchased new phones and word processors.

The Judge reluctantly approved our contract at twenty percent. And we were ready to sue.

Tip-off was at seven thirty-five – Georgetown versus Syracuse. Mordecai somehow squeezed two tickets. My flight arrived at National on time at six-twenty, and thirty minutes later I met Mordecai at the east entrance of the U.S. Air Arena in Landover. We were joined by almost twenty thousand other fans. He handed me a ticket, then pulled from his coat pocket a thick, unopened envelope, sent by registered mail to my attention at the clinic. It was from the D.C. bar.

'It came today,' he said, knowing exactly what it contained. 'I'll meet you at our seats.' He disappeared into a crowd of students.

I ripped it open and found a spot outside with enough light to read. My friends at Drake & Sweeney were unloading everything they had.

It was a formal complaint filed with the Court of Appeals accusing me of unethical behavior. The allegations ran for three pages, but could have been adequately captured in one good paragraph. I'd stolen a file. I'd breached confidentiality. I was a bad boy who should be either (1) disbarred permanently, or (2) suspended for many years, and/or (3) publicly reprimanded. And since the file was still missing, the matter was urgent, and therefore the inquiry and procedure should be expedited.

There were notices, forms, other papers I hardly glanced at. It was a shock, and I leaned on a wall to steady myself and contemplate matters. Sure, I had thought about a bar proceeding. It would have been unrealistic to think the firm would not pursue all avenues to retrieve the file. But I thought the arrest might appease them for a while.

Evidently not. They wanted blood. It was a typical big-firm, hardball, take-no-prisoners strategy, and I understood it perfectly. What they didn't know was that at nine the following morning, I would have the pleasure of suing them for ten million dollars for the wrongful deaths of the Burtons.

According to my assessment, there was nothing else they could do to me. No more warrants. No more registered letters. All issues were on the table, all lines drawn. In a small way, it was a relief to be holding the papers.

And it was also frightening. Since I'd started law school ten years earlier, I had never seriously considered work in another field. What would I do without a law license?

But then, Sofia didn't have one and she was my equal.

Mordecai met me inside at the portal leading to our seats. I gave him a brief summary of the bar petition. He offered me his condolences.

While the game promised to be tense and exciting, basketball was not our top priority. Jeff Mackle was a part-time gun at Rock Creek Security, and he also worked events at the arena. Sofia had tracked him down during the day. We figured he would be one of a hundred uniformed guards loitering around the building, watching the game for free and gazing at coeds.

We had no idea if he was old, young, white, black,

fat, or lean, but the security guards wore small nameplates above their left breast pockets. We walked the aisles and portals until almost halftime before Mordecai found him, hitting on a cute ticket clerk at Gate D, a spot I had inspected twice.

Mackle was large, white, plain-faced, and about my age. His neck and biceps were enormous, his chest thick and bulging. The legal team huddled briefly and decided it would be best if I approached him.

With one of my business cards between my fingers, I walked casually up to him and introduced myself. 'Mr. Mackle, I'm Michael Brock, Attorney.'

He gave me the look one normally gets with such a greeting and took the card without comment. I had interrupted his flirting with the ticket clerk.

'Could I ask you a few questions?' I said in my best homicide detective impersonation.

'You can ask. I may not answer.' He winked at the ticket clerk.

'Have you ever done any security work for Drake & Sweeney, a big law firm in the District?'

'Maybe.'

'Ever help them with any evictions?'

I hit a nerve. His face hardened instantly, and the conversation was practically over. 'Don't think so,' he said, glancing away.

'Are you sure?'

'No. The answer is no.'

'You didn't help the firm evict a warehouse full of squatters on February fourth?'

He shook his head, jaw clenched, eyes narrow. Someone from Drake & Sweeney had already visited Mr. Mackle. Or, more than likely, the firm had threatened his employer.

At any rate, Mackle was stonefaced. The ticket clerk was preoccupied with her nails. I was shut out.

'Sooner or later you'll have to answer my questions,' I said.

The muscles in his jaw flinched, but he had no response. I was not inclined to push harder. He was rough around the edges, the type who could erupt with a flurry of fists and lay waste to a humble street lawyer. I had been wounded enough in the past two weeks.

I watched ten minutes of the second half, then left with spasms in my back, aftereffects of the car wreck.

The motel was another new one on the northern fringe of Bethesda. Also forty bucks a night, and after three nights I couldn't afford any more lockdown therapy for Ruby. Megan was of the opinion it was time for her to return home. If she was going to stay sober, the real test would come on the streets.

At seven-thirty Tuesday morning, I knocked on her door on the second floor. Room 220, per Megan's instructions. There was no answer. I knocked again and again, and tried the knob. It was locked. I ran to the lobby and asked the receptionist to call the room. Again, no answer. No one had checked out. Nothing unusual had been reported.

An assistant manager was summoned, and I convinced her that there was an emergency. She called a security guard, and the three of us went to the room. Along the way, I explained what we were doing with Ruby, and why the room wasn't in her name. The assistant manager didn't like the idea of using her nice motel to detox crackheads.

The room was empty. The bed was meticulous; no sign of use during the night. Not a single item was out of place, and nothing of hers had been left behind.

I thanked them and left. The motel was at least ten miles from our office. I called Megan to alert her, then fought my way into the city with a million other commuters. At eight-fifteen, sitting in stalled traffic, I called the office and asked Sofia if Ruby had been seen. She had not.

The lawsuit was brief and to the point. Wilma Phelan, trustee for the estates of Lontae Burton and her children, was suing RiverOaks, Drake & Sweeney, and TAG, Inc., for conspiring to commit a wrongful eviction. The logic was simple; the causal connection obvious. Our clients would not have been living in their car had they not been thrown out of their apartment. And they wouldn't have died had they not been living in their car. It was a lovely theory of liability, one made even more attractive because of its simplicity. Any jury in the country could follow the rationale.

The negligence and/or intentional acts of the defendants caused the deaths, which were foreseeable. Bad things happened to those living on the streets, especially single mothers with little children. Toss them out of their homes wrongfully and you pay the price if they get hurt.

We had briefly considered a separate lawsuit for Mister's death. He too had been illegally evicted, but his death could not be considered foreseeable. Taking hostages and getting shot in the process were not a reasonable chain of events for one civilly wronged. Also, he had little jury appeal. We put Mister to rest, permanently.

Drake & Sweeney would immediately ask the Judge to require me to hand over the file. The Judge might very well make me do it, and that would be an admission of guilt. It could also cost me my license to practice law. Further, any evidence derived from anything in the stolen file could be excluded.

Mordecai and I reviewed the final draft Tuesday, and he again asked me if I wanted to proceed. To protect me, he was willing to drop the lawsuit entirely. We had talked about that several times. We even had a strategy whereby we would drop the Burton suit, negotiate a truce with Drake & Sweeney to clear my name, wait a year for tempers to cool, then sneak the case to a buddy of his on the other side of town. It was a bad strategy, one we ditched almost as soon as we thought of it.

He signed the pleadings, and we left for the courthouse. He drove, and I read the lawsuit again, the pages growing heavier the farther we went.

Negotiation would be the key. The exposure would humiliate Drake & Sweeney, a firm with immense pride and ego, and built on credibility, client service, trustworthiness. I knew the mindset, the personality, the cult of great lawyers who did no wrong. I knew the paranoia of being perceived as bad, in any way. There was guilt for making so much money, and a corresponding desire to appear compassionate for the less fortunate.

Drake & Sweeney was wrong, though I suspected the firm had no idea how very wrong it was. I imagined Braden Chance was cowering behind his locked door praying fervently that the hour would pass.

But I was wrong too. Perhaps we could meet in the middle somewhere, and cut a deal. If not, then Mordecai Green would have the pleasure of presenting the Burton case to a friendly jury one day soon, and asking them for big bucks. And the firm would have the pleasure of pushing my grand larceny case to the limit; to a point I didn't care to think about.

The Burton case would never go to trial. I could still think like a Drake & Sweeney lawyer. The idea of facing a D.C. jury would terrify them. The initial embarrassment would have them scrambling for ways to cut their losses.

Tim Claussen, a college pal of Abraham's, was a reporter for the *Post*. He was waiting outside the clerk's office, and we gave him a copy of the lawsuit. He read it while Mordecai filed the original, then asked us questions, which we were more than happy to answer, but off the record.

The Burton tragedy was fast becoming a political and social hot potato in the District. Blame was being passed around with dizzying speed. Every department head in the city blamed another one. The city council blamed the mayor, who blamed the council while also blaming Congress. Some right-wingers in the House had weighed in long enough to blame the mayor, the council, and the entire city.

The idea of pinning the whole thing on a bunch of rich white lawyers made for an astonishing story. Claussen – callous, caustic, jaded by years in journalism – couldn't suppress his enthusiasm.

The ambushing of Drake & Sweeney by the press did not bother me in the least. The firm had established the rules the prior week when it tipped a reporter that I had been arrested. I could see Rafter and his little band of litigators happily agreeing around the conference table that, yes! it made perfect sense to alert the media about my arrest; and not only that but to slip them a nice photo of the criminal. It would embarrass me, humiliate me, make me sorry, force me to cough up the file and do whatever they wanted.

I knew the mentality, knew how the game was played.

I had no problem helping the reporter.

THIRTY

Intake at CCNV, alone, and two hours late. The clients were sitting patiently on the dirty floor of the lobby, some nodding off, some reading newspapers. Ernie with the keys was not pleased with my tardiness; he had a schedule of his own. He opened the intake room and handed me a clipboard with the names of thirteen prospective clients. I called the first one.

I was amazed at how far I'd come in a week. I had walked into the building a few minutes earlier without the fear of being shot. I had waited for Ernie in the lobby without thinking of being white. I listened to my clients patiently, but efficiently, because I knew what to do. I even looked the part; my beard was more than a week old; my hair was slightly over the ears and showing the first signs of unkemptness; my khakis were wrinkled; my navy blazer was rumpled; my tie was loosened just so. The Nikes were still stylish but well worn. A pair of horn-rimmed glasses, and I would have been the perfect public interest lawyer.

Not that the clients cared. They wanted someone to listen to them, and that was my job. The list grew to seventeen, and I spent four hours counseling. I forgot about the coming battle with Drake & Sweeney. I forgot about Claire, though, sadly, I was finding that easier to do. I even forgot about Hector Palma and my trip to Chicago.

But I couldn't forget about Ruby Simon. I somehow managed to connect each new client to her. I wasn't worried about her safety; she had survived on the streets far longer than I could have. But why would she leave a clean motel room with a television and a shower, and strike out through the city to find her abandoned car?

She was an addict, and that was the plain and unavoidable answer. Crack was a magnet, pulling her back to the streets.

If I couldn't keep her locked away in suburban motels for three nights, then how was I supposed to help her get clean?

The decision was not mine to make.

The routine of the late afternoon was shattered by a phone call from my older brother Warner. He was in town, on business, unexpectedly, would've called sooner but couldn't find my new number, and where could we meet for dinner? He was paying, he said before I could answer, and he'd heard about a great new place called Danny O's where a friend had eaten just a week earlier – fantastic food! I hadn't thought about an expensive meal in a long time.

Danny O's was fine with me. It was trendy, loud, overpriced, sadly typical.

I stared at the phone long after our conversation was over. I did not want to see Warner, because I did not want to listen to Warner. He was not in town on business, though that happened about once a year. I was pretty sure my parents had sent him. They were grieving down in Memphis, heartbroken over another divorce, saddened by my sudden fall from the ladder. Someone had to check on me. It was always Warner.

We met in the crowded bar at Danny O's. Before we could shake hands or embrace, he took a step backward to inspect the new image. Beard, hair, khakis, everything.

'A real radical,' he said, with an equal mixture of humor and sarcasm.

'It's good to see you,' I said, trying to ignore his theatrics.

'You look thin,' he said.

'You don't.'

He patted his stomach as if a few extra pounds had sneaked on board during the day. 'I'll lose it.' He was thirty-eight, nice-looking, still very vain about his appearance. The mere fact that I had commented on the extra weight would drive him to lose it within a month.

Warner had been single for three years. Women were very important to him. There had been allegations of adultery during his divorce, but from both sides.

'You look great,' I said. And he did. Tailored suit and shirt. Expensive tie. I had a closet full of the stuff.

'You too. Is this the way you dress for work now?'

'For the most part. Sometimes I ditch the tie.'

We ordered Heinekens and sipped them in the crowd.

'How's Claire?' he asked. The preliminaries were out of the way.

'I suppose she's fine. We filed for divorce, uncontested. I've moved out.'

'Is she happy?'

'I think she was relieved to get rid of me. I'd say Claire is happier today than she was a month ago.'

'Has she found someone else?'

'I don't think so,' I said. I had to be careful because most, if not all, of our conversation would be repeated to my parents, especially any scandalous reason for the divorce. They would like to blame Claire, and if they believed she'd been caught screwing around, then the divorce would seem logical.

'Have you?' he asked.

'Nope. I've kept my pants on.'

'So why the divorce?'

'Lots of reasons. I'd rather not rehash them.'

That was not what he wanted. His had been a nasty split, with both parties fighting for custody of the kids. He had shared the details with me, often to the point of being boring. Now he wanted the same in return.

'You woke up one day, and decided to get a divorce?'

'You've been through it, Warner. It's not that simple.'

The maître d' led us deep into the restaurant. We passed a table where Wayne Umstead was sitting with two men I did not recognize. Umstead had been a fellow hostage, the one Mister had sent to the door to fetch the food, the one who'd barely missed the sniper's bullet. He didn't see me.

A copy of the lawsuit had been served on Arthur Jacobs, chairman of the executive committee, at 11 A.M., while I was at the CCNV. Umstead was not a partner, so I wondered if he even knew about the lawsuit.

Of course he did. In hurried meetings throughout the afternoon, the news had been dropped like a bomb. Defenses had to be prepared; marching orders given; wagons circled. Not a word to anyone outside the firm. On the surface, the lawsuit would be ignored.

Fortunately, our table could not be seen from Umstead's. I glanced around to make sure no other bad guys were in the restaurant. Warner ordered a martini for both of us, but I quickly begged off. Just water for me.

With Warner, everything was at full throttle. Work, play, food, drink, women, even books and old movies.

281

He had almost frozen to death in a blizzard on a Peruvian mountain, and he'd been bitten by a deadly water snake while scuba diving in Australia. His post-divorce adjustment phase had been remarkably easy, primarily because Warner loved to travel and hang-glide and climb mountains and wrestle sharks and chase women on a global scale.

As a partner in a large Atlanta firm, he made plenty of money. And he spent a lot of it. The dinner was about money.

'Water?' he said in disgust. 'Come on. Have a drink.'

'No,' I protested. Warner would go from martinis to wine. We would leave the restaurant late, and he would be up at four fiddling with his laptop, shaking off the slight hangover as just another part of the day.

'Candy ass,' he mumbled. I browsed the menu. He examined every skirt.

His drink arrived and we ordered. 'Tell me about your work,' he said, trying desperately to give the impression that he was interested.

'Why?'

'Because it must be fascinating.'

'Why do you say that?'

'You walked away from a fortune. There must be a damned good reason.'

'There are reasons, and they're good enough for me.'

Warner had planned the meeting. There was a purpose, a goal, a destination, and an outline of what he would say to get him there. I wasn't sure where he was headed.

'I was arrested last week,' I said, diverting him. It was enough of a shock to be successful.

'You what?'

I told him the story, stretching it out with every detail because I was in control of the conversation. He was critical of my thievery, but I didn't try to defend it. The file itself was another complicated issue, one neither of us wanted to explore.

'So the Drake & Sweeney bridge has been burned?' he asked as we ate.

'Permanently.'

'How long do you plan to be a public interest lawyer?'

'I've just started. I really hadn't thought about the end. Why?'

'How long can you work for nothing?'

'As long as I can survive.'

'So survival is the standard?'

'For now. What's your standard?' It was a ridiculous question.

'Money. How much I make; how much I spend; how much I can stash away somewhere and watch it grow so that one day I'll have a shitpot full of it and not have to worry about anything.'

I had heard this before. Unabashed greed was to be admired. It was a slightly cruder version of what we'd been taught as children. Work hard and make plenty, and somehow society as a whole would benefit.

He was daring me to be critical, and it was not a fight I wanted. It was a fight with no winners; only an ugly draw.

'How much do you have?' I asked. As a greedy bastard, Warner was proud of his wealth.

'When I'm forty I'll have a million bucks buried in mutual funds. When I'm forty-five, it'll be three million. When I'm fifty, it'll be ten. And that's when I'm walking out the door.'

We knew those figures by heart. Big law firms were the same everywhere.

'What about you?' he asked as he whittled on free-range chicken.

'Well, let's see. I'm thirty-two, got a net worth of

five thousand bucks, give or take. When I'm thirty-five, if I work hard and save money, it should be around ten thousand. By the time I'm fifty, I should have about twenty thousand buried in mutual funds.'

'That's something to look forward to. Eighteen years of living in poverty.'

'You know nothing about poverty.'

'Maybe I do. For people like us, poverty is a cheap apartment, a used car with dents and dings, bad clothing, no money to travel and play and see the world, no money to save or invest, no retirement, no safety net, nothing.'

'Perfect. You just proved my point. You don't know a damned thing about poverty. How much will you make this year?'

'Nine hundred thousand.'

'I'll make thirty. What would you do if someone forced you to work for thirty thousand bucks?'

'Kill myself.'

'I believe that. I truly believe you would take a gun and blow your brains out before you would work for thirty thousand bucks.'

'You're wrong. I'd take pills.'

'Coward.'

'There's no way I could work that cheap.'

'Oh, you could work that cheap, but you couldn't live that cheap.'

'Same thing.'

'That's where you and I are different,' I said.

'Damned right we're different. But how did we become different, Michael? A month ago you were like me. Now look at you – silly whiskers and faded clothes, all this bullshit about serving people and saving humanity. Where'd you go wrong?'

I took a deep breath and enjoyed the humor of his question. He relaxed too. We were too civilized to fight in public.

'You're a dumb-ass, you know,' he said, leaning low. 'You were on the fast track for a partnership. You're bright and talented, single, no kids. You'd be making a million bucks a year at the age of thirty-five. You can do the math.'

'It's already done, Warner. I've lost my love for money. It's the curse of the devil.'

'How original. Let me ask you something. What will you do if you wake up one day and you're, let's say, sixty years old. You're tired of saving the world because it can't be saved. You don't have a pot to piss in, not a dime, no firm, no partners, no wife making big bucks as a brain surgeon, nobody to catch you. What will you do?'

'Well, I've thought about that, and I figure I'll have this big brother who's filthy rich. So I'll give you a call.'

'What if I'm dead?'

'Put me in your will. The prodigal brother.'

We became interested in our food, and the conversation waned. Warner was arrogant enough to think that a blunt confrontation would snap me back to my senses. A few sharp insights from him on the consequences of my missteps, and I would ditch the poverty act and get a real job. 'I'll talk to him,' I could hear him say to my parents.

He had a few jabs left. He asked what the benefit package was at the 14th Street Legal Clinic. Quite lean, I told him. What about a retirement plan? None that I knew of. He embraced the opinion that I should spend only a couple of years saving souls before returning to the real world. I thanked him. And he offered the splendid advice that perhaps I should search for a like-minded woman, but with money, and marry her.

We said good-bye on the sidewalk in front of the restaurant. I assured him I knew what I was doing, that I would be fine, and that his report to our parents should be optimistic. 'Don't worry them, Warner. Tell them everything is wonderful here.'

'Call me if you get hungry,' he said in an effort at humor.

I waved him off and walked away.

The pylon grill was an all-night coffee shop in Foggy Bottom, near George Washington University. It was known as a hangout for insomniacs and news addicts. The earliest edition of the *Post* arrived each night just before twelve, and the place was as busy as a good deli during lunch. I bought a paper and sat at the bar, which was an odd sight because every person there was buried in the news. I was struck by how quiet the Pylon was. The *Post* had just arrived, minutes before me, and thirty people were poring over it as if a war had been declared.

The story was a natural for the *Post*. It began on page one, under a bold headline, and was continued on page ten where the photos were – a photo of Lontae taken from the placards at the rally for justice, one of Mordecai when he was ten years younger, and a set of three, which no doubt would humiliate the bluebloods at Drake & Sweeney. Arthur Jacobs was in the center, a mug shot of Tillman Gantry was on the left, and on the right was a mug shot of DeVon Hardy, who was linked to the story only because he'd been evicted and got himself killed in a newsworthy fashion.

Arthur Jacobs and two felons, two African-American criminals with little numbers across their chests, lined up as equals on page ten of the *Post*.

I could see them huddled in their offices and conference rooms, doors locked, phones unplugged, meetings canceled. They would plan their responses, devise a hundred different strategies, call in their public relations people. It would be their darkest hour.

The fax wars would begin early. Copies of the trio would be sent to law offices coast to coast, and every big firm in the world of corporate law would have a laugh.

Gantry looked extremely menacing, and it scared me to think we had picked a fight with him.

And then there was the photo of me, the same one the paper used the Saturday before when it announced my arrest. I was described as the link between the firm and Lontae Burton, though the reporter had no way of knowing I'd actually met her.

The story was long and thorough. It began with the eviction, and all the participants therein, including Hardy, who surfaced seven days later at the offices of Drake & Sweeney where he took hostages, one of whom was me. From me it went to Mordecai, then to the deaths of the Burtons. It mentioned my arrest, though I had been careful to tell the reporter little about the disputed file.

He was true to his word – we were never referred to by name, only as informed sources. I couldn't have written it better myself.

Not a word from any of the defendants. It appeared as if the reporter made little or no effort to contact them.

THIRTY-ONE

Warner called me at 5 A.M. 'Are you awake?' he asked. He was in his hotel suite, hyper, bouncing off the walls with a hundred comments and questions about the lawsuit. He'd seen the paper.

Trying to stay warm in my sleeping bag, I listened as he told me exactly how to proceed with the case. Warner was a litigator, a very good one, and the jury appeal of the Burton case was more than he could stand. We hadn't asked for enough in damages – ten million wouldn't cut it. The right jury, and the sky was the limit. Oh, how he'd love to try it himself. And what about Mordecai? Was he a trial lawyer?

And the fee? Surely we had a forty percent contract. There might be hope for me after all.

'Ten percent,' I said, still in the darkness.

'What! Ten percent! Are you out of your mind?'

'We're a nonprofit firm,' I tried to explain, but he wasn't listening. He cursed me for not being greedier.

The file was a huge problem, he said, as if we had not thought about it. 'Can you prove your case without the file?'

'Yes.'

He howled with laughter at the sight of old man Jacobs sitting there in the paper with a convict on each side. His flight to Atlanta left in two hours. He'd be at his desk by nine. He couldn't wait to pass around the

288

photos. He would start faxing them to the West Coast immediately.

He hung up in the middle of a sentence.

I'd slept for three hours. I turned a few times, but further sleep escaped me. There had been too many changes in my life to rest comfortably.

I showered and left, drank coffee with the Pakistanis until sunrise, then bought cookies for Ruby.

There were two strange cars parked at the corner of Fourteenth and Q, next to our office. I drove by slowly at seven-thirty, and my instincts told me to keep going. Ruby was not sitting on the front steps.

If Tillman Gantry thought violence would somehow help his defense of the lawsuit, he wouldn't hesitate to use it. Mordecai had cautioned me, though no warning was necessary. I called him at home and told him what I had seen. He would arrive at eight-thirty, and we agreed to meet then. He would warn Sofia. Abraham was out of town.

For two weeks my primary focus had been on the lawsuit. There had been other significant distractions – Claire, moving out, learning the ropes of a new career – but the case against RiverOaks and my old firm was never far from my mind. There was a prefiling frenzy with any large case, then a deep breath and a pleasant calmness after the bomb hit and the dust settled.

Gantry didn't kill us the day after we sued him and his two co-defendants. The office was quite normal. The phones were no busier than usual. The foot traffic was the same. With the lawsuit temporarily set aside, my other cases were easier to concentrate on.

I could only imagine the panic in the marbled halls of Drake & Sweeney. There would be no smiles, no gossip by the coffeepot, no jokes or sports talk in the hallways. A funeral parlor would be rowdier.

In antitrust, those who knew me best would be especially somber. Polly would be stoic, detached, and forever efficient. Rudolph wouldn't leave his office except to huddle with the higher-ups.

The only sad aspect of slandering four hundred lawyers was the inescapable reality that almost all of them were not only innocent of wrongdoing but completely ignorant of the facts. No one cared what happened in real estate. Few people knew Braden Chance. I was there seven years before I met the man, and then it was only because I went looking for him. I felt sorry for the innocent ones – the old-timers who'd built a great firm and trained us well; the guys in my class who would carry on the tradition of excellence; the rookies who had awakened to the news that their esteemed employer was somehow responsible for wrongful deaths.

But I felt no sympathy for Braden Chance and Arthur Jacobs and Donald Rafter. They had chosen to go for my jugular. Let them sweat.

Megan took a break from the rigors of keeping order in a house filled with eighty homeless women, and we went for a short drive through Northwest. She had no idea where Ruby lived, and we didn't really expect to find her. It was, however, a good reason to spend a few minutes together.

'This is not unusual,' she said, trying to reassure me. 'As a rule, homeless people are unpredictable, especially the addicts.'

'You've seen it before?'

'I've seen everything. You learn to stay level. When a client kicks the habit, finds a job, gets an apartment, you say a little prayer of thanks. But you don't get excited, because another Ruby will come along and break your heart. There are more valleys than mountains.'

'How do you keep from being depressed?'

'You draw strength from the clients. They are remarkable people. Most were born without a prayer or a chance, yet they survive. They trip and fall, but they get up and keep trying.'

Three blocks from the clinic, we passed a mechanic's garage with a collection of wrecked vehicles behind it. A large, toothy dog with a chain around its neck guarded the front. I had not planned on poking around rusty old cars, and the dog made the decision to keep going an easier one. We figured she lived in an area between the clinic on Fourteenth and Naomi's on Tenth near L, roughly from Logan Circle to Mount Vernon Square.

'But you never know,' she said. 'I'm constantly amazed at how mobile these people are. They have plenty of time, and some will walk for miles.'

We observed the street people. Every beggar came under our scrutiny as we drove slowly by. We walked through parks, looking at the homeless, dropping coins in their cups, hoping we would see someone we knew. No luck.

I left Megan at Naomi's, and promised to call later in the afternoon. Ruby had become a wonderful excuse to keep in touch.

The congressman was a five-termer from Indiana, a Republican named Burkholder who had an apartment in Virginia but liked to jog in the early evenings around Capitol Hill. His staff informed the media that he showered and changed in one of the seldom-used gyms Congress built for itself in the basement of a House office building.

As a member of the House, Burkholder was one of 435; thus virtually unknown even though he'd been in Washington ten years. He was mildly ambitious, squeaky clean, a health nut, forty-one years old. He served on Agriculture and chaired a sub-committee of Ways and Means.

Burkholder was shot early Wednesday evening near Union Station as he jogged alone. He was wearing a sweat suit – no wallet, no cash, no pockets with which to carry anything valuable. There appeared to be no motive. He encountered a street person in some manner, perhaps a collision or a bump or a harsh word given or received, and two shots were fired. One missed the congressman, the other struck him in the upper left arm, then traveled into his shoulder and stopped very near his neck.

The shooting occurred not long after dark, on a sidewalk next to a street filled with late commuters. It was witnessed by four people, all of whom described the assailant as a male black homeless-looking type, almost a generic description. He vanished into the night, and by the time the first commuter could stop, leave his car, and rush to the aid of Burkholder, the man with the gun was long gone.

The congressman was rushed to the hospital at George Washington, where the bullet was removed during a two-hour surgery, and he was pronounced stable.

It had been many years since a member of Congress had been shot in Washington. Several had been mugged, but with no permanent damage. The muggings typically provided the victims with wonderful pulpits to rail against crime and the lack of values and the general decline of everything; all blame, of course, being laid at the feet of the opposing party.

Burkholder wasn't able to rail when I saw the story at eleven. I'd been napping in my chair, reading and watching boxing. It was a slow news day in the District, slow until Burkholder got shot. The news anchorperson breathlessly announced the event, giving the basics with a nice photo of the congressman in the background, then went Live! to the hospital where a reporter stood shivering in the cold outside the ER entrance, a door Burkholder had passed through four hours earlier. But there was an ambulance in the background, and bright lights, and since she could not produce blood or a corpse for the viewers, she had to make it as sensational as possible.

The surgery went well, she reported. Burkholder was stable and resting. The doctors had released a statement which said basically nothing. Earlier, several of his colleagues had rushed to the hospital, and somehow she had been able to coerce them into appearing before the camera. Three of them stood close together, all looking sufficiently grave and somber, although Burkholder's life had never been in danger. They squinted at the lights and tried to appear as if it was a major invasion of their private lives.

I had never heard of any of them. They offered their concerns about their buddy, and made his condition sound far worse than the doctors. Without prompting, they gave their assessments of the general decline of Washington.

Then there was another live report from the scene of the shooting. Another goofy reporter standing on the Exact Spot! where he fell, and now there was really something to see. There was a patch of red blood, which she pointed to with great drama, right down there. She squatted and almost touched the sidewalk. A cop stepped into the frame and offered his vague summary of what went on.

The report was live, yet in the background there were flashing red and blue lights of police cars. I noticed this; the reporter did not.

A sweep was under way. The D.C. police were out in force cleaning the streets, shoveling the street people into cars and vans and taking them away.

Throughout the night, they swept Capitol Hill, arresting anyone caught sleeping on a bench, sitting in a park, begging on a sidewalk, anyone who obviously appeared to be without a home. They charged them with loitering, littering, public drunkenness, panhandling.

Not all were arrested and taken to jail. Two van loads were driven up Rhode Island, in Northeast, and dumped in the parking lot next to a community center with an all-night soup kitchen. Another van carrying eleven people stopped at the Calvary Mission on T Street, five blocks from our office. The men were given the choice of going to jail or hitting the streets. The van emptied.

THIRTY-TWO

I vowed to get a bed. I was losing too much sleep floundering on the floor, trying to prove a point to no one but myself. In the darkness long before dawn, I sat in my sleeping bag and promised myself I'd find something softer to sleep on. I also wondered for the thousandth time how people survived sleeping on sidewalks.

The Pylon Grill was warm and stuffy, a layer of cigarette smoke not far above the tables, the aroma of coffee beans from around the world waiting just inside the door. As usual it was filled with news junkies at 4:30 A.M.

Burkholder was the man of the hour. His face was on the front page of the *Post*, and there were several stories about the man, the shooting, the police investigation. Nothing about the sweep. Mordecai would give me those details later.

A pleasant surprise was waiting in Metro. Tim Claussen was evidently a man on a mission. Our lawsuit had inspired him.

In a lengthy article, he examined each of the three defendants, beginning with RiverOaks. The company was twenty years old, privately held by a group of investors, one of whom was Clayton Bender, an East Coast real estate swinger rumored to be worth two hundred million. Bender's picture was in the story, along with a photo of the corporate headquarters in Hagerstown, Maryland. The company had built eleven office buildings in the D.C. area in twenty years, along with numerous shopping centers in the suburbs of Baltimore and Washington. The value of its holdings was estimated at three hundred fifty million. There was also a lot of bank debt, the level of which could not be estimated.

The history of the proposed bulk-mailing facility in Northeast was recounted in excruciating detail. Then, on to Drake & Sweeney.

Not surprisingly, there was no source of information from within the firm. Phone calls had not been returned. Claussen gave the basics – size, history, a few famous alumni. There were two charts, both taken from *U.S. Law* magazine, one listing the top ten law firms in the country by size, and the other ranking the firms by how much the partners averaged last year in compensation. With eight hundred lawyers, Drake & Sweeney was fifth in size, and at $910,500, the partners were number three.

Had I really walked away from that much money?

The last member of the unlikely trio was Tillman Gantry, and his colorful life made for easy investigative journalism. Cops talked about him. A former cellmate from prison sang his praises. A Reverend of some stripe in Northeast told how Gantry had built basketball hoops for poor kids. A former prostitute remembered the beatings. He operated behind two corporations – TAG and Gantry Group – and through them he owned three used-car lots, two small shopping centers, an apartment building where two people had been shot to death, six rental duplexes, a bar where a woman had been raped, a video store, and numerous vacant lots he'd purchased for almost nothing from the city.

Of the three defendants, Gantry was the only one

willing to talk. He admitted paying eleven thousand dollars for the Florida Avenue warehouse in July of the previous year, and selling it for two hundred thousand to RiverOaks on January 31. He got lucky, he said. The building was useless, but the land under it was worth a lot more than eleven thousand. That was why he bought it.

The warehouse had always attracted squatters, he said. In fact, he had been forced to run them off. He had never charged rent, and had no idea where that rumor originated. He had plenty of lawyers, and he would mount a vigorous defense.

The story did not mention me. Nothing was said about DeVon Hardy and the hostage drama. Very little about Lontae Burton and the allegations of the lawsuit.

For the second day in a row, the venerable old firm of Drake & Sweeney was maligned as a conspirator with a former pimp. Indeed, the tone of the story portrayed the lawyers as worse criminals than Tillman Gantry.

Tomorrow, it promised, there would be another installment – a look at the sad life of Lontae Burton.

How long would Arthur Jacobs allow his beloved firm to be dragged through the mud? It was such an easy target. The *Post* could be tenacious. The reporter was obviously working around the clock. One story would lead to another.

It was twenty minutes past nine when I arrived with my lawyer at the Carl Moultrie Building, on the corner of Sixth and Indiana, downtown. Mordecai knew where we were going. I had never been near the Moultrie Building, home of civil and criminal cases in the District. The line formed outside the front entrance, and it moved slowly as the lawyers and litigants and criminals were searched and scanned for

297

metal devices. Inside, the place was a zoo – a lobby packed with anxious people, and four levels of hallways lined with courtrooms.

The Honorable Norman Kisner held court on the first floor, room number 114. A daily docket by the door listed my name under First Appearances. Eleven other criminals shared space with me. Inside, the bench was vacant; lawyers milled about. Mordecai disappeared into the back, and I took a seat in the second row. I read a magazine and tried to appear utterly bored with the scene.

'Good morning, Michael,' someone said from the aisle. It was Donald Rafter, clutching his briefcase with both hands. Behind him was a face I recognized from litigation, but I could not recall the name.

I nodded and managed to say, 'Hello.'

They scooted away and found seats on the other side of the courtroom. They represented the victims, and as such had the right to be present at each stage of my proceedings.

It was only a first appearance! I would stand before the Judge while he read the charges. I would enter a plea of not guilty, be released on my existing bond, and leave. Why was Rafter there?

The answer came slowly. I stared at the magazine, struggled to remain perfectly calm, and finally realized that his presence was merely a reminder. They regarded the theft as a serious matter, and they would dog me every step of the way. Rafter was the smartest and meanest of all litigators. I was supposed to shake with fear at the sight of him in the courtroom.

At nine-thirty, Mordecai emerged from behind the bench and motioned for me. The Judge was waiting in his chambers. Mordecai introduced me to him, and the three of us settled casually around a small table.

Judge Kisner was at least seventy, with bushy gray hair and a scraggly gray beard, and brown eyes that burned holes as he talked. He and my lawyer had been acquaintances for many years.

'I was just telling Mordecai,' he said, waving a hand, 'that this is a very unusual case.'

I nodded in agreement. It certainly felt unusual to me.

'I've known Arthur Jacobs for thirty years. In fact, I know a lot of those lawyers over there. They're good lawyers.'

They were indeed. They hired the best and trained them well. I felt uncomfortable with the fact that my trial judge had such admiration for the victims.

'A working file stolen from a lawyer's office might be hard to evaluate from a monetary point of view. It's just a bunch of papers, nothing of real value to anyone except the lawyer. It would be worth nothing if you tried to sell it on the streets. I'm not accusing you of stealing the file, you understand.'

'Yes. I understand.' I wasn't sure if I did or not, but I wanted him to continue.

'Let's assume you have the file, and let's assume you took it from the firm. If you returned it now, under my supervision, I would be inclined to place a value on it of something less than a hundred dollars. That, of course, would be a misdemeanor, and we could sweep it under the rug with a bit of paperwork. Of course, you would have to agree to disregard any information taken from the file.'

'And what if I don't return it? Still assuming, of course.'

'Then it becomes much more valuable. The grand larceny sticks, and we go to trial on that charge. If the prosecutor proves his case and the jury finds you guilty, it will be up to me to sentence you.'

The creases in his forehead, the hardening of his eyes, and the tone of his voice left little doubt that sentencing would be something I would rather avoid.

'In addition, if the jury finds you guilty of grand larceny, you will lose your license to practice law.'

'Yes sir,' I said, very much chastised.

Mordecai was holding back, listening and absorbing everything.

'Unlike most of my docket, time is crucial here,' Kisner continued. 'This civil litigation could turn on the contents of the file. Admissibility will be for another judge in another courtroom. I'd like to have the criminal matter resolved before the civil case progresses too far. Again, we're assuming you have the file.'

'How soon?' Mordecai asked.

'I think two weeks is sufficient time to make your decision.'

We agreed that two weeks was reasonable. Mordecai and I returned to the courtroom where we waited another hour while nothing happened.

Tim Claussen from the *Post* arrived with a rush of lawyers. He saw us sitting in the courtroom, but did not venture over. Mordecai moved away from me, and eventually cornered him. He explained that there were two lawyers in the courtroom from Drake & Sweeney, Donald Rafter and another guy, and perhaps they might have a word for the paper.

Claussen went right after them. Voices could be heard from the back bench where Rafter had been killing time. They left the courtroom and continued their argument outside.

My appearance before Kisner was as brief as expected. I entered a plea of not guilty, signed some forms, and left in a hurry. Rafter was nowhere in sight.

'What did you and Kisner talk about before I got back there?' I asked as soon as we were in the car.

'Same thing he told you.'

'He's a hard-ass.'

'He's a good judge, but he was a lawyer for many years. A criminal lawyer, and one of the best. He has no sympathy for a lawyer who steals the files of another.'

'How long will my sentence be if I'm convicted?'

'He didn't say. But you'll do time.'

We were waiting for a red light. Fortunately I was driving. 'All right, Counselor,' I said. 'What do we do?'

'We have two weeks. Let's approach it slowly. Now is not the time to make decisions.'

THIRTY-THREE

There were two stories in the morning *Post*, both prominently displayed and accompanied by photos.

The first was the one promised in yesterday's edition – a long history of the tragic life of Lontae Burton. Her grandmother was the principal source, though the reporter had also contacted two aunts, a former employer, a social worker, a former teacher, and her mother and two brothers in prison. With its typical aggressiveness and unlimited budget, the paper was doing a splendid job of gathering the facts we would need for our case.

Lontae's mother was sixteen when she was born, the second of three children, all out of wedlock, all sired by different men, though her mother refused to say anything about her father. She grew up in the rough neighborhoods in Northeast, moving from place to place with her troubled mother, living periodically with her grandmother and aunts. Her mother was in and out of jail, and Lontae quit school after the sixth grade. From there, her life became predictably dismal. Drugs, boys, gangs, petty crime, the dangerous life on the street. She worked at various minimum-wage jobs, and proved to be completely unreliable.

City records told much of the story: an arrest at the age of fourteen for shoplifting, processed through juvenile court. Charged again three months later for public drunkenness, juvenile court. Possession of pot at fifteen, juvenile court. Same charge seven months later. Arrested for prostitution at the age of sixteen and handled as an adult, conviction but no jail. Arrested for grand larceny, stealing a portable CD player from a pawnshop, conviction but no jail. Birth of Ontario when she was eighteen, at D.C. General with no father listed on the birth certificate. Arrested for prostitution two months after Ontario arrived, convicted but no jail. Birth of the twins, Alonzo and Dante, when she was twenty, also at D.C. General, also with no father listed. And then Temeko, the baby with the wet diaper, born when Lontae was twenty-one.

In the midst of this sad obituary, a glimmer of hope sprang forth. After Temeko arrived, Lontae stumbled into the House of Mary, a women's day center similar to Naomi's, where she met a social worker named Nell Cather. Ms. Cather was quoted at length in the story.

According to her version of Lontae's last months, she was determined to get off the streets and clean up her life. She eagerly began taking birth control pills, provided by the House of Mary. She desperately wanted to get clean and sober. She attended AA/NA meetings at the center, and fought her addictions with great courage, though sobriety eluded her. She quickly improved her reading skills, and dreamed of getting a job with a steady paycheck to provide for her little family.

Ms. Cather eventually found her a job unpacking produce at a large grocery store; twenty hours a week at $4.75 an hour. She never missed work.

One day last fall she whispered to Nell Cather that she had found a place to live, though it must be kept a secret. As part of her job, Nell wanted to inspect the place, but Lontae refused. It wasn't legal, she explained. It was a small, two-room squatter's apartment with a roof and a locked door and a bathroom nearby, and she paid a hundred dollars a month in cash.

I wrote down the name of Nell Cather, at the House of Mary, and smiled to myself at the thought of her on the witness stand, telling the Burtons' story to a jury.

Lontae became terrified at the thought of losing her children, because it happened so often. Most of the homeless women at the House of Mary had lost theirs, and the more Lontae heard their horror stories, the more determined she became to keep her family together. She studied harder, even learned the basics of a computer, and once went four days without touching drugs.

Then she was evicted, her meager belongings tossed into the street along with her children. Ms. Cather saw her the next day, and she was a mess. The kids were hungry and dirty; Lontae was stoned. The House of Mary had a policy forbidding the entry of any person obviously intoxicated or under the influence of drugs. The director was forced to ask her to leave. Ms. Cather never saw her again; not a word until she read about the deaths in the paper.

As I read the story, I thought of Braden Chance. I hoped he was reading it too, in the early morning warmth of his fine home in the Virginia suburbs. I was certain he was awake at such an early hour. How could a person under so much pressure sleep at all?

I wanted him to suffer, to realize that his callous disregard for the rights and dignities of others had caused so much misery. You were sitting in your nice office, Braden, working hard by the golden hour, shuffling papers for your rich clients, reading memos from paralegals you sent to do the dirty work, and you made the cold, calculated decision to proceed with an eviction you should have stopped. They were just squatters, weren't they, Braden? Lowly black street people living like animals. There was nothing in

304

writing, no leases, no papers, thus no rights. Toss 'em. Any delay in dealing with them might hinder the project.

I wanted to call him at home, jolt him from his morning coffee, and say, 'How do you feel now, Braden?'

The second story was a pleasant surprise, at least from a legal point of view. It also meant trouble.

An old boyfriend had been found, a nineteen-year-old street tough named Kito Spires. His photo would frighten any law-abiding citizen. Kito had a lot to say. He claimed to be the father of Lontae's last three children – the twins and the baby. He had lived with her off and on over the last three years; more off than on.

Kito was a typical inner-city product, an unemployed high school dropout with a criminal record. His credibility would always be questioned.

He had lived in the warehouse with Lontae and his children. He had helped her pay the rent whenever he could. Sometime after Christmas, they had fought and he had left. He was currently living with a woman whose husband was in prison.

He knew nothing about the eviction, though he felt it was wrong. When asked about conditions in the warehouse, Kito gave enough details to convince me he had actually been there. His description was similar to the one in Hector's memo.

He did not know the warehouse was owned by Tillman Gantry. A dude named Johnny collected rent, on the fifteenth of each month. A hundred bucks.

Mordecai and I would find him soon. Our witness list was growing, and Mr. Spires might well be our star.

Kito was deeply saddened by the deaths of his children and their mother. I had watched the funeral very carefully, and Kito was most certainly not in attendance.

Our lawsuit was getting more press than we could have dreamed of. We only wanted ten million dollars, a nice round figure that was being written about daily, and discussed in the streets. Lontae had sex with a thousand men. Kito was the first prospective father. With that much money at stake, other fathers would soon appear and claim love for their lost children. The streets were full of prospects.

That was the troubling part of his story.

We would never get the chance to talk to him.

I called Drake & Sweeney and asked for Braden Chance. A secretary answered the phone, and I repeated my request. 'And who's calling, please?' she asked.

I gave her a fictitious name and claimed to be a prospective client, referred by Clayton Bender of RiverOaks.

'Mr. Chance is unavailable,' she said.

'Tell me when I can talk to him,' I said rudely.

'He's on vacation.'

'Fine. When will he return?'

'I'm not sure,' she said, and I hung up. The vacation would be for a month, then it would become a sabbatical, then a leave of absence, and at some point they would finally admit that Chance had been sacked.

I suspected he was gone; the call confirmed it.

Since the firm had been my life for the past seven years, it wasn't difficult to predict its actions. There was too much pride and arrogance to suffer the indignities being imposed.

As soon as the lawsuit was filed, I suspected they got the truth from Braden Chance. Whether he came forth on his own, or whether they pried it out of him, was immaterial. He had lied to them from the beginning, and now the entire firm had been sued. Perhaps he showed them the original memo from Hector, along with the rent receipt from Lontae. More than likely, though, he had destroyed these and was forced to describe what he had shredded. The firm – Arthur Jacobs and the executive committee – at last knew the truth. The eviction should not have occurred. The verbal rental agreements should have been terminated in writing, by Chance acting for RiverOaks, with thirty days' notice given to the tenants.

A thirty-day delay would have jeopardized the bulk-mail facility, at least for RiverOaks.

And a thirty-day delay would have allowed Lontae and the other tenants time to survive the worst of winter.

Chance was forced out of the firm, undoubtedly with a generous buy-out package for his partnership share. Hector had probably been flown home for briefings. With Chance gone, Hector could tell the truth and survive. He would not, however, tell of his contact with me.

Behind locked doors, the executive committee had faced reality. The firm had enormous exposure. A plan of defense was devised with Rafter and his litigation team. They would defend vigorously on the grounds that the Burton case was based on materials stolen from a Drake & Sweeney file. And if the stolen materials couldn't be used in court, then the lawsuit should be dismissed. That made perfect sense, from a legal perspective.

However, before they were able to implement their defense, the newspaper intervened. Witnesses were being found who could testify to the same matters protected in the file. We could prove our case regardless of what Chance had concealed.

Drake & Sweeney had to be in chaos. With four

hundred aggressive lawyers unwilling to keep their opinions to themselves, the firm was on the verge of an insurrection. Had I still been there, and been faced with a similar scandal in another division of the firm, I would have been raising hell to get the matter settled and out of the press. The option of battening down the hatches and riding out the storm did not exist. The exposé by the *Post* was only a sample of what a full-blown trial would entail. And a trial was a year away.

There was heat from another source. The file did not indicate the extent to which RiverOaks knew the truth about the squatters. In fact, there was very little correspondence between Chance and his client. It appeared as though he was given instructions to close the deal as soon as possible. RiverOaks applied the pressure; Chance steamrolled ahead.

If we assumed RiverOaks did not know the evictions were wrongful, then the company had a legitimate claim for legal malpractice against Drake & Sweeney. It hired the firm to do a job; the job was botched; and the blunder was to the detriment of the client. With three hundred fifty million in holdings, RiverOaks had sufficient clout to pressure the firm to remedy its wrongs.

Other major clients would also have opinions. 'What's going on over there?' was a question every partner was hearing from those who paid the bills. In the cutthroat world of corporate law, vultures from other firms were beginning to circle.

Drake & Sweeney marketed its image, its public perception. All big firms did. And no firm could take the hammering being inflicted upon my alma mater.

Congressman Burkholder rallied magnificently. The day after his surgery, he met the press in a carefully staged exhibition. They rolled him in a wheelchair to a makeshift podium in the lobby of the hospital. He stood, with the aid of his pretty wife, and stepped forward to issue a statement. Coincidentally, he wore a bright red Hoosier sweatshirt. There were bandages on his neck; a sling over his left arm.

He pronounced himself alive and well, and ready in a few short days to return to his duties on the Hill. Hello to the folks back home in Indiana.

In his finest moment, he dwelt on street crime, and the deterioration of our cities. (His hometown had eight thousand people.) It was a shame that our nation's capital was in such a sorry state, and because of his brush with death he would from that day forward devote his considerable energies into making our streets safe again. He had found a new purpose.

He blathered on about gun control and more prisons.

The shooting of Burkholder had put immense, though temporary, pressure on the D.C. police to clean up the streets. Senators and representatives had spent the day popping off about the dangers of downtown Washington. As a result, the sweeps started again after dark. Every drunk, wino, beggar, and homeless person near the Capitol was pushed farther away. Some were arrested. Others were simply loaded into vans and transported like cattle to the more distant neighborhoods.

At 11:40 P.M., the police were dispatched to a liquor store on Fourth Street near Rhode Island, in Northeast. Gunshots had been heard by the owner of the store, and one of the sidewalk locals had reported seeing a man down.

In a vacant lot next to the liquor store, behind a pile of rubble and cracked bricks, the police found the body of a young black male. The blood was fresh, and came from two bullet holes to the head.

He was later identified as Kito Spires.

THIRTY-FOUR

Ruby reappeared Monday morning with a ferocious appetite for both cookies and news. She was waiting on the doorstep with a smile and a warm hello when I arrived at eight, a bit later than usual. With Gantry out there, I wanted the extra daylight and the increased activity when I got to the office.

She looked the same. I thought perhaps I could study her face and see the evidence of a crack binge, but there was nothing unusual. Her eyes were hard and sad, but she was in a fine mood. We entered the office together and fixed our spot on Ruby's desk. It was somewhat comforting to have another person in the building.

'How have you been?' I asked.

'Good,' she said, reaching into a bag for a cookie. There were three bags, all bought the week before, just for her, though Mordecai had left a trail of crumbs.

'Where are you staying?'

'In my car.' Where else? 'I sure am glad winter is leaving.'

'Me too. Have you been to Naomi's?' I asked.

'No. But I'm going today. I ain't been feeling too good.'

'I'll give you a ride.'

'Thanks.'

The conversation was a little stiff. She expected me

to ask about her last motel visit. I certainly wanted to, but thought better of it.

When the coffee was ready, I poured two cups and set them on the desk. She was on her third cookie, nibbling nonstop around the edges like a mouse.

How could I be harsh with one so pitiful? On to the news.

'How about the paper?' I asked.

'That would be nice.'

There was a picture of the mayor on the front page, and since she liked stories about city politics, and since the mayor was always good for some color, I selected it first. It was a Saturday interview in which the mayor and council, acting together in a shaky and temporary alliance, were asking for a Justice Department investigation into the deaths of Lontae Burton and family. Had there been civil rights violations? The mayor strongly implied that he thought so, but bring in Justice!

Since the lawsuit had taken center stage, a fresh new group of culprits was being blamed for the tragedy. Fingerpointing at City Hall had slowed considerably. Insults to and from Congress had stopped. Those who'd felt the heat of the first accusations were vigorously and happily shifting blame to the big law firm and its rich client.

Ruby was fascinated with the Burton story. I gave her a quick summary of the lawsuit and the fallout since it had been filed.

Drake & Sweeney was battered again by the paper. Its lawyers had to be asking themselves, 'When will it end?'

Not for a while.

On the bottom corner of the front page was a brief story about the Postal Service's decision to halt the bulk-mail project in Northeast Washington. The controversy surrounding the purchase of the land, the warehouse, the litigation involving RiverOaks and Gantry – all were factors in the decision.

RiverOaks lost its twenty-million-dollar project. RiverOaks would react like any other aggressive real estate developer who'd spent almost a million dollars in cash purchasing useless inner-city property. RiverOaks would go after its lawyers.

The pressure swelled some more.

We scanned world events. An earthquake in Peru caught Ruby's attention, and we read about it. On to Metro, where the first words I saw made my heart stop. Under the same photo of Kito Spires, the same except twice as large and even more menacing, was the headline: KITO SPIRES FOUND SHOT TO DEATH. The story recounted Friday's introduction of Mr. Spires as a player in the Burton drama, then gave the scant details of his death. No witnesses, no clues, nothing. Just another street punk shot in the District.

'You okay?' Ruby asked, waking me from my trance.

'Uh, sure,' I said, trying to breathe again.

'Why ain't you reading?'

Because I was too stunned to read aloud. I had to quickly scan every word to see if the name of Tillman Gantry was mentioned. It was not.

And why not? It was obvious to me what had happened. The kid had enjoyed his moment in the spotlight, said too much, made himself too valuable to the plaintiffs *(us!)*, and was too easy a target.

I read the story to her, slowly, listening to every sound around us, watching the front door, hoping Mordecai would arrive shortly.

Gantry had spoken. Other witnesses from the streets would either remain quiet or disappear after we found them. Killing witnesses was bad enough. What would I do if Gantry came after the lawyers?

In the midst of my terror, I suddenly realized the

story was beneficial to our side of the case. We had lost a potentially crucial witness, but Kito's credibility would have caused problems. Drake & Sweeney was mentioned again, in the third story of the morning, in connection with the killing of a nineteen-year-old criminal. The firm had been toppled from its loftiness and was now in the gutter, its proud name mentioned in the same paragraphs as murdered street thugs.

I took myself back a month, before Mister and everything that followed, and I pictured myself reading the same paper at my desk before sunrise. And I imagined that I had read the other stories and had learned that the most serious allegations in the lawsuit were indeed true. What would I do?

There was no doubt. I would be raising hell with Rudolph Mayes, my supervising partner, who likewise would be raising hell with the executive committee, and I would be meeting with my peers, the other senior associates in the firm. We would demand that the matter be settled and laid to rest before more damage was inflicted. We would insist that a trial be avoided at all costs.

We would make all sorts of demands.

And I suspected most of the senior associates and all the partners were doing exactly what I would be doing. With that much racket in the hallways, very little work was being done. Very few hours were being billed. The firm was in chaos.

'Keep going,' Ruby said, again waking me.

We raced through Metro, in part because I wanted to see if perhaps there was a fourth story. No such luck. There was, however, a story about the street sweeps being conducted by the police in response to the Burkholder shooting. An advocate for the homeless was bitterly criticizing the operation, and threatening litigation. Ruby loved the story. She thought it wonderful that so much was being written about the homeless.

I drove her to Naomi's, where she was greeted like an old friend. The women hugged her and passed her around the room, squeezing and even crying. I spent a few minutes flirting with Megan in the kitchen, but my mind was not on romance.

Sofia had a full house when I returned to the office. The foot traffic was heavy; five clients were sitting against the wall by nine o'clock. She was on the phone, terrorizing someone in Spanish. I stepped into Mordecai's office to make sure he had seen the paper. He was reading it with a smile. We agreed to meet in an hour to discuss the lawsuit.

I quietly closed my office door and began pulling files. In two weeks, I had opened ninety-one of them, and closed thirty-eight. I was falling behind, and I needed a hard morning fighting the phone to catch up. It would not happen.

Sofia knocked, and since the door would not latch, she pushed it open while still tapping it. No Hello. No Excuse me.

'Where is that list of people evicted from the warehouse?' she asked. She had a pencil stuck behind each ear, and reading glasses perched on the end of her nose. The woman had things to do.

The list was always nearby. I handed it to her, and she took a quick look. 'Bingo,' she said.

'What?' I asked, rising to my feet.

'Number eight, Marquis Deese,' she said. 'I thought that name was familiar.'

'Familiar?'

'Yes, he's sitting at my desk. Picked up last night in Lafayette Park, across from the White House, and dumped at Logan Circle. Got caught in a sweep. It's your lucky day.'

I followed her into the front room, where in the center Mr. Deese sat next to her desk. He looked remarkably similar to DeVon Hardy – late forties, grayish hair and beard, thick sunshades, bundled heavily like most homeless in early March. I examined him from a distance as I walked to Mordecai's office to give him the news.

We approached him carefully, with Mordecai in charge of the interrogation. 'Excuse me,' he said, very politely. 'I'm Mordecai Green, one of the lawyers here. Can I ask you some questions?'

Both of us were standing, looking down at Mr. Deese. He raised his head, said, 'I guess so.'

'We're working on a case involving some people who used to live in an old warehouse at the corner of Florida and New York,' Mordecai explained slowly.

'I lived there,' he said. I took a deep breath.

'You did?'

'Yep. Got kicked out.'

'Yes, well, that's why we're involved. We represent some of the other people who were kicked out. We think the eviction was wrongful.'

'You got that right.'

'How long did you live there?'

''Bout three months.'

'Did you pay rent?'

'Sure did.'

'To who?'

'Guy named Johnny.'

'How much?'

'A hundred bucks a month, cash only.'

'Why cash?'

'Didn't want no records.'

'Do you know who owned the warehouse?'

'Nope.' His answer came without hesitation, and I had trouble concealing my delight. If Deese didn't

315

know Gantry owned the building, how could he be afraid of him?

Mordecai pulled up a chair, and got serious with Mr. Deese. 'We'd like to have you as a client,' he said.

'Do what?'

'We're suing some people over the eviction. It's our position that you folks were done wrong when you got kicked out. We'd like to represent you, and sue on your behalf.'

'But the apartment was illegal. That's why I was paying in cash.'

'Doesn't matter. We can get you some money.'

'How much?'

'I don't know yet. What have you got to lose?'

'Nothing, I guess.'

I tapped Mordecai on the shoulder. We excused ourselves and withdrew into his office. 'What is it?' he asked.

'In light of what happened to Kito Spires, I think we should record his testimony. Now.'

Mordecai scratched his beard. 'Not a bad idea. Let's do an affidavit. He can sign it, Sofia can notarize it, then if something happens to him, we can fight to get it admitted.'

'Do we have a tape recorder?' I asked.

His eyes shot in all directions. 'Yeah, somewhere.'

Since he didn't know where it was, it would take a month to find it. 'How about a video camera?' I asked.

'Not here.'

I thought for a second, then said, 'I'll run get mine. You and Sofia keep him occupied.'

'He's not going anywhere.'

'Good. Give me forty-five minutes.'

I raced from the office and sped west toward Georgetown. The third number I tried from my cell phone found Claire between classes. 'What's wrong?' she asked.

316

'I need to borrow the video camera. I'm in a hurry.'

'It hasn't been moved,' she said, very slowly, trying to analyze things. 'Why?'

'A deposition. Mind if I use it?'

'I guess not.'

'Still in the living room?'

'Yes.'

'Have you changed the locks?' I asked.

'No.' For some reason, this made me feel better. I still had a key. I could come and go if I wanted.

'What about the alarm code?'

'No. It's the same.'

'Thanks. I'll call you later.'

We placed Marquis Deese in an office empty of furniture but crowded with file cabinets. He sat in a chair, a blank white wall behind him. I was the videographer, Sofia the notary, Mordecai the interrogator. His answers could not have been more perfect.

We were finished in thirty minutes, all possible questions served up and answered. Deese thought he knew where two of the other evictees were staying, and he promised to find them.

Our plans were to file a separate lawsuit for each evictee we could locate; one at a time, with plenty of notice to our friends at the *Post*. We knew Kelvin Lam was at the CCNV, but he and Deese were the only two we'd been able to locate. Their cases were not worth a lot of money – we would gladly settle them for twenty-five thousand each – but their filing would heap more misery upon the beleaguered defendants.

I almost hoped the police would sweep the streets again.

As Deese was leaving, Mordecai warned him against talking about the lawsuit. I sat at a desk near Sofia and typed a three-page complaint on behalf of our new client, Marquis Deese, against the same three defendants, alleging a wrongful eviction. Then one for Kelvin Lam. I filed the complaints in the computer's memory. I would simply change the names of the plaintiffs as we found them.

The phone rang a few minutes before noon. Sofia was on the other line, so I grabbed it. 'Legal clinic,' I said, as usual.

A dignified old voice on the other end said, 'This is Arthur Jacobs, Attorney, with Drake & Sweeney. I would like to speak to Mr. Mordecai Green.'

I could only say, 'Sure,' before punching the hold button. I stared at the phone, then slowly rose and walked to Mordecai's door.

'What is it?' he said. His nose was buried in the U.S. Code.

'Arthur Jacobs is on the phone.'

'Who is he?'

'Drake & Sweeney.'

We stared at each other for a few seconds, then he smiled. 'This could be the call,' he said. I just nodded.

He reached for the phone, and I sat down.

It was a brief conversation, with Arthur doing most of the talking. I gathered that he wanted to meet and talk about the lawsuit, and the sooner the better.

After it was over, Mordecai replayed it for my benefit. 'They would like to sit down tomorrow and have a little chat about settling the lawsuit.'

'Where?'

'At their place. Ten in the morning, without your presence.'

I didn't expect to be invited.

'Are they worried?' I asked.

'Of course they're worried. They have twenty days before their answer is due, yet they're already calling about a settlement. They are very worried.'

THIRTY-FIVE

I spent the following morning at the Redeemer Mission, counseling clients with all the finesse of one who'd spent years tending to the legal problems of the homeless. Temptation overcame me, and at eleven-fifteen I called Sofia to see if she had heard from Mordecai. She had not. We expected the meeting at Drake & Sweeney to be a long one. I was hoping that by chance he had called in to report everything was proceeding smoothly. No such luck.

Typically, I had slept little, though the lack of sleep had nothing to do with physical ailments or discomfort. My anxiety over the settlement meeting outlasted a long hot bath and a bottle of wine. My nerves were jumping.

As I counseled my clients, it was difficult to concentrate on food stamps, housing subsidies, and delinquent fathers when my life was hanging in the balance on another front. I left when lunch was ready; my presence was far less important than the daily bread. I bought two plain bagels and a bottle of water, and drove the Beltway for an hour.

When I returned to the clinic, Mordecai's car was parked beside the building. He was in his office, waiting for me. I closed the door.

The meeting took place in Arthur Jacobs' personal

conference room on the eighth floor, in a hallowed corner of the building I'd never been near. Mordecai was treated like a visiting dignitary by the receptionist and staff – his coat was quickly taken, his coffee mixed just right, fresh muffins available.

He sat on one side of the table, facing Arthur, Donald Rafter, an attorney for the firm's malpractice insurance carrier, and an attorney for RiverOaks. Tillman Gantry had legal representation, but they had not been invited. If there was a settlement, no one expected Gantry to contribute a dime.

The only odd slot in the lineup was the lawyer for RiverOaks, but it made sense. The company's interests were in conflict with the firm's. Mordecai said the ill will was obvious.

Arthur handled most of the talking from his side of the table, and Mordecai had trouble believing the man was eighty years old. The facts were not only memorized but instantly recalled. The issues were analyzed by an extremely sharp mind working overtime.

First they agreed that everything said and seen in the meeting would remain strictly confidential; no admission of liability would survive the day; no offer to settle would be legally binding until documents were signed.

Arthur began by saying the defendants, especially Drake & Sweeney and RiverOaks, had been blindsided by the lawsuit – they were rattled and reeling and unaccustomed to the humiliation, and to the battering they were taking in the press. He spoke very frankly about the distress his beloved firm was suffering. Mordecai just listened, as he did throughout most of the meeting.

Arthur pointed out that there were a number of issues involved. He started with Braden Chance, and revealed that Chance had been expelled by the firm. He did not withdraw; he was kicked out. Arthur spoke

320

candidly about Chance's misdeeds. He was solely in charge of all RiverOaks matters. He knew every aspect of the TAG closing, and monitored every detail. He probably committed malpractice when he allowed the eviction to proceed.

'Probably?' Mordecai said.

Well, okay then, beyond probably. Chance did not meet the necessary level of professional responsibility by proceeding with the eviction. And he doctored the file. And he attempted to cover up his actions. He lied to them, plain and simple, Arthur admitted, with no small amount of discomfort. Had Chance been truthful after Mister's hostage crisis, the firm could have prevented the lawsuit and its resulting flood of bad press. Chance had embarrassed them deeply, and he was history.

'How did he doctor the file?' Mordecai asked.

The other side wanted to know if Mordecai had seen the file. Where, exactly, was the damned thing? He was not responsive.

Arthur explained that certain papers had been removed.

'Have you seen Hector Palma's memo of January twenty-seventh?' Mordecai asked, and they went rigid.

'No,' came the response, delivered by Arthur.

So Chance had in fact removed the memo, along with Lontae's receipt, and fed them to the shredder. With great ceremony, and relishing every second of it, Mordecai removed from his briefcase several copies of the memo and receipt. He majestically slid them across the table, where they were snatched up by hardened lawyers too terrified to breathe.

There was a long silence as the memo was read, then examined, then reread, then finally analyzed desperately for loopholes and words which might be lifted out of context and slanted toward their side of

321

the table. Nothing doing. Hector's words were too clear; his narrative too descriptive.

'May I ask where you got this?' asked Arthur politely.

'That's not important, at least for now.'

It was obvious they had been consumed with the memo. Chance had described its contents on his way out the door, and the original had been destroyed. But what if copies had been made?

They were holding the copies, in disbelief.

But because they were seasoned litigators they rallied nicely, laying the memo aside as if it were something they could handle effectively at a later date.

'I guess that brings us to the missing file,' Arthur said, anxious to find more solid footing. They had an eyewitness who had seen me near Chance's office the night I took the file. They had fingerprints. They had the mysterious file from my desk, the one that had held the keys. I had gone to Chance demanding to see the RiverOaks/TAG file. There was motive.

'But there are no eyewitnesses,' Mordecai said. 'It's all circumstantial.'

'Do you know where the file is?' Arthur asked.

'No.'

'We have no interest in seeing Michael Brock go to jail.'

'Then why are you pressing criminal charges?'

'Everything's on the table, Mr. Green. If we can resolve the lawsuit, we can also dispose of the criminal matter.'

'That's wonderful news. How do you propose we settle the lawsuit?'

Rafter slid over a ten-page summary, filled with multicolored graphs and charts, all designed to convey the argument that children and young, uneducated mothers are not worth much in wrongful-death litigation.

With typical big-firm thoroughness, the minions at Drake & Sweeney had spent untold hours spanning the nation to survey the latest trends in tort compensation. A one-year trend. A five-year trend. A ten-year trend. Region by region. State by state. City by city. How much were juries awarding for the deaths of preschoolers? Not very much. The national average was forty-five thousand dollars, but much lower in the South and Midwest, and slightly higher in California and in larger cities.

Preschoolers do not work, do not earn money, and the courts generally do not allow predictions about future earning capacity.

Lontae's estimate of lost earnings was quite liberal. With a spotty employment history, some weighty assumptions were made. She was twenty-two, and she would one day very soon find full-time employment, at minimum wage. That was a generous assumption, but one Rafter was willing to grant. She would remain clean, sober, and free of pregnancy for the remainder of her working life; another charitable theory. She would find training somewhere along the way, move into a job paying twice as much as minimum wage, and keep said job until she was sixty-five. Adjusting her future earnings for inflation, then translating to present dollars, Rafter arrived at the sum of $570,000 for Lontae's loss of earnings.

There were no injuries or burns, no pain and suffering. They died in their sleep.

To settle the case, and admitting no wrongdoing whatsoever, the firm generously offered to pay $50,000 per child, plus the full sum of Lontae's earnings, for a total of $770,000.

'That's not even close,' Mordecai said. 'I can get that much out of a jury for one dead kid.' They sank in their seats.

He went on to discredit almost everything in

323

Rafter's pretty little report. He didn't care what juries were doing in Dallas or Seattle, and failed to see the relevance. He had no interest in judicial proceedings in Omaha. He knew what he could do with a jury in the District, and that was all that mattered. If they thought they could buy their way out cheaply, then it was time for him to leave.

Arthur reasserted himself as Rafter looked for a hole. 'It's negotiable,' he said. 'It's negotiable.'

The survey made no allowance for punitive damages, and Mordecai brought this to their attention. 'You got a wealthy lawyer from a wealthy firm deliberately allowing a wrongful eviction to occur, and as a direct result my clients got tossed into the streets where they died trying to stay warm. Frankly, gentlemen, it's a beautiful punitive damages case, especially here in the District.'

'Here in the District' meant only one thing: a black jury.

'We can negotiate,' Arthur said again. 'What figure do you have in mind?'

We had debated what number to first place on the table. We had sued for ten million dollars, but we had pulled the number out of the air. It could've been forty or fifty or a hundred.

'A million for each of them,' Mordecai said. The words fell heavily on the mahogany table. Those on the other side heard them clearly, but it took seconds for things to register.

'Five million?' Rafter asked, just barely loud enough to be heard.

'Five million,' boomed Mordecai. 'One for each of the victims.'

The legal pads suddenly caught their attention, and all four wrote a few sentences.

After a while, Arthur reentered the fray by explaining that our theory of liability was not absolute. An intervening act of nature – the snowstorm – was partly responsible for the deaths. A long discussion about weather followed. Mordecai settled the issue by saying, 'The jurors will know that it snows in February, that it's cold in February, that we have snowstorms in February.'

Throughout the meeting, any reference by him to the jury, or the jurors, was always followed by a few seconds of silence on the other side.

'They are horrified of a trial,' he told me.

Our theory was strong enough to withstand their attacks, he explained to them. Either through intentional acts or gross negligence, the eviction was carried out. It was foreseeable that our clients would be forced into the streets with no place to live, in February. He could convey this wonderfully simple idea to any jury in the country, but it would especially appeal to the good folks in the District.

Weary of arguing liability, Arthur moved to their strongest hand – me. Specifically, my actions in taking the file from Chance's office, and doing so after being told I couldn't have it. Their position was not negotiable. They were willing to drop the criminal charges if a settlement could be reached in the civil suit, but I had to face disciplinary action on their ethics complaint.

'What do they want?' I asked.

'A two-year suspension,' Mordecai said gravely.

I couldn't respond. Two years, non-negotiable.

'I told them they were nuts,' he said, but not as emphatically as I would have liked. 'No way.'

It was easier to remain silent. I kept repeating to myself the words *Two years. Two years.*

They jockeyed some more on the money, without closing the gap. Actually, they agreed on nothing, except for a plan to meet again as soon as possible.

The last thing Mordecai did was hand them a copy

of the Marquis Deese lawsuit, yet to be filed. It listed the same three defendants, and demanded the paltry sum of fifty thousand dollars for his wrongful eviction. More would follow, Mordecai promised them. In fact, our plans were to file a couple each week until all evictees had been accounted for.

'You plan to provide a copy of this to the newspapers?' Rafter asked.

'Why not?' Mordecai said. 'Once it's filed, it's public record.'

'It's just that, well, we've had enough of the press.'

'You started the pissing contest.'

'What?'

'You leaked the story of Michael's arrest.'

'We did not.'

'Then how did the *Post* get his photograph?'

Arthur told Rafter to shut up.

Alone in my office with the door closed, I stared at the walls for an hour before the settlement began to make sense. The firm was willing to pay a lot of money to avoid two things: further humiliation, and the spectacle of a trial that could cause serious financial damage. If I handed over the file, they would drop the criminal charges. Everything would fold neatly into place, except that the firm wanted some measure of satisfaction.

I was not only a turncoat, but in their eyes I was responsible for the entire mess. I was the link between their dirty secrets, well hidden up in the tower, and the exposure the lawsuit had cast upon them. The public disgrace was reason enough to hate me; the prospect of stripping them of their beloved cash was fueling their hunger for revenge.

And I had done it all with inside information, at least in their collective opinion. Apparently, they did not know of Hector's involvement. I had stolen the file, found everything I needed, then pieced together the lawsuit.

I was Judas. Sadly, I understood them.

THIRTY-SIX

Long after Sofia and Abraham had left, I was sitting in
the semi-darkness of my office when Mordecai walked
through the door and settled into one of two sturdy
folding chairs I'd bought at a flea market for six bucks.
A matching pair. A prior owner had painted them
maroon. They were quite ugly, but at least I had
stopped worrying about clients and visitors collapsing
in mid-sentence.

I knew he had been on the phone all afternoon, but
I had stayed away from his office.

'I've had lots of phone calls,' he said. 'Things are
moving faster than we ever thought.'

I was listening, with nothing to say.

'Back and forth with Arthur, back and forth with
Judge DeOrio. Do you know DeOrio?'

'No.'

'He's a tough guy, but he's good, fair, moderately
liberal, started with a big firm many years ago and for
some reason decided he wanted to be a judge. Passed
up the big bucks. He moves more cases than any trial
judge in the city because he keeps the lawyers under
his thumb. Very heavy-handed. Wants everything
settled, and if a case can't be settled, then he wants the
trial as soon as possible. He's obsessive about a clean
docket.'

'I think I've heard his name.'

'I would hope so. You've practiced law in this city for seven years.'

'Antitrust law. In a big firm. Way up there.'

'Anyway, here's the upshot. We've agreed to meet at one tomorrow in DeOrio's courtroom. Everybody will be there – the three defendants, with counsel, me, you, our trustee, everybody with any interest whatsoever in the lawsuit.'

'Me?'

'Yep. The Judge wants you present. He said you could sit in the jury box and watch, but he wants you there. And he wants the missing file.'

'Gladly.'

'He is notorious, in some circles I guess, for hating the press. He routinely tosses reporters from his courtroom; bans TV cameras from within a hundred feet of his doors. He's already irritated with the notoriety this case has generated. He's determined to stop the leaks.'

'The lawsuit is a public record.'

'Yes, but he can seal the file, if he's so inclined. I don't think he will, but he likes to bark.'

'So he wants it settled?'

'Of course he does. He's a judge, isn't he? Every judge wants every case settled. More time for golf.'

'What does he think of our case?'

'He kept his cards close, but he was adamant that all three defendants be present, and not just flunkies. We'll see the people who can make decisions on the spot.'

'Gantry?'

'Gantry will be there. I talked to his lawyer.'

'Does he know they have a metal detector at the front door?'

'Probably. He's been to court before. Arthur and I told the Judge about their offer. He didn't react, but I

329

don't think he was impressed. He's seen a lot of big verdicts. He knows his jurors.'

'What about me?'

There was a long pause from my friend as he struggled to find words that would be at once truthful yet soothing. 'He'll take a hard line.'

Nothing soothing about that. 'What's fair, Mordecai? It's my neck on the line. I've lost perspective.'

'It's not a question of fairness. You took the file to right a wrong. You did not intend to steal it, just borrow it for an hour or so. It was an honorable act, but still a theft.'

'Did DeOrio refer to it as a theft?'

'He did. Once.'

So the Judge thought I was a thief. It was becoming unanimous. I didn't have the guts to ask Mordecai his opinion. He might tell me the truth, and I didn't want to hear it.

He shifted his considerable weight. My chair popped, but didn't yield an inch. I was proud of it. 'I want you to know something,' he said soberly. 'You say the word, and we'll walk away from this case in the blink of an eye. We don't need the settlement; no one does really. The victims are dead. Their heirs are either unknown or in jail. A nice settlement will not affect my life in the slightest. It's your case. You make the call.'

'It's not that simple, Mordecai.'

'Why isn't it?'

'I'm scared of the criminal charges.'

'You should be. But they'll forget the criminal charges. They'll forget the bar complaint. I could call Arthur right now and tell him we would drop everything if they would drop everything. Both sides walk away and forget it. He would jump at it. It's a piece of cake.'

'The press would eat us alive.'

330

'So? We're immune. You think our clients worry about what the *Post* says about us?'

He was playing the devil's advocate – arguing points he didn't really believe in. Mordecai wanted to protect me, but he also wanted to nail Drake & Sweeney.

Some people cannot be protected from themselves.

'All right, we walk away,' I said. 'And what have we accomplished? They get away with murder. They threw those people in the street. They're solely responsible for the wrongful evictions, and ultimately responsible for the deaths of our clients, yet we let them off the hook? Is that what we're talking about?'

'It's the only way to protect your license to practice law.'

'Nothing like a little pressure, Mordecai,' I said, a bit too harshly.

But he was right. It was my mess, and only fitting that I make the crucial decisions. I took the file, a stupid act that was legally and ethically wrong.

Mordecai Green would be devastated if I suddenly got cold feet. His entire world was helping poor folks pick themselves up. His people were the hopeless and homeless, those given little and seeking only the basics of life – the next meal, a dry bed, a job with a dignified wage, a small apartment with affordable rent. Rarely could the cause of his clients' problems be so directly traced to large, private enterprises.

Since money meant nothing to Mordecai, and since a large recovery would have little or no impact on his life, and since the clients were, as he said, either dead, unknown, or in jail, he would never consider a pretrial settlement, absent my involvement. Mordecai wanted a trial, an enormous, noisy production with lights and cameras and printed words focused not on him, but on the declining plight of his people. Trials are not always about individual wrongs; they are sometimes used as pulpits.

My presence complicated matters. My soft, pale face could be the one behind bars. My license to practice law, and thus make a living, was at risk.

'I'm not jumping ship, Mordecai,' I said.

'I didn't expect you to.'

'Let me give you a scenario. What if we convince them to pay a sum of money we can live with; the criminal charges are dropped; and there's nothing left on the table but me and my license? And what if I agree to surrender it for a period of time? What happens to me?'

'First, you suffer the indignity of a disciplinary suspension.'

'Which, unpleasant as it sounds, will not be the end of the world,' I said, trying to sound strong. I was horrified about the embarrassment. Warner, my parents, my friends, my law school buddies, Claire, all those fine folks at Drake & Sweeney. Their faces rushed before my eyes as I saw them receive the news.

'Second, you simply can't practice law during the suspension.'

'Will I lose my job?'

'Of course not.'

'Then what will I do?'

'Well, you'll keep this office. You'll do intake at CCNV, Samaritan House, Redeemer Mission, and the other places you've already been to. You will remain a full partner with the clinic. We'll call you a social worker, not a lawyer.'

'So nothing changes?'

'Not much. Look at Sofia. She sees more clients than the rest of us combined, and half the city thinks she's a lawyer. If a court appearance is necessary, I handle it. It'll be the same for you.'

The rules governing street law were written by those who practiced it.

'What if I get caught?'

'No one cares. The line between social work and social law is not always clear.'

'Two years is a long time.'

'It is, and it isn't. We don't have to agree on a two-year suspension.'

'I thought it was not negotiable.'

'Tomorrow, everything will be negotiable. But you need to do some research. Find similar cases, if they're out there. See what other jurisdictions have done with similar complaints.'

'You think it's happened before?'

'Maybe. There are a million of us now. Lawyers have been ingenious in finding ways to screw up.'

He was late for a meeting. I thanked him, and we locked up together.

I drove to the Georgetown Law School near Capitol Hill. The library was open until midnight. It was the perfect place to hide and ponder the life of a wayward lawyer.

THIRTY-SEVEN

DeOrio's courtroom was on the second floor of the Carl Moultrie Building, and getting there took us close to Judge Kisner's, where my grand larceny case was awaiting the next step in a cumbersome process. The halls were busy with criminal lawyers and low-end ham-and-eggers, the ones who advertise on cable TV and bus stop benches. They huddled with their clients, almost all of whom looked guilty of something, and I refused to believe that my name was on the same docket with those thugs.

The timing of our entry was important to me – silly to Mordecai. We didn't dare flirt with tardiness. DeOrio was a fanatic for punctuality. But I couldn't stomach the thought of arriving ten minutes early and being subjected to the stares and whispers and perhaps even the banal pregame chitchat of Donald Rafter and Arthur and hell only knew who else they would bring. I had no desire to be in the room with Tillman Gantry unless His Honor was present.

I wanted to take my seat in the jury box, listen to it all, and not be bothered by anyone. We entered at two minutes before one.

DeOrio's law clerk was passing out copies of the agenda. She directed us to our seats – me to the jury box, where I sat alone and content, and Mordecai to the plaintiff's table next to the jury box. Wilma

Phelan, the trustee, was already there, and already bored because she had no input into anything about to be discussed.

The defense table was a study in strategic positioning. Drake & Sweeney was clustered at one end; Tillman Gantry and his two lawyers at the other. Holding the center, and acting as a buffer, were two corporate types from RiverOaks, and three lawyers. The agenda also listed the names of all present. I counted thirteen for the defense.

I expected Gantry, being an ex-pimp, to be adorned with rings on his fingers and ears and bright, gaudy clothing. Not so. He wore a handsome navy suit and was dressed better than his lawyers. He was reading documents and ignoring everyone.

I saw Arthur and Rafter and Nathan Malamud. And Barry Nuzzo. I was determined that nothing would surprise me, but I had not expected to see Barry. By sending three of my fellow ex-hostages, the firm was delivering a subtle message – every other lawyer terrorized by Mister survived without cracking up – what happened to me? Why was I the weak sister?

The fifth person in their pack was identified as L. James Suber, an attorney for an insurance company. Drake & Sweeney was heavily insured against malpractice, but I doubted if the coverage would apply. The policy excluded intentional acts, such as stealing by an associate or partner, or deliberately violating a standard of conduct. Negligence by a firm lawyer would be covered. Willful wrongdoing would not. Braden Chance had not simply overlooked a statute or code provision or established method of practice. He had made the conscious decision to proceed with the eviction, in spite of being fully informed that the squatters were in fact tenants.

There would be a nasty fight on the side, out of our

335

view, between Drake & Sweeney and its malpractice carrier. Let 'em fight.

At precisely one, Judge DeOrio appeared from behind the bench and took his seat. 'Good afternoon,' he said gruffly as he settled into place. He was wearing a robe, and that struck me as odd. It was not a formal court proceeding, but an unofficial settlement conference.

He adjusted his microphone, and said, 'Mr. Burdick, please keep the door locked.' Mr. Burdick was a uniformed courtroom deputy guarding the door from the inside. The pews were completely empty. It was a very private conference.

A court reporter began recording every word.

'I am informed by my clerk that all parties and lawyers are now present,' he said, glancing at me as if I were just another rapist. 'The purpose of this meeting is to attempt to settle this case. After numerous conversations yesterday with the principal attorneys, it became apparent to me that a conference such as this, held at this time, might be beneficial. I've never had a settlement conference so soon after the filing of a complaint, but since all parties agreed, it is time well spent. The first issue is that of confidentiality. Nothing we say today can be repeated to any member of the press, under any circumstances. Is that understood?' He looked at Mordecai and then at me. All necks from the defense table twisted for similar scrutiny. I wanted to stand and remind them that they had initiated the practice of leaking. We'd certainly landed the heaviest blows, but they had thrown the first punch.

The clerk then handed each of us a two-paragraph nondisclosure agreement, customized with our names plugged in. I signed it and gave it back to her.

A lawyer under pressure cannot read two paragraphs and make a quick decision. 'Is there a problem?' DeOrio asked of the Drake & Sweeney crowd.

They were looking for loopholes. It was the way we were trained.

They signed off and the agreements were gathered by the clerk.

'We'll work from the agenda,' the Judge said. 'Item one is a summary of the facts and theories of liability. Mr. Green, you filed the lawsuit, you may proceed. You have five minutes.'

Mordecai stood without notes, hands stuck deep in pockets, completely at ease. In two minutes, he stated our case clearly, then sat down. DeOrio appreciated brevity.

Arthur spoke for the defendants. He conceded the factual basis for the case, but took issue on the question of liability. He laid much of the blame on the 'freak' snowstorm that covered the city and made life difficult for everyone.

He also questioned the actions of Lontae Burton.

'There were places for her to go,' Arthur said. 'There were emergency shelters open. The night before she had stayed in the basement of a church, along with many other people. Why did she leave? I don't know, but no one forced her, at least no one we've been able to find so far. Her grandmother has an apartment in Northeast. Shouldn't some of the responsibility rest with the mother? Shouldn't she have done more to protect her little family?'

It would be Arthur's only chance to cast blame upon a dead mother. In a year or so, my jury box would be filled with people who looked different from me, and neither Arthur nor any lawyer in his right mind would imply that Lontae Burton was even partially to blame for killing her own children.

'Why was she in the street to begin with?' DeOrio asked sharply, and I almost smiled.

Arthur was unfazed. 'For purposes of this meeting,

Your Honor, we are willing to concede that the eviction was wrongful.'

'Thank you.'

'You're welcome. Our point is that some of the responsibility should rest with the mother.'

'How much?'

'At least fifty percent.'

'That's too high.'

'We think not, Your Honor. We may have put her in the street, but she was there for more than a week before the tragedy.'

'Mr. Green?'

Mordecai stood, shaking his head as if Arthur were a first-year law student grappling with elementary theories. 'These are not people with immediate access to housing, Mr. Jacobs. That's why they're called homeless. You admit you put them in the street, and that's where they died. I would love to discuss it with a jury.'

Arthur's shoulders slumped. Rafter, Malamud, and Barry listened to every word, their faces stricken with the notion of Mordecai Green loose in a courtroom with a jury of his peers.

'Liability is clear, Mr. Jacobs,' DeOrio said. 'You can argue the mother's negligence to the jury if you want, though I wouldn't advise it.' Mordecai and Arthur sat down.

If at trial we proved the defendants liable, the jury would then consider the issue of damages. It was next on the agenda. Rafter went through the motions of submitting the same report on current trends in jury awards. He talked about how much dead children were worth under our tort system. But he quickly became tedious when discussing Lontae's employment history and the estimated loss of her future earnings. He arrived at the same amount, $770,000, that they had offered the day before, and presented that for the record.

'That's not your final offer, is it, Mr. Rafter?' DeOrio asked. His tone was challenging; he certainly hoped that was not their final offer.

'No sir,' Rafter said.

'Mr. Green.'

Mordecai stood again. 'We reject their offer, Your Honor. The trends mean nothing to me. The only trend I care about is how much I can convince a jury to award, and, with all due respect to Mr. Rafter, it'll be a helluva lot more than what they're offering.'

No one in the courtroom doubted him.

He disputed their view that a dead child was worth only fifty thousand dollars. He implied rather strongly that such a low estimation was the result of a prejudice against homeless street children who happened to be black. Gantry was the only one at the defense table not squirming. 'You have a son at St. Alban's, Mr. Rafter. Would you take fifty thousand for him?'

Rafter's nose was three inches away from his legal pad.

'I can convince a jury in this courtroom that these little children were worth at least a million dollars each, same as any child in the prep schools of Virginia and Maryland.'

It was a nasty shot, one they took in the groin. There was no doubt where their kids went to school.

Rafter's summary made no provision for the pain and suffering of the victims. The rationale was unspoken, but nonetheless obvious. They had died peacefully, breathing odorless gas until they floated away. There were no burns, breaks, blood.

Rafter paid dearly for his omission. Mordecai launched into a detailed account of the last hours of Lontae and her children; the search for food and warmth, the snow and bitter cold, the fear of freezing to death, the desperate efforts to stay together, the

339

horror of being stuck in a snowstorm, in a rattletrap car, motor running, watching the fuel gauge.

It was a spellbinding performance, given off the cuff with the skill of a gifted storyteller. As the lone juror, I would have handed him a blank check.

'Don't tell me about pain and suffering,' he snarled at Drake & Sweeney. 'You don't know the meaning of it.'

He talked about Lontae as if he'd known her for years. A kid born without a chance, who made all the predictable mistakes. But, more important, a mother who loved her children and was trying desperately to climb out of poverty. She had confronted her past and her addictions, and was fighting for sobriety when the defendants kicked her back into the streets.

His voice ebbed and flowed, rising with indignation, falling with shame and guilt. Not a syllable was missed, no wasted words. He was giving them an extraordinary dose of what the jury would hear.

Arthur had control of the checkbook, and it must've been burning a hole in his pocket.

Mordecai saved his best for last. He lectured on the purpose of punitive damages – to punish wrongdoers, to make examples out of them so they would sin no more. He hammered at the evils committed by the defendants, rich people with no regard for those less fortunate. 'They're just a bunch of squatters,' his voice boomed. 'Let's throw them out!'

Greed had made them ignore the law. A proper eviction would have taken at least thirty more days. It would have killed the deal with the Postal Service. Thirty days and the heavy snows would've been gone; the streets would've been a little safer.

It was the perfect case for the levying of punitive damages, and there was little doubt in his mind a jury would agree with him. I certainly did, and at that moment neither Arthur nor Rafter nor any other

340

lawyer sitting over there wanted any part of Mordecai Green.

'We'll settle for five million,' he said as he came to an end. 'Not a penny less.'

There was a pause when he finished. DeOrio made some notes, then returned to the agenda. The matter of the file was next. 'Do you have it?' he asked me.

'Yes sir.'

'Are you willing to hand it over?'

'Yes.'

Mordecai opened his battered briefcase and removed the file. He handed it to the clerk, who passed it up to His Honor. We watched for ten long minutes as DeOrio flipped through every page.

I caught a few stares from Rafter, but who cared. He and the rest were anxious to get their hands on it.

When the Judge was finished, he said, 'The file has been returned, Mr. Jacobs. There is a criminal matter pending down the hall. I've spoken to Judge Kisner about it. What do you wish to do?'

'Your Honor, if we can settle all other issues, we will not push for an indictment.'

'I assume this is agreeable with you, Mr. Brock?' DeOrio said.

Damned right it was agreeable with me. 'Yes sir.'

'Moving right along. The next item is the matter of the ethics complaint filed by Drake & Sweeney against Michael Brock. Mr. Jacobs, would you care to address this?'

'Certainly, Your Honor.' Arthur sprang to his feet, and delivered a condemnation of my ethical shortcomings. He was not unduly harsh, or long-winded. He seemed to get no pleasure from it. Arthur was a lawyer's lawyer, an old-timer who preached ethics and certainly practiced them. He and the firm would never forgive me for my screwup, but I had been, after all, one of them. Just as Braden Chance's actions had been a reflection on the entire firm, so had my failure to maintain certain standards.

He ended by asserting that I must not escape punishment for taking the file. It was an egregious breach of duty owed to the client, RiverOaks. I was not a criminal, and they had no difficulty in forgetting the grand larceny charge. But I was a lawyer, and a damned good one, he admitted, and as such I should be held responsible.

They would not, under any circumstances, withdraw the ethics complaint.

His arguments were well reasoned, well pled, and he convinced me. The folks from RiverOaks seemed especially hard-nosed.

'Mr. Brock,' DeOrio said. 'Do you have any response?'

I had not prepared any remarks, but I wasn't afraid to stand and say what I felt. I looked Arthur squarely in the eyes, and said, 'Mr. Jacobs, I have always had great respect for you, and I still do. I have nothing to say in my defense. I was wrong in taking the file, and I've wished a thousand times I had not done it. I was looking for information which I knew was being concealed, but that is no excuse. I apologize to you, the rest of the firm, and to your client, RiverOaks.'

I sat down and couldn't look at them. Mordecai told me later that my humility thawed the room by ten degrees.

DeOrio then did a very wise thing. He proceeded to the next item, which was the litigation yet to be commenced. We planned to file suit on behalf of Marquis Deese and Kelvin Lam, and eventually for every other evictee we could find. DeVon Hardy and Lontae were gone, so there were fifteen potential plaintiffs out there. This had been promised by Mordecai, and he had informed the Judge.

'If you're conceding liability, Mr. Jacobs,' His

342

Honor said, 'then you have to talk about damages. How much will you offer to settle these other fifteen cases?'

Arthur whispered to Rafter and Malamud, then said, 'Well, Your Honor, we figure these people have been without their homes for about a month now. If we gave them five thousand each, they could find a new place, probably something much better.'

'That's low,' DeOrio said. 'Mr. Green.'

'Much too low,' Mordecai agreed. 'Again, I evaluate cases based on what juries might do. Same defendants, same wrongful conduct, same jury pool. I can get fifty thousand per case easy.'

'What will you take?' the Judge asked.

'Twenty-five thousand.'

'I think you should pay it,' DeOrio said to Arthur. 'It's not unreasonable.'

'Twenty-five thousand to each of the fifteen?' Arthur asked, his unflappable demeanor cracking under the assault from two sides of the courtroom.

'That's right.'

A fierce huddle ensued in which each of the four Drake & Sweeney lawyers had his say. It was telling that they did not consult the attorneys for the other two defendants. It was obvious the firm would foot the bill for the settlement. Gantry seemed completely indifferent; his money was not at stake. RiverOaks had probably threatened a suit of its own against the lawyers if the case wasn't settled.

'We will pay twenty-five,' Arthur announced quietly, and $375,000 left the coffers of Drake & Sweeney.

The wisdom was in the breaking of the ice. DeOrio knew he could force them to settle the smaller claims. Once the money started flowing, it wouldn't stop until we were finished.

For the prior year, after paying my salary and

343

benefits, and setting aside one third of my billings for the overhead, approximately four hundred thousand dollars went into the pot of gold the partners divided. And I was just one of eight hundred.

'Gentlemen, we are down to two issues. The first is money – how much will it take to settle this lawsuit? The second is the matter of Mr. Brock's disciplinary problems. It appears as though one hinges on the other. It's at this point in these meetings that I like to talk privately with each side. I'll start with the plaintiff. Mr. Green and Mr. Brock, would you step into my chambers?'

The clerk escorted us into the hallway behind the bench, then down to a splendid oak-paneled office where His Honor was disrobing and ordering tea from a secretary. He offered some to us, but we declined. The clerk closed the door, leaving us alone with DeOrio.

'We're making progress,' he said. 'I've got to tell you, Mr. Brock, the ethics complaint is a problem. Do you realize how serious it is?'

'I think so.'

He cracked his knuckles and began pacing around the room. 'We had a lawyer here in the District, must have been seven, eight years ago, who pulled a similar stunt. Walked out of a firm with a bunch of discovery materials that mysteriously ended up in a different firm, which just so happened to offer the guy a nice job. Can't remember the name.'

'Makovek. Brad Makovek,' I said.

'Right. What happened to him?'

'Suspended for two years.'

'Which is what they want from you.'

'No way, Judge,' Mordecai said. 'No way in hell we're agreeing to a two-year suspension.'

'How much will you agree to?'

'Six months max. And it's not negotiable. Look,

Judge, these guys are scared to death, you know that. They're scared and we're not. Why should we settle anything? I'd rather have a jury.'

'There's not going to be a jury.' The Judge stepped close to me and studied my eyes. 'You'll agree to a six-month suspension?' he asked.

'Yes,' I said. 'But they have to pay the money.'

'How much money?' he asked Mordecai.

'Five million. I could get more from a jury.'

DeOrio walked to his window, deep in thought, scratching his chin. 'I can see five million from a jury,' he said without turning around.

'I can see twenty,' Mordecai said.

'Who'll get the money?' the Judge asked.

'It'll be a nightmare,' Mordecai admitted.

'How much in attorneys' fees?'

'Twenty percent. Half of which goes to a trust in New York.'

The Judge snapped around and began pacing again, hands clenched behind his head. 'Six months is light,' he said.

'That's all we're giving,' Mordecai retorted.

'All right. Let me talk to the other side.'

Our private session with DeOrio lasted less than fifteen minutes. For the bad guys, it took an hour. Of course, they were the ones forking over the money.

We drank colas on a bench in the bustling lobby of the building, saying nothing as we watched a million lawyers scurry about, chasing clients and justice.

We walked the halls and looked at the scared people about to be hauled before the bench for a variety of offenses. Mordecai spoke to a couple of lawyers he knew. I recognized no one. Big-firm lawyers did not spend time in Superior Court.

The clerk found us and led us back to the court-room, where all players were in place. Things were tense. DeOrio was agitated. Arthur and company looked exhausted. We took our seats and waited for the Judge.

'Mr. Green,' he began, 'I have met with the lawyers for the defendants. Here's their best offer: the sum of three million dollars, and a one-year suspension for Mr. Brock.'

Mordecai had barely settled into his seat, when he bounced forward. 'Then we're wasting our time,' he said and grabbed his briefcase. I jumped up to follow him.

'Please excuse us, Your Honor,' he said. 'But we have better things to do.' We started for the aisle between the pews.

'You're excused,' the Judge said, very frustrated.

We left the courtroom in a rush.

THIRTY-EIGHT

I was unlocking the car when the cell phone rattled in my pocket. It was Judge DeOrio. Mordecai laughed when I said, 'Yes, Judge, we'll be there in five minutes.' We took ten, stopping in the rest rooms on the ground floor, walking slowly, using the stairs, giving DeOrio as much time as possible to further pummel the defendants.

The first thing I noticed when we entered the courtroom was that Jack Bolling, one of the three attorneys for RiverOaks, had removed his jacket, rolled up his sleeves, and was walking away from the Drake & Sweeney lawyers. I doubted if he had physically slapped them around, but he looked willing and able.

The huge verdict Mordecai dreamed about would be lodged against all three defendants. Evidently RiverOaks had been sufficiently frightened by the settlement conference. Threats had been made, and perhaps the company had decided to chip in with some cash of its own. We would never know.

I avoided the jury box and sat next to Mordecai. Wilma Phelan had left.

'We're getting close,' the Judge said.

'And we're thinking of withdrawing our offer,' Mordecai announced with one of his more violent barks. We had not discussed such a thing, and neither the other lawyers nor His Honor had contemplated it. Their heads jerked as they looked at each other.

'Settle down,' DeOrio said.

'I'm very serious, Judge. The more I sit here in this courtroom, the more convinced I am that this travesty needs to be revealed to a jury. As for Mr. Brock, his old firm can push all it wants on the criminal charges, but it's no big deal. They have their file back. He has no criminal record. God knows our system is overloaded with drug dealers and murderers; prosecuting him will become a joke. He will not go to jail. And the bar complaint – let it run its course. I'll file one against Braden Chance and maybe some of the other lawyers involved in this mess, and we'll have us an old-fashioned spitting contest.' He pointed at Arthur and said, 'You run to the newspaper, we run to the newspaper.'

The 14th Street Legal Clinic couldn't care less what was printed about it. If Gantry cared, he wouldn't show it. RiverOaks could continue to make money in spite of bad press. But Drake & Sweeney had only its reputation to market.

Mordecai's tirade came from nowhere, and they were completely astonished by it.

'Are you finished?' DeOrio asked.

'I guess.'

'Good. The offer is up to four million.'

'If they can pay four million, then they can certainly pay five.' Mordecai pointed again, back to Drake & Sweeney. 'This defendant had gross billings last year of almost seven hundred million dollars.' He paused as the numbers echoed around the courtroom. 'Seven hundred million dollars, last year alone.' Then he pointed at RiverOaks. 'And this defendant owns real estate worth three hundred and fifty million dollars. Give me a jury.'

When it appeared that he was silent, DeOrio again asked, 'Are you finished?'

'No sir,' he said, and in an instant became remarkably calm. 'We'll take two million up front, a million for our fees, a million for the heirs. The balance of three million can be spread over the next ten years – three hundred thousand a year, plus a reasonable interest rate. Surely these defendants can spare three hundred thousand bucks a year. They may be forced to raise rents and hourly rates, but they certainly know how to do that.'

A structured settlement with an extended payout made sense. Because of the instability of the heirs, and the fact that most of them were still unknown, the money would be carefully guarded by the court.

Mordecai's latest onslaught was nothing short of brilliant. There was a noticeable relaxing in the Drake & Sweeney group. He had given them a way out.

Jack Bolling huddled with them. Gantry's lawyers watched and listened, but were almost as bored as their client.

'We can do that,' Arthur announced. 'But we keep our position regarding Mr. Brock. It's a one-year suspension, or there's no settlement.'

I suddenly hated Arthur, again. I was their last pawn, and to save what little face they had left, they wanted all the blood they could squeeze.

But poor Arthur was not negotiating from a position of power. He was desperate, and looked it.

'What difference does it make?!' Mordecai yelled at him. 'He's agreed to suffer the indignity of surrendering his license. What does an extra six months give you? This is absurd!'

The two corporate boys from RiverOaks had had enough. Naturally afraid of courtrooms, their fear had reached new heights after three hours of Mordecai. There was no way on earth they would endure two weeks of trial. They shook their heads in frustration and whispered intensely to one another.

Even Tillman Gantry was tired of Arthur's nitpicking. With the settlement so close, finish the damned thing!

Seconds earlier, Mordecai had yelled, 'What difference does it make?' And he was right. It really made no difference, especially for a street lawyer like me, one whose job and salary and status would remain wonderfully unaffected by a temporary suspension.

I stood, and very politely said, 'Your Honor, let's split the difference. We offered six months; they want twelve. I'll agree to nine.' I looked at Barry Nuzzo when I said this, and he actually smiled at me.

If Arthur had opened his mouth at that point, he would've been mugged. Everyone relaxed, including DeOrio. 'Then we have a deal,' he said, not waiting for a confirmation from the defendants.

His wonderfully efficient law clerk pecked away at a word processor in front of the bench, and within minutes she produced a one-page Settlement Memorandum. We quickly signed it, and left.

There was no champagne at the office. Sofia was doing what she always did. Abraham was attending a homeless conference in New York.

If any law office in America could absorb five hundred thousand dollars in fees without showing it, it was the 14th Street Legal Clinic. Mordecai wanted new computers and phones, and probably a new heating system. The bulk of the money would be buried in the bank, drawing interest and waiting for the lean times. It was a nice cushion, one that would guarantee our meager salaries for a few years.

If he was frustrated by the reality of sending the other five hundred thousand to the Cohen Trust, he concealed it well. Mordecai was not one to worry about the things he couldn't change. His desk was covered with the battles he could win.

It would take at least nine months of hard labor to sort out the Burton settlement, and that was where I would spend much of my time. Heirs had to be determined, then found, then dealt with when they realized there was money to be had. It would get complicated. For example, the bodies of Kito Spires and those of Temeko, Alonzo, and Dante might have to be exhumed for DNA tests, to establish paternity. If he was in fact the father, then he would inherit from the children, who died first. Since he was now dead, his estate would be opened, and his heirs located.

Lontae's mother and brothers posed intimidating problems. They still had contacts on the streets. They would be paroled in a few years, and they would come after their share of the money with a vengeance.

There were two other projects of particular interest to Mordecai. The first was a pro bono program the clinic had once organized, then allowed to slip away as federal monies evaporated. At its peak, the program had a hundred lawyers volunteering a few hours a week to help the homeless. He asked me to consider reviving it. I liked the idea; we could reach more people, make more contacts within the established bar, and broaden our base for raising funds.

That was the second project. Sofia and Abraham were incapable of effectively asking people for money. Mordecai could talk people out of their shirts, but he hated to beg. I was the bright young Waspy star who could mix and mingle with all the right professionals and convince them to give annually.

'With a good plan, you could raise two hundred thousand bucks a year,' he said.

'And what would we do with it?'

'Hire a couple of secretaries, a couple of paralegals, maybe another lawyer.' As we sat in the front after

351

Sofia left, watching it grow dark outside, Mordecai began dreaming. He longed for the days when there were seven lawyers bumping into each other at the clinic. Every day was chaos, but the little street firm was a force. It helped thousands of homeless people. Politicians and bureaucrats listened to the clinic. It was a loud voice that was usually heard.

'We've been declining for five years,' he said. 'And our people are suffering. This is our golden moment to turn it around.'

And the challenge belonged to me. I was the new blood, the new talent who would reinvigorate the clinic and take it to the next level. I would brighten up the place with dozens of new volunteers. I would build a fund-raising machine so that we could lawyer on the same field as anyone. We would expand, even knock the boards off the windows upstairs and fill the place with talented advocates.

The rights of the homeless would be protected, as long as they could find us. And their voices would be heard through ours.

THIRTY-NINE

Early Friday I was sitting at my desk, happily going about my business as a lawyer/social worker, when Drake & Sweeney, in the person of Arthur Jacobs, suddenly appeared at my door. I greeted him pleasantly, and cautiously, and he sat in one of the maroon chairs. He didn't want coffee. He just wanted to talk.

Arthur was troubled. I was mesmerized as I listened to the old man.

The last few weeks had been the most difficult of his professional career – all fifty-six years of it. The settlement had given him little comfort. The firm was back on track after the slight bump in the road, but Arthur was finding sleep difficult. One of his partners had committed a terrible wrong, and as a result innocent people had died. Drake & Sweeney would be forever at fault for the deaths of Lontae and her four children, regardless of how much money it paid into the settlement. And Arthur doubted if he would ever get over it.

I was too surprised to say much, so I just listened. I wished Mordecai could hear him.

Arthur was suffering, and before long I felt sorry for him. He was eighty, had been contemplating retirement for a couple of years, but wasn't sure what to do now. He was tired of chasing money.

'I don't have a lot of years left,' he admitted. I suspected Arthur would attend my funeral.

He was fascinated by our legal clinic, and I told him the story of how I'd stumbled into it. How long had it been there? he asked. How many people worked there? What was the source of funding? How did we operate it?

He gave me the opening, and I slipped in. Because I couldn't practice law for the next nine months, the clinic had decided that I should implement a new pro bono volunteer program using attorneys from the big firms in town. Since his firm happened to be the largest, I was thinking of starting there. The volunteers would work only a few hours a week, under my supervision, and we could reach thousands of homeless people.

Arthur was aware of such programs; vaguely aware. He hadn't performed free work in twenty years, he admitted sadly. It was normally for the younger associates. How well I remembered.

But he liked the idea. In fact, the longer we discussed it, the larger the program grew. After a few minutes, he was talking openly of requiring all four hundred of his D.C. lawyers to spend a few hours a week helping the poor. It seemed only fitting.

'Can you handle four hundred lawyers?' he asked.

'Of course,' I said, without any idea as to how to even begin such a task. But my mind was racing. 'I'll need some help, though,' I said.

'What kind of help?' he asked.

'What if Drake & Sweeney had a full-time pro bono coordinator within the firm? This person would work closely with me on all aspects of homeless law. Frankly, with four hundred volunteers, we'll need someone on your end.'

He pondered this. Everything was new, and everything was sounding good. I plowed ahead.

354

'And I know just the right person,' I said. 'He doesn't have to be a lawyer. A good paralegal can do it.'

'Who?' he asked.

'Does the name Hector Palma ring a bell?'

'Vaguely.'

'He's in the Chicago office, but he's from D.C. He worked under Braden Chance, and got pinched.'

Arthur's eyes narrowed as he struggled to remember. I wasn't sure how much he knew, but I doubted if he would be dishonest. He seemed to be thoroughly enjoying his soul-cleansing.

'Pinched?' he asked.

'Yeah, pinched. He lived in Bethesda until three weeks ago when he suddenly moved in the middle of the night. A quickie transfer to Chicago. He knew everything about the evictions, and I suspect Chance wanted to hide him.' I was careful. I was not about to break my confidential agreement with Hector.

I didn't have to. Arthur, as usual, was reading between lines.

'He's from D.C.?'

'Yes, and so is his wife. They have four kids. I'm sure he'd love to return.'

'Does he have an interest in helping the homeless?' he asked.

'Why don't you ask him?' I said.

'I'll do that. It's an excellent idea.'

If Arthur wanted Hector Palma back in D.C. to harness the firm's newly acquired passion for homeless law, it would be done within a week.

The program took shape before our eyes. Every Drake & Sweeney lawyer would be required to handle one case each week. The younger associates would do the intake, under my supervision, and once the cases arrived at the firm they would be assigned by Hector to the other lawyers. Some cases would take fifteen minutes, I explained to Arthur, others would take several hours a month. No problem, he said.

I almost felt sorry for the politicians and bureaucrats and office workers at the thought of four hundred Drake & Sweeney lawyers suddenly seized with a fervor to protect the rights of street people.

Arthur stayed almost two hours, and apologized when he realized he had taken so much of my time. But he was much happier when he left. He was going straight to his office with a new purpose, a man on a mission. I walked him to his car, then ran to tell Mordecai.

Megan's uncle owned a house on the Delaware shore, near Fenwick Island on the Maryland line. She described it as a quaint old house, two stories with a large porch that almost touched the ocean, three bedrooms, a perfect spot for a weekend getaway. It was the middle of March, still cold, and we could sit by the fire and read books.

She slightly stressed the part about three bedrooms, so there would be plenty of space for each of us to have privacy, without matters getting complicated. She knew I was limping away from my first marriage, and after two weeks of cautious flirting we had both come to realize that things would proceed slowly. But there was another reason for mentioning the three bedrooms.

We left Washington Friday afternoon. I drove. Megan navigated. And Ruby nibbled on oatmeal cookies in the backseat, wild-eyed at the prospect of spending a few days outside the city, off the streets, on the beach, clean and sober.

She had been clean Thursday night. Three nights with us in Delaware would make four. Monday afternoon we would check her into Easterwood, a small women's detox center off East Capitol. Mordecai had leaned heavily on someone there, and Ruby would have a small room with a warm bed for at least ninety days.

Before we left the city, she had showered at Naomi's and changed into new clothes. Megan had searched every inch of her clothing and bag looking for drugs. She found nothing. It was an invasion of privacy, but with addicts the rules are different.

We found the house at dusk. Megan used it once or twice a year. The key was under the front doormat.

I was assigned the downstairs bedroom, which Ruby thought odd. The other two bedrooms were upstairs, and Megan wanted to be near Ruby during the night.

It rained Saturday, a cold, blowing shower that came from the sea. I was alone on the front porch, rocking gently in a swing under a thick blanket, lost in a dream world, listening to the waves break below. The door closed, the screen slammed behind it, and Megan walked to the swing. She lifted the blanket and tucked herself next to me. I held her firmly; if not, she would've fallen onto the porch.

She was easy to hold.

'Where's our client?' I asked.

'Watching TV.'

A strong gust threw mist in our faces, and we squeezed tighter. The chains holding the swing squeaked louder, then faded as we became almost still. We watched the clouds swirl above the water. Time was of no importance.

'What are you thinking?' she asked softly.

Everything and nothing. Away from the city, I could look back for the first time and try to make sense of it all. Thirty-two days earlier I had been married to someone else, living in a different apartment, working in a different firm, a complete stranger to the woman I

357

was now holding. How could life change so drastically in a month?

I didn't dare think of the future; the past was still happening.

AUTHOR'S NOTE

Before writing this book, I had not worried too much about the homeless. And I certainly didn't know anyone who worked with them.

In D.C., I found my way to the Washington Legal Clinic for the Homeless, where I met Patricia Fugere, the Director. She and her colleagues – Mary Ann Luby, Scott McNeilly, and Melody Webb O'Sullivan – introduced me to the world of the homeless. Many thanks to them for their time and assistance.

Thanks also to Maria Foscarinis of the National Law Center on Homelessness and Poverty, and to Willa Day Morris at Rachael's Women's Center, and Mary Popit at New Endeavors by Women, and Bruce Casino and Bruce Sanford of Baker & Hostetler.

Will Denton once again read the manuscript and suggested changes to keep it lawyerly. Jefferson Arrington showed me the city. Jonathan Hamilton did the research. Thanks.

And to the real Mordecai Greens, a quiet tribute for your work in the trenches.

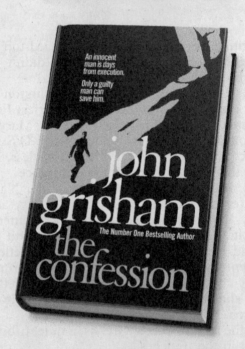